THE PRINCE OF THE SOVIETS

THE RUSSIAN TREASURES SERIES

BOOK THREE

ELVIRA BARYAKINA

Translated from Russian by Rose France

This book is a work of fiction. Any references to historical events, real people, or real places are used fictitiously. Other names, characters, places, and events are products of the author's imagination, and any resemblance to actual events or places or persons, living or dead, is entirely coincidental.

Copyright © 2018 Elvira Baryakina
All rights reserved, including the right to reproduce this book or portions thereof in any form whatsoever. For information, visit http://www.baryakina.com/en/

ISBN: 978-1-7325840-4-4

PROLOGUE

1

TO KLIM ROGOV, the ungrateful wretch I foolishly harbored in my bosom

FROM FERNANDO JOSE BURBANO, the boss and owner of this damn radio station, the devil take it

Regarding your willful resignation

September 28, 1927
Shanghai, Republic of China

Note from O. Harper, secretary:
Sorry, Klim. I'm just typing what the boss dictates to me.

YOU UNGRATEFUL WRETCH:

You had no right to resign from your job at my outstanding radio station and go charging off to the very devil itself—Soviet Russia. You're the best radio presenter we have, and you're causing us no end of trouble with our commercials.

We've only just signed a contract with the makers of Sedat-Eze sleeping tablets. I promised them you'd do them proud. Instead, it turns out you have done a runner. I detest you heartily for it, damn your eyes!

You can rest assured that I wouldn't take you back even if you came crawling back on your belly asking my forgiveness for a whole year.

Why the devil are you going back to that den of vipers anyway? You only just got out by the skin of your teeth after the revolution.

Have you forgotten that it is run by the Bolsheviks, a godless crowd, who confiscate private property belonging to decent traders and businessmen?

If you haven't taken complete leave of your senses, I advise you to buy yourself a big packet of Sedat-Eze and avoid the place like the plague—I'll organize you a discount. However, if you're serious about this crazy scheme, I hope the Bolsheviks string you up from the nearest tree.

Your friend,
Fernando

2

To my boss, friend, and owner of this damn radio station, Fernando Jose Burbano

From the ungrateful wretch, Klim Rogov

Regarding my resignation

September 29, 1927
Shanghai, Republic of China

MY DEAREST FRIEND:

Please don't be angry with me. I am only doing what I have to do. My wife is in trouble: the Bolsheviks have deported her to Moscow, and she is in mortal danger there. I know for a fact that the Soviet political police, the OGPU, is seizing any White Russians who return to the USSR and sending them off to prison camps somewhere in the far north of the country. The OGPU don't care if the people they arrest are guilty or not—their policy is to "neutralize" them in any case.

I have to save Nina.

I know in advance what you'll say: "People like this lady friend of yours are nothing but bad news." And you're right: if I go back to Soviet Russia, I also risk falling into the hands of the OGPU—I'm also a White émigré like my wife.

And even if I do manage to get her back, I can't expect any sort of domestic idyll in the future. Such a life isn't possible with a woman as passionate and headstrong as Nina.

How can I explain it all to you so that you'll understand and not take offense?

I've had the good fortune to find a marvelous, unique woman, and for her sake, I'm prepared to go straight into the lion's mouth. When I'm beside her, I feel alive.

We all have something we prize above all else, Fernando. You'd risk everything for profit, but I haven't any enthusiasm for gold mining or for creating commercial empires. If I do anything, I do it for the sake of my wife and my little daughter. I'm sorry, but it's just a defect of my character.

Please don't try to persuade me not to go. I know Nina and I are completely at odds at the moment; our relations are at a dead end, and I don't see any way out. But it's too late for me to go back now.

Your friend, colleague, and companion in arms,

Klim Rogov

3

TO KLIM ROGOV

FROM FERNANDO JOSE BURBANO

On the subject of your *** explanatory note.

September 29, 1927
Shanghai, Republic of China

Note from O. Harper, secretary: The asterisks indicate where Mr. Burbano used unprintable expressions. Please accept my apologies if this letter is not to your liking.

GO TO THE *** DEVIL, YOU ***!

By the way, if you ever come back alive from the USSR, how about making a radio program about your adventures? I think it could be popular with our listeners. If the team that makes Sedat-Eze haven't gone bust by then, they could be our sponsors.

You can tell our listeners about running away from the Bolsheviks, and during the commercial break, you can advise them to take tablets to calm their nerves.

Make sure you write down everything that happens to you anyway. If you find you're about to be killed, take a moment to send us all your stories, and we'll broadcast them.

If you need a funeral service, send a telegram. You may be a *** Orthodox Christian and not a Catholic, but I'll say a prayer for you and do what needs to be done.

Your friend,
Fernando

1. ESCAPE FROM CHINA

1

The window of Nina Kupina's room was decorated with an intricate pattern of thin red wooden strips. At one time, the room had been occupied by the wife of an important Chinese official, and the window lattices had been a sign of success and prosperity. For Nina, however, they were nothing more than the bars of a prison, serving only to remind her of her captivity. Ever since the Bolsheviks had brought her here, she had been forbidden to leave the house, and for two months now, her world had been reduced to an inner courtyard with a weed-covered pond and a high stone wall.

Officially, the building was occupied by a scholar specializing in Oriental studies. Unofficially, it was the headquarters of the Soviet secret service, sent to Peking to organize workers mutinies and to create a new hotbed of world revolution.

It was very early in the morning, but the entire household was already up. Employees ran back and forth; abandoned possessions and forgotten documents lay scattered among the puddles.

Nina looked anxiously at the cars, which stood at the gates with their doors wide open, while young stenographers hurriedly loaded them with bundles and suitcases.

So, it was true, Nina thought. *Moscow had given the order to evacuate.*

It had been hot and muggy since dawn, but she kept shivering. If the Bolsheviks left, what would become of her? She hoped fervently that they would leave her behind or simply forget about her, and then she could smash the wooden lattices on the window and escape.

Recently, life for the Soviet workers in Peking had been like sitting on a powder keg. Efforts to incite revolution in China had failed, the Soviet embassy had been ransacked, and now, local communists were being executed without trial. Their severed heads were displayed in town squares as a warning to the public. By August 1927, it became clear that the Soviets were fighting a losing battle.

Moscow had spent vast amounts on propaganda and civil war in China, and somebody had to be held accountable for the disaster. The Soviet agents working in Peking found themselves caught in the middle; to one side of them were the Chinese police officers with their curved swords, and to the other side were their stern colleagues from the Bolshevik party.

The idea of returning to the USSR was an alarming prospect to say the least.

Borisov, the party instructor, came out onto the porch, and Nina shuddered. Whenever the swine had a drink inside him, he would pound at her door, slurring, "How about some class war tonight? Just you and me." She had had to barricade herself in her room with furniture to keep him out.

Now, Nina watched two men come running up to Borisov with a map. They spread it out on the bonnet of a car and began to argue about something, pointing at different locations.

Please, let them forget about me, she prayed silently.

Six months earlier, she had, as ill luck would have it, ended up on a steamer together with a number of Soviet agents who had been arrested too. The Chinese authorities had not bothered to find out which of the passengers were communists and which were White Russians, those who had fled the country for China after the Bolshevik's had seized power. The prisoners had been spared from execution only because Moscow had paid an enormous bribe to the judge, who had let them out of custody.

But Nina had fallen straight from one prison into another. The ruler of Peking announced a manhunt for the conspirators, and they had been forced to go into hiding in an old mansion on the edge of the city. One after the other, Nina's "partners in crime" had been sent back to the USSR, the house's inhabitants kept changing, and still, Nina sat in her room waiting for her invisible superiors to decide her fate.

She had been to Borisov more times than she could count, pleading him to let her go home. She had told him that she had left behind a husband and a small child in Shanghai, but Borisov would not be moved. He knew that Nina had adopted a Chinese orphan girl and refused to believe that she might really have grown attached to Kitty. As for her husband, he simply laughed at Nina's face at the first mention of him. "I know you White whores—you sell yourselves to the first capitalist pig you can find."

Had Borisov known Nina was in charge of a large security organization consisting of several hundred armed White Army men, he would have been the first to put her up against the wall to be shot. It was only in the eyes of the Russian émigrés that Nina had made a brilliant career for herself. The Bolsheviks saw things differently. In their opinion, if some young lady who had run off to China after the revolution suddenly became rich, it could mean only one thing. After all, it was a well-known fact that nobody could achieve success through their own brains and hard work in a capitalist country.

Things were made worse by the fact that Nina had managed to get American passports for herself and Klim, as an exceptional case, without having set foot in the country. Clearly, she was a spy and an enemy of the workers.

Borisov raised his head and looked in at Nina's window. Then, with a decisive air, he set off inside the house toward her.

Nina's heart lurched. What should she do now? Make another barricade? What if Borisov started shooting, or, worse still, set the building on fire? Just a few days ago, the Bolsheviks had been saying that the house would have to be burned after they left because it would be impossible to take all their secret documents with them.

Borisov burst into the room and seized Nina by the arm. "You're coming with us."

"Where to?" Nina gasped.

"To the Soviet Union. We'll hammer all the bourgeois nonsense out of you."

She tried to make a dash for it, but two guards came running to help Borisov. They pulled Nina from the house and pushed her into the back seat of one of the waiting cars.

Borisov thrust a large, blue-tattooed fist up close to her face. "Just one sound out of you, you bitch, and you're dead."

2

The small procession left Peking in mid-August, and for some weeks, they traveled a circuitous route along country roads, trying to throw the police off the scent.

All this time, the Bolsheviks continued to keep a close eye on Nina. They were tired, their nerves frayed, and they took out their anger on whoever happened to be on hand. For them, letting Nina go would have meant giving the

"White bitch" a chance. This was something, in their eyes, she did not deserve.

When they had got as far as Inner Mongolia, they were joined by more cars carrying Chinese communists and their Russian advisers. These newcomers frightened the fleeing Soviet agents by telling them of the in-fighting that had begun among top party officials in Moscow.

Joseph Stalin had unexpectedly begun to build up authority. In casting around for someone to blame for the foreign policy debacle, he had singled out none other than Leon Trotsky—one of the main organizers of the Bolshevik Revolution and the founder of the Red Army. Those who supported Trotsky were now openly referred to as counter-revolutionaries and were being hounded by the press. This was a bad sign. The agents who had worked in Peking had, almost to a man, been supporters of Trotsky.

Nina shuddered to hear the news. If loyal Bolsheviks were seriously concerned about their own fate, what might lie in store for her? Though, truth be told, she was not at all sure she would even reach Soviet Russia. Borisov made no secret of the fact that he was planning to teach her a lesson. He had recently bought himself a chain metal whip at a village market, and he had promised Nina that he would soon be trying out his new acquisition on her.

Once the convoy had crossed the low mountains, they saw the great Gobi Desert stretching to the horizon, but they were not able to travel far across the stony, trackless waste. One of the cars broke down, and as they tried to mend it, night fell.

For the first time since they had left Peking, the fugitives allowed themselves to relax a little. Borisov had some rice vodka in his luggage, and he passed his flask around the circle.

Nina realized that this was her last chance to make a run for it. They had still not gone too far from the last Chinese village.

As the revolutionaries, warmed by the drink, sat around the fire reminiscing about their life in China, Nina hurriedly gathered her possessions. She took only a compass, a blanket, some bread rusks, and a water flask. There was no point in taking more—if she got lost, she would never survive in any case.

Nina tried not to think about what would happen if she managed to make it to a Chinese settlement. She did not know any Chinese, she had no documents, and it would be impossible to send a message to Shanghai—the nearest telegraph office was more than a hundred miles away. But it would be better to rot in remote Chinese backwater than to fall into Borisov's clutches.

A little the worse for the drink, the Bolsheviks went off to their tents one by one, and when the first light appeared in the sky above the mountains, Nina quietly stole away from the camp.

Hardly a thing could be seen in the gray half-light. Nina made her way across the flat, stony plain by looking at the stars. All around, it was deathly quiet. Twisting an ankle, stepping on a scorpion, or simply grazing a heel—any of these would be enough to spell death.

"Just wait for me—that's all I ask," whispered Nina.

For several months now, she had been keeping up a constant conversation with her husband as if Klim could hear every word she said. When the Chinese had arrested her, Klim had rushed to Peking to make all possible efforts to get her released, and this despite all their quarrels and offenses of the past. No matter what happened between them, he never deserted her when she was in trouble.

The Bolsheviks had almost certainly not told Klim where they had taken Nina after the trial, and she could only guess what he had done after that. Had he gone back to Shanghai? Or had he perhaps stayed in Peking?

"Just you wait. I'll come back to you," Nina kept saying. "I'll make everything right again. Just give me a chance."

3

When a huge, red sun rose over the desert, Nina was so tired that she felt a constant ringing in her ears and a sharp pain in her side. But she could not stop trudging uphill—she had to walk as far as she could before the heat of the day set in.

Suddenly, the deafening sound of a gunshot broke the silence, and a fountain of small stones erupted right beside Nina. Flinching, she looked around, and her blood ran cold—down below at the foot of the hill stood a familiar, dust-covered Buick.

The German flight instructor, Friedrich, lowering the barrel of his gun, beckoned to Nina. "Come here!"

There was nowhere to hide. Nina sank to the ground and hid her face in her hands. Let them carry her back to the car if they had to.

Borisov came running up, grabbed her by the shoulder, and forced her to her feet.

"Idiot!" he shouted, dealing her a great slap in the face. "Do you know how much petrol we've wasted because of you?"

Nina tried to get away, but Borisov twisted her arm and pulled her toward the car.

"You're for it now," he hissed. "You backstabber! What if they'd caught you? You'd have handed us all over to the Chinese, wouldn't you?"

He was about to hit Nina again, but Friedrich stopped him. "We should go," Friedrich said. "We still have to catch up with the others."

Nina, sobbing, was bundled into the Buick between boxes of tinned food and a shining gramophone speaker.

"Oh, don't worry," said Borisov. "I'll set you free in a week—without food and water. But first, I'll thrash the living daylights out of you."

Friedrich glanced at Nina in the rearview mirror. "Get into the truck with Magda," he said suddenly in English. "And don't leave her for a minute, or this scoundrel will beat you to death."

Nina was bewildered. She had had no idea that any of the Bolsheviks sympathized with her.

Borisov frowned. "What did you just say to her?" He knew no English, despite having spent three years in the Peking Legation Quarter.

"I was just telling her to get into the baggage truck," said Friedrich. "I don't want her in my car."

4

Englishwoman Magda Thomson felt like a pariah among the Bolsheviks. She had an inherent and irreparable defect in their eyes—she was the heiress of a large soap factory near Liverpool. Tall and heavily built, she looked more like a butcher's daughter than a "soap princess," but that did not help—the Bolsheviks looked askance at her. Sometimes they would even mock her openly.

Magda had traveled the world at her leisure before settling in Peking. She took a room in a hotel not far from the Legation Quarter, and one night as she sat reading in her room, she had heard a suspicious scuffle outside the door. Looking out into the corridor, she saw a man clutching a bloody wound on his arm.

"The Chinese police are after me," he panted. "Could I hide out here with you for a while? My name is Friedrich. And yours?"

At the sight of this Teutonic knight with his haughty stare and close-cropped head of graying hair, Magda had been unable to resist. She let Friedrich stay and began helping him in any way she could: driving him to the apartments of fellow conspirators and organizing the evacuation of Chinese communists and their Russian advisers. At night, they would make love.

Magda asked Friedrich about his plans for the future.

"I'm going to Moscow," he said.

"But why? You're a German. What is there for you in Moscow?"

"A new life is dawning there. As for your beloved West, it has nothing to offer but vulgarity, tedium, and moneymaking."

Friedrich told Magda of how he had been taken prisoner by the Russians during the Great War and how he had become friendly with Bolsheviks and realized that it was his fate to try to bring about world revolution. In China, he had instructed National Revolutionary Army pilots in aerial warfare.

Magda gave Friedrich a nickname in private: Friedrich der Große (Frederick the Great). He knew no fear and was less concerned for his own welfare than he was for that of his comrades and for the general good—as he understood it. He was the first man that Magda had ever met who cared nothing for her fortune. In fact, he thought of it as a burden that she should get rid of as soon as possible.

"I can't," Magda explained apologetically. "It's not my money, you see. It's my father's. He just pays all my bills."

Friedrich never spoke to Magda of love. He assumed that she wanted to help not him personally but his cause, and he was grateful to her for it.

One day, he clasped her tightly by the hand and told her that he was leaving for the Soviet Union.

"The Party will never forget your kindness, Miss Thomson."

"I'm coming with you," declared Magda without a second thought.

Friedrich was dumbstruck. He told Magda she had lost her senses and hinted that, as a British capitalist, she might run into some serious problems in the USSR. In reply, Magda said that she was not really scared of anything. She had been traveling around South America and met an Indian medicine man who had given her a special herb to smoke and put a charm over her that was supposed to protect her from a violent death.

Next day, Magda went to see new friends she had made in the Soviet Embassy and managed to get herself a visa.

"Have they lost their minds?" Friedrich yelled, furious, when he found out. "How did you talk them into it?"

Magda smiled enigmatically. She had offered Friedrich's comrades in arms a large medical truck that they could use to take personal possessions out of China. The Soviet government was only providing enough money to evacuate people, the party archive, and weapons. Everything else was to be left behind.

Friedrich warned Magda not to come near him. The other Bolsheviks kept their distance from her too as if she might infect them with "British imperialism."

The journey from China was a long one, and Magda, worn out from fear and loneliness, was overjoyed when Nina Kupina was put into the truck with her, especially as this new fellow passenger spoke excellent English. It was a good thing that Nina was thin too as it meant she could squeeze into the space behind the passenger seat. There was no room in the back; the van was crammed full with bundles, baskets, and boxes.

Day after day, the medical truck trundled across the desert like a solid, stony sea. Watermelons rolled about underfoot while feathers from a number of ladies' hats nodded overhead, pinned to the ceiling of the driver's cabin. The embassy women were hoping to sell them for a profit in Moscow, opting to forget about their anti-capitalist convictions for a while.

Their Chinese driver sang songs, interrupting his singing now and again to curse their guides, who kept getting confused and more than once led the column of vehicles in the wrong direction completely.

"What are we going to do if we run out of gas?" the driver muttered now and again. "Or if there's a sandstorm?"

Magda was listening with only one ear. Up ahead of them was the Buick driven by Friedrich der Große. She would have given anything on earth to be next to him right now. If there were some disaster, she thought how good it would be to die at his side in a single moment. The sands would cover them, and three-hundred years later, they would be discovered by some archeologist, sitting side by side and holding hands. Even death would be powerless to separate them.

But Friedrich had taken Borisov in his car with him, together with an extra water cask—there was nothing there to delight the archeologists of the future.

Magda could not understand why Friedrich was rejecting her. It was true that she was no beauty; it was true that she was English, but these things had never bothered him in the past. What if he had no desire to make it up to her when they got to Moscow? What if he just disappeared, leaving her to do whatever she wanted?

Magda had no idea what to expect in Soviet Russia. There had been a revolution there ten years ago, followed by civil war and a famine that had claimed the lives of five million people. One of her friends had been in Petrograd in 1921 and told her of rats running around in the hotels. Hotel guests had been issued with a bucket of water a day to wash and to prepare food.

"When did you leave Russia for China?" Magda asked Nina now.

"In October 1922," Nina said. "There was a terrible shortage of food back then."

It's safe to assume, thought Magda, *that things wouldn't have changed too much in five years.*

Magda felt anger rising up in her like a wave. The Bolsheviks could not get their own house in order, but here they were trying to teach the world how to create a bright future.

She turned to Nina, who was sitting on the floor of the truck and holding on to the armrest of Magda's seat as the truck kept lurching and bouncing.

"Do you have a place to stay in Moscow?" Magda asked.

Nina shook her head. "No."

"Would you like to be my interpreter? I don't know a word of Russian."

Nina was silent for a moment. "How long are you planning to stay in Moscow?" she asked. "Until Friedrich changes the anger to mercy?"

Magda had not realized that it was so easy to guess her state of mind.

"I don't know yet," she replied, embarrassed.

She had been studying Nina for some time and had noticed that anything and everything merely enhanced this woman's beauty—she looked lovely even in a shabby skirt and blouse, even with that ever-present look of sadness in her eyes.

Nina attracted attention without any effort on her part. It was just the way she was with her large gray-green eyes, wavy dark hair, and the graceful lines of her neck and shoulders. She was like a fascinating porcelain figurine found at an antique market; to see her was to want her.

Magda, on the other hand, had always had to strive her utmost to prove to others that she was deserving of love and attention.

"I wonder what it would be like to be like you?" she asked, staring quizzically at Nina. "Men are attracted to you immediately. Don't tell me it isn't true."

Nina frowned. "I can't choose who is attracted to me, and there's nothing I can do about it."

Magda smiled. She had the same problem exactly.

2. THE WORKERS' CAPITAL

1

A month later, the fugitives crossed the border with the USSR and reached a nameless outpost where an international sleeping car sent from Moscow awaited them.

The Bolshevik agents began to breathe more easily. If they were being welcomed in this manner, surely they were not about to be reprimanded? Perhaps this was a sign that the party leadership knew they had done everything they could in China to further the world revolution and had failed only through force of circumstance.

They were gripped by a childlike excitement. Here they were, back home at last, among their own people. They had survived the journey across the desert and had met neither soldiers nor the Honghuz bandits who preyed on trade caravans. Now, they felt sure, everything would be all right.

Covered head to foot in dust, their faces burned dark by the desert sun, the fugitives began to stow their baggage onto the overhead racks of the sleeping car.

"The train will leave in five minutes!" shouted the attendant, a handsome old man with impressive gray whiskers.

Nina and Magda got into the compartment allotted to them.

There were bundles of stiffly starched bed linens on the seats. A vase holding a single flower and a menu for the restaurant car were on the window table.

On the other side of the compartment came the sound of laughter and water splashing. One of their fellow passengers was clearly marveling at the fact that there was running water on the train.

Nina walked up to the mirror on the back of the door and lifted a strand of curly hair above her head where it stayed stiffly standing on end.

"When we finally take a proper bath, we'll wash away a ton of dirt," said Magda. "I hope they still have bathtubs in Moscow."

Somebody knocked at the window, and Magda opened it. It was Borisov.

"Get Nina for me," he ordered.

Nina walked reluctantly to the window. "What do you want?"

Borisov took a newspaper from his pocket and tossed it to her. "Look at this. I just bought it in the station."

On the first column was a large headline: "Trotsky expelled from the list of candidates for the Comintern Executive Committee." The same article told of the arrest of several traitors who had "undermined the very basis of the party's social construction project" and "introduced division among the Bolshevik cadres."

"It would be suicide to go to Moscow," Borisov whispered. "If they've got rid of Trotsky, they'll eat us alive. And you into the bargain." Borisov looked about him to make sure nobody was listening.

"Come with me to Khabarovsk," he said under his breath. "I have money—we'll be all right. Don't tell me you want to go with that great English heifer to the slaughter."

Nina closed the window with a rattle.

"What did he say?" asked Magda as the train began to move.

Nina sat down on the seat and hugged herself as if she were cold.

"Miss Thomson," she said, "it's dangerous to go to Moscow. Why don't we get out at the very first station and go to Vladivostok? We could get a steamer to Shanghai from there."

Magda refused point-blank. "I understand you're anxious to get back to your husband, but I don't want to lose Friedrich either. I can take care of you. My father has lots of friends in parliament. We can send Klim a telegram, and he can wire you the money for the return trip."

"The Bolsheviks couldn't care less about your parliament," Nina said. "You won't find any diplomats here or any legal system to speak of. They can just accuse you of spying and shoot you on the spot."

Low hills covered in reddish grass stretched away outside the window. From time to time, a chain of railcars would pass, and they would glimpse horses' faces and the broadcloth helmets of Red Army soldiers. Troops were being sent off somewhere.

Magda slurped at the tea that the attendant had brought in for them. "I don't know whom Frederick thinks he's trying to fool," she said. "Nobody can live without love. He's just worried about getting me into trouble. But I told him straight away that I'm not afraid of anything…well, perhaps except my father when he's angry. We just need time to get to know one another better."

Nina sat in silence. All she could think of was that every second was taking her farther and farther away from Klim.

2

The train flew across half the length of Russia and eventually arrived in Moscow.

Nina was preparing herself for the worst. Any minute, officers from the OGPU might come to the door of their compartment and begin to question her: How had she ended up in China? What had she been up to there?

Magda was also looking as if she had seen a ghost. She was staring through the window at a porter stamping about on the station platform, an enormous man with a brutish face, a matted beard, and a lighted cigarette dangling from his thick lips. He was the spitting image of the Bolsheviks on political posters shown making their way toward a horrified Europe.

"If they try to arrest us," Nina said in a trembling voice, "jump out onto the rails and hide under the train. Then we'll run in different directions: you go toward the station, and I'll go over there to that freight train. We can meet in twenty-four hours on the square in front of the station—in the place where the cab drivers wait for fares."

There was a knock at the door. Nina pressed her hand to her lips. That was it. They were done for.

But it was only Friedrich.

"What are you doing sitting around in here?" he said. "Go to the Second House of Soviets. They're expecting you there."

"And what about you?" fretted Magda. "Where are you going?"

"To the Comintern Hostel."

Friedrich called a porter, who tied Marga's suitcases with a leather strap and hoisted them onto his shoulder.

"Where to?" the porter asked.

"To the exit," ordered Friedrich as he led Magda and Nina through the crowds of passengers.

Nina wondered whether she ought to make a run for it before it was too late. Or would it be better to stay close to Magda? If she were to run away, where could she hide, and how could she survive when she knew no one in the city? And then there was Magda's influential father who could mobilize the British Parliament if anything were to happen—or so she claimed.

"Friedrich?" said Nina. "What's the Second House of the Soviets?"

"You'll see in a minute," he answered.

Nina assumed it was the place foreigners were taken for interrogation.

3

Nina had been expecting Moscow to be like some abandoned citadel ransacked by the enemy, but it was quite different. The smart station building had been recently refurbished, and there were lots of people on the streets, although nobody here was dressed in the European manner.

Moscow had its own distinctive style of dress. The men wore trousers of woolen cloth, Russian shirts, and peaked hats while the women were all in calico dresses and headscarves tied low over their foreheads.

Friedrich took Nina and Magda out into the square outside the station and pointed to a small Renault parked close by.

"Get yourselves a cab," he said.

"When will I see you again?" asked Magda with a pleading note in her voice.

"I'll come and find you."

Once they were in the car, Magda began her ruminations about love again, but Nina wasn't listening; she was watching the twilight city as it rushed by outside the window of the cab. So, here it was, the city that was talked of the world over as the embodiment of all evil.

There were crowds of people streaming along the narrow pavements and into open shop doorways. But every minute, it was harder for Nina to make out the shop signs, which were not illuminated as they had been in Shanghai.

There were far fewer cars in Moscow than there had been in China. People got around using horse-cabs or trams, which were full to overflowing. The windows in the buildings were lit up from top to bottom, and even the basement windows below pavement level threw out yellow rectangles of light.

"Why are all the lights on?" Nina asked their driver.

"There are tenants in every room," he said. "Before you might have had some gentleman taking up a whole apartment by himself. But things are different now. Every family gets a room, and there's no waste."

Nina translated his words to Magda.

"Could you imagine if you had to share your house with strangers?" she asked.

"I wouldn't mind if one of them was Friedrich," answered Magda

The magic charms of the medicine man in South America had done more than protect Magda from violent death, it seemed. They had also cured her of common sense.

4

The Second House of Soviets turned out to be the former Hotel Metropol. Before, it had been used by members of the government. Now, they had been given private apartments, and the hotel rooms were being rented out to foreigners once again.

Magda's spirits lifted immediately when she saw the lobby, which was more than respectable with its marble floors and glittering chandeliers.

"There. You see?" she said to Nina. "Things are looking up."

On the downside, the prices at the Metropol were extortionate. They had to pay as much to stay a night as they would have paid for a whole month in a Peking hotel.

"The country needs hard currency," explained the receptionist bluntly.

When he asked for their documents, Magda gave him her passport with a five-pound-note inside it.

"This woman is my guest," she said, indicating Nina.

"I see," said the receptionist quietly, dropping the note into a desk drawer.

As it was elsewhere, so it was in the land of the Soviets: money might not buy you everything, but it certainly helped solve most problems.

5

Nobody thought to arrest Nina and Magda. They stayed in the Metropol, dining in the restaurant on the ground floor and getting to know the foreigners who had come to the capital to celebrate the tenth anniversary of the Bolshevik Revolution.

Magda kept asking after Friedrich, hoping that some foreign communists might know where to find him, but the days passed without a word or sign of him. Friedrich clearly had no intention of resuming relations with his old sweetheart.

"He's just very busy," Magda kept saying. "He needs time to sort out his affairs, and he knows where to find me."

Nina had also had bad news. She had sent a telegram to Klim at home and at his workplace, but they had come back marked *"Addressee not known here."* She was beside herself now at the thought that something might have happened to Klim and Kitty.

The telegrams she had sent to her friends had also gone unanswered. There was unrest in Shanghai, and a many of the white settlers had decided to leave, to be on the safe side.

There was nobody to help her out, and Nina would have to find the money for her journey home herself. It would take months to save up the sum needed on the salary she was getting from Magda, and then she had to get the necessary documents to get across the border—a seemingly impossible task.

Magda could not increase Nina's pay. She did not have enough money herself as her father had refused to pay her bills.

"Come back to England immediately," he sent back a cable in reply to her request. He did not want to invest a single penny in Bolshevik Russia.

For days on end, Nina and Magda would walk about Moscow looking at the sights, from the wooden mausoleum in which Lenin's embalmed body lay on show to the Anti-Religious Museum, which had been set up in the old Strastnoy Monastery.

The whole of the city was preparing for the 7th of November when the tenth anniversary of the Bolshevik revolution would be celebrated. Buildings were being repaired and refurbished right and left, and columns of workers armed with training rifles or wearing gas masks were marching the streets—in a rehearsal of the coming military parade.

The Soviet Union was living in expectation of imminent war. It could be felt everywhere, in the headlines of the papers and the conversations at the markets.

Posters had been put up all around the town:

The Red Army is the ever-vigilant guard of the Land of the Soviets. Strengthen the Union of Workers and Peasants, and the USSR will be invincible!
Death to the blood-soaked Imperialists!

"Who are the Bolsheviks preparing to fight?" asked Magda, puzzled.

"Why, the English, of course. Who else?" Nina said with a smile. "After all, you're planning to attack the USSR—all the newspapers are talking about it."

Magda was terribly upset when she found out that the USSR was seriously expecting English warplanes to appear in the skies at any moment.

"But that's absolute nonsense!" she argued. "The Soviet government knows that it's physically impossible. Why are they deliberately misleading the population?"

Nina knew very well why. For years now, the Bolsheviks, dreaming of world revolution, had been spending huge amounts of money on financing strikes and armed uprisings around the globe. As a result, the Soviet Union was now looked upon as a criminal state that supported radicals and thought nothing of carrying out sabotage in neighboring countries while it talked about "friendship between nations."

Britain had cut off diplomatic relations with the USSR; France had expelled the Soviet ambassador; in Poland, the Soviet ambassador had been killed; in China, communists were hunted down like rabid dogs. Moreover, newspapers around the world were printing documents to prove that the Bolsheviks had carried out subversive action not only in Europe but also in Asia.

All this had been interpreted by the Kremlin as the "eagerness of the imperialists to stifle the new Soviet state," and they were now preparing for a major war. It was vital too for the government to whip up war hysteria so that the Soviet people would rally around their leaders and don't complain about the empty shops and queues for bread. It may have been peacetime, but now, ten years after the revolution that had promised prosperity for the working class, the country was back in the same state of economic crisis it had experienced in 1917.

Magda went to the department store to buy Nina warm clothes, but it turned out that she would have to pay forty rubles for a pair of ugly shoes with crooked seams, seven rubles for a pair of cotton stockings, and a hundred and fifty rubles for a winter coat.

"Remember, you told me that the average salary for a Moscow worker is seventy-five rubles a month?" Magda said, puzzled. "How do ordinary people manage?"

Nina sighed. "I wish I knew."

They left the shop empty-handed, and Magda made Nina a present of a velvet coat she had brought herself as a souvenir in Peking. It was an enormous, bright red horror with a folded collar and dragons embroidered on the back.

"You can alter it as you like," she told Nina. "You can't go about without a warm coat, and it would be mad to buy one at Soviet prices."

Nina worked on it for several days and transformed it into an elaborate but smart oriental-style cropped coat and a beret.

When she wore her new winter clothes, Nina was repeatedly mistaken for a participant in one of the fancy-dress performances staged to discredit the English. Young people from a propaganda brigade would wheel an enormous effigy of an Englishman about the streets of the city. From time to time, they would prop it on its knees, read some fiery, passionate speeches, and then begin to beat the cursed "Anglo-Saxon" over the head. Once, one of these Soviet youngsters even handed Nina a wooden mallet and told her to deal the effigy a blow on behalf of the Chinese insurgents.

Magda was trying to think how she could earn enough money to support herself. Every day, the Soviet papers and pamphlets brought into the Metropol carried announcements about how the USSR was planning to modernize its industry and how the country needed urgent help to acquire and develop the latest technology.

Magda wrote a short instruction book on soap making and asked Nina to translate it into Russian. But to her surprise, none of the publishers she approached offered her a contract.

"It's an interesting topic," the editor from the state publishing house, Gosizdat, told Magda, "but we need permission from the Administration for Literary Affairs."

Elsewhere, she was asked for a piece of paper from the People's Commissariat for Education, from the Supreme Soviet for Domestic Economy, or even from the OGPU.

"Do they think I've written something wrong?" fumed Magda. "They can submit it for scrutiny if they like. Let them send it to a specialist!"

"They won't be submitting anything for scrutiny," Nina said, wearily. "They just don't want any problems with foreigners. Who knows? You could be a foreign agent or a saboteur. And if so, they'll have to answer for it."

Although Nina tried to convince herself that she had nothing to do with the Land of the Soviets, she felt ashamed in front of Magda on account of the publishers, the effigy of the Englishmen, and the ugly shoes on sale for forty rubles.

6

Nina was also trying to think of ways to earn money.

The All-Union Society for Cultural Relations with Foreign Countries was handing out free tickets to the Bolshoi Theater to the guests at the Metropol so that foreign visitors could get a taste of Soviet culture. But far from all of them were interested in going to the opera, and some were happy to sell their tickets to Nina.

They did not realize that the Bolshoi Theater was the bastion of Soviet high society. This was where the country's elite gathered—the wives of people's commissars, famous writers, and sometimes members of the Central Committee. Many Russians would give their back teeth for a seat in the stalls; as for a ticket for a box reserved for foreigners, it was nothing short of a passport to paradise.

Nina came back to her hotel room after concluding another successful deal with the ticket traders and spread out her profits on the bed. One hundred and thirty rubles—not a great deal, perhaps, but at least now she could sense a glimmer of hope on the horizon.

Tucking the money away into her knitted purse, Nina looked out of the window. The clock in the middle of Sverdlov Square said five o'clock. Where could Magda have got to?

Magda had begun gathering material for a book she was planning to write about the Soviet Union. She had already come to the gypsies who lived in Petrovsky Park, and on another occasion, she had visited a flophouse that was home to hundreds of criminals, prostitutes, and down-and-outs. Given her formidable size and strength, she had decided she had nothing to fear.

Darkness fell, and a light autumn rain began to drum against the window pane. Several times, Nina picked up the novel borrowed from the hotel library, but all her thoughts were of Magda. Where had she got to this time? To interview the cleaners of public toilets, or to attend a meeting of Trotsky's supporters?

It was one in the morning when Nina heard heavy footsteps in the corridor followed by a knock at the door.

"H'llo—I'm back," Magda said in a drunk voice.

She stomped damply across the room and fell onto her bed without taking off her boots or her coat.

"What's the matter with you?" gasped Nina.

"Not with me. With Friedrich. He *does* care about me after all."

Magda had found the Comintern Hostel, gained entrance in through the kitchens, and arrived in Friedrich's room just in time for a celebration. The Party had forgiven him all his Chinese transgressions, both voluntary and involuntary, and appointed him pilot of a new passenger airplane.

"A Fokker-Grulich F II!" exclaimed Magda with relish. "Now Friedrich will be flying from Moscow to Berlin three times a week."

Suddenly, she blanched, got to her feet, and rushed to the toilet. Soon, dreadful groans could be heard from behind the door.

Magda was in such a bad way that Nina stayed by her side all night. When Magda was feeling a little better, she began to describe her meeting with Friedrich, her voice full of affection.

"Tomorrow, there'll be a parade in honor of the anniversary of the revolution. Friedrich has given me a special pass for the tribune, for important foreign guests. He told me it will be a military parade by the Red Army to show enemies—well, to show *us*, I suppose—that the Soviet people fear nothing. Oh, I need to go to the lavatory!"

Nina went to the floor manager and brought some clean towels.

"If you can't hold your drink, you've no business drinking!" she scolded Magda. "Did you talk to Friedrich about your relationship?"

"We didn't have a chance," said Magda in a weak voice. "We—I mean Friedrich has had a hard time of it. He's a loyal supporter of Trotsky, but he was forced to denounce him. He had to sign a document saying that the Chinese revolution was failed on account of the Trotskyites, who were part of a worldwide capitalist plot. Otherwise, he could have been sent to prison."

So, that's why they've given him a Fokker Grulich, thought Nina.

She had already heard, however, that all Trotsky's supporters had been given exactly the same choice—to betray their leader or face disgrace and persecution.

She helped Magda to bed and lay down herself but was unable to sleep. Deep down, she hoped that her English benefactress would become disillusioned with Friedrich and come with her to China. Everything would be much easier given Magda's large, confident presence. But it looked as though that was not going to happen.

"I don't think I can go to the parade tomorrow," Magda whispered barely audibly. "But I really need to take some photographs. I want to put them in my book."

"Just go to sleep, for goodness sake," said Nina.

The bedsprings set up a doleful creaking.

"You'll find the pass in the pocket of my coat," Magda continued. "Please go instead of me."

"But I'm not even a foreigner!"

"If you go in your Chinese coat, nobody will imagine for a moment that you're a Russian. The main thing is not to open your mouth and give yourself away. Please!"

Magda stopped suddenly, leaned over the side of the bed, and was sick on the floor.

Nina was ready to agree to anything just to get Magda to calm down and go to sleep.

3. THE ANNIVERSARY OF THE BOLSHEVIK REVOLUTION

1

The city was shrouded in a damp mist. On every side, trucks rattled past, and soldiers marched along wordlessly in felt helmets with the ear flaps down. Armored cars crouched darkly in the lanes and alleyways, and from time to time, the sound of a horse's whinny or the hollow echo of hooves could be heard as the Red Cavalry prepared for the parade.

Nina walked along in the crowd, clutching Magda's camera in its case to her chest. Magda had only one roll of film left and had instructed Nina to guard it with her life.

Everybody was gawping at Nina's ridiculous coat. One little girl was so distracted by the sight that she dropped her bunch of chrysanthemums on the ground.

Her mother immediately fetched her a clip on the back of the head. "Look after those flowers," she scolded. "What are you going to wave at the parade if you lose them?"

At the approach to Red Square, all was excitement and anticipation as if before a battle. Huge banners and portraits of Soviet leaders swayed in the swirling mist; military instructors made their rounds of the workers' brigades, giving instructions about the order of procession, while the shivering men hopped from foot to foot in an effort to keep warm.

Nina was also shivering, but more from anxiety than cold. She was certain that at any minute, she would be accosted by a policeman who would ask her to explain just how she had managed to get ahold of a foreigner's pass for the tribune.

But all went well. At the Iversky Gates, Nina showed her pass and walked out onto Red Square where the unpaved ground had frozen hard during the night.

A scarlet flag fluttered above the Kremlin wall. On the ancient spires of the Kremlin towers, the golden Imperial eagles, still untouched by the Bolsheviks, gleamed faintly through the mist. At the other end of the square, on the building of the State Department Store, GUM, an enormous canvas with a portrait of Lenin with his bulbous forehead and bourgeois suit and tie was flapping and billowing in the wind. As vast, mighty, and eternal as an Egyptian pharaoh, he looked down sadly at his own mausoleum built in the shape of a truncated pyramid. It was a strange quirk of history that twentieth-century Russia had revived the customs of Ancient Egypt.

Nina mounted the tribune and sat down on a wooden seat in the corner. Nobody seemed to be paying her any attention.

Gradually, the tribune filled up with foreign guests: Europeans and Americans, Indians and Arabs, but Chinese above all. Nina even saw some familiar faces among them. They were the men with whom she had traveled across the Gobi Desert. They appeared quite unsurprised by Nina's presence on the tribune.

The foreign guests kept up a stream of lively chatter, blowing on their frozen fingers and trying to find a good position from which to take photographs and film the parade. A tall, round-shouldered man wearing a pince-nez moved between them, switching between various foreign languages to greet his esteemed guests and ask if he could do anything to help them.

"And who are you?" he asked amiably when he came to Nina.

She acted as if she had not understood the question.

The man in the pince-nez stamped around a little longer before sitting down on the bench behind Nina.

"Who is that?" she heard him ask somebody. "The woman in the red coat?"

"I don't know, Comrade Alov," said a young voice. "I don't recognize her."

"Well, find out then," Nina heard Alov say.

He was almost certainly an agent from the OGPU, and Nina cursed herself for having agreed so thoughtlessly to Magda's request. What if this Alov were to ask for her documents? Or what if one of the Chinese guests told him that she was Russian?

Just then, some members of the Soviet government came out onto their tribune, and all the foreigners jumped to their feet and began to take photographs. Nina had no idea who they were, but she took some pictures too just in case they might come in useful to Magda. It was strange how small and unimposing they all looked; in their military-style suits, they resembled a crowd of provincial clerks dressed up as war heroes.

A moment later, a woman holding a folder rushed up to Alov and began to whisper to him. Nina could make out the words "Trotsky" and "spontaneous demonstration."

"Damn!" muttered Alov. Running down the steps, he disappeared into the crowd of soldiers standing in the cordoned off area.

Nina breathed a sigh of relief. She decided to take a few more photographs and leave while the going was good.

The bells of the Spassky Tower began to peal, and the roar of thousands of voices went up from the streets around Red Square. "Hurra-a-ah! Hurra-a-ah!"

To the strains of the "Internationale," the Soviet anthem, the first columns of demonstrators began to file out onto the square.

2

Announcements blared from the loudspeakers fixed to the lampposts around the square:

"Now, at the time of this celebration, greater than any in the course of human history, our thoughts are of our great leader, Lenin, who led the victorious troops of workers in their fearless attack on the bastions of capitalism!"

The government representatives smiled, saluted, and waved to the demonstrators with their leather-gloved palms.

Then a column of young people came level with the mausoleum—students, apparently. They stopped, and a moment later, a banner unfurled above their heads emblazoned with the words, "Down with Stalin!"

The orchestra fell silent, and a deathly hush descended on the square. All that could be heard was the chirruping of the sparrows that had flown in to peck at the horse manure.

"Long Live Trotsky!" shouted a young man's voice. "Down with opportunism and party separatism!"

His comrades sent up a ragged cheer.

A moment later, policemen came running in on the demonstrators from all sides.

Nina raised her camera and took a photograph. The foreigners around her were also snapping away.

"Stop! No photographs!" shouted a voice, and Alov came bounding up the stairs of the tribune two steps at a time.

His gaze fell on Nina. "I said no photographs!" he barked and snatched away her camera.

"What are you doing?" gasped Nina, forgetting that she was not supposed to speak Russian. "Give that back!"

"So, you're Russian, are you?" Alov grabbed Nina by the shoulder. "How did you get onto the tribune? And who are you, anyway?"

Nina broke free of his grasp, beside herself with fear, and rushed down the steps.

"Stop that woman!" roared Alov, but the police were too busy to apprehend Nina. A fierce struggle between the police and demonstrators had broken out in front of the mausoleum.

3

Nina wandered about the city all day, at a loss as to what to do. She could not go back to her hotel room—the OGPU had almost certainly worked out already who she was and where she lived. For them, an emigrant who had returned to Russia to take pictures of a pro-Trotsky demonstration could only be a spy, and Nina would be arrested without fail.

She felt guilty about Magda. How would she manage now without her camera or her interpreter? Moreover, Alov was almost certain to question her about Nina. Nina hoped fervently that Magda herself would not be suspected of espionage.

Nina knew that she had to get away from the capital. She decided to buy a ticket to a city as far away from Moscow as she could afford and then work out how to get to Vladivostok and then to China. But at the station, she was told that all the tickets for the next few months had been sold.

Nina walked out of the station and boarded the first tram that came along. Her mind was racing. Where could she go now? Where could she spend the night? On a park bench? Even if she found a place to shelter, she would, in any case, get through all the money she had managed to save in less than a month. And what then?

"Fares, please, comrades," said the conductor, pushing his way through the tightly packed passengers.

Nina reached into her pocket and froze. Her purse had disappeared.

"Are you going to buy a ticket or not?" asked the conductor.

"My purse has been stolen," Nina said.

The conductor grabbed her roughly by the collar. "Off the tram with you. Look at you, dressed up to the nines in velvet without a kopeck to pay for your ticket."

"The lady's had a fight with her lover, I reckon," grinned a blue-eyed soldier standing beside Nina. "And he sent her packing, skint."

The passengers began to laugh.

Nina pushed her way to the door and, as the tram slowed down, jumped from the footplate out into the muddy street.

It was already dark. The howls of chained dogs in nearby yards echoed in the night air. The street lights were not lit, and the only glimmer of light came from the open door of a small church nearby.

So, that's that, thought Nina. *There's no way I'll get back to Vladivostok or to China. I'll have to sell my coat tomorrow to eat, and then I'll throw myself in the Moscow River.*

She stood for a moment, looking distractedly about her. Then she headed toward the church. Surely she could find shelter there?

The church was almost empty. There was only a server in felt boots topping off the icon lamps with oil.

"You should be ashamed of yourself!" he whispered angrily at someone behind Nina.

She turned her head and saw the blue-eyed soldier she had seen on the tram.

"You should take off your hat when you come into a church!" the server told him.

"But I'm a woman, and women have to cover their heads in church," said the newcomer, throwing open her greatcoat. "You can check if you like."

The server faltered. "Good gracious…and I thought—but what a face!"

It was, indeed, difficult to tell from her face that she was a woman. She had no eyebrows to speak of, her throat sagged, and half of her front tooth had been broken off. She had the look of a heavy drinker.

Nina approached the icon of St. Nicholas the Miracle Worker, the protector of those in trouble, and began to pray under her breath. "Help me, desperate and sinful as I am, to find a way to live."

As she was praying, the blue-eyed soldier-woman stood behind her, scrutinizing her intently.

"What's your name?" she asked at last.

"Nina."

"Really? That's my name too. Only I don't like it—everyone calls me Shilo."

She stroked the golden dragon on the back of Nina's coat. "That's some coat. Present from your man, is it?"

Nina shook her head. "No, I made it myself."

"So, you're one of us, are you? A working-class girl? I thought you had a lover working for the state department store. I knew a guy who was the boss of a chemist's shop; he gave all sorts of presents to his girlfriends—condoms, douche bulbs, you name it. A nice guy, but he got shot for fraud."

"I don't have a lover," said Nina.

"You must have someone! Is it a husband?" Shilo opened her eyes wide and nodded sympathetically. "So, they've arrested him, have they? And confiscated his property? The police have gone crazy lately. They're picking up every profiteer they can find and arresting them under Article 7 of the Criminal Code."

Nina did not bother to contradict her. The woman was clearly unhinged.

"Here, will you sell me your coat?" asked Shilo suddenly. "I love it."

"I don't have anything else to wear though," Nina replied.

"We can swap. I'll get a coat for you. I can give you some money too."

"Citizens, the church is closing," they heard the server say.

Shilo grabbed Nina by the arm. "Let's go back to mine—I can sort it out."

"Where?"

"You can stay over at my place. You don't have anywhere else to go, do you?"

Nina glanced in wonder at the icon. St. Nicholas had sent her a miracle after all.

4

Shilo led Nina to an ancient monastery in the center of the city. A lantern hung above the iron-bound gates, and from time to time, its faint light fell on the writing of a notice on the gate: "—Corrective Labor."

Nina was too hungry and too cold to feel anything, including fear. She did not care where Shilo was taking her, to a monastery or a homeless shelter.

Shilo knocked quietly at a side gate. "Zakhar, open up!" she called.

Behind a metal grille in the window, a head appeared for a moment. "Is that you, Shilo?"

"That's right."

"And who's that with you?"

"A seamstress. Fyodor Stepanych asked me to find one."

The bolt rasped, and the gate opened. "Come in."

Under a low stone arch, a guardhouse had been set up, lit dimly by a paraffin light. The gatekeeper, a strapping young soldier, looked at Nina with suspicion.

"Show me your documents!" he demanded.

"She doesn't have any," said Shilo. The next minute, Nina saw her take a purse out of her pocket—Nina's own—and count off a couple of rubles for the soldier.

So, she was the one who robbed me, Nina thought, amazed.

What should she do? Demand her money back? But Shilo would never give it back, and then Nina would end up out on the street.

"Well, what are you waiting for? Let's go," ordered Shilo.

"Don't be afraid if you see a skull lying about," she added a moment later as they walked over a board that had been put down over a puddle. "This used to be an old cemetery for noble families. Some of our girls messed it up a bit. Time was, you'd dig up some dead fellow out, and there's enough gold on him to open a jewelry store. Then we'd have a party with Fyodor Stepanych; he'd bring vodka and food, and we'd have a feast that went on for days. But there are no more graves left to rob now—nothing but bones. Fyodor Stepanych keeps telling us to bury them, but they keep coming up again. Seems they don't like being in a common grave, so they come climbing up out of the ground."

"Who's Fyodor Stepanych?" asked Nina

Shilo laughed. "He's in charge of this center of corrective labor—prison, that is. I've been in here two weeks. It's not bad."

"You've *been in* here?" asked Nina in shock. "Do you mean to say you're a prisoner?"

"That's right. It's fine so long as they give you a sentence without solitary confinement, taking into account your 'low cultural level and difficult material circumstances.' Fyodor Stepanych sends us out to make money, and we share it with him."

"Doesn't anyone run away?"

"We'd have to be fools to run away from here. Just you try finding a room to yourself outside with free food! They even take us to the bathhouse on Fridays, and the children even hold concerts for us to help reform us quicker."

Nina gave a nervous laugh, despite herself. Well, she would have to live in a corrective workhouse for the time being. At least Alov would be unlikely to find her here.

Shilo walked onto the porch of a low one-story building and opened the door with a squeak. "In you come. Make yourself at home."

The dark room smelled of candle wax and dust. Nina looked around. The room with its barred window was empty except for a pot-bellied stove, a bundle of firewood, and a trestle bed covered with a blanket.

"It's a good place here," Shilo said, spreading her greatcoat on the floor in front of the stove. "The angels often come and visit me in this room. I sit here with them at the window. We have a smoke, and they take all my sins away. It's better than stain remover, I tell you."

"Please," asked Nina, "couldn't you give me back my money? Everything I had was in that purse."

"All right. But I get your coat. Deal?" Shilo tossed Nina her purse. "And I'll find you another. Don't you worry."

"Are you going to steal one?"

Shilo did not answer. She reached under the mattress and took out a hunk of bread and a battered flask.

"Here," she said, handing Nina the bread. "This is for you. And this is for me."

She took a swig from the flask, and Nina caught an acrid whiff of home-brewed vodka.

"I like you, you know," said Shilo a moment later. "It's not even the coat. It's just something about you."

"What about me?" Nina asked.

"You're like me, you see," said Shilo. "Before they threw me out the window."

Nina chewed away at the bread, feeling that nothing would surprise her any more.

5

They were awoken the next morning by a loud male voice. "So, who's this then?"

Nina, who had slept on the greatcoat on the floor, sat up with a start to see a small, gray-haired Chinese man with a sheepskin coat over his shoulders.

"Hello, Fyodor Stepanych," Shilo greeted the man cheerfully. "I've brought you a seamstress. Just look at what she can do!"

She handed the man Nina's velvet coat. He examined it critically.

"Who taught you to sew?" he asked Nina.

"My parents were tailors," she explained.

"Listen, boss. Take her on, why don't you?" pleaded Shilo. "She can live here. She don't have a place to go anyway—her husband's been arrested for profiteering."

Fyodor Stepanych scratched his chin thoughtfully. "I'll need to give her a job and see how she manages. If you show you can do it," he told Nina, "we'll take you on. You can run courses in cutting and sewing. Let's go!"

Nina could hardly believe her luck. If they let her stay here and paid her for her work, she would be able to raise the money for a ticket to Vladivostok.

Shilo gave her a blanket to keep her warm. Nina wrapped herself up in it and set off after Fyodor Stepanych.

In the daytime, the monastery did not look at all sinister. Nina saw brick walls with whitewash crumbling off in places, bare bushes, and puddles. It was clean and tidy, and the paths bore the traces of having been swept by a broom. There were no skulls anywhere to be seen.

In front of the ancient cathedral, a row of women stood performing exercises, supervised by a prison guard with a loudhailer. As she shouted out the order, they all raised their arms.

"Up on your toes!" she boomed. "Now breathe out!"

The prisoners obligingly breathed out small clouds of steam.

"I've introduced morning exercises to keep them fit," Fyodor Stepanych said. "All our women here are victims of capitalism. Thieves and prostitutes, you know, and I reform them through labor. Nobody here is idle."

With his captive women, he was like an estate owner with two hundred serfs. Some he used as groundskeepers and domestic staff, but most had been set to work making funeral wreaths and foot wrappings for Red Army soldiers.

Fyodor Stepanych made no secret of the fact that he sent the most accomplished pickpockets out to ply their trade.

"They only steal from the *Nepmen*," he said. "And their number's up soon, anyway."

Nina knew already that "Nepmen" was the name for entrepreneurs who had been given permission to engage in manufacturing and trade since 1921. The NEP, or New Economic Policy, had been introduced to restore the economy to its prewar level. After this, the idea was that the class of Nepmen was to be "liquidated," and the country would begin to build a truly socialist society in which all the means of production belonged to the state, and private enterprise would be forbidden by law.

Fyodor Stepanych took Nina to the vestry, which was in an outbuilding next to the church. Here, in a cold room smelling of mice, was a table with a sewing machine and some old trunks, black with age, on which were piles of church vestments.

"Here is your workstation," said Fyodor Stepanych. He handed Nina a purple cassock. "I'd like you to make a couple of skirts out of this. I think there should be enough material."

Nina looked at him, bewildered. "But that's sacrilege—"

"The priests don't need any of this stuff anymore," said Fyodor Stepanych with a wave of his hand. "They've all been sent to the Solovki labor camp long ago—to speed them on their way to the Kingdom of Heaven."

He began to lay out cassocks, surplices, and albs on the table.

"We'll use the velvet for skirts," he said, "the brocade for belts and collars, and we can use the winter robes to make coats for the proletarian women. You can sleep here on the trunks. I'll give you a couple of logs a day to keep you from freezing."

4. BARON BREMER'S TREASURE

1

Nina made an excellent job of the sewing task she had been set, but Fyodor Stepanych told her she would not be getting paid for her work.

"Can't you already sit by a warm stove and eat in our canteen?" he said. "What more do you want?"

Nina realized that she had fallen into a trap. Shilo had still not brought her the promised coat, and now the weather had turned so cold that Nina could not even put her nose outside, let alone go to the market and buy herself something warm.

"I've been put in prison without a trial!" she protested.

Fyodor Stepanych only laughed. "But you're free to go. Nobody's keeping you here."

He was only too happy to have a seamstress who could handle expensive material and would work for him free of charge. Nina's handiwork provided outfits for the prostitutes, bringing in a good profit for Fyodor Stepanych.

He watched Nina like a hawk to make sure that she did not help herself to offcuts and came in from time to time to count the leftover scraps of material. If he was in a good mood, he would sit for a while in the vestry, reminiscing about his youth.

He told Nina he had lived in Khabarovsk, working as a peddler who went door to door selling petty goods. His dream at that time had been to go to Canada. He had heard that the Canadian National Railways needed people to maintain the tracks that ran through remote forested regions. A family with two adult males could get an electric saw and an interest-free loan for twenty-five years. But it turned out that Canada would not take Chinese workers, only whites, and Fyodor Stepanych, smarting from the insult, had joined the Bolshevik party and enlisted in the fight against imperialism by becoming a warden of a women's prison.

Shilo would sometimes come to see Nina too. If she had a drink or two in her, she would always start telling stories of her past.

"We're like sisters, you and me," Shilo told Nina, perching on the cutting table. "Only my family's grander than yours. Have you heard of the Barons Bremer? Well, that's us."

She would describe in detail the luxury life she had once enjoyed and relatives so distinguished they had all but served in the court of the Tsar himself. But in all these stories, there was only one detail that rang true: during the revolution, Shilo had been raped by a group of soldiers and thrown out of a window. Her mind had been affected ever since.

"We had a great big house on Petrovka Lane," Shilo enthused. "Beautiful—like a palace. There were these carved oak panels in the dining room commissioned by my mother with portraits of all of us children as angels."

"So, what happened to your siblings?" asked Nina

"My brothers were shot in 1918, and my mother never got over the shock. She had a heart attack on the spot. But my father survived the revolution and the war. He worked as a shoeshiner on Pervomaisky Street, right opposite our apartment block. Only this summer, he was run down and killed by a cart."

Nina sighed. Everybody, it seemed, had lost loved ones.

"I had a fiancé once, you know," Shilo said one day. "He was a military attaché from France."

Suddenly, she began to speak French—correctly and with barely a trace of an accent. As she told the story of her romance with Jean Christophe, how they had met at the racetrack and later begun a correspondence, Nina listened, dumbstruck, glancing now and again at Shilo's raddled face. Who knew, perhaps she really had been a baroness? Nowadays, there were any number of doormen who had once been army colonels and cleaners who had been born princesses. They all survived as best they could, changing not only their appearance but also their very nature.

All the same, Shilo, with her fevered imagination, was capable of dreaming up any number of extraordinary things: an aristocratic past, angels in army helmets, or a samovar that whistled the "Internationale."

"Do you know what else I remember?" Shilo said. "I hid some sweets under the windowsill in the library. My brother Mishka was always stealing them from me, and I made a secret hiding place—I was clever, see. There was a panel you could pull out and hide things behind."

Shilo grabbed a pencil and began to draw a plan on a scrap from an old sewing pattern. "So, this is Petrovsky Lane, and this is our house. This is the gate and the courtyard. You go in and go upstairs…"

She told the story in such detail that Nina did not know what to think.

"You don't believe me, don't you?" Shilo asked. "I can prove it! I know where all our papers are. Father buried them in the yard after the revolution. There's a whole treasure trove there. If you go and dig it up, you'll see for yourself."

Only the day before, Nina had read an article in a newspaper about treasure hidden away by the "bourgeoisie" for a rainy day. Workers who were repairing former townhouses belonging to the nobility would sometimes find collections of porcelain, old embroideries, gold coins, and family silver.

"Do you remember exactly what your father buried in the yard?" Nina asked cautiously.

Shilo shrugged. "There was definitely a photograph album. There's a picture in it of me at seventeen." Shilo laughed and hugged Nina. "When I saw you on the tram, I stared and stared, and I couldn't believe my eyes; you were so like me on this picture!"

"Wait," Nina slipped out of her embrace. "Do you know where the treasure is hidden?"

"You bet I do. You go in the yard and count out five bricks on the wall to the right. The fifth one has a chip in it where Mishka threw a horseshoe and knocked a bit off. You need to dig right under it—" Shilo cut herself short. "But I'm not going there. There are evil spirits there."

Nina frowned. "Which evil spirits?"

"Those devils who threw me out of the window."

"But that was ten years ago!"

"I'm not going, I tell you. Go yourself if you want. I can take you there."

"But I don't have a coat."

"I'll let you have your coat for a bit. Listen. If you get our photograph album back, I'll be grateful for the rest of my life. I'll do anything for you! I'd love to have another look at my family after all these years."

That night, Nina could not get to sleep. Maybe this was her chance to escape? If the treasure really existed, it might contain something valuable. She could sell it to pay for her ticket back to Shanghai and return the money to Shilo later.

But who knew what was happening now in the Bremers' former mansion? There might be a police station there or worse.

2

Shilo went to Petrovsky Lane to see how the land lay.

"They've moved some government office into our house," she said to Nina. "They don't have a sign, and there are no dogs or groundskeeper. But there's a motor car parked in the coach house."

In the evening, Shilo brought Nina her Chinese coat. She also produced a small shovel. "Look at what I got from our grave robbers! Their business is bad these days. They're going around the city cemeteries, but there's only poor folk buried there—they don't even have gold teeth. Recently, they went to the funeral of a commissar specially, to have a look, and they saw him lying in his coffin with his boots on. But when they opened up his grave, the boots had gone. Someone had already taken them."

Nina could not imagine climbing into somebody else's yard—it was a sin after all. But then again, she had nothing to lose now, not after making church robes into dresses for prostitutes. She would never get into heaven with her record anyway.

"What if I'm caught?" Nina asked.

Shilo grinned. "The police will decide you're a thief and put you back in here."

Nina decided that if she was successful, she would not come back to Fyodor Stepanych. So, before she left, she changed into a dress she had made out of a gray priest's robe, trimmed with dark red velvet panels. It was comical to set off on a treasure hunt dressed for a cocktail party, but it would be a shame to leave the dress for the prostitutes—it was the best piece Nina had made.

As it got dark, Nina and Shilo set off for Petrovsky Lane. Snow began to fall. There was nobody about and no light from the windows—luckily for the treasure hunters, all the electricity in the district had been turned off.

"There's my house," said Shilo, pointing to a recently refurbished house opposite the Korsh Theater. "Do you see the window on the second floor? That's my window. I wonder who has that room now. It's a good thing they've put an office in there. If they'd put in tenants, they'd have messed the place up already."

Nina nodded.

Now that proletarian tenants were being packed into former mansions, they would alter them to their own taste without a thought for the architecture. In Moscow now, at every step, you could see the disfigured facades of buildings—their windows bricked up and their balconies destroyed.

Shilo tugged at Nina's sleeve. "Come on. I'll show you the best place to climb over. There's a woodpile on the other side of the fence here. You can get up on that and jump into the yard."

Nina looked doubtfully at her. "Maybe we should go together after all?"

"Are you starting that again?" snapped Shilo. "I've told you!"

"But what if I don't find anything?"

"You will."

"But what if someone catches me?"

"Just hit him in the face with your shovel, and that'll be the end of it."

Good lord, thought Nina. *What on earth am I doing?*

Shilo helped her climb onto the snow-covered woodpile. "Come on, St. Nicholas the Wonderworker—don't let us down!" She made the sign of the cross over Nina. "When you dig up the treasure, give me a shout, and I'll help you get out of there."

Nina felt like Aladdin sent by the evil sorcerer into the magic cave to find the lamp.

She jumped down into the snowdrift, and a minute later, the shovel came flying over the fence after her.

The small yard was covered in snow. All that could be seen on the ground were the dark marks of car tracks by the coach house.

Holding her breath, Nina stole along the stone wall. She reached the gate and began to look for the chipped brick. It was snowing more heavily now, and she could see very little in front of her.

At least it will cover my tracks, Nina thought as she ran her hands hastily over the brickwork.

At last, she found a deep pit in one of the bricks. She got down and began to clear away the snow beneath the fence. The ground had not frozen solid, but her shovel kept hitting some roots. Nina chopped away at them with the shovel, and the blows were so loud that they could have been heard a mile away.

Then there was a scraping of metal, and the shovel slipped along a flat surface. Nina threw it aside and began to dig with her hands. Her heart was beating fast with excitement and a sort of superstitious fear. She felt as if she was about to dig up not buried treasure but a coffin.

With a final effort, she pulled out a large metal box, its surface rough with rust. But it was too early to celebrate. She still had to get out of the yard.

Nina stood up, brushed the dirt from the hen of her dress and…froze in horror. Before her stood a huge, strapping man with a shaven head and dressed in an unbuttoned greatcoat.

"Do you need some help?" he asked with a grin.

Nina rushed to the fence, forgetting all about the box.

"Get me out of here!" she called, but there was no answer from Shilo.

Nina dashed to the locked gate and again to the fence.

The terrifying shaven-headed man came striding out of the swirling snow, grabbed Nina by the arm, and dragged her toward the house without a word. She started to scream, but he shook her like a doll. "Stop yelling!"

They were met in the dark entrance hall by two more people: a young man in a silk dressing gown and a large black woman—a servant with a paraffin lamp in her shaking hands.

"Oscar, we should call the police," barked the shaven-headed man. "I've caught a thief."

The young man took the lamp from the servant and began to examine Nina as if she were some exotic animal. Her red velvet coat, now covered in earth and snow, clearly made an impression on him.

"What are you doing here?" asked the man with a strong American accent.

Nina gawked at him, trying to catch her breath. This Oscar looked quite civilized. He had a well-groomed, pale face, close-set hazel eyes, and a fashionable pencil mustache.

"I didn't want to steal anything," Nina said in English. "I just needed some documents."

"What documents?" snarled the shaven-headed man, who clearly knew English but preferred to speak in Russian.

"I left a box out there in the snow—"

"Yefim, bring it in," ordered Oscar.

"Then the girl will do a runner!"

"No, she won't. Theresa and I will watch her."

Yefim went outside, and Nina took a look around her. She was not in an office but in a rich private house. The hall had parquet floors, and there was a whole array of expensive canes in a carved umbrella stand by the door and a crystal chandelier hanging from the ceiling.

Nina turned her gaze on Oscar.

Who is this man? she wondered. He was living in the center of Moscow like some lord. He even had a black servant.

Yefim came back with the rusty box, put it down on a pier table, and began to take out yellowed envelopes and paperwork. There was no sign of any money or valuables.

Oscar picked up a leather-bound photograph album.

"Property of Baroness Nina A. Bremer," he read the inscription on the cover.

On the first page was a picture of a young girl in a fancy dress and a fetching hat pulled down over one eyebrow.

"Look! It's her!" exclaimed Theresa, pointing at Nina.

Clearly, the photograph showed a young Shilo, and there was a definite resemblance to Nina. They did indeed look like sisters.

"So, you're a baroness, are you?" asked Oscar, looking at Nina with interest. "Well, I'm very pleased to meet you. Will you have dinner with me?"

Nina had expected that the evening might end in any number of ways—scandal, hue and cry, police procedures—but she had not expected an invitation to dinner.

"Th-thank you," she stammered. "I'd be delighted."

"Theresa, lay another place at the table, would you?" asked Oscar.

"Very good, Mister Reich."

They can think what they like about me, thought Nina, *so long as they don't call the police.*

3

Nina followed Oscar through a succession of rooms, and she was barely able to believe her eyes. Here, in the heart of communist Moscow, was a veritable oasis of capitalism. Every chair and every vase was a work of art.

What is Oscar Reich's line of work? she wondered. Was he a foreign diplomat? How could the Soviet government allow him to live in such dazzling splendor?

Nina had many questions she wanted to ask, but she bit her tongue. She had a feeling this man might be able to help her. The important thing was not to frighten him off.

As she went past a large mirror, Nina felt secretly pleased that she had decided to wear the beautiful dress. It would have been horribly awkward to dine with Oscar in her darned skirt and faded blouse.

Theresa ladled out soup into bowls. Nina tried a spoonful—it was real New England Clam Chowder served with thin pieces of melba toast and fresh herbs. She was prepared to act the imposter for a while for the sake of pleasures such as this. Shilo's grand title clearly opened the door to certain privileges.

Nina pointed out the wooden panels around the ceiling to Oscar. "Do you see those angels? They're portraits of me with my brothers. Mother had them carved specially. That's Mishka, and those two are Ilya and Anton," she said, naming the other brothers off the top of her head. Who knew their names, anyway?

Oscar looked at her with a mixture of amazement and disbelief. "So, where have you been living all this time?"

Nina improvised a tragic story about how she had spent many years roaming the country after the revolution and had finally decided to go abroad.

"There's nothing for me here," she said woefully. "I need money and documents, so I dug up my box."

"I understand," Oscar nodded.

Everything seemed to be going to plan.

I'll flirt with him for a bit and then ask him for a loan, thought Nina. *It'll be nothing to him to give me some money with his fortune.*

4

After dinner, Oscar told Theresa to light a fire in the library and to bring in a bottle of wine and two glasses.

Nina was delighted. This was a good sign!

In the library, she went straight to the window. As Shilo had said, under the windowsill was a tiny hiding place covered with a small piece of wood. Nina moved the wood to one side, reached into the crack, and took some sweets in silver wrappers, hardened with age.

"Help yourself," she said, holding one out to Oscar.

He laughed. "Antique sweets! Whatever next."

He had unnaturally white teeth that looked as if they were made of porcelain. *How much do crowns like that cost?* Nina wondered. They had to be more expensive than gold ones.

"Will you join me in a drink?" asked Oscar, opening the bottle. "Wine isn't like sweets—it gets better with time."

They chinked glasses and drunk to Nina's health.

Encouraged, she could not resist asking a question. "Tell me, who are you? What do you do?"

"I'm a Red capitalist," answered Oscar. "When there was famine in Russia, I brought a fully equipped field hospital over from the States and sixty thousand dollars' worth of canned goods. After that, the Soviet government gave me a concession, and now I have my own pencil factory at the Dorogomilovskaya Gate."

Nina was bewildered. The fight against capitalism was the mainstay of Bolshevik ideology. Why was an American allowed to own a factory in Moscow?

Seeing her confusion, Oscar laughed. "The Bolsheviks want to build a new kind of society, but they don't have the technical specialists they need: they've all either run away or died during the war. Currently, eighty-five percent of the population of the USSR live in rural areas, and half of them can't read and write. The first thing the country needs is to fight against illiteracy, and there's a huge demand for pencils and pens. So, they made an exception for me."

"Aren't you afraid that the Soviet government could just take away your factory?" Nina asked.

"You shouldn't confuse politics with the propaganda aimed at the man in the street. You may have noticed that the Bolshevik press likes to attack the English, the French, the Poles, and the Chinese, but they hold up the USA as an example—a model of modernization and business acumen. They're no fools in the Kremlin; they know very well that to get industry back on its feet, they need close ties with the United States. Europe is still recovering from the Great War, and America is the only country that will provide technology and long-term loans. The success of my business is like a pledge—a guarantee that one day Washington will acknowledge the USSR and create an embassy here. And as soon as that happens, foreign investors will start to move in."

"You're a brilliant diplomatist, it seems," Nina said, delighted.

Oscar shrugged. "I guess I just have a feel for business. I earned my first million when I was nineteen years old."

They sat on the divan and talked. Nina now felt completely relaxed, perhaps from the warmth and comfort or the excellent Italian wine. When all was said and done, she thought that had to be one of the greatest pleasures in life: to sit and chat with an intelligent man who clearly showed an interest in her.

She did not want to think about the future at all, not even the immediate future. But still, she glanced at the clock on the mantelpiece above the fire. It was already long after midnight. She hoped Oscar would let her stay the night in his house. Surely, he would not throw her out—Nina hinted several times that she had nowhere to go.

Oscar took a last sip of wine, put his glass down on the floor, and, without a word, pushed Nina down on the divan.

"What are you doing?" she cried out in a muffled voice.

He put his hand over her mouth and began fumbling hastily at the buttons of his trousers.

5

Yefim, his cigarette in his mouth, took aim at a ball with his cue and sent it rattling into the far pocket.

"You'll get yourself a dose of syphilis one of these days," he said, sullenly, as Oscar came whistling into the billiard room.

Oscar waved him away impatiently. "Skip it. Turns out this one was a nice little lady. Just a little shy for my liking."

Yefim put his billiard cue back in the rack. "I wanted to show you something."

He brought in one of the large gray envelopes belonging to Baron Bremer and tipped out its contents onto the green baize of the billiard table. It was a bundle of securities in German and Swedish firms along with a will registered with a solicitor, stating that all the baron's property was to pass to his children on his death.

Oscar looked at Yefim with amazement. "Do you think these papers are genuine?" he asked. "Is our baroness a millionairess?"

"It's possible."

Oscar scratched his head. "Well, it's impossible to get ahold of this fortune in the USSR, anyway."

"You need to think how to go about it," said Yefim. "We need all the money we can get."

Oscar liked to tell everyone that his business was going well, but in fact, things were getting worse every day. According to the original plan, he was to become a model concession-holder and attract foreign investors into the USSR, but nothing had come of it mainly because in the Bolshevik camp, the right hand did not know what the left was doing. One government department would hand out guarantees of private capital while another would threaten to destroy every last capitalist on earth. Who would start up a business in Moscow under such conditions?

But worst of all was the fact that the Bolsheviks kept altering the rules in their own favor. When Oscar had come to Russia, he had been promised that he could change Soviet money into foreign currency at the greatly reduced official rate and transfer the profit from his business into foreign bank accounts. But now there was a foreign currency crisis in the country, and the State Bank was doing all it could to prevent Oscar from taking a single cent out of the country.

Besides all this, Oscar was constantly hounded by various commissions connected with the trade unions or the police or the Chief Committee for Concessions. All these officials pretended to be concerned about the conditions of his workers when their real mission was simply to extort bribes.

Yefim had been the first to suggest to Oscar that they needed to get out of the USSR, and the sooner the better. He had never had any illusions about the Bolsheviks. Before the revolution, he had been the owner of a luxury bathhouse with private suites and had been through all the cycles of nationalization. He had had his accounts and property confiscated and eventually lost his house. If Oscar had not taken him on as his assistant, Yefim would have taken to drink long ago.

Oscar too understood that it was time to fold up his business and get out. But he had put everything he owned into his factory, and it was impossible to sell. He felt like a foolish child who has been warned countless times not to play with fire. Oscar had never heeded such warnings—he was a business genius after all. But now the genius had lost.

The securities belonging to Baroness Bremer could be just what Oscar needed to save him, but he had ruined everything.

A week of courtship, flowers, and chocolates, and Nina would have fallen for him hook, line, and sinker. Instead, he had treated her as just another victim of the revolution—a *lishenets* girl with whom he could do whatever he wanted.

Lishentsy was the name given in the USSR to former aristocrats, priests, and other "socially hostile elements" who had been stripped of their electoral rights. They could not find a job or receive credit, so in order to survive, young and attractive women in this position often resorted to working as escorts or sometimes even prostitutes. This was something of which Oscar took full advantage. Deep down, he was engaged in his own class struggle. He was Jewish, and once upon a time, princes and barons would not have let him past their thresholds. Now, their daughters were submitting themselves willingly to his embraces.

But this time, he had made a serious mistake.

He hurried back to the library. He had to convince Nina that he had been swept off his feet by a fit of uncontrollable passion.

5. THE GERMAN JOURNALIST

1

What could have happened to Nina? wondered Magda fearfully. *Had she been robbed and killed?*

It was more than likely. Magda's camera and Nina's velvet coat were valuable enough to attract thieves, and crime in Moscow was rife.

Magda could not make up her mind to go to the police. As sworn enemies of capitalism and White émigrés, they might decide to pursue the victims rather than the criminals. In a country ruled by a dictatorship of the proletariat, "class enemies" could not count on the state to protect them.

The only one who could help Magda was Friedrich; after all, he had friends in high places. But since he had been assigned to his new post, he would disappear abroad for three days at a time, come back, and catch up on his sleep before setting out again.

"I could come out to Germany," Magda suggested, "and we could meet there if you want."

But Friedrich did not want anything. He had only just managed to extricate himself from the trouble in China and had no wish to jeopardize his position by associating with an Englishwoman.

To add to her problems, Magda's visa was about to expire. She pestered all her acquaintances, asking if they could help her find work in the city until at last, a German journalist, Heinrich Seibert, told her that he had some good news.

"On Thursday," he said, "I'm meeting Edward Owen, the vice-president of the United Press news agency. His Moscow correspondent has broken a leg and gone abroad to get medical treatment, so Owen is on the lookout for a replacement."

Magda was hugely excited to hear this. Mr. Owen was a legendary reporter. It was said that his London headquarters was hung with photographs of him in the company of royalty, heads of state, and army generals. He earned a king's ransom and for good reason—under his leadership, the European section of the United Press was flourishing.

If Magda secured the post as the Moscow correspondent, she would not only have her visa renewed but also be able to move out of the despised Metropol into an apartment of her own. Moreover, she would no longer be a member of the bourgeoisie; she would be a member of the working class, and Friedrich would not have to hide from her.

For the first time in many years, Magda had her hair cut and said a prayer or two. She also bought a Kodak camera from another hotel guest just in case. She wanted to be able to show Owen the full scope of her talents not only as a writer but also as a photographer.

2

Heinrich Seibert had come to Moscow soon after the Bolshevik revolution and fallen on his feet; he had a wonderful apartment on the premises of the former Neapolitan Café, a car, and a large circle of friends. With his short, top-heavy body and his large forehead, he looked like an aging satyr. In Germany, no girl would have looked at him twice; but in Moscow, he attracted interest merely by virtue of being a foreigner who possessed countless treasures out of the reach of ordinary mortals: a wristwatch, shampoo powder, sunglasses, and the like.

That evening, Seibert sat at the window of the half-empty restaurant of the Bolshaya Moskovskaya Hotel (formerly the Grand Hotel), celebrating a small victory of his own. A friend of his, an engineer, had smuggled out an article he had written on the reasons behind the current economic crisis in the Soviet Union, and it had caused quite a stir.

The Bolsheviks took great care to prevent material "denigrating the Soviet system" getting out of the country, and articles of this sort had to be published under a false name unless you wanted your visa canceled. But Seibert was still pleased; it tickled him to hoodwink the Soviet censors and to publish an article saying exactly what he thought.

A waiter arrived, bringing Seibert a dish of cold sturgeon with horseradish and a decanter of chilled vodka.

It was already getting dark; the elegant chandeliers and white cloth-covered tables were reflected in the dark blue of the great windows of the restaurant. Seibert poured himself a shot of vodka and raised a glass to his own reflection. "To freedom of speech!"

In his article, he had written about how it was unprofitable for Soviet citizens to engage in industry of any sort whatsoever, let alone agriculture. In order to feed the Red Army, the police, and Soviet officials, the government was deliberately lowering the procurement prices for grain, and each year, the peasants were sowing less and less. What was the point in working for such a paltry sum?

When the Kremlin spread rumors of an imminent English attack on the USSR, the frightened peasants had begun to hide everything edible and to distil their grain into the time-honored Russian "hard currency" of bootleg vodka or *samogon*. As a result, the markets and shops in the cities were now empty.

Soviet officials had the right to use special cooperative shops attached to each government department, and people had quickly realized that the safest bet was to find work as a civil servant. Meanwhile, the Kremlin, rather than taming this bloated bureaucratic machine, was fighting political opposition and the surviving remnants of private enterprise. Naturally, the country was in the grip of an economic crisis. It was unavoidable.

Glancing out of the window, Seibert saw a taxi draw up at the hotel entrance. Out stepped an elegant foreigner in a dark gray suit and Homburg hat. A smartly dressed little girl of about four years old stepped out after him, holding a toy horse under one arm.

A minute later, the pair came into the restaurant, and Seibert almost choked on his sturgeon: the daughter of this modishly dressed foreigner was Chinese. She had rosy cheeks still flushed from the cold and shiny black eyes, and her spiky hair, which had been pressed flat by her hat, stuck out comically on the back of her head. She brought the toy horse with her and sat it down at a table just a few feet away from Seibert.

The girl's father was about thirty-five or forty years old. He was slim, tanned, and well-groomed and had the look of a European aristocrat. *How could he have married a Chinese woman?* Seibert wondered. Now, the man would not be accepted into any respectable company. And his daughter, who had clearly taken after her mother, would encounter all sorts of difficulties.

"Kitty, put your horse on the floor, please," said the man. He spoke in English but with quite a strong accent. "Horses don't sit at the table."

"They do!" said the little girl.

"Is that so? And who decided that?"

"I did. I'm big. I know that two plus two is four."

"What about two plus three?"

Kitty frowned for a moment but then laughed. "All right. I'll feed my horse in the hotel room."

They were speaking in a mixture of three languages: Russian, English, and what sounded like some Chinese dialect.

While they were waiting for their order, Kitty's father performed tricks for her with a sugar lump, hiding it in his fist and then producing it from out of his cuff or behind his ear.

Kitty let out peal after peal of laughter. "Again! Again!"

Seibert could not resist. "Excuse me," he asked, leaning toward them. "I'm curious. Are you by any chance with a theater?"

The man turned around. "No," he answered. "I'm a journalist." He handed Seibert a card on which was written "Klim Rogov."

"Oh, you're Russian, are you?" asked Seibert, still more surprised.

"By birth, yes. But I have American citizenship, and Kitty and I live in Shanghai. I work at an English-language radio station there."

"And I work at the Wolffs Telegrafische Bureau news agency," said Seibert. "So, how do you find Moscow?"

Klim gave a shrug. "I came here to find people who took part in the civil war in China, but everywhere I'm told that the Soviet Union sent no agents out there."

Seibert gave a knowing smile. "What do you expect? Politics is nothing but a collection of myths and legends we are told we must believe."

"Somehow I'm not convinced," said Klim. "A friend of mine left for the USSR together with a group of political advisers who had been working in China, and they all seem to have vanished into thin air. I've been trying to find them for a month but with no luck."

"You should come to my house tomorrow," said Seibert. "I'm having a bit of a gathering at five o'clock, and there will be an English lady there, Magda Thomson. She knows some people who used to work in China."

"Thank you! You've been a great help!" Klim turned to his daughter. "You see, Kitty? Didn't I tell you everything would be all right?"

Seibert felt like some kind of magician who could grant the wishes of ordinary mortals with one click of his fingers.

3

KLIM ROGOV'S NOTEBOOK

Keeping a secret diary is like putting a notice on your door saying, "Keep out!" and then deliberately leaving it slightly open.

It's a bad habit, and I've tried to give it up many times, but what can I do? I'm a scribbler by nature, one of that writerly tribe whose chief pleasure in life lies in hunting out words and collecting meanings. Without this pleasure, I don't think I could survive. Anyway, I've promised to give a detailed account of my adventures in Soviet Russia to Fernando, so let that be my excuse.

I caught sight of this notebook in a kiosk in Vladivostok. It was only after I'd bought it that I noticed it included a note of "memorable events" for every date: executions of revolutionaries, forcible dispersal of demonstrations, assassination attempts on the Tsars, etc. This diary could quite easily be called the "Book of the Dead," but I hope for me it will tell a story of survival, not of disaster.

My wife has disappeared without a trace. The only clue I have to her whereabouts is an article in *Pravda* newspaper announcing that the "Chinese group" with which she was traveling has arrived in Moscow.

When my friends in Shanghai heard I was coming to Russia, they thought I had lost my mind. As the

Bolsheviks see it, any foreigner with a Russian name is a White émigré, and a White émigré is, by definition, an enemy.

But nobody stopped me at the border. My American passport and respectable coat were enough to mark me out as a VIP. Clearly, the petty Soviet officials were afraid to stick their necks out. Who knows who I might be—a famous engineer or a foreign scientist invited to attend the tenth anniversary of the Bolshevik Revolution?

It took Kitty and me sixteen days to reach Moscow, and what sights we saw on the way! The train was accompanied as far as Khabarovsk by a convoy of Red Army soldiers who stood on duty on the platforms between the railcars and on the locomotive. They were there to protect us from the gangs of armed bandits that often attack passenger trains in the Far East just like the Indians in films about the Wild West.

There were still several rusty, derailed trains lying about from the time of the civil war. A number of bridges had been blown up, and the Bolsheviks had replaced them with temporary wooden structures. It is quite terrifying crossing these makeshift bridges; the train inches across, the beams groaning and cracking from the weight, and all the passengers hold their breath, praying it will hold out till they reach the other side. Once, the bridge did actually start to break up under us, and the locomotive only just succeeded in dragging the last car across to the opposite bank. It was the strangest feeling as if we had crossed the Rubicon.

I don't know how long my search will last and how long my money will hold out. I never had access to Nina's bank account, so Kitty and I are living off my own modest savings.

My friends are right, of course. It is madness to stake everything you own on one card and to set off of your own accord to this bogeyman of a country, which émigré mommies use to frighten their naughty children. Even if I do find Nina, the chances are that we'll only break up again. Even before she left, we both realized that our life together wasn't working out, and we were only heading for some inevitable catastrophe.

So, why am I chasing after the ghost of this long-lost love?

I have always admired Nina's energy, her dignity, and her ability to rise up out of the ashes like a phoenix, but there's more to it than that. She has her own distinctive feminine charm, which I find quite irresistible. And I'm not the only one by any means. I've seen how other men look at her. Where will I find another woman like her? If I hadn't come to Moscow, I'd be doomed to loneliness or a pointless search for someone exactly like her, and I don't even want to think about that.

I am like a passenger on the *Titanic* after the shipwreck, freezing in the icy water, refusing to believe that the ship is doomed, convinced that the whole thing was just some emergency drill. Any minute now, the ship will rise up from the depths, the holes in its hull will close up, and the captain will steer it off on its original course.

4

Klim could not wait for the meeting with Magda.

He hailed a cab at the hotel and helped Kitty into an old-fashioned sleigh.

"Pray that everything works out for us," he whispered in Kitty's ear. "God will hear your prayers, I'm sure."

"Please let everything work out for us!" shouted Kitty at the top of her voice. Then she turned to Klim. "Do you think he heard that? Or should I say it louder?"

The cab driver laughed into his frost-covered beard and took up the reins. "Giddy up now, girl, as fast as a motorcar!"

The evening sky over Moscow blazed with a crimson sunset. The sleigh rushed on, its runners squeaking in the snow. Wind blew in their faces and clumps of dirty snow flew up from under the horse's hooves.

As they came out onto Lubyanka Square, the cab driver turned to his passengers and pointed at a high building with a clock on its facade. "Have a look at that, comrade foreigner. That building used to be the central office for the Rossia Insurance Company, but now it's the headquarters of the OGPU, the political police."

The clock face reflected the scarlet of the setting sun, and Klim found himself wincing. He felt as if he were being closely watched by some fiery eye, all-seeing and dispassionate.

Kitty fell asleep on the way to the party.

The driver stopped at a single-story house with high windows. On the walls of the house was a frieze showing blue sea, rose bushes, and dancing girls with tambourines. Meanwhile, a palisade of enormous Moscow icicles hung from the roof.

Klim lifted Kitty in his arms and walked up the porch steps. He knocked at the door, which bore an inscription in Gothic script: "*Aufgang nur für Herrschaften*"—"Only the noble may enter here."

"Look who's here!" cried Seibert as he threw open the door, and lowering his voice to a whisper, added quickly, "Come with me into my bedroom. You can put your daughter down there."

Klim looked around. The hall was hung from the floor to the ceiling with gilt-framed paintings. Seibert collected them, apparently.

A coat-stand groaned under the weight of a mountain of furs and coats, and a whole flotilla of galoshes was arrayed on the floor. From the living room came the sounds of music and bursts of laughter. Somebody was playing the piano.

Klim felt awkward coming to this party where he knew no one, bringing his daughter, creating bother for strangers. But what could he do?

His host led him deep into the dimly lit apartment with high arched ceilings and narrow winding corridors. Any noble guests who reached Seibert's bedroom would find themselves in cramped quarters hung with dark blue wallpaper. In the middle of the room was a colossal bed with a carved headstand and orange pillows. A mirror gleamed on the ceiling, and on the chest of drawers beside the bed was a china figurine of the devil with an enormous phallus.

Seibert gave an embarrassed chuckle and turned the figurine to the wall. "Just a bit of fun, you know."

Klim laid Kitty on the bed and pulled off her felt boots, hat, and coat.

There was a crash from the kitchen behind the wall as if somebody had dropped a metal tray.

"Your little girl's lucky to be able to sleep through that noise," said Seibert in an indulgent tone. "As for me, I wake up at the sound of a broom on the pavement outside.

"Let me take you to meet my guests. Magda should be here any minute."

5

Magda was half an hour late. The windows of her tram had been white with hoarfrost, and she had missed her stop.

"Owen is here already," said Seibert when Magda stumbled into the hall, frozen through, her nose streaming from the cold. "Have you got everything prepared?"

Magda sniffed. "I think so, yes."

Glancing in the mirror, she straightened her dress—dark blue with a pink collar and square buttons on the sleeves. She should have hung her camera case around her neck so that it would be clear straight away that she was a professional journalist and photographer.

"Come on then. I'll introduce you," said Seibert, and Magda followed him into the living room.

The room was already full of people all talking at once in a mixture of German, English, and Russian. A pair of Frenchmen, already mellow with drink, were playing a duet on a grand piano and singing "Valentina," and a few couples were dancing. Wreaths of tobacco smoke spread out in the orange light of the lamps.

"Not long ago, we were at war with one another," Seibert told Magda, "and now, here we are in the heart of snowy Moscow, drinking wine, and none of us bearing a grudge against the others."

"Where's Owen?" asked Magda in a trembling voice.

Seibert pointed out a stout gentleman in a circle of guests.

Magda went a little closer and listened to the conversation.

"When I crossed the border, the customs officials made me declare my fur coat and galoshes," Owen said. "Can anyone explain why the Soviets do this?"

"It's their way of fighting unemployment," answered a dark-haired gentleman in an elegant three-piece suit. "If there aren't enough jobs, they make some up on the spot. Just imagine how many people you can employ counting all the galoshes that come in and go out of the country."

"Who's that?" Magda asked Seibert.

"His name is Klim Rogov. He wanted to talk to you, actually."

"Why? I don't know him. Or perhaps I do—"

Magda was interrupted by another loud crash from the kitchen.

"Is that you again, Lieschen?" barked Seibert. "What an infernal nuisance that girl is! Always breaking things!"

He ran from the room.

Magda glanced again at Klim Rogov. She had just remembered that was the name of Nina Kupina's husband. Could it really be him?

"Soviet power is like a pyramid," Klim said, turning to Owen. "You have all these leaders at the very top, and each of them picks his vassals—not the best men but the most loyal; those who will always do their bidding. As a reward for their loyalty, the vassals are given profitable official positions, and they are allowed to live off them. All these people have their own vassals, a rung lower down, and the ones lower down have others beneath them, and so on. Everybody's welfare depends on the strength of the pyramid, so they do their best to reinforce it."

Klim began to talk about the members of the Soviet government and who belonged to which camp.

"How do you know all this?" asked Owen in amazement.

"I make it my professional habit to be interested in all the details," Klim said.

"Do you speak Russian?"

Kim nodded. "I have fluent Russian, English, and Spanish, and I can also speak the Shanghai dialect."

"Could you write me a short piece now on approval?"

"Of course."

From the next room came the sound of a child crying, and Seibert came rushing in, looking harassed.

"Your daughter has woken up in the other room," he told Klim.

"I'll be right back," Klim said, growing pale.

"You've got ten minutes," shouted Owen after him. "I'm leaving soon."

Seibert took Magda by the elbow. "Mr. Owen, I'd like to introduce you to Miss Magda Thomson."

"Excuse me," Magda interrupted him. "I have to powder my nose." She set off toward the door.

Magda had already realized that Owen was hoping to hire Klim Rogov as his correspondent, and there was no way she could get around it. No amount of photographs would make up for the fact that she knew no Russian.

6

Kitty was sitting on the bed howling, her head flung back. "Da-a-a-ddy!"

Klim switched on the night light and took her in his arms. "What is it, little one? I'm here."

Kitty put her arm around his neck and tried to say something but just kept sobbing and hiccupping.

Klim sat her on his knees. "There, there, little one. Shh…"

He should never have left Kitty alone. How awful for a four-year-old to wake up in an unfamiliar, dark room!

Klim took a notebook from his pocket and, still hugging his daughter, began to write a short article about the currency profiteers who haunted the Moscow markets.

The state bank, Gosbank, exchanged money at the official rate of one ruble, ninety-four kopecks for one US dollar, but in Riga, a dollar was worth four rubles. The unofficial course was used by foreigners living in the USSR as well as thousands of underground traders and smugglers.

"I want to go home," sobbed Kitty.

"Soon you'll be at home in your own bed. I promise," whispered Klim, kissing her on the back of the head, still warm from sleep. "I'll think of something."

"What about Mommy?"

"We'll find her."

Klim had not even dreamed of finding work in Moscow. It was more than he could have hoped for. With a press card, it would surely be easier for him to find Nina.

After all, it was one thing to ask questions as an individual but quite another to ask them on behalf of a respectable news agency.

Klim finished his article, took Kitty in his arms, and went out into the hall.

Owen was already putting on his coat while Seibert rummaged through the pile of coats for the lost gloves.

"Is the article ready?" Owen asked.

Klim handed him the open notebook.

As Owen read the article, his face lit up. "Could you change the money for office expenses on the black market too?"

"Most likely," said Klim.

Owen handed him his business card. "I think you're going to work out twice as cheap as your predecessor. Give me a call tomorrow at the hotel, and we can go over the details."

Owen's gaze fell on Kitty, and like many others, he could not resist asking about her. "Excuse me. Is that your child?"

Klim nodded. He was annoyed by the way people were always so curious about his daughter's oriental appearance.

"Well, your personal life is no business of mine," said Owen, putting out his hand. "I'll see you soon."

As the door closed behind Owen, Klim turned to Seibert. "Has Miss Thomson arrived yet?"

Seibert gave a startled blink. "Oh, dear, you should have had a word with her. Magda was hoping to work at United Press, you see, and I think you've just stolen her job."

"And where is she now?" Klim asked, alarmed.

"I don't know. Go and have a look for her. She's a big, tall young woman."

Still holding Kitty, Klim rushed into the living room, then the kitchen, and then began to search through a number of dimly lit rooms full of furniture. *Damn it all*, he thought. Now Miss Thomson would refuse to speak to him!

He found her in Seibert's bedroom, sitting on the bed and sobbing, rubbing at her wet cheeks with her hands.

"Get out of here!" she shouted when she saw Klim.

Kitty, frightened, began to whimper, and Klim retreated with her into the corridor.

"You sit here. I'll be back in a minute," he said, handing her his gold watch that Nina had given him as a present long ago. Kitty had had her eye on it for some time and was overjoyed now to receive this unexpected prize.

Klim headed back into the bedroom, pulled the door almost shut behind him, and sat down in an armchair opposite Magda.

"Miss Thomson," he said, "my wife has gone missing, and I hope you might be able to help me find her."

"I have no intention of helping you," cried Magda. "You stole my job!"

"I won't take the job if that's what you want."

Magda reached into her pocket for a handkerchief and blew her nose loudly.

"Go to hell, you and your noble gestures! After speaking to you, Owen will never hire me. And you won't find your wife, anyway."

"Why not?"

Through angry curses, Magda told him of her friendship with Nina and about her disappearance.

"She was wearing a red velvet Chinese coat with dragons embroidered on the back," Magda said. "It was very noticeable. I suppose somebody may have spotted her."

"Thank you," said Klim, his head lowered.

"You're very welcome, I'm sure," Magda muttered as she left the room, slamming the door so hard that the china devil fell off the chest of drawers and shattered into pieces.

THE PRINCE OF THE SOVIETS

6. MOSCOW SAVANNAH

1

BOOK OF THE DEAD

I've signed a contract for the next eleven months and am now officially head of the Moscow Office at United Press. It's an impressive title, but in fact, the office consists of only one person. So, I have been put in charge of myself.

The first thing I had to do was to pay a visit to the People's Commissariat of Foreign Affairs and fill out a sheaf of forms. In order not to arouse undue curiosity, I introduced myself as a New Yorker of Russian origin who had lived several years in China. This seemed to do the trick.

Next, I went to the so-called Press Department, which is the name for the Soviet censors' office, through which every single article sent abroad must pass.

The Soviet censors seemed a pleasant, well-educated bunch. They all wear spectacles, speak three or four foreign languages, and every one of them is a distinguished revolutionary. Once upon a time, they escaped the evils of Tsarism by going into exile in Europe and spent their time denouncing all those who stifled freedom in Russia. They came back after 1917, and now, they are the ones trying to rid the country of any ideas that offend the powers that be.

The head of the department, Yakov Weinstein, immediately explained the official line to me to forestall any foolish questions on my part.

"True freedom of speech is only possible here in the USSR," he said. "Ours is the only country in which workers can freely have their say in the press without fearing for their lives. No other nation publishes letters from peasants in its newspapers."

I have read some of these letters, according to which the inhabitants of remote villages in Siberia use the modern metric system to measure their land, and a proud Don Cossack calls himself a *muzhik*, a commoner. What does it matter that for a genuine Cossack warrior, such an epithet would be an insult? Such minor details mean nothing to the average reader of *Pravda*.

"Censorship is a measure we find unavoidable, or at least, necessary," Weinstein told me, stroking his impressive, tightly curled beard, which made him look rather like a priest. "Unfortunately, foreign journalists are doing their best to damage the reputation of our country in the eyes of the international proletariat. Sometimes, they have no bad intentions; they simply misunderstand the situation. One reporter, for instance, reported that troops had been brought into Moscow after seeing soldiers on the street. In fact, what he saw was merely a group of cadets on their way to the bathhouse. But sometimes foreign journalists deliberately distort the facts. Not long ago, the *Daily Telegraph* reported that the OGPU was shooting workers. Now tell me—have you seen a single execution or dead body in Moscow?"

I admitted I've not seen anything of the sort. And how am I to know what goes on in the cellars of the Lubyanka?

"I'm glad to see you take such a level-headed view of the situation," said Weinstein, delighted. "We like to lend a helping hand to foreign correspondents and relieve them of the responsibility of digging out information for themselves. Every time a noteworthy event takes place, we send out a communiqué. Journalists write their articles on the basis of our bulletins, and then the material is sent to press. As you can see, we have no intention of standing in your way."

He also added that if I reported objectively on events, he would help me make a career for myself as a journalist.

"I trust you realize," he said, "that any success you may have had with a Chinese radio station is neither here nor there. As soon as your contract expires, you will have to find a new job. Stay on the right side of Owen and our department, and you can be assured of glowing references."

I'm sure this is what he tells every new correspondent. Basically, it was a warning: should I get on the wrong side of Weinstein, the censors will make it impossible for me to work, and my employers will fire me for failing to reach an agreement with the local authorities.

As a matter of fact, Owen also demanded absolute objectivity just before he left Moscow, telling me that if I had anything important that would not get past the censor, I should smuggle it out to London.

"You'll have to find your own way of sending articles abroad," he said. "But you have to be very careful. If you're caught, you could be expelled from the Soviet Union. We've already had some cases of expulsion. The Soviet officials are convinced that only the 'enemies of the working class' are capable of criticizing their actions, and they believe these enemies should be 'neutralized.' So, don't take unnecessary risks."

2

Seibert advised Klim to rent an apartment from a friend of his, Elkin.

Elkin was a small man, all angles and sharp edges, with a hooked nose and a ginger toothbrush mustache. He had grown rich during the NEP years and brought a decaying mansion in the elite district of Chistye Prudy in the center of Moscow. Soon, he had opened a secondhand bookstore called Moscow Savannah on the ground floor while renting the rooms on the floor above to foreigners.

"We still haven't finished refurbishing the building," he said apologetically as he showed Klim and Kitty around the apartment. "But there's nothing I can do about it. It's impossible to get ahold of building materials at the moment."

It was true that the living room had patches of crumbling plaster on the walls, and the parquet floor was scored and scratched as though heavy furniture had been dragged across it. But it also had arched windows of colored glass and a fireplace decorated with sky-blue ceramic tiles. Elkin had also thrown in some extra pieces of furniture—a piano in need of tuning, a divan, and a ladies' dressing table with candlesticks in the shape of giraffes.

There were a great many giraffes in the apartment; they adorned everything in sight, from the door handles to the lace curtains.

"What do you think?" Klim asked Kitty. "Would you like to live here?"

"Yes!" Kitty was staring wide-eyed at the bronze heads and horns on the light fitting. "Look at all the funny horses!"

Elkin asked for an astronomical sum in rent—two thousand American dollars for eleven months. "At present, I am in some financial difficulty," he said. "I'm afraid I can't take any less."

In the course of the next few days, he and Klim haggled over the rent in a series of telephone calls.

"I'd be better off in the Grand Hotel," Klim protested. "It's cheaper there, and the plaster isn't falling off the walls."

"I'm asking a reasonable price," Elkin kept repeating in a tedious voice. "You won't find a private apartment anywhere else in Moscow. The house has a telephone, a stove in the kitchen, a storeroom, and a bathroom. You'll need a bathroom for your daughter."

"But you're asking more in rent than I earn!"

Eventually, Klim knocked the price down to a thousand dollars. United Press agreed to give him an advance on his future salary, and he moved into the apartment on Chistye Prudy.

That evening, a tousle-headed old man dressed in a torn padded jacket appeared at Klim's door and introduced himself in a deep voice, "My name's Afrikan. I'm the yard keeper here. And this old girl is Snapper." He pointed to a fat white dog skulking at his felt boots. "She's our guard dog. We've brought you a present, see? We thought you might need something to sit on to play the piano." He held out a stool cobbled together from pieces of birch wood.

Klim gave the yard keeper a ruble, and Afrikan promised he would make three more stools for "his excellency" so that Klim could receive visitors.

"Did you see our new tenant, Snapper?" he muttered admiringly as they went downstairs. "A prince—a Soviet prince! I thought there were no more of his kind left."

The dog whined as if in agreement. The new tenants had won her respect straight away as Kitty had treated Snapper to the skin from her salami.

3

BOOK OF THE DEAD

United Press has more than a thousand clients throughout the world, and every day, I have to send dispatches to New York, London, Berlin, and Tokyo. Then my cables are sorted and sent out to the local papers—our subscribers.

It turns out that, as a foreign correspondent in Moscow, finding a story is a devil of a job. All the material sent out by the Press Department consists of dull accounts of government sessions and decrees, so I have to rely on my own wits.

I was wrong to think that Soviet citizens would be happy to speak to me if I showed them a press pass. Foreigners in Moscow are kept apart from the local population not only by the language barrier but also by the fear of the OGPU. After all my years abroad, I have developed a slight foreign accent, and besides that, my clothes give the game away completely, so people here are wary of me as they are with any "guest from overseas."

The only Soviet citizens prepared to talk to me are the simplest souls. Yesterday, I interviewed a delegate to the All-Union Communist Party Congress from the Yakutia in the east of Siberia. I asked him what they were voting on, and it turned out he knew nothing about politics whatsoever but was so grateful to the Party that he was willing to approve anything.

"Before the revolution, I was nothing but a reindeer herder," he explained. "The Party brought me up in the world. I've come to Moscow! Why would I go against them?"

He wandered around the gilded corridors of the Tsar's palace that had once played host to royal receptions, putting out a finger to touch the huge mirrors and laughing in delight.

"Now I've seen everything!" he said as we parted. "I can go to my grave happy."

The censor didn't like my interview with the reindeer herder.

"What is this?" Weinstein said, frowning when I brought him the papers to sign. "We sent you a communiqué. Isn't that enough for you?"

The communiqué had been on the subject of "the fight against political bias in the interests of improving the organizational work of the Party."

No matter how hard I tried, I couldn't get Weinstein to pass my article.

"We don't know yet if we can count on you," he said. "Don't think of taking any liberties before you have our trust."

4

There are around forty foreign correspondents in Moscow. We visit each other often to dance, play poker, and exchange gossip. The strict censorship and the dearth of information only heighten the thrill of the chase for us. We all compete to see who can be the first to dig up some story and send it out to a foreign press office.

It may not be as prestigious to work in the USSR as in Europe, but my journalist colleagues all agree that they wouldn't change Soviet Russia for anything. We enjoy unheard-of privileges here: we earn huge salaries by local standards, live in private apartments, and have access to embassy doctors and cooperative stores of the People's Commissariat of Foreign Affairs where you can buy coffee, cocoa, different cheeses, and even exotic fruits. We're not afraid of all the local petty tyrants or the secret police. After all, we can leave the country at any moment.

There's a word for what we have—FREEDOM, the same freedom that was a cherished dream for several generations of Russian revolutionaries. Oddly enough, since 1917, the only people in the USSR who enjoy any sort of freedom are the foreign diplomats and journalists.

Even high-ranking Party officials are not immune to high-handed treatment from those at the top. A few days ago, I rang the former Central Committee member, Grigory Zinoviev, who, like Trotsky, has been placed under house arrest. When I asked him how he was, he said in a trembling voice, "Wait a minute. I need to have a word with my comrades."

Without permission from his superiors, he can't even complain of a cold. Outside his gilded cage, he has nowhere to run.

No other job I have had has aroused such a whirlwind of conflicting emotions. Soviet Russia is an extraordinary amalgam of the most benighted superstition and ignorance and the most advanced ideas, inspired creativity, and belief in the future. Despite everything, many people believe that here, in the USSR, it will be possible to build a new world, a world in which all the dreams of mankind will somehow be realized.

I am going to public lectures at the university, and I am struck by the intelligence and inventiveness of Soviet scholars. Architects are designing extraordinary buildings, Sergei Eisenstein is making astonishing films, and meanwhile, the crudest, most vile propaganda is being disseminated on all sides. The disenfranchised are being hounded mercilessly, and nobody seems capable of an ounce of fellow feeling. There's a lot of talk of a "sacred struggle" or a "sacred war," and it seems that the majority of the population approve.

My biggest problem though is that I have no time to search for Nina. Life here is a constant mad rush: my telephone never stops ringing, couriers from the People's Commissariat of Foreign Affairs are always bringing new communiqués, and I keep having to run off somewhere to attend some event or other.

While I am away, Afrikan is keeping an eye on Kitty, who has already decided she wants to be a yard keeper when she grows up. Now her favorite game is sweeping the floor, muttering in a deep voice, "The Russian people have gone to the dogs. New this, new that—you mark my words, the only thing that comes of new boots is aching feet."

Kitty has also become friendly with Snapper. The two of them share an interest in hunting out the boot grease, which Afrikan hides. It is made with bacon fat. Snapper can sniff it out, Kitty gets it out, and they both have a treat.

I have been around all the kindergartens in the area and found out a number of shocking things: The nursery teacher in the Golden Fish makes the children stay out in the freezing cold on purpose so that they get sick. The less children she has to look after every day, the less work for her. The nanny in the Rowan Tree tells the children she can take her eyes out and put them up on a high shelf so that they can see everything that is going on. The thought of these eyes, separated from their owner, is enough to induce nervous hiccups in the children.

In the third kindergarten, a good one, there are no free places, and in the fourth, they refused to take Kitty because she was a foreigner. Apparently, the director was afraid my daughter was some tiny spy who might force her to disclose important strategic information about her high chairs and bibs.

I advertised for a helper: a responsible woman who spoke fluent English with teacher training, typing skills, and excellent references, good with children, and a good knowledge of Moscow in case I had to send her off on some errand. I also stipulated that she should be able to cook and clean and take on the running of a household.

It soon became apparent that angels of this sort are simply not to be found. Even if they did exist, they would hardly be tempted by the modest salary I was offering of thirty rubles and the tiny storeroom in which I hoped to install my new helper.

Seibert told me that in any case, I would not be allowed to hire outside help—apparently, you need special permission to do so.

"The Soviet authorities want to know what goes on in the houses of foreigners," Seibert said. "So, they'll send you from pillar to post for all sorts of official documents. And then, when they've finally weakened your morale, they'll plant an OGPU agent in your house."

"What about your Lieschen," I asked, remembering his maid. "Does she work for the OGPU too?"

"Naturally," said Seibert. "But she's very fond of me, all the same."

5

Afrikan appeared at the entrance to Klim's room accompanied by a dark-browed girl in a peasant coat and a paisley headscarf.

"I've brought someone to see you, sir," he said.

The girl held a rolled mattress under her arm, a knapsack on her back, and from her elbow hung a string of ring-shaped rolls.

"Hello, mister prince, sir," said the girl, bowing from the waist.

Klim looked quizzically at Afrikan. "And who might this be?"

"A serving girl for you, that's who," he said. "Her name is Kapitolina. She's a fool of a girl, I grant you, but you'll find she's a hard worker. And she's got a certificate."

The certificate was a "Certification of the Right to Operate a Stove and Boiler," and it stated that Comrade Kapitolina Ignatevna Kozlova was "trained in the rules of operation of heating appliances and in safety procedures."

"She can watch the little one," said Afrikan, "and cook you breakfast. And she's handy with a needle too. She's my own niece, from Biruylevo village—I can vouch for her. She came to the city to earn money for her dowry, but mind you don't pay her anything—it's against the law unless you get permission. Instead, just get her a nice piece of cloth the next time you're at that cooperative of yours. And if anyone comes from the Labor Inspectorate, you can tell them she's visiting me and helping you out."

Klim looked the blushing serving girl up and down. "Do you know Moscow well?" he asked her.

"I do indeed!" she exclaimed. "It's the best city on earth. This is the third time I've been. There's so much to see!"

"Can you read and write?"

Kapitolina hung her head, her brow furrowed.

Afrikan took Klim aside. "Look at her!" he whispered, gesturing toward Kapitolina's generous buttocks. "Time was, you'd have had to keep a fine girl like that under lock and key. But now there are no men in the village to speak of—half of them dead in the war, and nothing left but the scrapings of the pot: old men, drunks, and cripples. Without a dowry, no decent man will take a wife."

"Is your niece good with children?" asked Klim.

"She has five younger brothers and looked after the lot of them, and not one of them died."

"Uncle Afrikan tells me you'll let me live in the storeroom," said Kapitolina. "If that's true, I'll do anything you like: I'll wash your dishes with my tears, whatever you say."

"I think that would be going a little too far," said Klim, and he asked her to make a start on the washing right way. Kitty hadn't a single clean pair of stockings left.

6

It could hardly be said that things began to run smoothly with Kapitolina's arrival in the house, but life took on added interest.

Kapitolina brought her possessions with her from the village—a huge metal-bound chest and a large icon so soot-blackened that the image of the saint it depicted was all but invisible.

"Who's that?" asked Kitty.

"That's my little god," Kapitolina said affectionately. That same evening, she taught Kitty to kneel before the icon and prostrate herself before it, which Kitty enjoyed hugely.

On top of the chest Kapitolina laid a mattress that had been stuffed with old banknotes—worthless since the currency reform. During the war, her father had earned a pile of money selling straw at inflated prices, and he had hidden it all in the mattress, intending it to serve as a dowry for his daughter.

"Well, at least I can sleep like a millionaire," she said, plumping up her treasured mattress.

From the trunk, she produced embroidery frames, knitting needles, crochet hooks, and balls of yarn and thread. Soon, the apartment began to fill up with decorative cloths and ornamental towels.

"It's prettier like this," she said, spreading a cloth embroidered with roosters over the typewriter.

Klim kept taking away the cloth, but the following day, there it would be again in the same place.

Kapitolina had firm ideas about domestic economy. "You should eat the stale bread before you start on the fresh," she lectured Klim.

"But if I do that, the fresh bread will have gone stale by the time I eat it," he objected. "Am I supposed to live on dry rusks?"

Kapitolina's cheeks reddened with indignation. "Fine then! Let the bread rot and the house burn, and let's all go to the devil!" she cried.

Klim did not back down, so Kapitolina would eat up the stale bread herself to not let good food go to waste. She did nothing by halves: if she was making soup, she would boil up a whole vat full of it; if she started on the washing, she would set all the linen to soak at once, not leaving a single dry sheet for the night.

"You great dolt!" Afrikan scolded her. "You donkey!"

Kapitolina would sometimes roar with laughter. At other times, she would snap back, "Stop your yelling! You're not living in the Tsarist regime now!"

One day, hearing Snapper barking and Kitty squealing, Klim went into the kitchen to see what was going on.

"Get rid of this fool of a girl!" Afrikan demanded. "She's just burned a pound of your coffee."

"Informer!" Kapitolina wailed. "Why are you such a backstabber?"

"I'm not a backstabber. I'm trying to see you do things right. What did you think—that the master wouldn't miss all that coffee?"

"Well, he didn't miss the cup, did he?"

"What cup?" asked Klim, frowning.

Kapitolina and Afrikan both fell silent. There was a tense pause.

"The cup was on the table, and they had a fight and started running around the table," Kitty explained. "And everything fell off. But there's no need to get mad, Daddy. Kapitolina gave me my milk in a tin."

Klim took some money from his wallet. "Kapitolina, go out for me and buy us some new cups."

"Don't go sending that great lummox out to a china shop!" cried Afrikan in horror. "She'll break everything in sight."

But Kapitolina was already winding the paisley scarf around her head. "Yes, sir, this minute, sir! I'll be quick, so I will—I swear to God."

Klim had wanted a guardian angel to relieve him of his household chores, but Kapitolina was more like a goddess of destruction. He could not use her as a courier either. She did not know Moscow, and in any case, she was not allowed to go anywhere. Anyone taking messages from a foreigner needed official permission.

Klim bit the bullet and went to the People's Commissariat of Foreign Affairs to ask permission to hire an assistant.

Weinstein was clearly delighted at this turn of events. "We'll find you somebody with just the right qualifications," he promised.

7

"Sir," Kapitolina hissed and ran up to Klim on tiptoe—she believed that this was less distracting. "There's a woman asking about a job as a courier. Her name is Galina Dorina."

Klim told Kapitolina to let the prospective courier in, and in walked a diminutive, shabbily dressed woman with an extraordinary face. She had almond-shaped eyes the color of honey, a long thin nose, and full, pale lips. With her looks, Comrade Dorina would have been well-suited to play the role of a Christian martyr from ancient Byzantine icons.

"Good afternoon," she said. "I've been sent from the People's Commissariat of Foreign Affairs."

"Sit down," said Klim, pointing to the divan, "and tell me about yourself."

Comrade Dorina asked Klim to call her Galina. She told him that there was nothing much to say about her life. She had worked until quite recently as a filing clerk. But now, the Commissariat was laying off staff, and she was looking for a new position.

"Have you ever worked as a courier?" asked Klim.

"No, but I know Moscow well—I grew up here. And I have a good pair of felt boots. If you don't take me on, you should ask the other candidates about their footwear. Without felt boots, you'll find your courier ending up in bed with a cold."

"Do you have any other skills?"

"I can type in Russian, English, and French and do shorthand."

"Could you type something for me as a test?"

Galina sat at the typewriter like a pianist at her instrument and shot an enquiring glance at Klim. He began to dictate the first article that caught his eye from the *Times*: "The Soviet Union's economic experiments are continuing to amaze the world…"

Galina clattered away confidently at the keys and, in just a few minutes, had typed out an article about the budget crisis in the USSR. Klim could not believe his eyes: there was not a single typing error in the whole text.

"And with your skills, you still want to be a courier?" he asked.

Galina shrugged. "I need any work. And I've heard that foreigners have their salary paid on time. Is it true?"

Klim nodded. So long as this Galina did not ask for too high a wage, there seemed little point in interviewing anyone else for the job.

As he looked at her, he noticed an ugly lilac scar on her neck, protruding from beneath the collar of her blouse.

"I see you're looking at my scar," Galina said. "Perhaps you'd better ask me right away how I got it. Otherwise, if I come and work for you, you'll only keep wondering about it."

Klim smiled. "How did you get it?" He rather liked this Galina.

"My husband was a commissar in the civil war," she said. "The White bandits set fire to our house down. I had to carry my daughter out in my arms, but my husband died. I was badly burned."

"How do you manage alone with your child?"

"What's there to manage? There's not much washing as we hardly have any clothes, not much cleaning as we live in one small room, and we don't have anything much to cook either."

She got up. "Well, I'll be going now. If you would like to take me on, you can call me—I have a telephone at home."

Klim saw her out.

In the hall, Galina pulled on a pair of huge men's felt boots. "Goodbye," she said.

Suddenly, she looked at Klim with a serious expression. "There's just one thing I want to say. There's a mistake in your paper, the *Times*. Socialism isn't an experiment; it's a necessary stage of human development."

"Let's look at it logically—" began Klim, but Galina interrupted him.

"We don't need your logic! What can you and the *Times* possibly know about us? You're trying to crush us, to undermine our belief in our own strength, but we don't care! We…" Galina put her hand on her heart. "We *know* that there is not a capitalist army in the world that can defeat us. We shall never surrender; we shall fight to the end for our bright future."

Suddenly, she became embarrassed. Her face reddened, and her lips began to tremble as if she were about to cry.

"I'm sorry," she said. "I know I've spoiled everything, and you won't employ me now. I just wanted to make you understand…"

There was no need for explanations. Klim could see that Galina lived a very hard life and that all her hopes were tied up in the idea of the "bright future," which the Soviet press continued to depict in such glowing colors. The article from the *Times* was challenging this belief, so Galina refused furiously to accept the facts cited by the foreign journalist.

"I'll take you on for the job," said Klim. "But let's agree on one thing: we all have a right to our own opinion: you, I, and the *Times* newspaper."

Galina nodded, bitterly. "You wouldn't happen to have a cigarette, would you? I'm badly in need of one, but I left my packet at home."

"I don't smoke," Klim told her. "I have a small daughter, so I won't allow cigarettes in the house."

"Of course. I'm sorry. I was just a little flustered."

Galina ran outside, and Klim went back to his room. He watched from the window as she cadged a cigarette from a young man loitering by the skating rink across the road. She smoked it hungrily, looking back now and again at the Moscow Savannah building.

Klim had no doubt that Galina would inform on him. Well, let her inform the authorities that he had sent off a dozen cables checked by the censor or that he had gone to a stationery store to buy blotting paper. Perhaps she might even earn a ruble or two for herself.

7. THE SECRET POLICE AGENT

1

Galina Dorina was a dentist's daughter. For as long as she could remember, her family's large apartment had been a meeting place for the revolutionaries welcomed into the house by Galina's mother, who was keen to be thought of as a progressive social reformer.

The badly dressed guests would eat and drink their fill before they began to give speeches declaring that the Tsar, the landowners, and the capitalists were bleeding the life out of the Russian people.

Galina's parents encouraged her to read books in which the idea of freedom was lauded to the skies; her own life, however, proceeded according to a strict and unvarying schedule from the moment she greeted her parents each morning to the moment she lay down to sleep at night in the position considered most conducive to healthy breathing.

When Galina turned sixteen, her mother made her a wardrobe of new clothes and started taking her daughter out to social engagements to make the acquaintance of important gentlemen with stout figures and gleaming bald heads. The family had run up debts, and Galina's parents were hoping to arrange a good marriage for her.

"You'll find her a very obliging girl," Galina's mother would assure them.

Galina had a keen instinct for what was required of her and generally lived up to her parents' expectations, whether it was a question of achieving good grades at school or disappearing into her room when she was not wanted.

If she fell short in any way, her father would hiss in her ear, "You're in for it this evening." Later, he would thrash her with a dog leash.

Her mother was given to periodic fits of rage, during which she would often pick up the first thing she could lay her hands on and hurl it at her daughter. The scar on Galina's neck had been caused by a pair of red-hot curling irons—the story about the fire was her own invention.

One day, Galina's mother had invited over to the house a revolutionary, Comrade Alov, who was under surveillance by the Tsarist police. He was twelve years older than Galina and wore a ridiculous pince-nez on a greasy ribbon. The cook took one look at him and dubbed him the Stick.

Comrade Alov's passionate speeches had a profound effect on Galina. He spoke of how, in the present cruel age, the country needed not men and women but "superhumans" free of the doubt, fear, and petty vices of ordinary mortals. This, he argued, was the only way to retain dignity and not to demean oneself before those in power.

Whenever Alov was invited to dinner by Galina's mother, he would criticize his hostess for her sentimental books and deplore her husband's desire to live "as well as the next man."

"We only live once on this earth," Alov said passionately. "And look at how you're wasting your lives! Aren't you ashamed of yourselves? Is that really all you want—to be narrow-minded, bourgeois conformists?"

"Oh, dear, I *am* ashamed," Galina's mother sighed, dabbing away a tear with a scented handkerchief.

"Hear, hear! Spoken like a true man!" her father exclaimed and scribbled down phrases from Alov's speech in the special notebook he used to note down words of wisdom.

A romance grew up between Galina and Alov, but when her parents found out, they threatened to take their daughter's young man to the police. Alov was not the son-in-law they had been hoping for.

He took Galina away with him to Paris, where the Bolshevik party had assigned him to go, and that was the last time she saw her parents. Many years later, she found out that they had died of hunger during the civil war.

2

Galina did everything Alov asked or even hinted, cooking and cleaning for him, typing out his articles and translating materials from English and French into Russian. Alov had no intention of marrying Galina, so he informed her that she was an emancipated woman and that marriage was a bourgeois institution, unthinkable for one who held his convictions.

In 1914, war broke out. As a foreigner, Alov was not required to sign up, but he went to the front nevertheless as a volunteer to spread revolutionary propaganda among the French troops.

Galina was convinced that he would be killed. Soon after Alov had come back for a few days' leave, she found herself pregnant and resolved to keep the child. Seven months later, her daughter Tata was born.

But despite Galina's fears, Alov survived the war. He was gassed in the trenches, and as a result, suffered periodical attacks of a mysterious, dreadful sickness that would leave him doubled up with pain, struggling for breath. He took to wearing amber beads on his wrist, saying that they helped when he had an attack.

Early in 1919, Alov returned to Moscow with his "family," found work with the political police, and was given a room in the ancient Select Hotel, which was now horribly dirty and run-down.

The revolution had rid the country not only of exploitation but also of all creature comforts: everyday essentials—screws for spectacles, costume hooks and eyes, or nail scissors—had become unattainable luxuries. But Galina did not complain: what was a little discomfort when they were fighting for a bright future for all mankind?

She was desperate to believe that their efforts would not be in vain. She wanted to think that soon she would have her own divan covered by a plaid blanket and her own painted porcelain cup from which to drink hot chocolate, a private kitchen and sink, and her own lavatory where she could leave the commode without worrying that it would be stolen by her neighbors.

But week followed week, year followed year, and nothing changed.

Galina was a useful addition to Alov's life; not only did she carry out his every wish without a word of complaint but she was also able to take care of herself. But little Tata and her screaming got on his nerves. The three of them were all cooped up together in one small room where there was nowhere to hide from the baby's cries. He would shoot accusing glances at Galina as if to say, "Because you took it into your head to have a baby, now we all have to suffer!"

The neighbors would knock on the wall and shout, "Keep your little pest quiet!"

Galina, flushed and hectic, would often slap Tata, which only made the little girl cry louder.

"Are you a complete fool, woman?" Alov would hiss miserably.

He would go out for a cigarette, and Galina would hug Tata and cry bitterly, "Forgive me, please, for God's sake!"

3

Alov had been charged with keeping an eye on what the foreign press was writing about the USSR. He carried out his work so well that finally he was given a room in an apartment on Bolshoi Kiselny Lane.

"We need to have a serious talk," he told Galina when he received the official warrant.

He began by thanking her profusely for having been such a faithful comrade and for her devoted work in the fight for communism.

Galina listened, wondering where all this was leading.

At last, Alov drew himself up and, unable to meet her eye, informed her that he was marrying an actress.

Galina was speechless. She could not imagine how Alov could have fallen in love with another woman, still less decide to get married. After all, he had always told her he was against marriage.

"I would like to do the right thing by you," added Alov, "so I am proposing that you and Tata take my new room. After all, I'm much in debt to you."

"But what about you?" blurted out Galina, still reeling from the shock. "They'll take away the room at the Select Hotel now, won't they?"

"I'll manage. Don't worry."

So, Galina and her daughter moved into Bolshoi Kiselny Lane, and Alov moved in with a friend, an OGPU agent, who had extra living space. Galina did not know whether to be pleased about her new situation or to weep with the humiliation of it all.

True to his word, Alov married his actress, and Galina decided to have a look at her rival.

This rising star was called Dunya Odesskaya. She had no permanent job and found work here and there as an understudy in the theaters. She was a pretty girl with huge, watery eyes and short blonde curls but had no talent to speak of. Galina wondered if while at the front, Alov might have received a serious blow to the head that had affected his judgment.

Tata soon forgot all about her father, who never even showed his face in Bolshoi Kiselny Lane, and Galina had made up the story about the commissar who had died in the fire so that Tata would not feel that her father had abandoned her.

Tata would tell the story to everyone she met with great pride before showing them an important family relic—a crystal ashtray with a broken corner, which Galina had bought at a street market.

"This was my father's," Tata would say. "He gave it to me on my third birthday."

To Galina's surprise, her relations with Alov did not come to an end. Once or twice a month, he would invite her to his office to "drink tea." Those visits would end with passionate sessions on the office divan, after which Galina would leave deeply satisfied, not so much by Alov's prowess as a lover but by the thought of having taken revenge on her cow-eyed rival.

She had three abortions, the last of which, to her relief, had made her blessedly infertile. This, at least, put an end to the twice a year visits to the midwife to be "cleaned out."

Galina was twenty-nine, and her face was already etched with the first faint lines of suffering. If anyone ever asked her what she liked to do best, she would answer, "Smoking."

4

Alov ordered Galina to go to work with the American journalist as an assistant. "We need someone to keep an eye on that character. Try to work your charms on him."

Now, they had been reduced to Alov acting as if he were Galina's pimp.

Every day, when she came home, she would complain of him to her imaginary partner, who she thought of as *her man*. She had lived side by side with this man for years now; falling asleep by his side, having breakfast together, going out for walks, and sharing her most precious and secret thoughts with him. Galina's man had strong hands, thick, dark eyebrows, and a long fringe that fell over his forehead. He was reliable and generous, able to laugh at himself, and quite incapable of displaying greed, selfishness, cruelty, or dull indifference to the troubles of others.

Galina had become resigned to the thought that she would never have such a man. Her lot in life was to scurry about like a mouse, trying to find a crumb to eat, to build her little nest, and bring up her daughter.

And yet all of a sudden, here *he* was, a man who appeared to have been created from her own dreams. A man too marvelous to be real—her new employer. This foreigner who spoke Russian with a slight accent; this man whom she was obliged to betray.

Nobody treated Galina like him before. Klim would offer her *real coffee* or sweets. From sheer force of habit, he would pull out a chair for Galina or open the door for her. When he gave her a parcel to take to the post office, his fingers brushed her own, and the mere touch of his hand would send waves of heat through her body that made her weak at the knees.

Alov asked her to tell him in detail what Klim got up to and what he thought about the politics of the Soviet government.

"He calls the revolution an experiment," she reported, her eyes lowered. "But he enjoys working here, and he likes Soviet people. He was born in Moscow, you see, but he left Russia as a child."

There was much more that Galina chose not to tell Alov. Sometimes, when she heard Klim talking about the USSR, she wanted to cover her ears.

"To hear the Bolsheviks speak, they're waging war on the capitalists," he told her once. "But they are actually at each other's throats. They produce nothing but hatred and are obliged to consume it themselves."

If Alov had found out about these conversations, he would immediately have included Klim on the list of enemy journalists and demanded that the Press Department deport him.

"Where's Rogov's wife?" asked Alov, making a note in the official file.

Galina herself would have liked to know. "He never talks about her. I tried to ask Kitty, but she told me that he had forbidden her to say anything about her mother. I didn't like to insist."

"You did the right thing," Alov nodded. "We don't want Rogov to get suspicious. Well, congratulations. You've done a good job, and you'll get a bonus this month. Come to the Trade Union Committee, and you can pick up a free ticket for a lecture on 'The Question of Rejuvenation and Immortality.'"

At night, Galina would lie in bed, eyes wide open, horrified at what she was doing.

I'm betraying the man I love—and not even for thirty pieces of silver but for tickets to lectures I don't want to go to.

But the next day, back she would go to Chistye Prudy, say good morning to Klim, and sit down at the typewriter to take dictation of the next article. Klim would walk to and fro, thinking aloud, and Galina would stare at him. Everything inside her would seem to contract into a single point of brilliant light.

"Dearest one," she would repeat to herself, "God give you happiness—that's all I ask."

5

Afrikan came in from the street, dragging in some fragrant pine logs after him, and began to lay a fire in the fireplace.

"The law courts are saying that sharing a primus stove counts as having a family with this person," he muttered. "Along comes some woman with a can full of paraffin, fries eggs for you, and you're done for."

Afrikan shot a glance toward the door to see if Galina was coming. Then he lowered his voice to a whisper. "You listen to me, sir," he said. "Don't let Galina near the primus, or she'll make mincemeat of you."

Klim laughed. "And what about Kapitolina? Can I trust her to use the stove?

Afrikan sighed. "Sorry, sir, but you don't understand anything." He shuffled about for a minute, tending to the fire, and then went off to the gatekeeper's lodge.

In fact, Galina had become indispensable to Klim. She was now his secretary, housekeeper, courier and, most importantly, a nanny to Kitty. Kapitolina had taken to calling her the "deputy mistress."

Klim handed over all the housekeeping money to Galina with a sense of relief. Before long, his apartment was utterly transformed. Every week, Galina would go to an auction at the Church of St. Pimen where goods left over from second-hand stores were put up for sale.

Soon, Klim was the owner of a wind-up gramophone, a pair of oriental jugs, and a bronze figurine of a shepherdess that served as an inkwell. His living room was furnished with elegant chairs and an enormous mirror that stretched from floor to ceiling while the holes in the plaster were covered with cinema posters featuring Pola Negri and Clara Bow. The table was laid properly for every meal, and a full dinner service with gold trim stood in the display cabinet. The general effect, while strange, was very comfortable and convivial.

Galina and Kitty hit it off almost immediately, but Klim wasn't sure how to act with Galina. He felt guilty to see her doing so much for him for the salary he paid. As a sign of his gratitude, he took her to a shoemaker who served the city's foreign embassy staff and had some elegant shoes and smart, fur-lined boots specially made for her.

Kapitolina gasped when she saw the new purchases.

"Don't let anyone see them!" she exclaimed. "You might get them pinched. Hide them in the trunk, quick!"

But Klim insisted Galina wore the boots. "A woman should give the impression of elegance at all times."

When Afrikan found out about the presents, he told Klim he was a dead man.

6

BOOK OF THE DEAD

I've given several interviews to newspapers and even gone on the radio talking about life in China in the hope that my wife will hear about me and get in touch. But there are so few radio sets in Moscow, and what are the chances of Nina passing a loudspeaker on the street at exactly the right moment?

I've tried going to the police to find out if anyone has heard anything about a Chinese coat decorated with embroidered dragons, but it's no use. The women in the offices are either too lazy to take on any extra work or don't want anything do with me.

Without connections in high places, it's impossible to fight your way through the red tape of Soviet bureaucracy, so I've decided to go to some high society functions in the hope of finding new friends.

These banquets are held in palaces confiscated from the Tsar and always attended by the same crowd: ambassadors and diplomats, senior officials, and People's Commissars with their wives. By way of entertainment, they invite along certain pet poets, actors, and musicians. We foreign correspondents have taken the place of the aristocracy and are now the embodiment of "polite society."

So far, things have not been going too well. I only have to mention the word "China" to be met by strange looks and vague mutterings: "I don't know," "I've never been there," or "Sorry. I haven't the time right now." Nobody wants to be associated with the Soviets' debacle in the Far East. Strange, as only a few months ago, every loyal Party member thought it his duty to support the Chinese revolution.

Duplicity is, in my opinion, the chief characteristic of the Soviet official. In public, the Party leaders try to look as much like workers as possible: they dress like workers, behave like workers, and even curse every time they open their mouths. But in private, in their own circle, they indulge in every extravagance imaginable.

Almost all the Soviet leaders have left their wives (old Bolshevik party members) and found themselves new girlfriends. Any respectable man these days, it seems, has to have a charming young lady on his arm.

If the masses only knew how their leaders amuse themselves! The functions I've been to have nothing in common with the workers' leisure activities praised in Party leaflets. Glittering chandeliers, the delicate tinkle of china bearing the royal monogram, and imperious waiters, who once served in the household of the emperor, slipping between the tables. These old servants go about their duties with a fastidious sense of detachment as if to announce that their new clients are not fit to use plates previously owned by grand dukes.

A jazz band, the only one in the whole of the city, plays popular western tunes—all this is to make a good impression on foreigners. But once they have a drink inside them, all the foreign guests want to hear something more exotic: revolutionary songs and gypsy romances.

Often at these banquets, I am approached by beautiful ladies who come up and sit beside me. The interesting thing is that these women are all different—some are blondes, some brunettes, some slim, some voluptuous. The same thing happens to all the foreign correspondents. The OGPU is clearly trying to work out what our tastes are.

Seibert laughs at me. "Stop being so difficult," he tells me. "The OGPU are at their wit's end. If you keep being so stubborn, they'll send you a handsome young boy one of these days."

He's quite happy to get acquainted with every last one of these women.

The cult of love has entirely vanished from the USSR. All the knights in shining armor have been killed or driven out of the country, and traditional patriarchal customs reign supreme. For those at the top, a woman is a symbol of success, rather like a medal or a ceremonial weapon, and among the workers, she is regarded as a "unit of labor"—and so has to be healthy, sturdy, and politically educated.

Sometimes, coming back from yet another of these Soviet society events, I feel so weary and sick at heart that I wonder what on earth I am doing here.

Galina always meets me at the door and gives me a full account of everything she has done for the household that day. Then she proudly shows me some decorated bottle or picture frame she has bought at auction and says, "Isn't it beautiful?"

We stand there in the middle of the room. I wait for Galina to go, and she waits for me to ask her to stay.

Naturally, I am the first to lose patience: I tell her I need to do some work. Galina nods, sighs, and leaves, closing the door quietly behind her.

7

In my native land, it is now quite forbidden to write the truth. If I am caught in the criminal act of doing so, everybody will be held to account—Galina, Weinstein, the women at the telegraph office, and all the other kind people who help me every day.

The worst of it is that even if I did write the truth, it would not interest anybody outside Russia. Statistics indicate that Americans are showing less and less interest in foreign news. If, a few years ago, nine percent of newspaper columns were devoted to reports from abroad, now it is only two and a half percent. And that's for all foreign countries, including Britain, Germany, Japan, and China—countries of far more interest to America than the USSR.

It's a vicious circle. Readers have no interest in Russia because they know nothing about it, and meanwhile, I can't tell them anything meaningful. What can foreign readers hope to find out from my censored reports? That far, far away in a snow-covered realm called the Soviet Union live strange people who like to torment themselves and others? "Well, why should we care as long as they stay away from us?" they might answer.

My reports lack a human face—they don't reflect what life is like in the USSR. And it's not only censorship that's to blame. A telegram to London costs fifteen cents a word, and everything I put in my bulletin has to fit the budget. It's useless to ask for more expenses: the only thing United Press is prepared to pay for without hesitation is an interview with Stalin.

When I asked to organize a meeting with Stalin, Weinstein looked at me as if I had lost my mind.

"Why on earth would Comrade Stalin be interested in speaking to you?"

"It would be good to hear about his views and his future plans," I said.

Weinstein began to lose his temper. "Can you imagine some correspondent from a Russian news agency going to Washington and, as soon as he gets there, asking for a meeting with President Coolidge?" he asked.

I told him that President Coolidge had press conferences with journalists twice a week, but it was no use.

"I expect the American president hasn't got much to do, and that's why he can chat to every Tom, Dick, and Harry who comes along," he said. "But Comrade Stalin has got enough on his hands without having to think about you."

I told Owen about our conversation, and he asked me to think of how I might be able to lure Stalin to an interview.

Unfortunately, there's nothing we can offer that might interest Stalin. The man isn't looking for fame: he keeps to himself, only appearing in public twice a year at the Revolution anniversaries and Worker's Day parades. He's rather like some phantom living in an ancient castle. All his portraits are carefully retouched. The only people who see him close up are the Kremlin domestic staff and a dozen or so close confidants.

I decided in any case that twice a month, I'll send an official request for an interview. I figure if I keep knocking at the same door for long enough, maybe somebody will open it up—at least to have a look at the tiresome pest outside and find out what he wants.

Seibert tells me he's been doing exactly the same for three years. The two of us now have a bet to see which of us will be the first to get an interview.

I've had a daring idea. If I do manage to get a meeting with Stalin, I'll ask for his help in finding Nina. One word from him will be enough to set all the Moscow bureaucrats in action.

Sometimes, I think it's my only hope.

8. A PROBLEM CHILD

1

As far as Galina knew, Klim had neither a wife nor a lover. He had no interest in prostitutes, but he clearly had an eye for female beauty; Galina would be driven to impotent fits of jealous rage when she saw him staring at some attractive girls from the Communist Youth organization. He never looked at *her* like that.

Galina was amazed at the change that had taken place in her. Until recently, she had heartily condemned foreign capitalists and their evil ways and been certain that the triumph of communism was all she needed to be happy. But no sooner had she gone to work for Klim than all her former convictions had vanished like smoke. She could not help herself: she realized now that she liked elegant manners, sophisticated tastes, intelligent conversation, and even something as vulgar as money.

Klim did not think himself rich and kept talking about how he could not afford this or that. He had no idea what real poverty was, of how it wore you down, day after day, year after year, to scrimp and save all the time—even when it came to buying bread.

Now, Klim was dreaming of buying an automobile so that he could race Seibert to the main telegraph office with his dispatches. Meanwhile, Galina could not save enough money to buy mittens for her daughter.

"Ask the master for a bit extra," Kapitolina had advised her. "He's kind. He won't refuse."

But Galina did not want to ask Klim for anything. She needed more than a crumb thrown her way in charity now and again. What she needed was a husband to drag her out of the morass she had fallen into years ago.

She and Klim were now on friendly terms, and Galina began to work toward a private plan. She would help Klim make a brilliant career for himself in Moscow, making herself indispensable so that when his contract with United Press expired, he would marry her and take her and Tata in with him.

"It's essential that Weinstein singles you out as a 'friendly journalist,'" she advised Klim. "Then the People's Commissariat of Foreign Affairs won't be afraid to help you. In Moscow, everything comes down to connections. If they see you as one of them, you'll become a real expert on Soviet affairs because you'll get to talk to all the right people."

"Even Stalin?" Klim asked.

"Even Stalin."

Galina surmised that the quickest route to Klim's heart was through Kitty. He loved his daughter and felt guilty that he was unable to give her a "normal" childhood.

Kitty was desperate to go and play outside with the other children, but Klim would not let her because the neighborhood kids would tease her, calling her "slit-eyed." However proudly Soviet papers wrote of the "inseparable friendship of nations," it was a different story in Moscow's yards and children's playgrounds. There was too much that was different about Kitty: her race, her clothes, and the foreign expressions she used when she spoke. All this aroused both curiosity and dislike among strangers, and invariably, some child or adult would start to pick on her when she went outside.

The casual racism they encountered every day drove Klim into a rage.

"Idiots," he would fume. "They don't understand that difference is a wonderful thing! Kitty knows games they've never even heard of. She can tell stories and show them things. She can let them play with her toys, but all they want to do is shove her into a snowdrift and laugh in her face."

Galina would nod in agreement. When the occasion presented itself, she told Klim that her own daughter, who was twelve, would be happy to play with children of any nationality. She was determined to introduce Kitty to Tata and do everything she could to encourage a friendship between them.

2

As a matter of fact, Galina was ashamed of her daughter. Tata was ugly and not very bright. Almost all the girls in her class at school were homely—they had grown up in the years of civil war and suffered from poor nutrition and constant bouts of illness. But even compared to them, Tata was puny—she was a whole head shorter than other girls her age, and with her straggly ginger braids, her snub nose, and her ear-to-ear grin, she looked like an underfed gnome.

But the girl's character was worse still. Tata would have tried the patience of a saint. She was lazy, disrespectful toward her elders, and always answering back. Sometimes, she would come out with such rubbish that it drove Galina to distraction.

Galina had hoped that the school would sort Tata out. However, it turned out that rather than teaching children geography or Russian, schools now taught them to fight the "relics of the Tsarist past." As Tata saw it, the first of these relics was her mother.

"Your religious belief brings our whole family into disgrace," she said, imitating the tones of her teacher. "As for keeping cactus plants on the windowsill, it's a bourgeois habit that should be stamped out once and for all."

Tata rejected everything her mother loved: comfort, convenience, beauty, and gentleness. Often, Galina would be pushed to breaking point, but even if she beat Tata, there was nothing she could do to knock some sense into the girl.

"You can kill me," Tata would yell, "but I will never give up on our radiant vision! And you can be sure that my comrades will avenge me!"

What comrades? Who would avenge what? Galina had given her daughter a spanking because Tata had not turned off the light in the lavatory, and at a residents' meeting, they had been given a public reprimand.

Like her mother, Tata lived in a fantasy world, but whereas Galina dreamed of love, her daughter dreamed of partisan brigades, of heroic deeds, faraway journeys, and world revolution.

Galina had told her daughter that she worked as a secretary in the OGPU. If Tata had found out what her mother actually did, she would have had a fit. At school, it was hammered into them that a good person should be humbly dressed and as simple as a spade. Any attempt to ask spiritual questions or to strive for intellectual development or even good manners was regarded as "bourgeois." And everything bourgeois was regarded as not only foolish but also evil and treacherous, the mark of a secret desire to destroy everything on earth that was real or alive.

It was out of the question to bring Tata to the house on Chistye Prudy: she had never in her life even seen a private apartment, and Galina was afraid it would be too much of a shock for her daughter. It was better to start gradually.

Tata herself suggested the solution to this problem. When Galina hinted that she knew somebody who had come from Shanghai, Tata jumped up in excitement. "Is he a revolutionary? A real live revolutionary?"

"No," Galina said. "He's a journalist."

"Oh, I see! It's a state secret."

Up until quite recently in Tata's school, they had been discussing the heroic struggle of the Chinese proletariat. The children had held political arguments and debates, learned some words in Chinese, and collected money to help the striking workers. Tata now believed that there were only two sorts of people in China: revolutionaries and imperialists. An imperialist could not have come to the USSR, so Klim Rogov had to be a freedom fighter for the workers.

Galina invented a quite plausible story about how Klim had to hide his true identity to win the trust of the bourgeoisie and bring its secrets to light. Just now, he was working with foreign journalists in Moscow and was obliged, like it or not, to adapt himself to their corrupt tastes.

When Tata found out that Klim Rogov had a little Chinese daughter, she was overjoyed. She loved to boss other children around, but she was too small and plain to be taken seriously by her peers and preferred to play with younger children.

"Mother, can Kitty come and play with me?" Tata whined. "Please? I'll do the washing-up for a whole week without being asked."

Galina "grudgingly" agreed to her daughter's request, but first, she made Tata swear not to pester Uncle Klim with questions about his revolutionary activities.

3

At one time, the large apartment building on Bolshoi Kiselny Lane had been home to eminent doctors and lawyers. But after the revolution, they had been turned out of the building, and new tenants had been moved in—ten families to each apartment.

In the old days, if people shared a house, they would have had something in common: a similar lifestyle, a similar level of education, or similar income. But now, academics lived cheek by jowl with alcoholics, policemen with petty thieves, and aristocratic old ladies with staunch young communists.

Galina's apartment was no better or worse than any of the others. For the most part, the residents got along, but the cramped conditions and differences in opinions would invariably end in rows.

Who had trampled dirt from the street all over the entrance hall? Who had been splitting firewood in the bathroom and cracked the floor tiles? Who had hung up their washing in the kitchen out of turn? While tenants had individual washing lines, the nails in the walls were shared by all, and it was strictly forbidden to break the rota.

On Sunday morning, Galina went to Klim and Kitty's house to pick them up, and they took a horse-cab to her house. All the way there, she felt horribly anxious, and despite herself, she kept noticing omens: church bells were ringing, which was lucky; but then a flock of crows flew up from a fence—a bad sign. She felt sick at heart, thinking of what Klim might say when he saw how wretchedly she lived. What if Tata blurted something out? What if the other tenants started a row and disgraced her in Klim's eyes forever?

Klim noticed how nervous she was. "Don't worry. It'll be fine," he reassured her. "The main thing is for the girls to enjoy themselves."

She smiled gratefully in answer. It was incredible how he could always guess exactly what she was feeling and thinking.

After paying the cab driver, they entered a stairwell plastered with old announcements and went up to the second floor.

The marble staircase had survived ten years of Soviet rule, but the wooden rails had long since been taken off the banisters—they had been used for firewood in 1918. Here and there, plaster was peeling off the walls, and the doors were disfigured by a rash of doorplates, bells, and wires.

"Just a minute," Galina said as she dug in her handbag for the key.

Kitty looked at the rows of electric doorbells in amazement. "Why do you have so many?"

"We all have our own doorbells," explained Galina. "They all play different notes, so we know straight away who has a visitor."

The door opened suddenly and out came one of Galina's cotenants, Mitrofanych, an archive assistant. He greeted the visitors and set off downstairs, glancing up over his shoulder as he went. Klim and Kitty had clearly made quite an impression on him.

They entered a dark corridor hung with washing. From within the apartment, they could hear the whirr of a sewing machine.

"Sasha, you can heat up that meat rissole," a female voice came from the kitchen. "It's on the saucer under the cloth."

They walked along the corridor past a row of trunks. Galina told her guests that some of the residents in the apartment had domestic helpers who had come in to Moscow from the countryside. In the daytime, they did the housework, and at night, they slept on these trunks.

"Please, come in," said Galina, throwing open the door to her room. "Make yourselves at home."

She had done what she could to brighten up her room. The walls were hung with decorated birdhouses and little cages that contained toy airplanes instead of birds. There was a lamp made of carefully assembled bits of glass, and instead of a divan, a garden bench stood in the corner of the room with a brightly colored mattress made of a patchwork of scraps. This was where Galina slept. Tata slept in the wardrobe under the clothes, but the guests did not have to know that.

Kitty looked spellbound at the wardrobe, which was decorated with pink-nosed white rabbits.

"They're so pretty!" she said.

"My daughter painted them," Galina said proudly.

"Where is she?"

"Here I am!"

Tata was standing in the doorway, looking like a child from an orphanage in her blue school smock and the ugly knitted cardigan.

Tata was holding an old ginger cat in her arms, Pussinboots, a wretched, communally owned creature who was fed by each of the tenants in turn.

For a second or two, Tata stared at her guests without saying a word. Galina tensed inside. What would happen now? But all went well. Tata greeted the visitors and, ignoring Klim, walked straight up to his daughter.

"What's your name? Kitty? That won't do. We'll have to think up a new revolutionary name for you. My name is Traktorina, but you can call me Tata for short. Would you like to stroke Pussinboots? "

"Yes, please!" said Kitty, delighted.

"She's called Tatyana," said Galina with irritation, but Klim paid no attention to Tata's fibs.

"Let them play," he said.

"Who's that?" asked Kitty, pointing at a portrait of Lenin that was hung above the desk. "Is it your father?"

Tata gaped at her. "He's not my father. Or rather, he's everybody's father, not just mine. He's the leader of the workers of the world!"

Kitty looked puzzled. "That's my daddy, right there." She pointed at Klim. "But I don't know that man."

"What?" Tata was lost for words. "But that's…that's…"

"Why do your servants sleep on trunks?" asked Kitty, suddenly. "In our house, Kapitolina sleeps on a sack of money. If you jump on it, you can hear it rustling."

Tata looked slowly from Kitty to Klim. "Mother!" she said in dismay. "Can I talk to you in private?"

Galina took Tata out into the corridor.

"Who are these people?" Tata hissed angrily at her mother. "Why have you brought them here? They have servants who sleep on sacks of money!"

Galina put her hand over Tata's mouth. "Quiet, for pity's sake! It's nonsense about the sacks. Kitty's making it up!"

"Really? And why doesn't she know who Lenin is?"

"They've only just come here from China. If Uncle Klim had told Kitty about Lenin, she might have said something in public, and it could have got them arrested."

Tata looked thoughtful. She knew all about the outrages committed by the Chinese police.

"All right," she agreed at last. "Let's go back in."

4

Tata taught Kitty to play political exiles—they perched on the windowsill and pretended they were on their way to Siberia. The cactus plants were the gendarmes who were standing guard over them.

Galina poured Klim some tea and got out some biscuits bought at a ridiculously high price from one of the other tenants. Everything seemed to be going well.

"I expect you're at the Lubyanka now and again, are you?" asked Klim suddenly in English.

Galina stopped with her teacup halfway to her mouth. "What makes you say that?"

Klim pointed to a letter stuck behind the wire for the light switch. "OGPU Trade Union. Overdue membership fees: final notice."

Galina's hands began to shake. That fool of a girl Tata! Galina had told her a hundred times to hide the mail.

There was no point in denying it now.

"I don't tell them anything bad about you," she said hurriedly. "You can see my reports if you like. I don't—"

Klim shook his head. "Don't worry. I've nothing to hide. But could I ask you a favor? I want to know if the OGPU has a file on a woman called Nina Kupina."

"Who's that?" Galina frowned.

"A friend of mine."

"Very well. I can find out."

Klim leaned forward and touched Galina's wrist, sending shivers through her body.

"Just don't tell anybody I asked you. Do you promise?"

Galina nodded.

5

More than anything else, Tata Dorina wanted to join the Young Pioneers, the organization of young builders of communism. But to do this, besides having an excellent school record, she needed to "harden herself up" physically, help workers in other countries, and organize other children to carry out socially useful work. More importantly still, she needed a recommendation from somebody who was a member of the Young Pioneers.

Tata had problems with all of these conditions: she did not enjoy schoolwork, cold showers made her ill, and she could not organize other children because they never listened to her.

Once, she had tried to help workers in other countries by bringing in a big roasting dish for scrap metal. As a result, she had received a thrashing from her mother for her efforts.

"But they gave me twenty-five kopecks!" she shouted, trying to avoid her mother's belt. "I gave it to the worker's fund!"

"And now I'm going to give *you* what for!" threatened her mother.

Tata found even simple tasks difficult, such as talking to older people about why they shouldn't believe in God.

"Mother, just remember," Tata said, "God doesn't exist. If you ever feel you need to make the sign of the cross, raise your hand to your forehead and give a Pioneer salute instead."

"What if I find it easier to live with God than without?" asked her mother.

This remark angered Tata. "You shouldn't think only of your own enjoyment. We need to put all our strength into the fight."

"I'm doing that already," her mother sighed. "And I feel as if I have no strength left."

Tata despised her mother for her degenerate morals, but she was scared of her all the same. Not so much because of her beatings but because of her tears and her long, dreary spells of melancholy. Sometimes, when her mother got back from work, she would lie straight down on the bench without having supper and turn her face to the wall.

"What's the matter, Mommy?" Tata would ask, alarmed.

"Nothing."

Tata felt sure that her mother was upset because of something she had done, and Tata was always doing the wrong thing.

Once, she had been sitting at the window when she had spotted her archenemy from school, Julia—a dark-haired girl with a heavy face, pale skin, and unhealthy-looking swollen eyelids. She had an urge to throw something at Julia, and as ill luck would have it, the first thing that fell to hand was a tray of eggs that Tata's mother had bought at the market. Tata had subjected Julia to such a bombardment that she had been forced to retreat in disgrace.

But Tata's mother chose that moment to come in with a basin of wet washing.

"You awful girl!" she wailed, grabbing a wet towel and starting to thrash Tata with it. "I was going to make you a birthday cake!"

Tata kept apologizing and told her mother that the Young Pioneers would definitely correct her bad character. They had managed to reform even worse offenders than herself.

"Nothing will change you!" her mother spat at her. "How did you turn out to be such an idiot? Where did you get it from?"

Tata really did feel stupid. A little later, she found out that Julia was a member of the Young Pioneers and was now doing all she could to prevent Tata from being accepted.

There was nobody to stick up for Tata as she had no friends.

6

Tata enjoyed playing with Kitty. That little girl was pretty and amusing just like a doll, and Tata had never had a doll.

Kitty looked at her with adoring eyes. "Can I come play with you again? We could play we're running away from the jond…the jor…from the cactus plants."

It was a pity that Kitty's father had such bourgeois habits. Tata understood that he had to wear those dreadful ties and fancy ribbed socks for work, but why did he have to go about dressed up like a bourgeois on the weekend? He probably just wanted to show off in front of other people. It was very antisocial and immature of him, she thought.

When Uncle Klim and Kitty left, the tenants gathered in the kitchen and asked Tata about her guests. Tata could not help adding some extra details of her own to Klim's biography.

"He's a progressive journalist from Shanghai. He fought on the barricades there and saved wounded Red Army soldiers."

The tenants exchanged respectful glances.

"Well, I hope you and your mother don't get too big for your boots now," said Mitrofanych. "You know the sort of thing. That foreigner gives you a stamp from one of his letters, and the next thing, you're too proud to say hello to us."

"Why should we care about his stamps?" Tata snorted, and immediately the thought struck her—maybe she should ask Klim for some old envelopes? Foreign stamps were worth their weight in gold at school. You could swap them for anything, even radio parts.

When Tata went back to their room, her mother had already gone to bed. Tata crawled into her sleeping quarters and stretched out. At last, she had grown tall enough for her head and feet to touch the opposite sides of the wardrobe.

The bench creaked, and her mother suddenly asked in an uncharacteristically affectionate voice, "How were things at school today?"

That was strange. She never asked questions like this. She would even sign Tata's report without looking at it.

Tata told her that they had all played a game called "The Privilege Catcher."

"They gave us balls that had things written on them: 'union budget,' 'tax relief,' and 'electoral rights.' We had to throw them to one another so that the churchman representative didn't catch them. And guess who was the churchman? Julia!"

Tata climbed out of the wardrobe and began to run excitedly around the room in the dark.

"I'm a priest. I'm the enemy of the Soviet system!" she growled in a threatening voice, playing at being Julia. "I want to get the same privileges as the workers!"

"So, what happened?" asked her mother. "Did she get them?"

"Of course not!"

Actually, Julia had managed to get her hands on all the "privileges"—she had been chosen as the churchman as she was faster and nimbler on her feet than all the other girls in the class.

After the game, the Young Pioneer leader Vadik had made the panting children line up and told them that the real enemy was just as cunning and clever as this and that the privileges that had been given to the working class needed to be guarded fiercely.

"I hit Julia on the head with 'tax relief,' and she got nothing!" fibbed Tata. "They even praised me for being vigilant."

There was a sigh in the darkness, and Tata fell silent, unsure if her mother felt proud or angry at her for her fight against the church.

"Did you like Kitty?" asked her mother.

"You bet!" said Tata. "I wish I had a sister like her."

"I'm so glad," said her mother and laughed a quiet and happy laugh that Tata had not heard for a long time.

9. COCAINE

1

Magda discovered a new way to get access to the Comintern hostel: she registered as a student on the Russian language courses for foreigners that had recently opened there.

The hostel was home to communists of all nationalities, from Norwegians to Indians. They shaved their heads, wore traditional Russian shirts, and spoke in a strange jargon of their own, peppered with the words "Lenin," "communism," and "primus." The Kremlin thought these foreigners were potentially useful—come the world revolution, new governments all over the world would be formed from their ranks.

That radiant day was still in the future, however, and meanwhile, the communists at the Comintern hostel lived at the expense of the Soviet authorities, spending their time arguing heatedly about politics and signing all sorts of resolutions.

At the entrance to the hostel, a receptionist asked for Magda's documents and entered her name in a ledger.

"First floor on your right," he told her, but Magda headed straight off to see Friedrich in room 66.

She walked down a damp, dimly lit corridor and stopped in front of the precious door. Some jokers had added another "6" to the number plate and scrawled on it, "Gates of Hell—Please knock."

Quietly, Magda tapped on the door with her fingernails. Nobody answered, so she pushed open one of the double doors, which was slightly ajar.

"How much do you want?" she heard Friedrich's voice coming from the bedroom.

Barely aware of what she was doing, Magda crept into the hall and then in the bathroom. She stood with her back to the water heater, her heart thumping, listening to what was going on in the bedroom.

"Let me tell you, you won't find better cocaine in Moscow," Friedrich said persuasively.

"But why is it so expensive?" asked a voice with a French accent.

"Well, if you don't like the price, you can go and buy hashish from the Uzbeks at the market."

Magda's head was spinning. The man she loved was a drug dealer!

Soon after, the Frenchman left, and Friedrich came into the bathroom. He was so startled to see Magda that he cried out in alarm.

"What are you doing here?" he snapped.

"I…I wanted to buy some cocaine," she blurted out, unable to think of anything better to say. "I heard you were selling it."

2

Magda began to make regular visits to room 666. It was madness to spend the last of her money on cocaine she neither wanted nor needed, but it was the only way she could meet Friedrich alone.

They would speak only briefly, and their conversations always began with Friedrich criticizing Magda for her "drug habit."

"I don't feel sorry for the others," he said. "They can poison themselves for all I care. But you saved me from the Chinese police. Do you know what's going to happen to you? First of all, you'll have hallucinations and fits of despondency; then, after a couple of months, you won't be able to think of anything except your next meeting with me."

Magda looked into his eyes. "You're quite right, you know."

But despite all his warnings, Friedrich provided her with liberal supplies of cocaine, issuing strict warnings not to buy it from street kids.

"The stuff they sell is contraband from Livonia—cut with chalk or soda."

She would go back to her hotel room and flush her purchase down the toilet.

One day, Magda asked Friedrich why he had started to deal in drugs. His reply amazed her. He told her that his superiors had given him a choice: either he would start transporting cocaine into the country or somebody else would be given the job of flying to Berlin, and Friedrich would join his friends the Trotskyites in exile or in prison.

Like vintage wines and brandy, expensive drugs came into the USSR mainly from Hamburg, Berlin, and Riga. The top quality stuff was brought in not by smugglers, who tended to manufacture their own substandard product, but by ships' captains, train guards, diplomatic couriers, and pilots. These groups could get through customs without having their baggage inspected, and their product would be sold straight to eminent Party dignitaries and "useful foreigners."

"Do you think I'm ashamed of what I do?" Friedrich asked Magda. "Not in the least! Half the people in the Kremlin either swill vodka or sniff cocaine. Those scoundrels have killed the revolution, and I've no sympathy for them. What I can't understand is why *you've* become a drug addict."

Magda assumed a tragic expression. "What else do I have to live for?"

Then she told him all about how Klim Rogov had taken the job she had set her heart on. In spite of all her efforts to find work, no Soviet editor had expressed an interest in hiring her, and she now had no visa and no money.

"Do you know how to do *anything*?" demanded Friedrich angrily.

Magda put her hand to her heart. "I can write books, and I'm a good photographer."

The next time Magda came to Friedrich, he gave her a letter from an editor in Berlin. This editor explained that Germany was very interested in what was going on in the USSR because many German firms were hoping to supply goods to the country. They had nowhere else to turn since the victorious allies had placed heavy restrictions on German foreign trade after the Great War. If Miss Thomson were willing to write a book about her life in Moscow, the publisher would take on the expense of having the book translated, even paying her an advance. All the editor asked was for her to send him a plan and a couple of sample chapters.

"It's one of my…well, my customers," muttered Friedrich. "You need to grab your chance with him while he can still think straight. Pretty soon, his family will have him committed to a clinic, and he won't be any use to you."

Magda was so moved that tears came into her eyes. "Of course I'll write to him! Let me have the address."

Friedrich told her that all correspondence should be directed through him. That way, it would be possible to get around the censors.

"I'm happy to help you," he said, "but on one condition. You must give up cocaine. And believe me; you won't be able to fool me. If you carry on taking it, I'll be able to sniff it out."

Magda swore in the name of all that was sacred that she would never again touch the dreaded white powder. She was overjoyed at the prospect of her new job.

3

Magda's plan was approved in Berlin, the contract was signed, and work began on the new book.

The Bolsheviks were very keen to attract tourists into the country, and Friedrich advised Magda to inform the People's Commissariat of Foreign Affairs that she was planning to write a travel guide for foreigners. Her visa was extended straight away, and she was allowed to rent the apartment of an opera singer who had left the country on a tour.

What a shame it was, thought Magda, that Nina was no longer with her! The interpreters sent to her by the state did their best to take her to places she did not care about, such as the Bolshoi Theater or the furniture museum. In the end, Magda decided she would go everywhere alone and explain herself to Russians using sign language if she had to.

For a chapter of her book devoted to Soviet children, she had to write about the street urchins, homeless waifs who had appeared in vast numbers as a result of the civil war, the recent famine, and widespread alcoholism among the working class.

They had their own turfs and professions. One might steal coal from the railroad yards while another specialized in pickpocketing, and still others ran errands for construction teams. Magda was keen to build up a picture of how these children lived, so she set off for the market to acquaint herself with the future characters of her book.

4

A huge street market had sprung up beneath the half-ruined wall of Kitai Gorod. Lookouts sat in the embrasures in the ancient towers, ready to give the signal if a police patrol arrived. Beneath them jostled crowds of unlicensed traders peddling all manner of goods—from counterfeit perfume to dried fish and from coarse cloth brassieres to rat poison. Many of them were selling identical goods, produced out in manufacturing workshops in the suburbs of Moscow.

An enormous peasant moved through the crowd festooned in toy pistols and swords. Every once in a while, he would shoot a cap into the air with a deafening bang.

"Cap-guns and pistols,
Sabers and rapiers,
Toys for your boys, mothers,
Get yours today!
Take home a gun for your son
Right away!"

Chinese traders waved bags and briefcases sewn from patchworks of colored scraps, calling, "Buy, buy! Latest fashion!"

"Fresh pi-i-ies! Get yer fresh pies he-e-ere!" called a woman wearing a dirty apron over her heavy cloth coat. Nearby, students fumbled in their pockets for a few kopecks to buy something to eat, dancing from leg to leg and shivering in the cold.

Old women measured out sunflower seeds with wooden tumblers and poured them into their customers' pockets. This was a risky trade: the citizens of Moscow consumed enormous amounts of sunflower seeds, spitting the shells all over streets, and the Moscow Soviet had recently threatened to impose huge fines on anyone selling the snack. But as usual in Russia, the severity of the official laws was tempered by the casual attitude of the populace toward them.

Magda snapped some pictures of various wares spread out on oilcloths on the ground—children's books, underwear, cigarette lighters, and strings of beads. It was frustrating not to have a movie camera to film the street barbers who shaved their customers' with lightning speed; something she could never capture with a photograph.

Soon she came across a very exotic sight: braids of hair of all colors—from bluish-black to auburn and golden. These days, peasant women from the villages cut off their hair to sell to fashionable city women to make artificial chignons.

A young street urchin in a torn hat with earflaps ran up to Magda, stretching out a bony hand, blue with cold. This was just what she had been looking for. She reached into her bag and took out a raisin bun.

"Here," she told the boy. "Take this!"

The boy, amazed at this unheard-of generosity, took a step backward and sat down in the snow. Then he tucked the bun under his shirt, put his fingers in his mouth, and gave a piercing whistle. A moment later, a whole flock of children dressed in indescribable rags had gathered around Magda.

She began to hand the children some of the treats she had brought beforehand in the café of the Metropol Hotel. They chattered excitedly and tugged at her skirt. The scene attracted some openly disapproving glances from passersby.

A man in a sheepskin coat came up and tried to explain something to Magda, but one of the street children lobbed a piece of broken brick at his back. He spat angrily and went on his way.

Magda took out a carefully prepared "crib" and read aloud in Russian: "I would like to find out how you live. I want to take photographs of your house."

The boy in the hat with earflaps grabbed Magda's arm. "Come on."

They set off with the mob of street children streaming off after them. The children led Magda to a crumbling tower in the fortress wall. Here, street cleaners were piling up pieces of ice chipped from the pavements, together with trash and horse manure, into an enormous mound of waste. After clambering over the mound, Magda found herself facing a small opening covered with a metal grating, leading into a cellar. Grayish blue smoke drifted out from inside.

A girl of about nine pulled away the grating and was first to dive into the damp, black hole.

The boy in the hat with earflaps poked Magda in the back. "Go!"

She looked around at the children who smiled back at her. Looking at their unkempt figures, their runny noses, and filthy faces, she shuddered, seized with a painful sense of pity. What lay in store for these wretched youngsters?

Bending double, Magda squeezed her way into the damp-smelling crawl space, but her clothes caught on something. She lost her balance and went sprawling onto a heap of broken bricks.

5

BOOK OF THE DEAD

I was coming out of the store with a bag of groceries when suddenly a street urchin with a crutch threw himself under my feet. He fell into the snow and sent up a howl: "Help! I'm being trampled underfoot!"

While I was helping him to his feet and apologizing, his little friends grabbed my groceries and ran off in all directions, and the invalid suddenly lifted up his crutch like a cudgel and came straight at me.

"What did I just hear you say about the Soviet authorities?" he yelled. "Citizens, this bourgeois scum should have got what's coming to him long ago. He just called Lenin a bastard!"

The lad took me for a Nepman and thought that I would take fright and run off. I explained to him that he had just disgraced his country horribly in front of a foreign journalist. Now I would have to write a report about how workers in the Soviet Union were prevented from going about their business and were even subject to attacks by children.

The young defender of Lenin was hugely embarrassed to hear this. "Tell you what. You come back to our base, and we'll give you your stuff back," he promised, leading me after his fugitive comrades.

As we walked back to his den, he introduced himself to me as Tsar Pest and told me a little about his life. His parents had taken to drink, and he had refused to go into an orphanage because, as he explained it, all those places were run by "bourgeois do-gooders."

Until a year or so ago, Tsar Pest had earned his keep by running around attics and rooftops stealing clothes and bed linen from washing lines, but one day, somebody had caught him at it and thrown him down a flight of stairs, breaking his leg. The break had healed badly, and he had walked with a crutch ever since.

He had earned his nickname thanks to his cocky attitude, his belligerent character, and his extraordinary love of power. He told me that he had more than a dozen "minions" over whom he enjoyed absolute authority. They aided and abetted all his criminal activities and were obliged to bring him something valuable every day. In exchange, he allowed them to sleep in a cellar under the Kitai Gorod wall and protected them from the police or from other street gangs.

To cut a long story short, today, I made the acquaintance of an underage feudal lord.

Tsar Pest led me to the cellar where his "minions" were hiding out. Their lair was like the home of prehistoric cave dwellers: broken brick battlements above and a stone floor below covered with straw, and on the walls, smutty drawings done in lamp black. Right in the middle of the floor stood an iron stove and a big chest labeled "Froot" into which the kids put their catch at the end of every day.

Tsar Pest kept his word and gave me back my groceries, except those that had already been eaten. He also offered me his girlfriend, a hideous girl of about twelve who was clearly pregnant. All the time I was in the den, the girl was sitting next to the stove draped in an old theater poster, sniffing at some faded artificial forget-me-nots plucked from a funeral wreath.

When I turned down his girlfriend, Tsar Pest showed me some women's clothing that was clearly not of Soviet provenance.

"Buy some of this, and you can give it to your girl," he said.

In the pile he offered me, I noticed a battered rust brown Kodak camera case—and then it struck me: I was looking at the belongings of Magda Thomson. I recognized the dress she had been wearing on the day I met her.

When I asked Tsar Pest where he had found the stuff, he flared up and told me to mind my own business. He didn't need to tell me though. It was quite clear that he had robbed poor Magda.

I decided it would be a good idea to return her possessions, so I proposed playing Tsar Pest at cards for them. He agreed, quite unaware of what a devious opponent he was about to face. As a young man, I had quite a passion for card tricks, and in my time, I mastered a few techniques that would earn me a battering with a candelabra if I ever tried them out in a casino.

We sat down to play, and soon, I won back Magda's camera. Next, I won back her dress, her coat, and all the rest.

As they watched our battle, the "minions" got quite carried away with excitement.

"Holy cow, look at that!" one or other would exclaim. "This guy's a pro and no mistake."

First, they were all rooting for Tsar Pest, but gradually, their sympathies switched to me. Clearly, the Tsar's subjects were enamored of their master.

"Watch out, or he'll have the shirt off your back," said the pregnant girl with a guffaw.

"Shut it, you," muttered Tsar Pest, who was puffing nervously at a roll-up, turning it around now and again to smoke with the lit end in his mouth. His cheeks were scarlet, and smoke came pouring from his nostrils.

Once or twice he went for me with a knife made from a piece of sharpened metal. "I'll rip out your guts, so I will!"

All the kids roared as we scuffled together.

"Had enough?" I asked, pinning Tsar Pest to the floor.

"No-o!" he wailed, and we got back to our game.

In the end, Tsar Pest lost everything he had—his crutch, his knife, his "minions," and even the box labeled "Froot." Burying his head in his shoulders, he got to his feet and shuffled to the hole in the wall.

The urchins, who had all fallen silent, stared at me with eyes like saucers. I have no idea whom they took me for: a savior or a new slave owner.

I told them I had no intention of exacting tribute from them, but I needed them to help me.

"I want you to go around all the market traders and ask them if they've seen a red velvet coat with Chinese dragons on it. I'll give a handsome reward to the one who finds it."

I had tied Magda's clothes into a bundle and was already on my way out when the pregnant girl called out to me.

"There's a foreign lady in the cesspool over there," the girl said. "She might be dead already. Tsar Pest went at her with his crutch."

It turned out that the foreign lady was Magda: she had come to visit the urchins two days before. They had battered her and thrown her into a shallow cesspool in the corner of the cellar.

The "minions" helped me drag Magda out. She was unconscious, her face was smeared with dried blood, and there was a gaping, wet wound on the back of her head.

The children assured me that they had attacked the foreigner on the orders of Tsar Pest; had it not been for him, they would have left her alone.

"She was kind," they told me. "She even gave us buns."

I was surrounded by underage murderers, unpunished by the law and quite unwilling to accept responsibility for their crime. To look at them, it was clear they really believed they had done nothing wrong.

I took Magda off to the hospital. The doctor's told me she had a bad concussion, a great many injuries, and generalized hypothermia. It was a miracle that she had survived her ordeal.

The whole affair left me deeply shaken. What incredible luck that I turned up at that place at that very moment!

Another thing: it gave me an insight into the nature of power—the power of one person over another.

The street urchins almost killed Magda because their feared leader told them to do so. They didn't hate her. And in any case, all the loot went straight to Tsar Pest, so they gained nothing for their wrongdoing. Their crime was simply a symbol of their obedience. "Do you see how much we respect you? We're prepared to murder or to stoop to any despicable act so long as you leave us alone."

Tsar Pest's authority stayed in place until he experienced his first symbolic defeat. After losing a few games of cards, the "minions'" mighty commander was transformed before their eyes into a pitiful failure, and his power melted away like snow. The "minions" had committed a horrible crime out of fear of a power that turned out to be entirely illusory.

Alas, all too often, the world of adults follows similar laws.

6

I visited Magda in the hospital. She is already looking more like herself again.

An investigator came to see her, but she told him she has no intention of reporting the crime to the police. In her opinion, the children who tried to kill her were not guilty—they had simply been unlucky enough to fall into a corrupt world of crime.

Soon, we were joined by a mutual acquaintance, a pilot by the name of Friedrich. I had met him once at Seibert's house: when Friedrich was sober, he had sworn allegiance to Stalin, but once he had a drink or two inside him, he began to sing Trotsky's praises. Clearly, he was one of the many oppositionists who quickly had to change their views in order not to share the fate of their leader, who, at the time, was about to be exiled either to Siberia or Central Asia.

Friedrich had not even got through the door before he began to curse Magda, calling her every name under the sun and accusing her of going to the street kids to buy cocaine. Eventually, I had to step in, and we left the ward together. Then, blushing, nervous, and shamefaced, he began to thank me for saving Magda's life.

"Would you like me to bring you some ketchup back from Berlin?" he asked. "Or Coca-Cola? You Americans like that, don't you?"

I asked him if he could smuggle abroad my article exposing the amorous exploits of the Bolsheviks, and after a few awkward moments, he agreed.

So, today, I had my second lesson about the nature of power. People may fear their leaders so much that they shake in their shoes at the sight of them and forget all their morals. But despite all this, they will still happily thumb their nose at their oppressors on the quiet. It's a very natural human impulse: you may have the right to airplanes, Berlin, ketchup, and Coca-Cola, but you can't be truly happy unless you are free.

7

Once Magda was out of the hospital, she sent me a long letter of thanks with a snapshot of Nina taken not long before her disappearance.

Just now, I'm sitting at my desk looking at this small black-and-white photograph printed on bad paper. This picture is all I have to show for my efforts after several months.

In the daytime, I can forget about my troubles for a while and can even feel happiness over little things. Friedrich took my article out of the country, and Owen has already sent a telegram: "Letter received from Berlin. Expect bonus." Of course, I should be happy.

But an obscure ache creeps into my heart every night. I try to distract myself with books and newspapers, but I can't get away from it.

I can recall everything so clearly: how Nina and I used to amuse ourselves at bedtime acting out idiotic romantic novels, trying to keep a straight face, and always end up crying from laughter. Or how I would walk past Nina as she was washing her face and put my arms around her waist for a few moments. I can still remember how it felt to run my hand over the silk of her open peignoir and the warm skin beneath.

How many moments of secret intimacy we enjoyed when we spoke to one another by touch alone!

Magda has captured Nina's beauty for me, but the photograph doesn't show even a tenth of what I have lost.

If you are enjoying *The Prince of the Soviets*,
please leave a review on Amazon and Goodreads.
Your feedback is very important for the author.

THANKS!

10. THE SMUGGLING ARTICLE

1

Alov arrived at work early to find crowds of people already in the entrance hall. It was payday. The OGPU was a sizable organization: it had two and a half thousand working in its central staff alone and another ten thousand agents in Moscow, and all of them needed to collect their wages.

Showing his pass at the door, Alov pushed through the turnstile and took the elevator up to the fourth floor where the Foreign Department was based.

His tiny office was furnished with a table, three chairs, a divan upholstered in oilcloth, and a coat stand. A courier had already brought in the mail and the latest copy of *Pravda*. All OGPU employees were expected to read the paper from cover to cover to make sure they kept informed on the latest Party directives.

Alov took off his greatcoat, changed into his felt slippers, and was about to sort through the mail when there was a shout in the corridor.

"All those in the Foreign Department, go collect your wage checks!" It was the secretary Eteri Bagratovna.

There was a banging of doors and the clattering of boots on the stairs. Within moments, a long line had formed at the cashier's office.

The employees of the Foreign Department fell into two groups of unequal status—the stick-at-homes and the travelers. Those who belonged to the first group never went anywhere and resembled impoverished teachers or clerks. Those in the second group enjoyed frequent trips abroad and returned decked out in the latest foreign clothes: sleeveless pullovers, shirts with pointed lapels, silk ties, and Oxford bags.

Alov did not particularly envy the *travelers*—his needs were simple: filterless cigarettes, strong tea, and perhaps medicine if he fell sick. But it vexed him that his beautiful wife had only two dresses, both of which had been bought second-hand.

Dunya Odesskaya was the sort of woman who should have been put on a pedestal and showered with presents. Comparing himself with her, Alov was at a loss to understand what she saw in him with his thinning hair, his pince-nez on a cord, his sunken chest, and the beginnings of a pot belly.

When his colleagues had had a drink or two, they would tease him, "You should watch out for that Dunya of yours. She's a real hot potato!"

"And just look at you—thin and bent as an old oven fork!"

Alov was sure that in calling him an "oven fork," they were hinting at cuckold's horns. Miserable and jealous, he hounded his wife with accusations and then locked himself in his office with Galina. These brief betrayals would leave him feeling temporarily avenged.

One day, in the Tretyakov Art Gallery, Alov saw a group of schoolchildren looking at the painting "The Unequal Marriage." The exhibition guide was explaining to the kids what torment it must be for the young bride to marry the rich but repulsive old man on the picture.

At least, Alov thought gloomily, *that old man could afford to give his young bride valuable jewelry and a gracious style of living.*

His own salary was circumscribed by the Party's rule on the maximum wage, and he could afford to bring Dunya nothing more exciting than a couple of sacks of potatoes.

If only he could find another position! He had heard rumors that some of his colleagues from the Economic Department had put together dossiers on the directors of various enterprises and forced them to pay up under threat of exposure. The OGPU employees who worked in the Transport Department did well for themselves too—they could always extort bribes from black market traders transporting goods from one region to another.

It sounded prestigious to work in the Foreign Department, but what did it actually mean? Alov could not even hope for a promotion: there was only one person above him in the whole department: the fearsome Drachenblut.

2

Standing behind Alov in the line was Zharkov, a small man with a rosy face, short graying hair, and a slightly crooked nose.

Zharkov played a minor role in the OGPU, but a very profitable one, supplying Russians living abroad with false documents, currency, codes, and so on. Every time he came back into the country, he would bring back with him a suitcase full of women's clothing and accessories.

"Did you bring it?" Alov mouthed the question silently.

"Mm-hm," Zharkov muttered in assent. "Come and see me after lunch."

The previous week, Alov had taken out a loan from the mutual aid bureau and asked Zharkov to bring him back some French perfume for Dunya. Dunya's birthday was coming up, and he needed to get her a decent present.

"Perhaps you want some lipstick too?" Zharkov enquired. "A young woman ordered it from me—she was close to Drachenblut at the time, but now he's got rid of her. So, I'm not allowed to give her anything."

Alov pulled at his beard. "Oh...all right. I'll take the lipstick too."

After drawing their wages, all the employees began sorting out what money they owed where and to whom. Everybody had debts of some sort, some going back more than a month.

A young girl from the Far East section darted about among them. "Who hasn't paid his subscription?" she called out. "Who's still short? Comrade Alov, you should be ashamed of yourself! You owe money to the International Society for Revolutionary Fighters and three other organizations. Do you want me to raise the issue at the next Party meeting?"

Grudgingly, Alov counted out what he owed. A huge number of "voluntary" organizations had sprung up in the Soviet Union offering support for everything you could imagine, from German workers' children to the chemical industry. Every good communist was obliged to be a member of these organizations and pay membership dues. Otherwise, he ran the risk of being expelled from the Party.

Alov made a quick calculation: after all these official payments had been made and he had paid his rent and given back what he owed to other people, he would have only fifty rubles left, hardly enough to buy food for the month.

On the stairs, he ran into Galina, who had also come to collect her paycheck.

"Hello, Pidge," he said gloomily. "Did you get your check? How about lunch in the canteen to celebrate? My treat."

There was no point trying to economize; he would still end up in debt before the month was out.

3

The canteen was in one of the basement rooms, and they had to cross the yard to get to it. On the other side of the yard, beyond a wooden fence, was the OGPU's holding prison, its windows partially screened with plywood panels. A guard was posted at the gate and beside him stood a battered Black Maria van, its doors wide open. The driver—a young, dark-browed man by the name of Ibrahim—jumped out as they passed.

Alov shook his hand. "How's it going?"

"I was working the night shift," said Ibrahim. "Wish I could sleep, but I can't. Got to clean up the car."

Alov peered inside the van—the floor, which had clearly been hurriedly wiped, was covered with brownish smears.

"Is that blood?" Galina gasped.

"Oh, no, Miss," said Ibrahim with a smirk. "That's fruit juice."

"Have you been beating someone again?"

Alov was annoyed at Galina acting the innocent when she had no qualms about accepting her OGPU paycheck or the vouchers for the organization's cooperative store.

Alov pulled at her arm. "Come on. Let's go. Otherwise, all the pies will have gone from the canteen."

Galina trailed obediently after him. Alov was sure she was already lost in some idiotic daydream: she was probably wondering about who had been arrested the night before and what he had done.

As they climbed the worn entrance steps, Galina could control herself no longer.

"I don't see why people have to be beaten when they're arrested," she burst out. "We're not savages after all!"

"We're surgeons. Spilling blood is part of what we do," growled Alov. "If nobody took it upon themselves to operate, our society would die from hidden diseases." He stopped and fixed Galina with a stern gaze. "You do see that, don't you?"

She nodded hurriedly. "Of course I do."

They entered a large echoing hall with tiled walls. All the tables were already occupied, but Alov was given a reserved place on the condition that they eat quickly before any of the management arrived.

A minute later, the waitress, Ulyana, came up to their table.

"What can I get for you today? We have rice and sausages. But the vodka and pies are gone. The Special Department finished the last of them this morning."

Ulyana's full lips were painted a bloodred, and her low-cut dress showed off her plump breasts and spectacular cleavage to full advantage.

Alov squinted across at Galina; beside Ulyana, she looked like some pale yellow moth beside a peacock butterfly. *And not so long ago, Galina had been a good-looking girl herself,* he thought. Where had it all gone?

She needs feeding up, thought Alov, and with a heavy sigh, he ordered a double portion of sausages.

When Ulyana had flitted away, Galina moved closer to Alov. "Listen, I was wondering, could you find out if we have a file on a certain woman? Her name's Nina Kupina."

Immediately, Alov remembered the young lady with the camera he had seen that day of the parade on the 7th of November. The Chinese guests on the tribune had recognized her; they had told him she was a White émigré from Shanghai. But at the time, all the OGPU officers had been taken up with the Trotsky supporters, and Alov had forgotten all about her.

"And what is she to you?" he asked Galina.

"Well, she's my…friend's neighbor, and she was asking, you see—"

"Pidge," said Alov gently, "I can see right through you. You're a terrible liar. Who's been asking you about this Nina Kupina?"

Galina looked at him sheepishly. "He asked me not to tell anyone."

"And who is *he*?"

As usual, it did not take long for Galina to cave in under pressure.

"Klim Rogov asked me to find out. But you mustn't think anything of it. He's on our side. He takes a very objective view of things…at least for the most part—"

Alov began to drum on the table with his fingers.

Very interesting, he thought. *Both Klim Rogov and Nina Kupina had lived in Shanghai, and they clearly knew one another. What might this mean?*

4

After lunch, Alov took Galina into his office and asked her to wait a minute. He told her he was going to check the archive, but instead, he headed to the office of a group of employees he referred to jokingly as "Their Royal Highnesses." These women were all from aristocratic families and knew several languages. Their job was to read through all the foreign papers and magazines to keep an eye on what was being written about the Soviet Union and by whom. Alov had specially picked out widows with children for the job, and they were among some of the most responsible employees of the OGPU. They were so afraid of losing their jobs that they would go to any lengths to please their employers.

"Do you have the file on Klim Rogov?" Alov asked Diana Mikhailovna, a tall woman of fortyish, her hair piled into an old-fashioned bun on top of her head.

"We've just been adding a new cutting to it from an English paper," she answered. "Have a look at this."

Alov began to read.

> In the space of the last ten years, the soldiers of the revolution have grown slowly older and more infirm, and now, they have begun to stare death in the face—not a heroic death on the battlefield but the most ordinary passing away in a hospital bed. Now that the romance of their youth has come to nothing, the Bolshevik leaders have begun to succumb feverishly to every temptation forbidden them. After all, the specter of communism may remain forever out of reach; must they forgo all life's pleasures in the meantime?
>
> The members of the old guard have acquired beautiful young wives, elegantly furnished apartments, German automobiles, and French wines.
>
> It is both sad and comical to compare the grand aims of the Bolsheviks with the reality to which they are now resigned. They dreamed of building a society in which everybody would have more than enough, but it seems they are incapable of doing more than feathering their own nests.

Alov was less surprised at the tone of the article than he was at the brazen cheek shown by its author. Klim Rogov had signed the piece with his *own name*.

"What's the matter with the man?" he asked. "Is he out of his mind?"

Diana Mikhailovna shrugged her stately shoulders. "I suppose he didn't think we'd read it."

Alov took Klim Rogov's file. According to the completed form, Rogov had emigrated from Russia some time before the revolution and received American citizenship and had spent several years in China. A few months ago, he had come back to the country of his birth as a tourist and found work with the United Press agency. That was all the information they had on him.

Alov stamped Rogov's file with the words "enemy journalist." Inadvertently, this reporter had hit a raw nerve with this article. Alov could recall how, as an impassioned young man, he had felt nothing but contempt for the hard-hearted, immoral, corrupt old bureaucrats he had seen around him. For him, these men were symbolic of the bourgeoisie that had to be wiped from the face of the earth. And now, he had become just like one of them, the only difference being that while the Tsar's officials had been well-off, Alov was condemned to a life of unrelenting poverty.

Alov never showed his feelings in front of "Their Royal Highnesses," but with Galina, he had no such qualms.

"What is this?" he yelled from the doorway, flinging the newspaper cutting in her face. "Why didn't you keep a closer watch on this Rogov? How could he have sent this article to London?"

Galina burst into tears on the spot. "I don't know!" she wailed.

"Oh, you don't know!" Alov mimicked sarcastically. "You mean you don't know how to do your job? Do you think we're paying you to do nothing? I want you to get to the bottom of this. I want to know everything about this Rogov—who his friends are, where he goes, and what's between him and Kupina! Is that clear?"

Galina sniffed. "I'll try. So, we do have a file on her, do we?"

"No, we don't! Now get out, and don't you dare come back without something to show for yourself."

Ten minutes later, there was already a file on Nina Kupina: Alov opened a new one, noting down his impressions from his own encounter with her and what he had heard from the Chinese people with whom she had crossed the Soviet border.

It was all a bit flimsy, but Alov decided that from now on, he would be on the alert and keep a close watch on Klim Rogov and his young lady friend.

5

BOOK OF THE DEAD

Galina brought me two pieces of news, one good and one bad. The good news is that the OGPU doesn't have a file on Nina. The bad news is that now I have been labeled an "enemy journalist."

Galina was so upset on my behalf that she started to cry. "Why did you do it? Now they're going to make life difficult for you in every way they can!"

She asked me how I had managed to get the article out of the country, but I lost my temper and sent her away.

I feel sorry for her; really I do—I know she's only trying to protect me, but her persistent solicitude drives me crazy.

I went to the censors' office to find out how much trouble I'm in and what they're planning to do about it.

As soon as I opened the door, Weinstein launched into me with a string of accusations.

"I really thought we understood one another, and this is how you repay me. If this happens one more time, there'll be hell to pay!"

I felt relieved to hear this. It seems that as it's the first such misdemeanor, I'm being forgiven and allowed to stay in Moscow. All the same, I felt like a schoolboy called in to the headmaster's office. What damn business is it of that devil Weinstein what I choose to publish abroad?

Still, there was no point in arguing with him.

I think I can forget about getting an interview with Stalin.

6

I have to face facts: Nina has disappeared without a trace, and I can't go on living on memories.

Kitty needs a mother, and I need a wife. But I can't imagine any other woman playing that part in my life.

For all her excellent qualities, Galina is too much of a cud-chewing herbivore for my liking. A cow may be a helpful animal, but I can't get excited about it.

Nina, on the other hand, was like a graceful twilight predator with glowing eyes. She would never agree to be anyone's servant. It wasn't always easy living with her, but I could never look at her without admiration. Who could take her place?

I can see quite clearly what Galina's up to. She's counting on the fact that I'll get used to all these home comforts. I suppose she thinks one day I'll just give in and I won't bother looking elsewhere for a wife. She wants to domesticate me, to put me in a nice warm stable with a straw for bedding and a bunch of hay. Sit and munch and forget about everything!

I would hate myself if I took up with a woman out of mere gratitude.

A later entry

What the hell? I was actually starting to plan my life without Nina.

7

The enemy article cost me dearly. Now the censors smile sweetly at me and cut half of everything I write. I have to work almost twice as hard as I used to.

In order to have at least something to write about, I have subscribed to the press cuttings office service. Every day now, a courier brings me a big pile of clippings. Once I've looked through some article which has passed the censor, I can insist that it's an official bulletin and needs to be sent abroad.

But my catch is getting smaller every day. Ever since the routing of the opposition, it's clear that it is not a good idea to argue about the direction the country should be taking. These days, countless congresses and meetings are held in Moscow, at which the speakers talk for hours without actually saying anything at all. To protect themselves against any accusations of freethinking, they cite the pronouncements of Lenin and Marx and stick to tried-and-true phrases such as "the fight against the recalcitrant core of the petty bourgeoisie" or "steering a course toward a union with the peasantry." Who can tell what they actually mean? Nobody. Wonderful!

Just to keep afloat, I am forced to shuffle words, people, and events on a regular basis. As for the moral implications of what I am doing, I have stopped even thinking about them. This is the only way I can hope to get a telegram through to the Press Office.

Mass repressions have begun, the main victims being profiteers who are accused by the government of pushing up prices. I come into the censors' office with a bulletin that reads, "Eighteen Men Shot," hoping that they'll at least allow something insipid, such as "Ruthless Purges," to be sent abroad.

"What's the point in that?" Weinstein is bound to object. "Who cares about profiteers? We can't send that out."

"It's an official announcement by *Izvestia*," I remind him. "Or do you think that *Izvestia* is giving a distorted picture of the Party line?"

Weinstein acts as if he has not heard what I just said. "We've opened up a factory canteen," he says, shoving a clipping across this desk toward me. "You say you're a friend of the Soviet Union. Why don't you write about how we're helping the working man?"

I also act as if I'm hard of hearing and put my briefcase on his clipping. For a while, we talk about the weather and what's on in the Moscow theaters. Then I come back to the subject of the profiteers.

"I know you want to write about the factory canteen," I say, "but I'm afraid my editors aren't interested in that sort of story."

"So, what do they want?" asks Weinstein in aggrieved tones.

I sigh heavily. "They just want blood and violence."

The censor eventually passes the title "Decisive Purges," puts his stamp on my report, and I run to the telegraph office.

This is how it works these days: "Flour Distribution at Standstill" is changed to "Delays in Dispatch of Bumper Grain Supplies"; "Meat Shortages" to "The Victory of Vegetarianism," and so on.

Seibert told me that when he found out about how rebellious Cossacks had been exiled to Siberia, he managed to get the news over the border by writing, "State Guarantees Resettlement for Cossack Families."

11. CHRISTMAS NIGHT

1

Kitty went several times to visit Tata. At first, Klim was pleased she had found herself a friend, but soon, his daughter began to use expressions like "a class-based attitude" and "rotten idealism." One day, instead of asking for Klim to read her a fairytale at bedtime, Kitty asked for the "Young Pioneer's Solemn Oath."

The following day, Tata rang Klim to demand that Kitty be given a topical, revolutionary name.

"I've made up a list of names," she said, "so you can choose: either Barricade, Progressina, Diamata, or Ninel. 'Diamata' comes from 'dialectical materialism,' and 'Ninel' is 'Lenin' backward."

Klim told Tata that his daughter was quite revolutionary enough.

"Actually," he said, "'Kitty' stands for 'Kill the Imperialist Traitors of Tomorrow's Youth.'"

"You don't say!" Tata gasped in admiration. "Kitty never told me that! I promise you, I'll make such a fine communist out of your daughter you won't believe it!"

2

Afrikan went out into the forest and bought back a moss-covered fir tree, which he put up in the living room. Galina and Kapitolina spent all Christmas Eve making paper lanterns while Kitty cut pictures at random from postcards and punched holes in them to make decorations.

The window panes were half coated in snow, but inside, the room was wonderfully warm and inviting, smelling of fir sap and the smoke of birch logs.

Klim picked up from the table a sealed envelope, which Galina had given him earlier, and opened it. It was Tata's Christmas present: an article from *The Pioneer's Pravda*.

The Christmas tree is a survival of the benighted past, which encourages children to destroy the forest. Besides which, pine forest is one of the mainstays of national industry in the USSR.

If by some chance you are unaware of this and have already bought a fir tree, be sure to decorate it with red stars and ribbons and, when you dance around the tree, sing Pioneer songs.

Santa Claus is a reactionary element; his place should be taken by a Red Army Commander or a OGPU worker who can tell the children about his heroic fight to free the Soviet people.

At the end of the article Tata had added a handwritten note:

Uncle Klim pleese read my letter to Kitty!

Tell yore dad that a Crissmas tree is just a stupid survival of the old rejeem. He shud know this or he is not with us the workers and only pretending to be. I am not coming to your Crissmas party. Come to mine and we will play storming the tsar's palase.

When Galina went out in the kitchen to check on the pastry for the pie, Klim followed her.

She lifted the pan lid, breathed in, and closed her eyes in pleasure.

"What a delicious smell!" she said. "When I was little, our cook would make a wonderful apple pie every year, and I would stuff myself so that I could barely move afterward."

She gazed at Klim, her eyes shining. "It's wonderful that you can cook on a proper range," she added. "At home, we have to use kerosene stoves. Coal is too expensive, and we never have enough of it."

"Your daughter seems to have taken it upon herself to educate Kitty and me," said Klim and held out Tata's letter to Galina.

She scanned the note and then threw it angrily into the range. "The little pest! She's incorrigible. No matter how much I thrash her—"

"What? Do you beat her?"

"I don't beat her badly. I just give her a taste of the belt from time to time. To keep her in line."

Klim felt his hands tightening into fists despite himself. He had been thrashed as a child, and the memory of it was a source of a profound sense of humiliation.

"Never beat people smaller and weaker than you are," said Klim, enunciating each word coldly and deliberately. "Don't you see how despicable it is?"

Galina realized that she should have held her tongue, but she still tried to defend herself. "It's the only language Tata understands!"

"No, it's that *you* have no idea how else to deal with her. Children simply stop listening to you if you punish them all the time. Tata can't live in a state of constant fear, believing that her mother thinks she's bad. She has only one way of protecting herself: to ignore all the insulting things you say."

For too long, Klim had concealed a growing annoyance with Galina.

"Adults who beat children," he said, "are like lackeys taking pleasure in the fact that for once, they can exert power over somebody else. They grovel to their bosses and then take it all out on some defenseless victim who can't get away from them."

Galina looked stricken. "Is that really what you think of me?"

"Well, isn't every word of it true?"

Galina's lips trembled. "It's easy enough to have scruples when you have plenty of everything and can be your own master. But my nerves are at their breaking point!"

"Why do you think that is? Tata's your only child, yet you spend days over here at my house. She doesn't have any idea how to get your attention."

Galina looked at Klim in horror. "But she…but I…"

Klim realized he had gone too far. What was the point in reminding Galina that she was a terrible mother? She knew already after all. And now Tata would be punished for her silly Christmas "gift."

Good god, thought Klim, *and that woman still holds out hope that something will happen between us!*

As he left the kitchen, his gaze fell on a parcel beside the door. It contained books that Klim had ordered for Elkin from a Swedish catalogue. It was much easier for foreigners to order things from abroad.

Klim did not want to go back into the living room. He knew that Galina would start apologizing and vowing never to lay a finger on Tata again.

He took the box of books and set off downstairs.

3

Elkin had once been a garage owner, but after the West had imposed a trade boycott on Soviet Russia, it was no longer possible to get spare parts. Forced to change profession, he had become a bookseller.

His bookstore, Moscow Savannah, had become popular with readers for its wonderful selection of prerevolutionary books. Visitors would rummage through dusty tomes, discussing the new finds unearthed in abandoned warehouses. Subversive conversations could be heard in the store about how the only worthwhile books were printed in the prerevolutionary script.

Elkin's shop, like Klim's apartment, was lavishly adorned with giraffes. Herds of painted giraffes paraded around the walls, and small wooden and bronze figurines stood on top of the bookcases. There was even a miniature giraffe with a parasol perched on the cashier's desk.

Until recently, business had been lively at the Moscow Savannah, but in the summer of 1927, the authorities had raised the taxes on private trade so that it was no longer profitable to run a store. Elkin was afraid he would have to close it.

Klim found him in a small room piled high with reference books, sketches, and all sorts of equipment. Elkin was listening to the radio with a pair of improvised headphones.

"It's a devilish business!" he exclaimed, removing his headphones when he caught sight of Klim. "Have you listened to the Comintern Radio lately? They're deliberately trying to give the whole country the jitters, scaring us with talk of saboteurs who want to sell the population into slavery to imperialists."

"Don't let it upset you," Klim said. "Intelligent people know that it's all propaganda."

"But that's the point!" Elkin exclaimed. "These good-for-nothings are turning the rabble against educated people. That's the Bolsheviks' state policy—to declare the workers the 'vanguard' and the 'hegemony' and make them believe their superior to all the 'bourgeois specialists.' Just read the papers! I tell you, it's civil war all over again—only this time not between the Reds and the Whites but between the schooled and the unschooled."

Elkin grabbed a magazine from the table and thrust it toward Klim. "Take a look at this! 'Machine Operator Exposes the Lies of a Technical Specialist.' Or here's another one: 'The Dirty Tricks of a State Fisheries Engineer.' They're throwing mud at anyone with higher education now. After all, we all studied under the Tsarist regime, so now we are 'alien class elements.' These social Darwinists have decided that the son of an alcoholic and uneducated peasant is made of better stuff than the son of a family of scholars."

With his hair standing up on end, Elkin resembled a large, disheveled bird.

"Do you have a parcel for me?" he said, finally noticing the box in Klim's arms. "Well, that's one bright spot in the gloom."

He began to dig around in the box, and soon all his woes were forgotten. "Well, just look at this!" he exclaimed delightedly as he leafed through a large textbook on the corrosion of metals. "This is excellent stuff!"

"Do you know Swedish?" asked Klim in surprise.

"It's not difficult. If you know three or four European languages, you can get the hang of the rest, especially when it comes to scientific material."

Elkin told Klim that these books would be sent to the Gosizdat, the state publishing house. They would be translated and printed there unofficially on paper earmarked for Party literature.

"The publishers are sent orders from those at the top to print a certain number of trade union anthologies or textbooks on 'Scientific Marxism.' But of course, there's no demand for that stuff. On the other hand, the authorities want publishers to make a profit, so the solution is to let them publish useful technical literature on the quiet. Officially, we're doing one thing, but in reality, it's a different picture."

"Do the Swedes know their books are going to be translated into Russian?" asked Klim.

Elkin regarded him with a wry smile. "My dear fellow, have you no *idea* of where you are living? The country of the Soviets is a kingdom of deception. The Bolsheviks have deceived themselves with their theory, but they stubbornly keep trying to make it real because they don't want to lose power. They can explain to the fools that 'everything *has* to be this way,' and meanwhile, they declare all intelligent people who doubt their propaganda as enemies and saboteurs. Everything here is lies and fakery, and no matter what scruples you may have, you can't get by here unless you lie and bend the rules. Have a look at me! If I didn't cheat, my business would go up in smoke tomorrow."

Just at that moment, they heard the piercing cry of a child from outside the building. "Daddy! Help!"

Klim rushed out into the corridor, flung open the door, and ran into the dark, snowy yard. There was nobody there, but he could hear bloodcurdling howls from the porter's lodge where Snapper was locked up.

"Daddy!" squealed the voice again.

A shadow flitted past the woodshed—a small man in a long greatcoat was trying to drag off Kitty, who was struggling with all her might. Klim caught up with them and knocked Kitty's kidnapper into the snow with a blow to the jaw before snatching up Kitty in his arms.

"Are you all right?" he asked her.

She was wearing nothing but her indoor dress—she was even without shoes.

Kapitolina ran up to them. "This man tried to steal our little girl!" she shrieked and began to kick the kidnapper, who was still spread-eagle in the snowdrift. The man's Red Army cap had fallen off his close shaved head, and blood was pouring from his split lip.

"Why are you attacking me?" the man wailed in a high pitched voice like a woman. "I'm just looking for a foreigner who asked about the Chinese coat with the dragons."

Klim's heart skipped a beat. He handed Kitty to Kapitolina. "Take her home," he said.

Klim took the kidnapper under the elbow and dragged him inside the house. The lobby was lit only by a dim bulb.

"What do you know about the Chinese coat?" he asked hotly. "Do you know the woman it belonged to? I'll let you go if you tell me the truth."

The man stared at Klim warily and sniffed. "They told me at the market that you'd give a reward for information about a Chinese coat. That was Nina's coat!"

"And where is she now?"

"How the devil should I know? She was taken away by those bourgeois opposite the Korsh Theater."

"What do you mean by 'taken away'? Where?"

The man did not seem to have heard Klim's question. "Your girl has a pretty dress," he said. "I had one like that when I was little."

He's completely insane, thought Klim, looking into the man's crazed eyes.

At that moment, Elkin ran out onto the landing, brandishing an ax. "Freeze! I'll call the police!"

"I'll kill you, you bastard!" roared the kidnapper, whipping a homemade blade out of his pocket and making a lunge at Klim, who leaped to one side.

The man ran headlong out into the street, and Klim and Elkin were unable to catch him.

4

Klim went back to his apartment, his heart hammering in his chest. Could it be that he had stumbled upon a clue to Nina's whereabouts? All the foreigners in Moscow knew who lived in the house opposite the Korsh Theater. It was Oscar Reich, an American who earned millions from business concessions in Soviet Russia. Klim had met him several times at official banquets.

Kitty's voice came from her room. "Daddy, where are you?"

"I'm coming," he said.

What if I hadn't heard Kitty cry out? thought Klim. *That madman would have carried her off, taken her dress, and left her somewhere in the snow.*

Galina, her eyes swollen with crying, came out of the living room and, catching sight of the bloodstains on Klim's shirt, stared at him, horrified.

"Were you in a fight? Who was it?"

"It doesn't matter," he said. "How could a stranger have just walked into our apartment?"

Galina gave a plaintive sob. "Kitty took a postcard with a picture of Comrade Stalin on it. She punched a hole through his forehead with a pencil to hang the picture on the tree, so I told her to go and sit outside in the corridor and think about what she had done. She was on her own out there—Kapitolina and I were laying the table. I think the door may have been open—you didn't slam it shut. And that character must have walked in—"

Hearing this, Klim felt another wave of anger at Galina. "What do you think you're doing? Punishing a child about a Stalin postcard! Why are you so keen to fall down and worship sacred objects? You're no better than a savage! Or were you just taking it out on Kitty because I had upset you before?"

Saying nothing more, Klim went into Kitty's room. She was lying on the bed.

"I thought the man was Santa Claus," she said, wiping away her tears. "He promised to give me a biscuit. And then he suddenly grabbed me and carried me off."

Klim sat down beside her on the bed. "But he didn't have a beard, did he?"

"I thought maybe he was a modern Santa. I thought maybe Santa shaves his beard nowadays." Kitty sat up on the bed and looked into Klim's eyes. "Daddy, I promise I won't…" She did not finish and flung her arms around his neck.

They assured each other several times how frightened they had been and how good it was that everything had ended happily.

"You must promise me never to go anywhere with a stranger," said Klim.

Kitty nodded. "I promise."

He sent her off to wash her face. Then he went back into the living room and dug an address book out of the desk drawer.

"Klim, it wasn't my fault," Galina began, putting her head around the door. "I didn't think—"

"It's fine," he said without looking up. "You can go home. Kapitolina will put Kitty to bed."

He was overcome by nervous excitement. What if he was about to find Nina after all? What if he was about to experience a simple, ridiculously ordinary miracle and receive the most precious gift possible on the night before Christmas?

He stood for a long time, unsure whether to pick up the telephone and make a call. This indecision surprised even himself. What was stopping him? Addiction to the misery that had now become his lot in life? Fear of the unknown?

Plucking up his courage in the end, he lifted the receiver and asked the operator for Oscar Reich's number.

The housekeeper answered the phone. "I'm sorry," she said with a sing-song intonation. "Mr. Reich isn't at home right now."

"When will he be back?" asked Klim.

"In four months," came the answer. "He's leaving for Europe tonight."

Klim's heart gave a lurch. "What time is his train?"

"At ten. If it's something urgent, you might still catch him at the station."

It was already five to nine—there was almost no time left.

Klim could not simply approach Reich empty-handed and ask him about Nina because that might attract unwanted attention. He picked up a few postcards from the floor, put them into an envelope, and wrote on it the first thing he could think of: "Central Post Office, London, for collection by Mr. Smith."

I'll say that I need to send this letter in a hurry, Klim thought, *and ask Reich to post it in the first post box he finds abroad.*

Galina appeared again in the doorway. "Please don't be angry with me—"

Klim rushed past her and began to pull on his coat. "I'll be back soon."

12. EX-WIFE

1

The sleigh was running along the busy Boulevard Ring. Snow was falling, soft, thick and gentle, covering the road and pavements under the bright light of the streetlamps.

"Come on. Hurry up!" pleaded Klim under his breath. But the driver seemed to dawdle deliberately, barely moving the reins.

At the crossroads, a street vendor had scattered his goods across the road, bringing traffic to a standstill.

"Hurry up, damn you!" Klim begged silently.

Chains of carts carrying firewood made their way slowly along Tverskaya Street with its magnificent buildings from the prerevolutionary era. The dray horses plodded on gravely, lifting great shaggy hooves caked in ice.

"Here we are!" the driver shouted, stopping the sleigh opposite the elegant tower of the station.

Klim paid the fare and dashed off through the crowds to the lacquered doors.

The train to Warsaw that took foreigners out of the country was still standing at the platform. The crew had not even begun to get up steam.

Klim made his way back to the station entrance. He needed to take a breath, to calm down. Oscar Reich still hadn't left Moscow, and all Klim had to do was just wait for him.

Traders from the countryside who had come into the city for the day were hurrying to catch trains out of town. Little boys ran about selling spare buttons, playing cards, and wire brushes for cleaning kerosene stoves.

At last, Klim saw Reich's dark green Chevrolet—the only one of its kind in Moscow. The chauffeur jumped out and pulled back the front seat to let out a passenger in an expensive fawn coat.

Klim set off to greet him.

"Mister Reich, I'm so glad I caught you before you left! I want to send a letter to London. Would you mind posting it for me in Warsaw?"

Oscar shook him by the hand. "Good to see you. Let's have the letter."

Klim held out the unsealed envelope. "There's nothing in it but postcards, so there won't be any problem with customs. Take a look if you like."

"The customs men won't bother me anyway."

Klim gave a tense smile, unsure how to steer the conversation around so that he could ask what he was dying to ask.

"I wonder…I wanted to…" Klim did not finish.

Giving her hand to the chauffeur, an elegant woman in a luxurious fur coat with a small felt hat pulled down over her forehead, emerged from the car.

It was Nina.

"Klim…" she whispered, her hand to her mouth. A large diamond ring glittered on her finger.

Oscar turned and handed Nina the envelope. "Could you put this into my briefcase, darling? By the way, Mr. Rogov, have you met my wife? We were married only a week ago."

Klim, still smiling, murmured some suitably polite words, thanking Oscar and wishing him a pleasant journey.

He even managed to bow to Nina, who stood dumbstruck, staring at him.

"You must call in on us when I get back from Europe," said Oscar and turned to the chauffeur. "Are the suitcases already on the train? Then let's get on. I haven't much time."

Klim turned on his heel and walked away.

Idiot! he cursed himself. *Why did you have to come here? Why did you come chasing after that…that….* He was lost for words.

A young driver in a leather coat came rushing up. "Taxi! Where can I take you, sir?"

Klim looked at him blankly. "To Chistye Prudy."

"With pleasure, sir. In you get!"

Klim got into the back seat and was about to close the door when Nina came running up.

"Please don't go, for God's sake!" she cried, panting for breath.

Without looking her way, Klim tugged the door shut.

"Drive on," he told the driver.

"Who was that young lady?" asked the driver as they came out onto the Garden Ring.

"Just some tramp," said Klim without expression.

He felt as a bomb had fallen straight into his heart, leaving nothing but a heap of smoking ruins.

2

Galina rang Tata and told her she would be late back from work. She had decided that she would not leave the house until she had made it up with Klim.

Galina put Kitty to bed and then, in order to get the servant out of the way, suggested that Kapitolina go to a Christmas service.

"Ever so grateful to you, ma'am!" Kapitolina said and a moment later ran off to church.

The minutes went by, and still, there was no Klim. Galina heated up the iron on the stove, spread a blanket on the kitchen table, and began to iron the linen. All sorts of anxious thoughts swarmed in her head. Something important had happened, clearly—otherwise, Klim would never have left Kitty right after some maniac had tried to kidnap her.

At half past nine, there was a ring at the door bell, but it turned out to be a dashing courier in a smart overcoat and a gray astrakhan hat with a red star. He held out a thick envelope decorated with the Soviet state emblem.

"Sign for this please, ma'am," he said.

Galina stared in awe at the large wax seal. "What's this?"

"Special delivery from the Kremlin," said the courier.

He got her signature, snapped a salute, and was gone.

Galina threw her coat over her shoulders, grabbed her cigarettes, and went out around the back of the building for a smoke. Just between its windowless wall and the fence of the neighboring house, there was a secluded spot where she could enjoy her cigarette without fear that Klim would come across her.

What if he doesn't marry me after all? she thought fretfully.

It was quiet and dark all around. The wind was whipping up clouds of glittering snow, and the clear winter stars hung motionless overhead.

Galina went back inside. Taking the pile of freshly ironed linen, she walked into the living room, turned on the light, and gasped. "Good lord!"

Klim was sitting on the windowsill, his arms folded over his chest.

"I didn't hear you come in," said Galina.

He did not look at her. His shoulders were oddly hunched as if it hurt him to move.

"Kitty and I are leaving the country," he said in a strange voice.

Galina stood aghast, the linen falling out of her hands. "Are you being expelled?"

"No."

"Is Owen getting rid of you?"

Klim dismissed her with an irritated gesture. "No, it's not that."

Galina saw that there was no point in plying Klim with questions—he was obviously not going to explain.

"But you can't just *leave*," she said miserably. "You have a contract! You've paid the rental on your apartment in advance!"

"That's nothing. It doesn't matter."

"What about me? Am I nothing to you too?" asked Galina, going up to Klim and looking into his eyes. "Don't you understand that if you do this, you'll destroy *everything*? Everything I have?"

"Spare me the hysterics, please!" said Klim through gritted teeth. "That's the last thing I need."

"Can't you see after all this time?" she asked quietly. "I love you!"

He looked at her for a long while and then suddenly pulled her toward him. Shivering with fear and unexpected joy, Galina kissed him.

As Klim led her to the divan, she turned out the light. She was horribly ashamed of her scar and of her old, darned underclothes.

3

Galina lay beside Klim listening to him breathing. It was difficult to believe what had just happened.

What now? she thought. *Would Klim really leave the country? No, that was impossible. He would never have done all that if he wanted to go. That would have been too dishonorable, and Klim is an honorable man.*

Galina felt the urge for a smoke but did not dare breathe a word to Klim about cigarettes.

"You should go home," he said. "Tata is probably out of her mind with worry."

Galina closed her eyes for a moment. Was Klim throwing her out? Or was he really concerned about Tata?

"Yes, I'm going. I'm going." She kissed Klim on the cheek and stood up.

It seemed there was something left unsaid. She wanted to explain to him how she felt, but there was only one thought in her head: *Please don't leave me!*

Klim reached for his trousers on the floor.

"I'll tell Afrikan to hire a cab for you," he said. "You shouldn't walk about alone at night."

He switched on the desk lamp, and Galina's fear grew—she saw no sign of tenderness, no interest in his eyes; nothing but a look of painful, inscrutable misery.

As Galina was getting dressed, Klim began to sort through the post on his desk. His movements were more abrupt than usual: he tossed the envelopes to one side carelessly, and a couple fell at Galina's feet.

She saw Klim opening the letter with the state emblem.

"What is it?" she asked.

He held out a piece of thick paper with a typewritten message on it:

Unfortunately, due to other demands on my time, I am unable to grant you an interview. I hope that the situation will change in the future.

—Joseph Stalin

Galina stared in amazement at the signature, written in blue ink.

"He sent you a *personal* answer?" she gasped. "Even though you're considered an 'enemy journalist'?"

"I've got a Christmas present after all," said Klim with a mirthless laugh.

"Look," said Galina, "he's written here that the situation might change in the future. You can't leave Moscow now! You'll lose your chance to somebody else."

"Galina, you don't understand—"

"And I never will!" she broke in. "Your life here is fine. You have a house, work, and friends. If you go abroad, you'll have to start all over from scratch. How do you think you're going to pay the money owing on the apartment? Right now, you have it on credit, and don't think Elkin will give you anything back—he's sunk everything into his business. Good god! You can't just ruin your whole life like this!"

Galina went up to Klim and put her arms around him. "Whatever happens to you, I'll be by your side. I'll always do what I can to help you."

"Thank you," he said and gave a deep sigh. "It was foolish, of course, to talk about leaving. All of this would pass eventually."

Galina suddenly realized that Klim was looking at her scar. In her haste, she had forgotten to button her dress.

Klim also had a scar on his chest from a deep wound, which, by the look of it, had not been stitched and had healed haphazardly.

"Do you mind me asking what that is?" Galina asked him now. "If I don't know, I won't be able to stop staring at it every time I see it."

"Spoils of war," he said.

"It must have almost hit your heart."

"Something like that."

Galina breathed a sigh of relief. She had hinted that this was not the last time she would see the scar, and Klim had not said anything to contradict her.

How could she find out what had happened? It was wrong to leave Klim all alone with his gloomy thoughts, but Galina understood that he did not want her around.

"All right. I'm going," she said.

Klim took Galina by the shoulders, took a step back, and looked at her as if for the first time.

"You know, you're a fine woman, Galina," he said.

She kissed him on the lips. "You're not so bad yourself."

4

So, Klim had become her lover after all, and Galina found it almost impossible to believe. She had to do her best not to ruin everything, not to make the mistake of blurting out something that would annoy him.

She should buy a new brassiere and new underwear too. Damn it all—she would have to get a loan from the OGPU cooperative again!

At the thought of the OGPU, Galina cringed inwardly. Would Alov realize that she had allowed this foreigner to take his place? Alov was terribly possessive and took the view that it was acceptable for men to be unfaithful, as it was in their nature, but that women should remain devoted all their lives to a single man.

What would happen now when Alov called her in to his office? It would be unthinkable to let him have his way with her now that she had become romantically involved with Klim. But should she try to make excuses, Alov would immediately suspect something was up.

I'll tell him I have women's problems, she decided. *I'll get a doctor to write me a note if I have to.*

As the sleigh took her home past the Church of the Archangel Gabriel, Galina lifted her eyes to the gold cross gleaming faintly in the darkness and swore that never again would she smoke or beat Tata.

This was the beginning of a new life filled with excitement, fear, and an amazing sense of hope.

5

Klim shut the door after Galina and went back into his room. He sat at his desk and opened the "Book of the Dead."

The entries in his diary did not correspond with the dates printed on the pages, and the last notes he had made in December had been written under April dates:

15 April, 1881: Execution by hanging of the revolutionaries who took part in the assassination of Tsar Alexander II.
17 April, 1912: Massacre of goldfield workers on the Lena River.

Klim dipped his pen into the inkwell and wrote beneath: "Nina is dead too."

He sat for some time looking at the damp violet letters. It was hot from the light of the electric lamp.

He noticed that his fingernails still bore the traces of dried blood from the man who had tried to kidnap Kitty. In his haste, Klim had not even had time to wash his hands properly.

Disgusted at the sight, he tried to wipe away the blood with blotting paper but soon gave up. What difference did it make anyway?

He remembered how Galina's kisses had smelled horribly of tobacco and some sort of medicine. She was no more than a dismal substitute, and what had happened between them had been a desperate attempt to burn his bridges and show himself that he had put the past behind him.

But Galina would not be disloyal to him, he felt sure. Or was it a mistake on his part to trust her? After all, she had already reported on him to the OGPU, and disloyalty was her professional duty.

The front door creaked open.

"Why aren't you in bed, sir?" he heard Kapitolina's voice. "Are you still working?"

She put her head around the door and looked with quizzical merriment at Klim. "Happy Christmas! I made you a new towel."

She ran back to her room and came back with a hand towel and a pair of mittens. "This is for you, and these are for Kitty. If I had any more yarn, I'd have made some for Tata too. Galina says the poor little one hasn't any mittens, and that's why her nose is always running."

Klim gave Kapitolina two rubles and then added another so she could buy some yarn and make Tata a pair of mittens.

"Oh, sir, you're too kind!" Kapitolina exclaimed. "You've made our day—all of us girls, I mean!"

She unwound her shawl, wrapped the money in it, and hid it beneath her shirt.

"I'll go to a witch and ask her for a love charm so as I can find me a husband," she said, blushing. "The best thing would be to get a worker from the state catering department or the member of some factory committee. I've got my eye on a soldier too—one of the guards at the Lenin Mausoleum. I've been twice now to stand in the queue and get a peek at him. Such a job he has, standing stock still all day and making sure nobody runs off with the body of our leader!"

"Don't tell me you believe in witches?" asked Klim.

Kapitolina put her hands on her hips. "There are some very powerful witches out there, you know! They can cast all sorts of spells."

She looked around the room for a fitting example and saw a book of fairy tales lying on the carpet. On the cover was a picture of Snow White sleeping in her coffin.

"You see what a spell can do?" said Kapitolina.

Klim gave a grim laugh. That was a good comparison. *His* Nina, the Nina he had once known, had tasted the forbidden fruit, and her true self had died. She was still breathing, her heart was still beating, but there was nothing left of his wife but an empty shell.

6

That night, Klim could not get to sleep. He kept remembering Nina standing next to her new husband, clear-eyed, gorgeous, and unattainable. He remembered how she had pounded with her palm on the window of the taxi, wanting, for some reason, to explain something to Klim.

What was there to explain? She had acted exactly as he might have expected—she had found the only millionaire in Moscow and married him. As for divorce, under Soviet law, a former spouse could be notified by post. All you had to do was pay the state tariff, send a letter recorded delivery, and you could consider yourself free.

That Christmas Eve, Klim had received a more valuable gift than a personal letter from Stalin. He had also got a clear reply to all the questions that had been plaguing him. He was afraid that Nina met her end in Moscow—and he had been right.

There was no point in going back to Shanghai. What sort of future could Kitty hope for there? The Europeans and Americans living in China regarded the Asian races as second class citizens, and in Chinese society, a woman was of about the same status as a piece of furniture.

There was only one way to overcome Kitty's "unfortunate" parentage, and that was to give her a brilliant education. By fair means or foul, Klim had to get Kitty a place in a good European school, and to do so, he needed money and a residency permit. It would be good if he were transferred to London, but Klim knew he had not been with United Press for long enough yet to be in line for a position in a European office.

Well, now his future plan of action was clear. First, he had to get an interview with Stalin, and then he could get out of the country to Europe.

And Nina? As far as Klim was concerned, she no longer existed.

13. WIFE OF A SOVIET MILLIONAIRE

1

That night, when Nina had ended up in Oscar's house, she had been faced with a choice. She could act like a rape victim, somebody who could be walked over, or like an artful courtesan who had deliberately seduced Mr. Reich.

She chose the latter course. Had she decided to play the part of victim, she would have had to go to the police, to give tearful explanations, and undergo humiliating medical examinations. As a courtesan, she could listen to Oscar's passionate declarations of love with a knowing smile and accept his invitation to stay in his house for as long as she liked without any loss of dignity.

However, one thing led to another. Oscar began to pay court to Nina, buying her flowers and gifts and showering her with compliments.

"Once I've wrapped the business up here, you and I will go to New York," he promised her. "It's a marvelous city, and you'll score a sensation over there."

Naturally, Nina shared Reich's bed. Having decided on this particular game, she was obliged to play by the rules. She consoled herself with the thought that this was not happening to her but to "Baroness Bremer," and that she had made the right choice in a difficult situation. Reich was the only person who could help her: he had money, connections, and most of all, a secure position in Bolshevik society.

But as it turned out, her calculations were wrong.

One day, Oscar came in drunk with tears in his eyes and began to tell her his family history.

His father had been a penniless émigré from a little shtetl in the western part of Russian Empire. Thirty years ago, he had made his way to America through Hamburg. While there, he had had so little money that he had been forced to spend several nights sleeping rough in the entrance to the Reichsbank. He had gazed at all the beautiful and rich people around him and decided that he would adopt the surname "Reich" to bring him luck.

In New York, he had married and opened a pharmacy but still found difficulty making ends meet. In frustration, he had begun to fraternize with the American socialists. He had frequented the underground meetings to hear speakers who had come over from Europe, collected funds for the great cause, and dreamed of a revolution in the USA.

At one of these meetings, Reich senior had met Leon Trotsky, and the two had quickly found common cause, discussing the Jewish question and social inequality.

In 1919, fortune had smiled on Reich at last. Prohibition had been introduced in the United States, and all products including alcohol had been withdrawn from sale except medicine. Tincture of ginger, which was used to treat indigestion, had not come under the ban, and so Reich had borrowed money and, together with his now grown-up son, brought up all the ginger available in the port of New York. The two had been the only legal traders of alcohol in the Bronx, and within a year, they had become millionaires. Soon after this, Trotsky had written to Oscar to suggest a business proposition in Russia.

"Nina," Oscar cried, "I'm such a damn fool! The Bolsheviks won't listen to anything I say anymore. As long as Trotsky was in charge, I could do what I liked, but now, they're accusing me of taking currency out of the country illegally. And that was the deal in the first place!"

Nina's heart sank. "But what about my exit papers? You told me you'd have no trouble getting hold of them for me."

"There's only one way I can take you out of the country," said Oscar, looking mournfully at Nina. "You'll have to marry me and sign a document giving me power of attorney. Then I can go to an American embassy somewhere in Europe on your behalf."

Nina felt out of her depth. "But I can't do that! I don't have any papers."

"We can sort out a Soviet passport for you," Oscar promised. "I've arranged it already. The most important thing is to get an American visa and permission to leave the country from the OGPU."

Nina asked Oscar to give her time to think.

In theory, she told herself, it would not be Nina Kupina who was getting married, but "Baroness Bremer." And the marriage would not harm Shilo as it would not be legally binding for her. As for Klim, he would never find out. In any case, what was the point of tormenting herself over a marriage of convenience when she had already betrayed her real husband, and it was too late to do anything about it?

I'll go back to Shanghai and start life afresh, Nina decided.

The next morning, she agreed to marry Reich and to sign over power of attorney to him.

2

It turned out that Klim had already left China for Moscow by the time Nina sent her telegrams, and that was why he had never answered any of them.

She could only imagine what he thought of her now. Klim could have forgiven her for just about anything—but not a marriage of convenience to another man.

After he had driven off, Nina had run back onto the platform to ask Oscar where he had met Klim, but Oscar did not remember.

"Take care!" he said, planting a kiss on Nina's lips. "I'll write to you soon."

Nina returned to the deserted house on Petrovsky Lane and sank feebly onto the bench that stood in the hall by the front door.

What should she do now? How could she find Klim? Her head felt as if it was filled with wet sand.

She heard the flick of a light switch, and Theresa appeared at the top of the stairs.

"Oh, so you're back already!" she said. "After you left, there was a call for Mr. Reich from Mr. Klim Rogov."

Nina jumped to her feet. "Did he leave his number?"

Theresa went to where the telephone hung on the wall and picked up a large address book from the shelf beside it.

"Here you are, ma'am. Last time Mr. Rogov rang, he left his address and his telephone number."

Her head spinning, Nina stared down at Theresa's penciled scrawl. Klim lived in Chistye Prudy, only a fifteen minute drive away.

3

Nina took a cab to the building that housed the Moscow Savannah bookstore. She entered the small, inviting courtyard and mounted the porch, but seeing her shadow on the door, she froze.

Everything she was wearing, from her cloche hat to her extravagant fur coat, had been bought with Oscar's money, and every bit of it was evidence of her crime. How could she appear before Klim in all this shameful finery?

Just then, the door flew open, and a red-haired man in an unbuttoned coat came out onto the porch.

"Is that you, Mrs. Reich?" he cried out delightedly. "Have you come to see me? Or is it Klim you're after?"

"Have we met before?" asked Nina frowning.

"Of course. I'm Elkin. Don't you remember me? I came to see your husband to discuss selling a car."

Nina had no memory of Elkin. Oscar had always had a constant stream of visitors.

"I used to have a garage," explained Elkin, "but I've packed it in now. I'm selling off all my stock."

He reached into his pocket and fished out a torn visiting card. "Here's my name and telephone number. Please, remember me to your husband!"

Nina nodded. "He's abroad at the moment, but I'll tell him when he comes back."

She walked quickly past Elkin and made her way up the stairs to the story above.

There was a small landing, a round window, and a smart door with a brass handle in the shape of a comical giraffe.

Nina crossed herself quickly as if she were about to jump into a hole in the ice and pushed the doorbell.

After a few agonizing minutes, Klim appeared at the door. He was wearing a white shirt with the collar unbuttoned, a dark gray waistcoat, and trousers of the same color. His hair was shorter than Nina remembered it.

"Hello," she said in a weak voice. "May I come in?"

Klim looked at her for a long time. "What do you want?"

"I want to talk."

The door below banged shut, and they heard Elkin's voice downstairs. "Please, don't forget about my car!"

"Come in then," Klim said shortly. Clearly, he did not want to start a domestic argument in front of his neighbor.

Nina took off her fur coat and began to unlace her overshoes. Klim made no move to help or show her where to hang her coat.

"Where's our daughter?" she asked.

"Kitty's not here."

Nina followed Klim into a living room with colored glass in the windows. He showed her to the divan and sat down on the windowsill as far away from her as possible. He looked at her with cold surprise as if to say "How on earth did you find the cheek to show your face here?"

"I sent you quite a few telegrams," Nina said. "I waited and waited for you to reply, but it seems you were right here in Moscow all the time."

"If I'm not mistaken, we separated a year ago," said Klim. "To tell you the truth, I have no desire to go raking around in the past. You have your life now, and I have mine."

Nina felt herself grow cold. "But you followed me to Moscow—"

"I think you should leave now," Klim interrupted.

"Won't you at least listen to my side of the story? I'm not going anywhere until I've spoken to you!"

"If you won't leave, I will." Klim got to his feet. "When you get tired of talking to the wall, you can close the door after you."

4

Klim left so quickly that Nina had no time to do anything to stop him. She stood in the middle of the room, crushed and miserable.

The day was coming to an end. The windows in Klim's living room shone like the stained glass windows in a church, but the bronze giraffe heads that decorated the curious branched light-fitting had the look of malevolent imps in the half-light.

Nina walked around the apartment, scrutinizing every last detail. In the typewriter on Klim's desk, there was an unfinished article in English, and files of newspapers, directories, and piles of telegraph forms were scattered everywhere. It looked as though Klim had found work in Moscow.

Clearly, he had plenty of friends. There was a globe in the corner of the room covered in signatures and good luck messages. And it seemed he had plenty of money too to judge by the freshly upholstered furniture and the expensive china in the cabinet.

Here and there, Nina came across some item Klim had brought to Moscow from Shanghai: the fountain pen she had bought for him in the Wing On department store, a pair of cuff links in the shape of scarab beetles, and a shirt with his initials embroidered on the cuffs. Looking at these things, she felt her heart turn over. Once, they had been as good as hers, but now, she did not even have the right to touch them.

She went into Kitty's bedroom, and tears came into her eyes. Kitty must have grown a lot, judging by her new dresses and stockings. Her drawings hung all over the walls, and there were toy horses and giraffes strewn across the rug.

Kitty probably doesn't even remember me, Nina thought bitterly. *Little children have short memories after all.*

There were two pairs of women's shoes in the hall, but they were different sizes and clearly belonged to two different women. One was a pair of homemade felt sleepers, the other a pair of elegant leather shoes.

Nina rushed into the bathroom but was relieved to find only two toothbrushes there, one large and one small. There were no women's clothes in the closets, but Nina found a nail file and a hairpin on the floor. It seemed unlikely that these things belonged to a servant who occupied the little room off the kitchen.

But there *was* another woman coming to see Klim regularly—she even kept a pair of indoor shoes there to wear around the house.

Nina sat down and buried her face in her hands. What if Klim had met somebody else?

It couldn't be true, she thought. If so, he would never have been so angry or adopted such a hostile manner with her. Instead, he would have asked her how she was and probably even offered to help her in some way.

"Klim will calm down," Nina said to herself, "and when he comes back, we'll sit down and discuss everything like adults."

Night fell, but he did not come. For minutes at a time, Nina would sit motionless in the armchair before jumping up and pacing the room, unable to bear it anymore. Why didn't he come back? Where was Kitty? And where was the servant girl? If only someone would come!

Evidently, Klim had decided to spend the night somewhere else.

Nina found a blanket and a pillow, turned off the light, and lay down on the divan in the living room. Not long ago, Klim himself had slept there, and perhaps not only that.

At last, she heard the key turn slowly in the door. Her whole body stiffened, and she strained her ears to catch the slightest sound. The blanket fell to the floor, but Nina did not dare pick it up.

The door creaked, and she heard the sound of cautious footsteps.

"How about a nightcap?" she heard Elkin's voice from the landing. "Do you have any of that brandy left?"

"Go to bed, for God's sake, man!" she heard Klim say. "You're drunk."

"I'm no more drunk than you are, my dear fellow!"

Apparently, Klim had been sitting with his neighbor downstairs, waiting for Nina to leave.

All was quiet out in the hall. Then at last, Klim came into the living room, bent over, and ripped the telephone cord out of the wall. Then he stood for a long time without saying a word, gazing at Nina.

A minute passed; two minutes; three. Nina was afraid to breathe.

Klim picked up the blanket that had fallen to the floor and carefully put it over her.

Feeling a pang of overwhelming tenderness, Nina touched his hand, but Klim grabbed her wrist and squeezed it so hard that she screamed in pain. "What are you doing? Let me go!"

His fingers continued to press on her wrist as if he wanted to break it.

"Stop!" she cried. "You're hurting me!"

He flung down her hand and left the room. Nina heard the door of Kitty's bedroom slam shut.

She ran out into the dark corridor and felt her way along the walls to the other room.

"Please, open up!"

There was no reply.

Nina hammered at the door panel with all her strength. "We need to talk! Klim, open up! I won't leave till you've heard what I have to say."

"Stop making a scene!" she heard Klim snap. "It's three o'clock in the morning."

"You can't hide from me forever!"

At last, the door opened, the light switch clicked, and a flood of bright light dazzled Nina for a moment.

Klim stood staring at her with icy rage. "Do you realize I have to go to work tomorrow? I didn't ask you to come here and have a fit of hysterics."

"But I didn't—"

"Go to bed now, or I'll put you out of the house! Good night."

The door slammed again.

Nina's head was throbbing from all the tears she had cried.

He's just drunk, she told herself. *He doesn't want to hear anything just now. But I'll explain. Tomorrow, I'll tell him everything.*

5

Nina managed to drift into a light sleep just before dawn. She dreamed that she was trying to cross a deep river in a small rowing boat full of holes. But with every stroke of the oars, the boat sank deeper in the water. She was in some silent, misty, deserted place, and she knew she would never reach the other side.

Nina woke from a loud rattling sound as if somebody had dropped something in the kitchen. Apparently, Klim was already up.

Nina sat up and gave a shudder as she caught sight of a pink shape moving in the corner of the room. It took her a moment to realize that it was only her own reflection in a large mirror on the wall. She looked a fright: her hair was tangled, and her eyes were swollen from crying. Not ideal, given that she was planning to talk about her feelings to the man she loved.

Klim was making coffee in the kitchen.

"Good morning," Nina said and sat down on a crooked, clumsily made stool.

Klim looked at her and nodded without a word. He was not looking his best either. He was rumpled and unshaven, his clothes in creases. Apparently, he had been up all night.

"Can I help with anything?" asked Nina.

"No."

Klim took a spoon and began skimming the froth from the coffee.

The silence was unbearable.

"Listen," began Nina, "don't I deserve a bit of respect, at least—"

Klim gave her such a look that she stopped mid-sentence.

"A woman who solves her problems by hopping from bed to bed can't ask to be treated with respect," he told her.

"Are you trying to make me suffer on purpose?"

"You've done a pretty good job of that yourself. In a few years, Reich will swap you for some seventeen-year-old girl, and then, for all your fine manners and fancy clothes, you'll be tossed aside like an old shoe."

At that moment, the coffee boiled over, flooding the stove.

"Damn it!" Klim took hold of the coffee pot, burned his fingers, and dropped it at his feet. Coffee poured out across the floor.

Nina let out a deep breath. "Listen. I came here so that—"

"No, you listen to me!" Klim turned toward her, furious and quite unrecognizable. "It just so happens that I have met somebody else. Now would you kindly stop interfering in our lives and just leave!"

Nina's chin quivered. "All right, I'll leave! Don't worry—I'll manage fine without you. And you will curse this day as long as you live!"

14. THE RIVAL

1

For a little while after the night of Christmas Eve, Galina was in seventh heaven, but her joyful mood soon passed. Klim did not seem at all like a man who had found the love of his life.

She was plagued by doubts. Perhaps he did not find her beautiful? Or was Tata the problem? Klim was probably reluctant to get involved with a woman who already had a child, particularly when that child was so difficult.

What had taken place that Christmas Eve was repeated several times, and Galina cursed the infertility she had once considered a blessing. If she had got pregnant, Klim would almost certainly have married her. He had told her many times that children were the most important thing in life.

She could not understand what was happening to Klim. He had become sullen, withdrawn, and sarcastic. Increasingly, he wanted to be left alone, and it was impossible to talk to him properly about anything besides work because he refused to answer any questions.

Alov was not making things any easier for Galina.

"Have you found out yet what this Nina Kupina means to Rogov?" he asked her.

Unfortunately, Galina could find out nothing from Klim, even about matters far closer to her heart than this Nina.

"You'll be in trouble at this rate," Alov warned her. "I could have you removed from your post. Staff reduction."

In order to be seen useful, Galina prepared reports on all of Klim's acquaintances: Elkin, Seibert, Magda, and others.

Alov carefully filed them away. Galina thought he looked like a praying mantis, waiting with expressionless eyes to pounce on an unsuspecting fly.

2

Galina delivered a package to a censor on the other side of Moscow. On the way back home, the tram broke down, and she arrived back at her apartment exhausted and chilled to the bone.

She found her room turned upside down. Tata and Kitty had been using one of her old aprons to make a toy horse, and the room was strewn with pieces of material, buttons, and tattered bast fibers for the horse's mane and tail.

Galina hadn't even the strength to scold them. All she wanted to do at that moment was to drink some hot tea and crawl under a warm blanket. She shivered at the thought that she would have to take Kitty home.

The telephone rang in the hall.

"Galina, it's for you!" called one of the other tenants.

It was Klim.

"Could Kitty stay the night with you?" he asked. "Kapitolina is out of town, and I have something to do."

"Of course," Galina replied.

Klim had never let his daughter spend a night away from home before now. It was all very strange.

3

In the morning, Galina tried several times to ring Klim, but there was no answer.

"Let's go home, Kitty," she said, dispirited. She could not bear the thought of waiting any longer in suspense.

All the way back home, Kitty pretended she was riding on her new toy horse. She was happy. She had gone to bed without washing her face the night before, and Tata had promised to take her to the circus the next time she got free tickets at her school.

They're just like sisters now, the two of them, thought Galina. If only Klim could be made to see sense, how happy they could all be together!

When they reached her house, Kitty climbed up onto the hillock of snow Afrikan had made for her in the yard.

"I want my horse to slide down with me!" she said.

Galina went up onto the porch and opened the front door. "Come on, Kitty, or I'm going in without you. I'll count to five: one, two—"

At that moment, there was a clatter of boots on the stairs, and a woman in a magnificent fur coat rushed out past Galina.

Galina's heart leaped into her mouth. That woman had been with Klim!

Galina dragged Kitty upstairs. The door to Klim's apartment was wide open, and from inside, there came the smell of burned coffee.

Klim was in the hall, his face ashen and his eyes like a madman's.

"What happened?" Galina gasped, but he did not even look her way.

"Daddy!" shouted Kitty, thrusting her toy horse toward him. "Look what I've got!"

"Yes, that's wonderful. Thanks," muttered Klim, clearly not taking in what she had said.

"Who was that woman?" asked Galina.

He met her eyes. "What do you mean?"

"I just saw a woman on the stairs. What was she doing here?"

Klim came to his senses at last. "She had the wrong address," he said. "Come on inside now that you're here. I need you to type something for me."

4

Birch logs blazed in the hearth. The room was as hot as an inferno, but Klim did not seem to notice.

"Portraits of Trotsky and his associates," he dictated, "have been taken down from walls of official buildings. Books written by Trotskyites have been removed from libraries. Streets previously named after their leader have been renamed after Marx, Lenin, and so on. There has been a spate of suicides. The most passionate Trotskyites are leaving notes declaring 'The counter-revolution has won. Farewell, comrades!.'"

"Perhaps there's no need to write all this?" pleaded Galina. "After all, it will never get past the censor."

"Keep typing, please," Klim told her. "When it was announced that Trotsky was being sent into exile in Alma-Ata, a huge crowd gathered at the station. A man resembling Trotsky was put onto the train under armed guard, but it later turned out this was an actor made up to look like the opposition leader. After standing in the freezing cold for several hours, the crowd dispersed."

Galina pulled the sheet of paper from the typewriter and dropped it by accident onto the floor. Bending down to pick it up, she noticed a crumpled pink chemise lying beside the divan.

Klim followed her gaze.

"Would you do me a favor and make me some coffee?" he asked.

As Galina was on her way out to the kitchen, she noticed that the telephone wire had been pulled out of its socket.

It was quite clear to her now what had happened. A woman had spent the night with Klim. This was why he had left Kitty with Galina and had not answered the phone.

Who can it be? thought Galina in dismay. *A foreigner? The wife of some Nepman? Has she been coming to see him for long?*

When Galina came back, there was no sign of the pink chemise, and the room smelled of scorched cloth. Klim had clearly thrown the garment onto the fire.

"Tell me the truth," Galina began in a trembling voice. "Who was it who came to see you last night?"

He glanced at her quickly and looked away. He had absolutely no talent for lying.

"Please don't ask me anything," he said at last. "I lost my wife not long ago. Since her death, I've been finding it difficult—"

So, *that* was it! Now Galina understood everything—Klim's misery and his detached, distant air. He had come to the Soviet Union to make a fresh start, but the wound was still too raw. He was not ready to marry again so quickly.

But who was that woman who had come to see him then? Galina guessed that it was probably one of the girls who hung around all day at the Commissariat of Foreign Affairs, trying to seduce wealthy foreigners. Klim must have let her stay the night, but then thrown her out, realizing that this was not at all what he wanted.

Galina was glad of one thing: she knew now that Klim's affections were not engaged elsewhere. All she had to do was to bide her time and make sure no other woman tried to steal her beloved.

15. A KINGDOM OF BOOKS

1

For a few days, Nina was reduced to a painful state of near-paralysis, trying to work out what to do. She had nothing left: no love, no child, no home, and no aim in life. Soon, Oscar would be back with her papers, and then what? Should she go with him to New York?

I'll get Klim back, she decided. *He still has feelings for me, so it isn't hopeless yet. And I'll deal with that lover of his too. She can't just come along and take what's mine.*

To start with, Nina had to do some detective work. She had to find out about Klim's way of life, his friends, and his new love interest. Then she would have a better idea what to do.

Nina dug out Elkin's business card and rang him. "I'd like to have a look at the car you're selling," she said. "Could that be arranged?"

Elkin was overjoyed. "Why, of course! Come any time!"

They agreed on a time to meet, but no sooner had Nina hung up than she was gripped by fear. What if it all went wrong? What if she went to see Elkin and ran into Klim? How shameful if he thought she was chasing him! And what if Kitty were there?

I'll cross that bridge when I get to it, thought Nina gloomily. *In any case, I've got nothing to lose.*

2

Nina arrived at the bookstore, and Elkin gave her a tour of his domain.

She looked around with interest at the motley shelves filled with information and cookery books, horoscopes, dream almanacs, miscellanies, and guide books.

Elkin kept his most valuable treasures—novels on the subject of love and war—in ancient metal-bound chests. Children's books lay strewn over on the rug, and handsome editions of encyclopedias and religious tomes stood in elegant rows on the shelves.

"It's like traveling back in time," said Nina, running her hands over the spines, which shone with gold leaf. "Don't you sell *any* modern books?"

Elkin showed her a stand in the corner of the shop, which contained the new Soviet books he was obliged to sell: propaganda leaflets and works of fiction with titles like *The Red Daredevils* and *Young Communists in Africa*.

Elkin gave a wry laugh when he saw Nina's bewildered expression. "A few years ago, the Party sent out a summons," he said. "'We need to have Soviet adventure stories of our own!' It annoyed them to see that young people only cared about 'bourgeois writers,' so they invested money in the scheme and got the wheels turning. Hungry young writers who arrive in Moscow from some far-off places are always happy to try their hand at writing something for a bit of money."

Nina picked up *Young Communists in Africa* and leafed through it. "Does anybody read this stuff?" she asked. "It's utter nonsense! It's quite obvious the author hasn't any idea what he's writing about."

"Well, what of it?" Elkin shrugged. "There's a whole generation of children in this country who have barely had any schooling. The Great War put a stop to decent education—all the teachers went off to the front, and after that, things went from bad to worse. Our young people have never traveled, they don't speak any foreign languages, they've never read any good books, and they have only the vaguest idea of what's what."

A customer asked for assistance, and Elkin ran off to serve him. Nina stood for some time looking at the illustrations in a large multi-volume edition of *Pictorial Russia*. She wondered how all these books had survived the war and revolution. Back then, books had been ruthlessly stripped of their leather bindings to make patches for boots.

At last, Elkin shut the door of the store and hung up the "Closed" sign in the window.

"These days, I have to do everything myself," he sighed. "I used to have three assistants, but I had to let them go. The labor inspection office was threatening to close me down for 'exploitation of the working classes.'"

"Why would they bother?" Nina asked, amazed. "There are no jobs in the country as it is. Why prevent people from earning a living?"

"You can't make an omelet without breaking eggs. In the Kremlin, they think the economic crisis is caused by the Nepmen cheating and swindling and not paying their taxes. But worst of all, we private traders create competition and take away customers from state businesses, thus getting in the way of the construction of socialism. We provide a better service. That's all. But the government thinks we're saboteurs and does everything possible to stifle us."

There was a burst of laughter and a clatter of feet from the apartment upstairs. Nina looked up: the silk giraffe-spotted lampshade hanging from the ceiling was jigging up and down. It looked as if Klim was having a party.

"Those foreigners are up to something every day," said Elkin. "Recently, they had a competition to see who could lose weight the fastest, Heinrich Seibert or Magda Thompson. But Seibert had a trick up his sleeve. The first time they weighed him, he wore his jacket and boots, and today, he came for the weigh-in with a haircut and without his glasses."

It was extraordinary how all the foreigners in Moscow knew one another, thought Nina. It was like a big village—even Magda, who had once shared a hotel room with Nina, was visiting Klim now.

"Would you like to go up and join them?" asked Elkin. "I expect Galina has made some pies."

Nina shivered. Galina—was that the name of Klim's lover?

"I'd rather have a look at your car," Nina said.

The car was in an old woodshed. Elkin flicked a switch, and the bulb on the ceiling lit up a smallish black car unlike any Nina had seen before. A figurine of a winged giraffe gleamed dully on the hood.

"Allow me to introduce you to Mashka," said Elkin with pride. "My own design. The challenge was to create an inexpensive model for use on Russian roads. But the authorities refused to back me, and I had to give up the whole idea."

"Why didn't they like Mashka?" asked Nina.

"Well, a car gives you personal freedom, you see. You can just jump behind the wheel and go wherever you like. Our leaders go everywhere by car, but they want the rest of us to travel by railroad—so we don't go off the beaten path. Nobody wants to invest money in private cars here. All they can think about is the metro. And in any case, I'm a Nepman, a private entrepreneur. What fool would go risking his career for my sake? Support an 'enemy class element,' and you're likely to share his fate."

Nina walked about the car, inspecting the wide-tired wheels and the engine with its tangle of wires.

Elkin waved his hands excitedly as he told her how he had invented the new boosting device and what he had done to alter the suspension.

"Please, buy my Mashka!" he said, putting his hand to his heart. "Perhaps your husband will take her out of the country and show somebody? Of course, I'd prefer to start production here in Russia, but I know that won't happen."

"Why did you decide to call her Mashka?" asked Nina.

"The Germans have their Mercedes, so why can't I have my Mashka?" replied Elkin.

He looked down at the floor. "Mashka was the name of my daughter. She loved giraffes, and we dreamed of going to Africa together one day to see them in real life. She was killed for her rabbit-fur hat. She was on the way to school, and somebody put a knife in her back."

Nina gasped. "My god!"

"Perhaps it was even for the best," said Elkin. "She died in an instant, and she won't have to put up with any bullying or harassment now. Her childhood was almost happy."

Nina felt that he was repeating something he had said many times before, both to himself and to others.

"You'll get along well with my Mashka," said Elkin warmly. "She's a bit like you—otherworldly—but in a good way."

"I'll have a word with Oscar when he comes back," Nina promised.

Elkin showed Nina out. Just after they had left the yard, a crowd of laughing people came running out and began a snowball fight.

Nina had a good view of the merrymakers. She saw Klim brushing the snow from the coat of a woman in a gray headscarf and then helping her to slide down the icy mound in the yard.

Elkin followed Nina's gaze. "Mr. Rogov is a lucky man," he said. "Galina's a good woman, and she's madly in love with him."

Nina pressed her lips together. So, now she knew.

"What do you say if I do some work in your store as a saleswoman?" she asked Elkin. "I'll work for free so that you don't get in trouble with any inspectors."

"But…I couldn't imagine…" Elkin was at a loss.

"I have nothing to do, anyway," said Nina. "And if I worked here, I could come to your store every day."

"Well…what can I say? I'd be delighted!"

"Good. We can start tomorrow."

Nina needed a good look-out post and some room for maneuver. Working as a saleswoman in the Moscow Savannah would be just what she needed.

3

It turned out that the Moscow Savannah was not only a store but a labor exchange for the Moscow intelligentsia. Elkin knew a great many people and helped skilled professionals find work—translating, writing articles, typing documents, and so on.

"Some people have workmates; I have *bookmates*," he said proudly to Nina. "And they're the best sort in the world."

Most of Elkin's customers were simple office workers, though occasionally professors or senior engineers would come into the store. Some venerable old man would unbutton his heavy overcoat and settle himself in an armchair, and Nina would bring him Jäger's *Universal History* or Brehm's *Life of Animals*. She would treat her guests to books like a diligent hostess. The cash register rang merrily, churning out receipt after receipt, and patrons would leave the store happy, clutching their precious haul.

Klim never came in to Elkin's store. Probably, somebody had told him that Nina was working there, and now, he was trying to avoid her.

At least Elkin enjoyed sharing stories about his tenants. Nina found out that Kitty would eat nothing but bread and cheese and candy, and Kapitolina was afraid of mice and would jump onto a stool at the slightest suspicious noise. She also heard that Galina had made a mobile in Kitty's room out of a child's bicycle wheel painted white and hung with paper airplanes on strings. According to Elkin, Kitty would spin the wheel and shout out at the top of her voice, "Airplane, airplane, take me there and back again!"

Nina was slowly boiling over with frustration and jealousy.

"What does Klim think about Galina?" she asked Elkin.

"It's not Galina he should think about," he said with a chuckle. "He needs to think about his sums. He wrote in one of his articles that a million people came out to take part in a parade to mark the Red Army anniversary. That was the figure the foreign journalists had been given in the press briefing. But there are only two million people in Moscow! Does Klim seriously believe that every second person went to that parade, including the elderly, the disabled, and the babies? He might be an American, but he doesn't care about getting his numbers right as Americans are supposed to do."

4

One day, a small, thin man in an old officer's greatcoat appeared in Elkin's store.

"I've just been dismissed from Gosizdat," he announced in a trembling voice.

Elkin took him into the back room and sat him down in an armchair.

"This is Count Belov, an exceptional translator who specializes in medical books," Elkin told Nina.

Gosizdat was the largest publishing house in the country, and apart from fiction, it published textbooks and scientific and technical literature. Belov's knowledge of the field was unique, but at a general meeting, a representative of the Party had announced that "former aristocrats" had no right to employment when so many Red Army soldiers who had fought bravely at the front in the civil war were without work.

Belov's supervisor tried in vain to explain that his team was working on a very important book on the prevention of epidemics. But the meeting decided to dismiss Belov and all his colleagues who had been hired through "class nepotism." Their place would be taken by brave Red Army soldiers.

Elkin groaned. "I've told you not to write on the application form that you were a count!"

Belov blushed to the roots of his hair. "Only a scoundrel could deny his own family history! My great-grandfather died on the battlefield during the Napoleonic Wars; my grandfather took part in the defense of Crimea, and my father was the commander of a battleship. How can I disown them?"

Elkin scratched his chin. "I suppose they've evicted you from your apartment too?"

Belov nodded mournfully. "We were given twenty-four hours to vacate the room. What do they care if six children end up on the street?"

Elkin spent some time making telephone calls, cursing, shouting, and cajoling.

"Go out to Saltykovka," at last he said to Belov. "It's a little place to the east of Moscow, a *dacha* settlement. My friend has a dacha there, though it's unheated and a bit of a mess. I'll look for some translation work for you to keep you and your family going."

When the count left, Elkin took an open bottle of cognac from his desk drawer and took a large gulp.

"Bastards!" he swore. "They'll be the end of Russia. They take everything of worth in the country and cut it off at the root! I don't know what the Belovs will live on when I leave."

"Are you planning to close down the Savannah?" asked Nina, alarmed.

"It's not me that wants to close it. It's the housing commission. They've already sent someone out to tell me I have no right to occupy an entire house like this one. The Bolsheviks may not have any specific plans for the development of the country, but they feel in their bones that if people's only source of income is the state, then nobody will want to smash the system. So, they're stifling everyone who has the desire or the ability to make money independently. They're not taking everything at once, but just cutting off a piece at a time, bleeding us slowly, so that we get used to the pain. And then they can do what they like."

Nina looked at Elkin in a daze. If Moscow Savannah closed, she would never have the chance to meet Klim and try to make it up with him.

"Where are you going?" she asked.

"Back home to Crimea," Elkin said. "It's nice there, mountains and sunshine. You walk along the beach, and the waves hiss and foam like champagne."

"But maybe you should oppose the housing committee? After all, there are people who speak up for you. They need you!"

Elkin shook his head. "Nobody will fight for me. My bookmates are out-and-out individualists…. Oh, we're all clever, worthwhile people, at least for ourselves, but we're not prepared to put our heads on the block for anyone. We're not lions; we're giraffes—outlandish, conspicuous, but capable of reaching certain heights, for all that."

5

BOOK OF THE DEAD

Fate is clearly having a joke at my expense. For months I was doing all I could to find out something, anything, about Nina. Now, almost every day, somebody gives me news of her.

She has begun working in the Moscow Savannah, and Elkin is in raptures over my ex-wife.

"How could a creature like that have survived in Soviet Russia?" he keeps saying.

Elkin is touched by the fact that Nina is elegant and well-dressed like the young ladies in Moscow before the revolution, and that she doesn't mangle her Russian with fashionable abbreviations.

"Brains, Mr. Rogov! Brains—that's the most important thing in a woman! Well, apart from all the rest."

I try to interrupt his enthusiastic outpourings, but he is unstoppable.

"I don't mean to say I'm making a play for her," Elkin says. "I'm no match for her millionaire husband. All the same, a healthy man can't stop thinking about these things. And don't come over all 'holier than thou' with me! You're just a hypocrite, whereas I tell it like it is. You know her, don't you?"

"No," I say. "And I have no intention of getting to know her."

"But I saw her go into your apartment that day. Sour grapes, is that it? Easy on the eye, but not so easy to catch?"

I am doing my best to ensure that Nina catches neither my eye nor Kitty's. I have ordered Afrikan to make a new gate in the fence in the yard behind the house, and now, we go out by this exit. I've also asked him to keep the gates locked so that unauthorized people (Nina that is) cannot come in to our stairwell.

I don't know what she is thinking. Is she bored without her husband perhaps? Is that why she's decided to play games with me? Or is it Kitty she's interested in? Maybe she's waiting for a good moment to take her away?

Galina is also puzzled. She asked me, "Did you know that that woman who visited you is working in Elkin's store?"

I told her I wasn't interested in gossip about the neighbors. However, this did nothing to reassure her. In fact, Galina has now begun to suspect me of being "unfaithful" to her. Every day, she asks Kapitolina where I've been while Galina was out and listens at the door when I'm on the telephone.

This has been going on for a few weeks now, and I'm living in a permanent state of tension. I pray that Nina will leave me alone, although this request to the heavenly powers seems utterly ridiculous since we never see one another and she doesn't interfere in my life.

The problem is me. I know Nina is somewhere nearby, and this thought is enough to drive me out of my senses.

What should I do? I can't leave Elkin's house any more than I can forbid Nina to come to the Moscow Savannah. The only thing I can do is to ask Galina to take my child when I go out to meetings. At least then, Kitty will not see Nina.

Tata is a bad influence on Kitty, of course, but at least it's the lesser of two evils.

16. THE RAID

1

Vadik, the Pioneer leader, promised Tata that if she took an active part in public service, she would be able to join the Pioneers that summer and go on a camping expedition.

Tata had never been anywhere in her life except Moscow and only to places within walking distance of her home. Her mother never gave her any money for the tram.

But a Pioneer camping expedition was a real adventure! The children would pile into an open truck, drive through the streets singing songs, and then set off with their backpacks far away into the unknown—perhaps even as far as the Moscow suburbs.

Tata was already in agonies of joy and suspense.

She registered on a three-person team or *troika* on a state-wide project to stamp out illiteracy, taking the place of a boy who had recently come down with tuberculosis. The members of the troika were to go around the neighborhood recruiting adults who could not read and write for literacy classes.

The thought of knocking on strangers' doors terrified Tata, but she told Julia and Inessa, the other members of the troika, that she was shivering from cold rather than fear and embarrassment. It was twenty degrees below outside.

Tata had a warm hat knitted with yarn from an unraveled old sweater, but her coat was a pitiful sight. It had been made from a plush mat decorated with squirrels. These squirrels were the cause of merciless taunting from her classmates.

The troika expedition was a disaster from the start. In the first building they went to, they were met with crude insults. In the next, they were stopped by a fierce dog in the yard. In the third, a maid told them to wait while she went to the store for kerosene, and they sat for two hours on the stairs for nothing. When the maid came back, she was visited by a fireman, and the shameless couple began kissing in front of the children.

Julia dug Tata in the ribs. "Say something!"

"Do you know that in 1920, six hundred and forty-five Russians out of every thousand couldn't read?" began Tata, stammering. "And now the figure is only four hundred and fifty-six."

"And do you know when you're not wanted?" barked the fireman and stamped his foot at the girls.

The troika fled outside.

"It's all your fault!" Julia said and gave Tata a cuff around the head.

It was getting dark over the boulevard, and the sound of a brass band could be heard from behind the trees. Despite the cold weather, the rink on Chistye Prudy was crowded with skaters.

"What do you think? Shall we keep going?" asked Tata, her teeth chattering.

"She said she wasn't afraid to go 'round houses on her own," said Julia to her friend. "Didn't she?"

"Yes, she did!" Inessa nodded.

Tata was taken aback. "What do you mean 'on my own'? Vadik said that the three of us should work as a team."

"She's a 'fraidy cat,'" snorted Inessa scornfully. "When we go camping, she'll probably start crying for her mommy."

"I'm not afraid!" Tata protested. "I can go 'round houses on my own!"

"Well, let's see you do it then," taunted Julia. "Do you see that house with the turret? Go and find out if there's anyone living there who can't read or write."

There was nothing for it. Hunching miserably, Tata shuffled toward her doom.

2

At the gate, Tata was met by a man with a ginger toothbrush mustache.

"I know just the person you need," he said,\ when Tata told him she was looking for anybody who could not read and write. "Come with me."

He took her across the yard and shown her the entrance door. "Go up one flight of stairs," he said. "There's only one apartment. It's impossible to miss."

Tata felt like a terrible fool. Luckily, she had a piece of paper with a speech on it, dictated by Julia. Without it, she would have been unable to say a word.

She reached the apartment, rang the doorbell, and when the door opened, she began to read aloud, unable to look the tenant in the eyes.

"Good afternoon, Comrade Tenant!" she said, struggling to decipher her own scribbles. "We are re-pre-sen-ta-tives from the troika of…oh, well, never mind that now…. What's your profession?"

She looked up and froze.

"My profession? Journalist," said Uncle Klim, smiling down at her.

"Can you read and write?" Tata heard herself saying in a small voice.

"Of course not!" came a voice from the staircase. It was the man with the ginger mustache. "Mr. Rogov, I sent this young lady up to you on purpose, so she could teach you to read and do your sums."

Tata wished the ground would swallow her up.

"I'm sorry," she said, blushing. "I just wanted to know if anybody here needed help learning the alphabet."

At that moment, Kitty came rushing out. "Here you are!" she cried delightedly, hugging Tata.

"Won't you come in?" suggested Uncle Klim.

Mother will hit the roof when she finds out I came to see the Rogovs without permission, thought Tata helplessly. Nevertheless, she entered the apartment.

"I'll just come in for a minute to warm up," she said.

As soon as she stepped inside, Tata realized that Uncle Klim was no revolutionary; he was a bourgeois. His home was a bastion of materialism—there was a mirror, a grand piano, and pictures of some fancy wenches on the walls. With a father like that, no wonder Kitty had some gaps in her education.

Uncle Klim brought in a samovar from the kitchen.

"Kapitolina isn't here, so we'll have to fend for ourselves," he said. He put down a dish of candy on the table. "Help yourself."

Tata gasped. Her mother always squirreled away sweets, and only once in a blue moon would she nibble on a toffee, letting Tata have half.

Tata reached out her hand to the dish, but at that moment, she remembered how all the children at school had been urged to eat only the right candies—the ones in ideologically sound wrappers which were called things like "Internationale," "Republican," or "Lives of the Peasants Then and Now."

But all Uncle Klim had were candies, their wrappers decorated with a picture of a girl bobbing a curtsey.

Tata looked at Kitty who had already put a candy in her mouth.

"How many can I have?" she asked, despising herself for her lack of character.

"As many as you like," Uncle Klim said.

Tata drank some delicious tea, ate candies and cookies, and began to feel that she was developing bourgeois tendencies.

"Let's see what books you have," she said, looking at Klim's bookshelves. "*Anna Karenina*, poetry…some sentimental rubbish! That's harmful literature. Self-indulgent drivel."

Uncle Klim looked at her with unfeigned curiosity. "So, what reading do you consider good for the soul?"

"There's no such thing as a soul," snapped Tata. Then she added, not entirely truthfully, "I'm interested in politics, not fiction. At the moment, our class is reading Lenin's speech to the third Young Communist Congress. I don't suppose you've ever inoculated yourself with the germ of revolution."

Uncle Klim burst out laughing and said that he would write down that phrase in his notebook; it would be useful for one of his articles. This ought to have pleased Tata; after all, it isn't every day adults want to make a note of your words. But she had an uneasy feeling the conversation was not going well.

"Come on. I want to show you something!" said Kitty, and, grabbing Tata by the hand, she led her into the other room.

Tata was amazed to see that Kitty had a bedroom to herself, and more toys than Tata had ever seen in her life. Kitty reached under the bed, brought out a colored magazine with a picture of a bourgeois lady on the cover, and settled down on the rug.

"Let's play. You can be her, and I'll be her."

One picture in the magazine showed the beach and some scantily clad girls, the other—a bride and groom at a wedding table laden with cakes.

"Let's eat all those!" said Kitty, beaming. "Yum-yum!"

Tata decided to take charge. She announced that they would play at a communist wedding.

"I'll be the secretary of a Young Communist organization, and you can be a worker bride who is getting married to...how about this teddy bear?"

Kitty shook her head. "No, he's too young for me. We bought him yesterday."

Tata spent a long time trying to pick out a potential husband: Kitty's rag horse, a wooden duck on wheels, and a progressive worker from the Liberated Labor factory whose portrait was in the paper. Eventually, Kitty agreed to marry a giraffe painted on her bedroom wall.

Tata read out a report about the new way of life in the Soviet Union and presented the newlyweds with a blanket from the women's union and a pillow from the factory management.

Uncle Klim knocked at the door. "Tata, I've been called out on business urgently. Would you mind staying here with Kitty?"

"Of course not," she said.

He pulled on his coat. "I'll be back in a couple of hours. Be good!"

"We will," promised Tata, a brilliant plan already taking shape in her head.

3

About thirty journalists were crowded into the press room. They sat around a long table, typewriters at the ready.

"What can it be at this time of night?" muttered Seibert irritably, yawning.

"I expect they've signed yet another report on the unbreakable alliance between the USSR and Afghanistan," replied Klim. He was sure they had all been brought here for nothing, for some story that presented no interest whatsoever to the world's news agencies.

Still, the journalists allowed themselves to dream of larger-than-life heroes and dangerous villains.

"We really are a bunch of vultures," said Seibert, looking around at his colleagues. "We feed off battles, plagues, and disasters. The more dead bodies, the happier we are."

At last, Weinstein came into the room. "Are you ready? This is the front page of tomorrow's *Pravda*." He began handing out mimeographed sheets to the journalists. "Familiarize yourselves with the facts and wire the story to your agencies as quickly as you can. All the censors are *in situ*, so you can start right away."

Klim scanned the text quickly. It was a report from the prosecutor of the Supreme Court about the discovery of a large clandestine counter-revolutionary organization in the Shakhty region in the south-east of Russia. The counter-revolutionaries, most of them engineers and technical specialists, had deliberately caused fires and explosions in mines. They had embezzled money allocated for construction, driven up costs, and spoiled production. Their objective was to reduce the USSR's defense capabilities in the event of a military attack. The coordinators of the plot were White émigrés from Russia who had close ties with German industrialists and Polish intelligence.

The journalists were dumbstruck. They had joked for years over the Bolsheviks' fears of some foreign power invading the Soviet Union. A poverty-stricken rural economy with almost no transport to speak of and no easily navigable waterways—what a prize! But if there really had been a plot, did that mean that the journalists had missed a trick?

Klim looked at the figures again. Of course, it was possible to fabricate some sensational crime and make a worldwide scandal out of it—it was just the sort of thing that could be expected from the Soviet secret police. But how could you fake the collapse of coal mining in an entire region?

The journalists all began to ask questions at once.

"How many people have been arrested?"

"A few hundred," said Weinstein. "The case is seen as one of national importance, and the most dangerous of the saboteurs will go on trial in Moscow."

Seibert was more agitated than anyone else. "Which German firms are suspected of financing the plot?"

"That's a state secret for now," Weinstein said. "There will be an open session of the panel of the Supreme Court, and we'll find out the facts then."

Seibert, stunned, turned to Klim. "It looks as if there'll be no shortage of dead meat."

The room filled up with the clatter of typewriters and the ringing of carriage bells.

Weinstein walked up to Klim and bent down to speak into his ear.

"This is your chance to improve your record," he said. "Just make sure you get everything down honestly and objectively."

Klim nodded without looking at him. The world seemed to have been turned upside down. A few minutes ago, everything had seemed clear: the Bolsheviks were ham-fisted cynics who blamed all their own ills on nonexistent foreign enemies. They used propaganda, lies, and the abuse of power as weapons and fed on ignorance and superstition of the majority of their countrymen. But now, everything seemed more complicated and more terrible. There was no rational explanation for what had happened in the Shakhty region. Why had the conspirators acted as they had? What was their objective?

Klim was the first to finish writing his dispatch. He rushed off to the censors' office.

Kogan, a censor notorious for his tireless harassment of journalists, beckoned Klim over and asked for the dispatch.

"Now let's see. What have we got here?" Kogan asked. "'Unconfirmed information about foreign links'…. Let me tell you that all our information is confirmed—backed up by evidence."

Rather than erasing the offending words, Kogan cut them out neatly with nail scissors, which took some time.

Seibert came rushing up to the next table, but he too did not get permission straight away.

"This has to be rewritten," ordered his censor. "The tone is completely unacceptable."

Kogan handed Klim his stamped dispatch, which now resembled a paper doily, and Klim rushed outside.

As luck would have it, there were no cabs to be seen, but a truck bearing the slogan "Live Poultry" was just coming around the corner.

Klim flagged down the truck. "Take me to the central telegraph office on Tverskaya Street, and I'll give you three rubles."

The driver opened the door of his cabin. "Jump in!"

They set off at top speed to the deafening sound of clattering cages and clucking chickens. A few minutes later, Klim, now covered in white feathers, had arrived at his destination.

Luckily, there was nobody at the window for Overseas Telegrams. But the next moment, a long line of journalists all panting for breath had formed there, Seibert right behind Klim.

"I should be the first in the queue!" Seibert grumbled. "But my car wouldn't start."

"Put your dispatches here, comrade foreigners," ordered the telegraph operator. "We'll send them right away."

She gathered together the stamped forms and picked up the one at the top of the pile.

"That's not fair!" the line exploded in indignant protests. "It's a form of the last one who came!"

To Klim's relief, the telegraph operator turned over the pile and took up his own form, which was now on top.

"Why do you have three addresses written here?" she asked in a stern voice.

Klim moved closer to the window. "The text has to be sent to London, New York, and Tokyo."

"That's not allowed." She handed him back his form. "You'll have to write it out three times."

"Didn't you know the rules had changed?" asked Seibert with feigned sympathy. "I was wondering how you managed to get here before me?"

The telegraph operator picked up Seibert's form.

"Listen," Klim pleaded with her, "yesterday, my courier brought you a form signed by the censor, and I called you and dictated seven addresses it had to be sent to. And there was no problem!"

"For the telephone, the rules are still the same," the telegraph operator cut him off. "Go back to the censor's office and write out your forms out again."

The journalists patted Klim's shoulder compassionately. "That's a shame, really."

Klim headed toward a nearby payphone on the wall, put a coin into the slot, and asked to speak to the operator at the window for Overseas Telegrams. He watched the woman picking up the phone.

"Hello," she said. "It's you, is it? Very well. Dictate the addresses to me."

"They're written on the form in front of you."

"Dictate them anyway. That's the rule."

The journalists laughed at Seibert who had turned green with envy. "Sometimes you have to lose, man!"

"Just you wait," he said, enraged. "I'll show the lot of you!"

4

Klim got home after seven. As he opened the door to the stair, he stopped short in amazement. Tata and Kitty were coming backward down the stairs, dragging a heap of objects wrapped in a tablecloth.

"Now, look here, young ladies—" Klim stopped them. "What on earth is going on?"

Kitty pushed up her cap, which had fallen over her eyes. "Tata and I are trying to put a stop to your bourgeois lifestyle!"

A crystal glass slipped out of the bundle, hit the stairs, and smashed to pieces.

"Private property degrades and corrupts!" lectured Tata. "You need to throw out all this useless junk, or soon, you'll be completely degenerate."

Without a word, Klim grabbed the bundle and took it back up the stairs.

"Acquisition of material objects is like a swamp!" Tata cried. "It swallows you up! You live among all your vases and serviettes and don't even notice how your own mind is in the grip of a hostile psychology!"

"Go home now, please," Klim said to her over his shoulder. "And don't dare show your face here again."

"Daddy!" yelled Kitty, rushing after him.

Klim let her into the apartment and slammed the door.

The apartment had been completely ransacked. Cinema posters were torn off the walls, curtains pulled away from the windows, and books lay all over the floor. It looked as if it there had been a raid by the police.

Klim felt himself shaking with fury at Tata. The girl needed to see a nerve doctor—there was clearly something wrong with her!

All the same, it occurred to him that a twelve-year-old girl should not be walking around Moscow on her own so late at night.

He went out to the stairs and called out to her, "Tata!"

But she was no longer on the stairs, and there was no sign of her in the yard either.

Klim went back to the apartment. Taking the sniveling Kitty in his arms, he sat down with her on the divan.

"I know you wanted the best for me," he said. "But look around you: are things better now or worse than they were?"

Kitty put her arms around his neck and burst into loud sobs. "Do you want me to go and stand in the corner?"

"No, I want you to come and wash your face and then go to bed. You didn't raid your own room, did you?

"No-o! I didn't want to give away my horses."

"Well, you see! You mustn't take other people's things without asking them."

Kitty nodded. "I understand. We mustn't take any of *your* things, but we can take Elkin's things. He's a Nepman and a criminal element."

"Who told you that? Is this Tata again?"

"Ye-es…"

"Don't listen to her."

Klim did not know what to do. Kitty was surrounded on all sides by barbarism and stupidity. Whether she liked it or not, it was starting to affect her.

He had to put a stop to the friendship with Tata. The raiding of the apartment was the thin end of the wedge. The next thing he knew, there would be denunciations to the authorities or worse.

5

When Tata got home, her mother was already asleep, and she was able to climb unnoticed into her wardrobe. The next morning, she did not breathe a word about what had happened but ran off to school.

She was furious with Uncle Klim; he had no right to inflict such damage on Kitty's young mind!

If Tata were an adult, she would have insisted on removing Kitty from her father's care and having her brought up by the Young Pioneer organization. Then Kitty could grow up to be a true Bolshevik.

But what could Tata do now as a little girl who had not even been accepted into the Pioneers?

After classes, there was a meeting of the school editorial committee, and Tata was given the task of putting together a *Stengazeta*, a newspaper in the form of a poster, to mark thirty-five years of literary work by Maxim Gorky.

She was entrusted with a large piece of white paper and some watercolor paints—hugely precious items.

"Look after those," Vadik warned her. "That's the last we have. If you do the job well, I'll give a good report on you to the Young Pioneers."

Tata promised to be as careful as she could.

As soon as she got home, she set to work. She wrote out the title "To Gorky from the Young Pioneers," and neatly pasted some articles by school reporters below it. It looked very good indeed.

There was a little room left in the bottom left-hand corner, and Tata decided to use it to make an important suggestion:

REFORM OF THE RASSIAN LANGUAGE

We, Pioneers and inovators, suggest that instead of greeting one another with the words "Good moning" we should use the greeting "Good Lenin."

Comrade Tata Dorina is collecting signaturs in support of this reform.

The door opened, and Tata's mother came in. She grabbed Tata by the collar, dragged her out from behind the table, and smacked her hard upside the head.

"What did you do that for?" wailed Tata.

"I'll give you 'what for,' you little brat!" her mother yelled. "Tell me why you ransacked the Rogov's apartment?"

Tata took a step back. "Uncle Klim is a class traitor…" she began in a trembling voice. "He's supposed to be educated, but he has portraits of filthy bourgeois all over his walls—"

"I'll give you 'filthy bourgeois'!"

Her mother looked around her, eyes wild. Her gaze fell on the poster.

"No, Mother, please!" squealed Tata, but it was too late. Her mother tore the poster to pieces, threw them to the floor, and stamped on them. "That'll teach you to touch things that don't belong to you! Out of my sight!"

Tata darted into the wardrobe. She heard her mother collapse onto the bench and weep bitterly.

"You fool!" her mother said in between sobs. "I hope you're satisfied! He said to me he won't let Kitty come to our house anymore because you're a bad influence."

"What?" Tata, in her astonishment, peeked out of the wardrobe.

"Shut that door this minute!" shouted her mother. "Or I swear, I'll thrash the living daylights out of you!"

Tata buried her face in the mattress. How could she go to school now? What would she tell them about the poster?

And what a beast Uncle Klim had turned out to be! An informer and a villain! How could he forbid children to play with one another? Didn't he feel sorry for his own daughter?

Tata felt that Kitty had become the most darling person in her life. She remembered how the two of them had been sitting on the windowsill in the evenings, playing that everything around them was different.

They had made believe that the dilapidated houses were beautiful glass and concrete buildings, the woodsheds were smart kiosks, and the linen hanging in the yard was the flags of different socialist republics. A milkman carrying a frost-covered churn on his sled was a famous Arctic explorer and researcher. Mitrofanych, one of the tenants of their apartment, had walked up to the milkman, and Kitty had wanted him to be a polar explorer too, but Tata disliked him. So, she had made him one of the sleigh dogs.

Then the girls had gone off on their own expedition beyond the fence to look for the Tunguska meteorite.

Had all this really come to an end?

17. THE MOSCOW ART THEATER

1

Oscar's journey had been a success. He had satisfied himself that his wife really was a rich heiress and instructed lawyers in Berlin and Stockholm to sort out her papers.

Now he had to think of how to get his precious wife over the border. There were Bremers in Germany, and they had got wind of the fact that Oscar had his eye on the family fortune and were demanding he produce Nina with proof that she really was Baroness Bremer.

Oscar sorted out documents for Nina at the American Embassy without too much difficulty. Now all he had to do was to get an exit visa from the OGPU.

As soon as his train got in to Moscow, he drove to the Lubyanka to see Comrade Drachenblut who was the head of the OGPU's Foreign Section.

A swarthy secretary showed Oscar into a spacious office with portraits of communist leaders on the walls. Although it was still afternoon, the windows were covered with heavy drapes with tiny holes in the material that let in thin rays of light. A lamp with a green shade lit up a desk littered with papers and intercoms.

Oscar beamed amicably at a pale, scrawny man with a high forehead and thinning brown hair, who was sitting at the desk, smoking a cigarette.

"How are you?" Oscar asked and held out a hand.

Drachenblut, however, ignored this greeting and indicated a chair against the wall. "Sit down."

He rummaged for a while through some yellow cards, plucking at his mustache and pushing up his spectacles with his middle finger when they slipped down his nose.

With each moment of tense silence, Oscar felt more and more uncomfortable. At last, Drachenblut put his yellow cards to one side and fixed his cold gray-blue eyes on Oscar.

"I'm very glad you came in to see me," he said frostily. "I've had some complaints about you."

"Who's been complaining?" asked Oscar, surprised.

"That doesn't matter. You were invited to the Soviet Union and provided with everything you needed to work to attract foreign capital into the country. And what's the result? Do you know what proportion of our industry is currently provided by foreign concessions? A grand total of 0.6 per cent."

"I can't help it if your government is always quarreling with the rest of the world," replied Oscar, trying to keep his voice steady. "You've backed the Chinese communists, and now, people in Washington don't even want to talk about recognizing the USSR."

"So, why haven't you persuaded those people that they need to improve relations with us? There's a democracy in the States, the American workers support us…you need to put pressure on the politicians."

Good god, thought Oscar, *what workers is he talking about?* In the Kremlin and in the Lubyanka, they judged what was happening in the USA from reports by intelligence agents who wrote whatever their bosses wanted to read and whatever was favorable to them.

If some agent reported that the workers in this or that US factory were on the verge of rebellion, he would be given money to help the revolutionary struggle. Then he would report back, saying he had invested all the money in the cause. How was anyone to know that he was lying through his teeth and had spent the lot on whoring and gambling?

The Soviet Union had nothing to offer American farmers or workers whose dreams were not of world revolution but of having their own house and car and of their favorite baseball team winning the next game. The only people in the States who raved about socialism were left-wing intellectuals. They lapped up the communist propaganda and had no idea what life was like in the USSR.

But Oscar found it impossible to convince Drachenblut of this.

"The US Department of Commerce," Oscar said, "released a report recently, saying that the Soviet state was on the point of collapse. All big businessmen in the States read those reports and trust them implicitly—"

"You were given several years to prove yourself useful to us!" Drachenblut interrupted, banging his desk. "You have not done so, and now, we shall have to liquidate you."

"What do you mean?" Oscar asked, jumping to his feet.

Drachenblut gave a chuckle. "I mean we're going to close down your company. The Soviet Union is moving to a planned economy. We're collecting data on capacity and demand within the country and allocating all work according to a centralized system. There's no place for you in the future Soviet state."

"You can't close my factory!" cried Oscar. "I have a contract with the Chief Concessions Commission!"

Drachenblut took a folder from his desk and, digging inside it, brought out a carbon copy of a typescript.

"Do you know what this is?" he asked. "It's a memorandum from the vice chairman of the OGPU, Yagoda, informing the Central Committee that the foreign employees in your factory are all spies."

Oscar gulped. Now he understood everything. In times of economic hardship, the secret police bosses had less money than usual. Recently, they had even had their monthly wages withheld at the Lubyanka. There were only two ways the secret police could improve its position: either by intimidating enterprise executives to extort money from them or to hint to the Kremlin that there were enemies on all sides and that the state should allocate more funds to fight them.

"I'll take you to court," said Oscar in a trembling voice.

Drachenblut smiled sarcastically. "Be my guest! You can declare war on me if you like."

He came out from behind his desk and, walking up to Oscar, put a hand on his shoulders. "Listen. I'm not your enemy, you know. I can save you from Yagoda if you do something for us. We need hard currency—badly!—and we're going to sell a large consignment of timber abroad. The Germans are building a new railroad. They need sleepers for it, but directors on their board are all fanatical anti-Soviets and won't have anything to do with us. We're looking for a go-between, someone to fix things for us. If you do the job properly, I'll arrange for your firm to be bought off, not confiscated, and we can part on good terms."

Never had Oscar Reich been spoken to in such an offhand manner!

"Have you thought about where *that* will get you?" he spat the words out furiously. "After a crude stunt like that, you won't be able to attract a single businessman into the USSR."

Drachenblut shrugged his shoulders. "As you please."

He sat at his desk again and took out another document from his folder.

"We have a story here on file; the story of a brilliant young man who was studying to be a pharmacist in New York. One day, he decided to give a sleeping draught to a rather attractive young lady friend—I suppose it was the only way he could think of to get her into bed with him. The young man raped her, and unfortunately, the girl never woke up. The unqualified young pharmacist had given her a fatal dose."

The room swam before Oscar's eyes. How had the ORGU found out about that story?

"You tell everyone you came to Russia to help people," said Drachenblut. "But in fact, you needed to hide out from the New York State Police for a while. That was why you jumped at Trotsky's suggestion. Your father arranged it so that another man went to jail in your place. But if you try to put a spanner in our works, I'm afraid I'll be forced to remember this story, and the papers will kick up no end of a fuss. How do you like the headline 'Famous Red Millionaire Revealed as Rapist and Murderer'?"

Oscar looked at the worn carpet at his feet. A single thought pounded in his brain over and over: "I'm done for…"

"So, what do you say?" asked Drachenblut. "Will you consider our timber project?"

Oscar nodded slowly.

There was no point now in asking for an exit visa for Nina. The OGPU would almost certainly keep her in the USSR as a hostage until he had made sure they would get their timber sale.

2

Oscar had taken Nina to the Bolshoi Theater—the bastion of the Soviet elite, but Elkin introduced her to another side of Moscow theatrical life.

"What do they have on at the Bolshoi?" he asked with a disdainful grimace. "*The Red Poppy*. And they call that art?"

Nina had gone to see this ballet, and it had amused her to see how under the Bolsheviks, even ballerinas had to fight against world imperialism. The *Red Poppy* was the story of Soviet "pale-faced brothers" saving Chinese natives from the yoke of English rule. The producers did not even realize how insulting this premise was to the Chinese, who considered their Celestial Empire a citadel of wisdom and culture, the center of the world. And the name of the ballet was comically incongruous too. In China, the red poppy was a symbol not of revolution but of narcotics because of the connection with opium while in Britain, it was a symbol of remembrance for the war dead.

Elkin, on the other hand, took Nina to the Moscow Art Theater to see *The Days of the Turbins*, a play about officers in the White Army—passionate, intelligent, and talented people who lost everyone and everything during the civil war. The Soviet critics lambasted the production, calling it "sentimental drivel," but nonetheless, the play was a resounding commercial success. Many Muscovites went to see it several times and began to pepper their conversations with quotes from the play.

According to Bolshevik ideology, happiness could only be found in collective labor and the battle against imperialists, and the heroes of the day were revolutionary martyrs with an iron will. *The Days of the Turbins*, however, was the story of *real* people who loved not the Party and the international proletariat but each other.

Nina and Elkin sat in the third row. She looked around at the audience—on all sides, she saw faces transfixed, eyes open wide in wonder. The audience was silent as if some unheard-of miracle were unfolding before them. After all, a play like this had no right to exist in Soviet Russia.

When the performance was over, the people filed down into the foyer in silence as if they were still taking in what they had just seen.

Elkin showed Nina the playwright, Mikhail Bulgakov, who passed them on his way up the stairs, a sad-looking gentleman with fair hair combed back from his forehead, wearing an old-fashioned monocle.

"The Last of the Mohicans," Elkin whispered. "The theater management only put up with him because they sell so many tickets for his plays. But he knows he's doomed. The Soviet government can't endure permanently such an obvious insult to their ideology."

"Good evening!" Nina heard a familiar voice say in English.

She looked around and froze. Oscar and Yefim were standing behind them.

"Your wife goes out every day to visit this character," Yefim informed Oscar, pointing at Elkin. "I've been following them."

Oscar took Nina roughly by the elbow. "Put on your coat and get into the car this minute!"

"Mr. Reich, it's not what you think!" cried Elkin desperately, but Oscar did not even look at him.

3

Oscar took Nina back to his house and launched into a blazing row, accusing her of unfaithfulness and ingratitude. It would have been wisest to have denied his accusations and tried to calm him down, but Nina hated to be shouted at.

"I won't have you telling me what to do!" she said through her teeth, walking away. "I'm leaving!"

Oscar caught up with her and shoved her so hard in the back that she fell forward, knocking her head on a marble sill.

For two weeks, she was forced to lie in bed, recovering. The doctor announced that she had received a linear fracture to her skull and a cerebral contusion.

"What a maniac!" grumbled Theresa as she applied homemade poultices to Nina's forehead. "And what were you thinking of? Why did you set him off like that?"

Oscar apologized to Nina once again, swearing undying love.

"I'll never let anyone else have you," he said, putting yet another bunch of flowers on her bedside table. "And if any other man so much as looks at you, I'll break his neck."

Whenever Oscar came in to see Nina, she would tense as if expecting to be hit. He would put his hand under the blanket to touch her, and she would go cold all over with helpless fury. This man had her completely in his power. He could rape her, beat her, even cut her throat, and he would get off scot-free. And she had no way of getting away from him.

Every day, Nina meant to find out what had happened to Elkin but could not bring herself to call the bookstore. While she was afraid of angering Oscar, she was still more afraid of what she might find out—that something terrible had happened to her friend, and all because of her.

4

A month had passed by the time Nina had plucked up the courage to leave the house and make her way to Chistye Prudy, taking great care not to be seen.

The snow had begun to melt, muddy water lay in the deep ruts in the road, and the rooks were clamoring in the ancient birches.

Nina went around to the back gate that led into the yard of the Moscow Savannah and bent down to look through the hole in the fence.

In the yard stood a truck spattered with mud. On its side, in crooked letters was written "Workers' and Peasants' Inspectorate." A group of youths, overseen by a woman in a red headscarf, were throwing bundles of books tied together with twine onto a bonfire.

"Why have you put Burroughs in the truck?" the woman shouted. "This lot's going to the Presnya library—they don't want any foreign dirt in translation there. And

Locke can go on the bonfire too. I told you to burn anything we don't need."

In a minute, a large bonfire was blazing merrily in the center of the yard. The young men kept piling more books onto it, and the woman hit at them with a broom handle, knocking out sparks and cinders.

A gust of wind blew a page over the fence, black and charred, like a bat with lacerated wings. Nina caught it with the toe of her boot, and it collapsed into ashes.

The gate swung open, and Afrikan came out into the alley carrying a trash pail.

"Excuse me," Nina said, approaching him, "do you know where Elkin is?"

Afrikan knitted his shaggy brows and sniffed loudly. "He's not here. He's left, and they've closed down his shop. They said he was opening at hours forbidden to private businesses and creating competition with state stores."

"So, what's going to happen now?"

"It's a mess," said Afrikan with conviction. "The whole of the ground floor has been taken over by the state. God knows who they'll put there. It's a good thing though that the gentleman upstairs took Mashka away. Elkin gave him the keys to the garage."

Afrikan went off to take out the trash, and Nina stood for a long time in the middle of the alley, overwhelmed by feelings of guilt and helplessness. She was certain it was Yefim who had called in the Workers' and Peasants' Inspectorate, following Oscar's order.

Nina looked up at the windows of the upper story, but she could see nothing through the colored panes of glass.
I don't have any right to try to meet Klim, she thought desperately. *No matter where I go, I bring nothing but bad luck.*

18. SOVIET PRIESTS

1

Galina spent a week repairing everything that Tata had destroyed but could do nothing about the net curtains her daughter had ripped clean out of Klim's wall. It was impossible to get ahold of curtain rods in Moscow.

Meanwhile, Klim kept his word: Kitty was no longer allowed to play with Tata.

"You have to understand," he said to Galina, "that my daughter will be going to a European school. She'll already face problems because of her appearance. If she starts a campaign against 'bourgeois values,' they'll single her out immediately."

These were painful words for Galina to hear. Clearly, it had never crossed Klim's mind to adopt Tata and help her get a place in a good school.

In a fit of desperation, Galina told Tata what her actions had cost them. "Now he'll never take us with him to Europe," she lamented.

"Why on earth would he take us to Europe?" asked Tata in alarm.

Suddenly, it dawned on her. "Have you lost your mind?" she yelled at her mother. "Don't tell me you've fallen in love with him of all people! It was all thanks to him I didn't finish the poster. Now the Young Pioneers won't have me in their organization."

Tata is just a little version of her father, Galina thought. With all those phony values and her hysterical hatred of anything she did not understand, Tata had no wish to know what lay beyond her own familiar world.

What could Galina do about her daughter? She racked her brain and at last came up with an idea.

"How would you like to go to the special school for artists in Leningrad?" Galina suggested. "It's a boarding school; children with a talent for drawing come from all over the Soviet Union to study there. And once you complete your final project, you can go straight to the Higher Art and Technical Institute."

To her amazement, Tata liked the idea. Now, whenever Galina thought about the future, her heart began to beat faster. If she could get Tata settled in some line of work, nothing would stand in the way of her own personal happiness.

I know I'm a bad mother, she thought without any particular regret. *But what else can I do for Tata?*

Klim was due a short period of leave from work, and Galina was already dreaming of how they would rent a dacha outside Moscow and live there together, far away from work, politics, and wayward children.

She was hoping that by that time, Klim might recover slightly from the loss of his wife. Things were starting to look up for him. Weinstein had indicated that he was prepared to bury the hatchet, Elkin had given Klim his car without demanding payment upfront, and the finance department in London had already agreed to fund this purchase later in the summer.

Things were starting to happen in the Soviet Union that could make front-page news in the world's newspapers, and the trial of the Shakhty saboteurs might bring Klim fame and money. The case would involve forty-two public prosecutors, fifteen defense lawyers, and fifty defendants, and the trial was to take place in the legendary Pillar Hall of the House of the Unions, formerly the Assembly of the Nobility, which was the setting for the balls in *War and Peace*.

Long before the proceedings were due to start, the Soviet press had begun to prepare the public for the trial. There was talk in the papers about the catastrophic situation in the coal industry and of how "bourgeois experts" had played a role in its collapse. The government had decided to keep even illiterate Soviet citizens informed about the trial by broadcasting radio reports through loudspeakers put up on the streets of Moscow.

The Bolsheviks were preparing the trial of the century, and Klim ought to have been pleased to have such an opportunity fall into his hands, but he seemed discontented.

Galina tried probing him gently. "What's the matter?"

In answer, Klim handed her a paper dated April 14, 1928, with a transcript of a speech by Stalin.

The facts tell us that the Shakhty affair is an economic counter-revolution plotted by bourgeois experts. Moreover, the facts state that these experts, who have formed a secret cell, have been receiving money for sabotage from their former masters, who are now in emigration, and from counter-revolutionary anti-Soviet organizations in the West.

"They've already made up their minds before the trial," said Klim. "Nobody has any doubt that the defendants are guilty."

"You mean to say you *don't* think they're guilty?" Galina stared at him, amazed.

"I'd just like to know…"

But Klim did not finish what he had begun to say. No matter what Galina did, Klim still saw her as a potential informer, and when he was with her, he was careful what he said. Galina suspected that this was why he seemed unable to love her.

But if she resigned her position at the OGPU, Klim would have had to find a new assistant. Galina was stuck in a vicious circle. She could not leave the OGPU until Klim married her, but he would never marry her because of the nature of her work.

2

To get Tata a place in the art school, Galina needed a recommendation from her employers. She set off to OGPU headquarters straight away, but nobody could tell her who was responsible for what.

The Lubyanka was in a state of confusion. An order had come from the Kremlin bosses stating that a purge was imminent and employees showing insufficient zeal in the fight against counter-revolution were to be flushed out.

Something similar was taking place across all the organizations in the country. Every sector of the economy was failing, and directors, rather than waiting for a Shakhty Trail of their own, were taking things into their own hands. If they too were not achieving, it must mean there was sabotage in the workplace.

The purge at the OGPU had not yet been scheduled, but Galina's friends from the administrative department were making haste to throw out all the fashion journals they had confiscated from Nepmen and to hide anything that might reveal a hankering for a bourgeois lifestyle. No longer could they collect pictures of foreign movie stars, bring knitting to work, or discuss how to do a permanent wave at home. Now, everyone was coming into work looking brisk and business-like and talking of nothing but the enemies of the state and support for the Party line.

Eteri Bagratovna, the secretary, whispered to Galina that Drachenblut had been receiving piles of anonymous denunciations every day. Alarmed at the prospect of dismissal, OGPU workers were starting to rat on any colleagues who might potentially cause problems for them during the purge. The personal files on staff members were growing fatter by the day. Everybody had some offence to their name. One had stolen rulers from work, another had arranged an unnecessary business trip for himself, and yet another had been heard to say something in favor of the opposition.

Galina went to see Alov in his office. She found him sitting on a windowsill and painting a lightbulb with nail varnish, the room full of the suffocating smell of solvent.

Alov looked at Galina with irritation. "What are you staring at? I'm marking the lightbulbs for our corridor. Somebody keeps unscrewing them and replacing them with burned-out ones. The supply manager is threatening to report us."

Galina squinted at the cluster of lightbulbs on the table, bearing the bloodred inscription, "Stolen from the OGPU."

"Where did you get the nail varnish?"

"Diana Mikhailovna gave it to me. 'Their Royal Highnesses' called a meeting and passed a resolution: they have decided not to paint their nails from now on. So, how about you? Any news?"

Galina told Alov that the building that had once housed the Moscow Savannah was now occupied by the League of Time. Its members were underfed, overworked students dedicated to the "scientific organization of labor," including their own. Everywhere they went, they carried little notebooks in which they wrote down exactly what they did.

"Has Rogov mentioned Kupina again?" Alov interrupted.

Galina shook her head. "No, not once."

"That's a shame. You need to uncover a plot, Pidge, or you'll have nothing to show for yourself when they start the purge. Keep a closer eye on those foreigners of yours, all right?"

Galina felt alarmed. Was Alov going to force her to make up some story about Klim? That was all she needed.

Alov studied her closely. "Why the long face? Has Mr. Rogov hurt your feelings?"

"No, of course not!" Galina quickly changed the subject. "I wanted to speak to you about Tata. She wants to try to get into the art school in Leningrad, but since it's a boarding school, she needs a document from our employment committee. Can you help?"

Galina showed Alov one of Tata's drawings.

"Wow!" His eyes became round in surprise. "I wonder which side of the family she got that from? Of course, I'll have a word with the employment committee. But won't the two of you be lonely without each other?"

"Of course we will," Galina said, "but after all, she's my child. I'd do anything for her."

Alov put a hand on her shoulder, and Galina flinched. Surely he wasn't about to try anything now? Oh, please, anything but that!

"I hope you won't take it too hard…" Alov hesitated for a moment and cleared his throat awkwardly. "But you and I can no longer be on intimate terms. Don't get me wrong. I'm fond of you, but I'm far too busy these days. And with this purge, anything could be used against us. It would be stupid to be dismissed from our job on account of low moral standards, wouldn't it?"

Galina almost wept from relief. "Don't worry," she told Alov in a shaking voice. "I understand perfectly."

Seeing tears in Galina's eyes, he was touched. "You and I are building a new life, Pidge. We can't carry on the way we used to."

Galina came out of the office feeling elated. Thank goodness, he was finally going to leave her alone! And if everything worked out with the plan for Tata, it would be wonderful.

The inner courtyard was flooded with spring sunlight, and the first blooms of coltsfoot were dotted about below the fence like yellow buttons.

"Hello!" Ibrahim waved to her as she crossed the yard.

This time, not one, but three Black Marias stood next to the OGPU holding cells. The door of one of them was heavily smeared with blood.

"Beautiful weather we're having!" Ibrahim shouted out happily. "We'll be down at the river soon, swimming and sunbathing!"

He screwed a canvas hose to a faucet in the yard and began to wash down the car.

Galina walked hurriedly past. There was no point thinking about Black Marias or about who had been taken away in them the night before. Anyway, more likely than not it had been profiteers anyway. None of that had anything to do with her or with Klim.

3

BOOK OF THE DEAD

I think Weinstein must have been some sort of priest in a former life, and a high priest at that. He has taken my conversion to the communist faith very seriously, and the two of us have been talking at length on "theological" subjects.

I don't dare try to dodge these conversations. It's very important for me to be seen as a "friendly journalist" again because they will be given access to special materials during the Shahkty Trial.

Weinstein claims that he was a romantic in his youth and regarded both censorship and lies in the press as an unmitigated evil. But his views have changed with time.

"You have to get your priorities right," he informed me with a condescending chuckle. "I ask you, what's more important: achieving the result you want or fighting for one's principles for the sake of it? The Soviet Union has to drag a hundred and fifty million people out of the middle ages and into the modern era. The Russian people are uneducated, and all your "basic human rights" mean nothing to them. We need to speak to Russians in a language the people understand."

"And what language might that be?" I asked.

"Proverbs, sayings, spells, and curses. We need to unite people behind a common cause and get them to work for nothing. Not because we're tightfisted but because the state has no money, and it won't have any until we've built up our own industry."

As Weinstein sees it, the purges that are taking place all over the country are a ritual cleansing before the great feat of industrialization. It's like the way warriors prepared for battle in the old days: first, they would fast, pray, and repent, and then they would charge at the enemy with their spears, confident that God was on their side. And often, they would be victorious. Spiritual strength is a great weapon.

"What if we were to get rid of all censorship and the papers were to print the truth?" Weinstein asked me with a crafty smile into his beard. "What do you think would happen then?"

I had to admit that that would result in widespread discontent.

"And how will your truth help us to solve the problem of industrialization?" Weinstein continued. "Do you really want to plunge the country into bloodshed and chaos again? No, my dear Mr. Rogov, we must choose another path."

However, this "other path" is hardly a shining example of humanity. The Soviet papers bristle with demands to "destroy the parasites," "crush the vermin," "tear the stings from their tails," and so on. The enemies (or rather those the Bolsheviks have declared enemies) are stripped of all human features. There is no need to feel sorry for these "subhumans" as they are "spawn," "scum," and "dross" that has no place in the Soviet Union. Actually, nobody feels sorry for them.

Owen often sends me to cover Party meetings that are effectively purges. At these meetings, a strange mass phenomenon can be observed: people repenting of crimes they could not possibly have committed.

Weinstein is probably right. Everyday magic and superstition is at work here. Many people believe that moral "purity" enables you to escape misfortune: by repenting and being cleansed of evil, you will be saved. It doesn't matter what the truth is—it's all about a relationship with mysterious higher powers, which can be appeased only with ritual and magic words.

I believe all of this is happening because people are utterly lost. They have no reliable information. Every decision about the future of the country is being taken in secret, way up in the corridors of power, and all you can do is pray that divine judgment will not suddenly descend like a bolt of lightning to strike you or your loved ones.

In some ways, I agree with Weinstein. The truth can be a force for destruction, but still, you can't stop people from wanting to know what's going on. If they have no way of reaching the truth, they begin to make up fairytales, and that won't solve anything.

I tried to explain to Weinstein that the latter is more dangerous, but he merely shook his head reproachfully.

"Imagine," he said, "we're traveling in a high-speed train, trying to catch up with the advanced capitalist nations. We don't have time to stop; our task is to get the state machine running smoothly, helping the engine to convert fuel and turn the wheels without any hitches."

"When you say fuel, I take it you mean people?" I asked.

But Weinstein wasn't bothered by such concerns. "You foreign journalists can either help us take this great leap into the future or try to throw a spanner in the works. Of course, your spanners won't stop us anyway. But think about it: how does it serve your interests to have our nation simply sitting and vegetating on the margins of Europe? Do you really bear us such ill will?"

"No, we don't," I answered, and Weinstein beamed.

"That's wonderful! Then there's no need to keep drawing attention to our shortcomings. All we ask of the West is that you help your readers like us. If you sow derision and hatred, it will lead to another war. Surely you don't want that?"

If I ever meet Comrade Stalin, I will definitely hint that Weinstein should be appointed patriarch of the new Bolshevik Church of the Sacred Spirit of the Proletariat. He would make a very good priest.

4

Everybody is waiting for the beginning of the Shakhty Trial. Much remains unclear. Why is such an enormous fuss being made of this affair, and why are preparations being made for it on the scale of those made for the Olympic Games in Amsterdam? What's the meaning of it all? Is it a scare tactic or criminal justice in action?

I receive a stream of instructions and orders from London. My professional future hangs in the balance, and I spend all my time running about Moscow trying to find answers to my editors' questions.

Everything I do, I do for Kitty's sake, but because I am so busy, I give her hardly any attention. She is desperately bored and lonely without me, particularly since I have forbidden her to play with Tata. But there is nobody to help me. Galina is traveling to and fro all the time, and whenever she puts in an appearance at our house, she is dropping from exhaustion.

Kapitolina is no use at all. She is frantic with worry about her relatives in the village. Terrible things are going on there: armed brigades of activists are coming out from the cities to search for hidden stores of grain and force the peasants to sell it to them at state procurement prices, which are too low to allow them to afford anything with their earnings. Sometimes, peasants have even been paid with government state bonds or receipts, that is to say, they have been robbed, purely and simply.

Several times, I have arrived home to find Kitty under the bed. She hides there and puts my gloves on her shoulders. "I'm pretending you're giving me a hug."

This makes me feel like a criminal, so I try to get ahold of treats for her—chocolates, toys, and books, but of course, none of it helps.

Every morning, I explain to Kitty that I have important business and I need to go to work. But what business could be more important than my own child feeling abandoned right now? Every day, Kitty is learning a lesson that her own feelings are unimportant and that it is wrong to ask for love and attention. Whether I like it or not, I am training her to expect pain and loneliness in life.

Kitty needs a mother, but I have cut off all ties with Nina because its simpler for me. At the merest mention of her name, I am thrown into a protracted gloom. I have to admit I was even pleased when Elkin was thrown out of his store.

But my former wife still haunts me. Recently, Kitty discovered her photograph in my diary and announced that she wanted to see her mother.

"Haven't you found her yet?" she asked me.

"We don't have a mother anymore," I replied, only to regret my words a moment later.

Kitty went into such hysterics that she made herself ill. "You've taken away everything I ever had!" she wailed. "You don't love me! Where's Mommy?"

She struggled in my arms like a captive animal. "Let me go! I hate you!"

She has been sick now for several days. She has come out in a rash, her face is swollen, and she has pains in her stomach.

The doctor from the German Embassy came out to have a look at her and shrugged. "It seems the Moscow climate is bad for your little girl. You need to take her to the seaside and get her some sunshine."

But I can't drop everything and go south. Who would grant me any leave from work now? As for resigning, it's out of the question. I haven't any savings, and if I quit my job, I lose my visa. And where could Kitty and I go then?

Nina was right when she said I would regret our quarrel. If we had parted on good terms, she could have helped me with Kitty. True, it would have meant mastering my feelings every day, but at least our daughter wouldn't be suffering now on account of my hurt pride.

I turned Nina's photograph over in my hands. On the back, Magda had written "Nina Kupina, November 1927." I crossed out the name of my ex-wife and wrote above it, "Mrs. Reich."

I still find it impossible to believe that this is the truth.

19. THE SHAKHTY TRAIL

1

On the morning of the 18th of May, 1928, the House of Unions was surrounded by a double police cordon, struggling to restrain the public from breaking through to the recently refurbished building with its pillared facade.

There were crowds milling about—journalists, children, and foreign tourists holding cameras. People kept arriving, and soon the pavement outside the building was overflowing, stopping the cars and cabs from passing and unleashing a chorus of motor horns.

Klim showed his press card and was allowed into the House of Unions. Last minute preparations were taking place there. Smartly dressed young men in OGPU uniform were dashing up and down the staircases, and catering assistants with lace headdresses pinned to their hair were wheeling trolleys furnished with decanters of water.

Klim walked into the Pillar Hall and felt as if he was in a theater on the night of a grand premier. Crystal chandeliers lit up rows of red seats for the spectators of the trial, and red cloth banners hung on all the balconies. Several powerful floodlights stood in the aisles, directed toward the stage. The carpet beneath them bulged with cables.

"Gangway!" called a workman wheeling in a huge, cumbersome movie camera.

Although people were fussing around nervously, the mood was generally one of excited anticipation. There were high hopes of the forthcoming show.

The foreign journalists exchanged greetings and handshakes.

"Don't expect to see any justice done here today. That's all I can say," the correspondent from the *Christian Science Monitor* told Klim. "The Soviet judges are quite openly guided by questions of class origin—with full official approval. If it turns out that the defendant is a former aristocrat or, God forbid, was born into a priest's family, then no proof of guilt is required whatsoever."

"But it would be stupid," a French correspondent intervened, "to pass an obviously wrongful verdict when the whole world is watching. Bolsheviks would never resort to such a thing."

"There will be executions, you mark my words," said Luigi, a little Italian with a beaky nose. "The authorities want to force poorly performing employees to work harder. Soviet industry is rife with substandard production. They want to tackle it."

Seibert would listen to no one and was loudly indignant about the fact that the OGPU had named among the saboteurs a number of German citizens who were working in the mines on contracts.

"When our ambassador reported to Berlin about this story," he said, "Germany almost broke off diplomatic relations with Russia. The country is up in arms. The Russian secret police have arrested my compatriots simply to show that the saboteurs had foreign connections. I don't know what the Kremlin is thinking of! The day after tomorrow, there will be an election to the Reichstag, and thanks to this scandal, the communists will lose a great many votes."

"Don't pretend to be so upset about it," laughed Luigi. "You've made a career for yourself out of the story."

Seibert had indeed become something of a celebrity in his own country. Following Germany's defeat in the Great War, patriotic feelings were running high, and any report on the sufferings of the German people brought forth a storm of protest. Seibert had been allowed personal access to the Germans who had been arrested, and he had gone to Berlin several times to give interviews about his visits to a Bolshevik jail. He had even been invited to the Ministry of Foreign Affairs and had decided that he would, in future, most definitely go in for politics. He had hugely enjoyed his role as spokesman for the German people.

At last, the spectators were allowed in, and the hall filled with a hubbub of excited voices and the urgent shouts of stewards directing people to their places. The wealthier spectators took out field glasses and opera glasses and, in the absence of the main players, began to inspect the foreigners. Klim felt uneasy as if all the glittering lenses were directed at him alone.

When the guards brought in the defendants, a gasp of disappointment went up in the hall. Seibert even took off his spectacles and wiped them with his handkerchief as if he could not believe his eyes.

"So, these are the criminals?" he asked.

Klim was also amazed by the appearance of the saboteurs. Without realizing it, he had been infected by the mood of his colleagues and begun to picture the accused as fanatical, menacing individuals prepared to risk their lives to challenge the Bolshevik system. But on the defendants' bench, he saw not proud counter-revolutionary conspirators but a bunch of ordinary-looking, disheveled men, glancing around them nervously.

If you picked out fifty passers-by at random, thought Klim, *arrested them, and held them in a cell, this is what they would look like.*

"All rise!" blared the loudspeakers. "This court is now in session."

A hush fell on the room. The judges, some in three-piece suits and others in military-style jackets, went up onto the stage and sat down in high-backed chairs. In the light of the floodlights, the tacks in the leather upholstery shone like strange, square haloes around the judges' heads.

According to the custom, everybody in the hall sang the "Internationale," and then the session began.

2

BOOK OF THE DEAD

During my chats with Weinstein, I occasionally allow myself to ask naïve questions.

"What do you think it cost the counter-revolutionaries to hire all those saboteurs, flood coal mines, and break equipment? It must have run into millions."

Weinstein nodded his head sadly and lamented the fact that our enemies will stop at nothing in their efforts to undermine the new Soviet state.

I continued to express disbelief. "And why, if they spent millions on all this, didn't they do it somewhere important? Why Shakhty—a town lots of Russians can't even find on a map? In any case, what were the conspirators hoping to achieve? All right. So, they damage industry in several towns. Then what?"

But for Weinstein, it's all a question of the cunning machinations of imperialism, or the devil, if you like. As he sees it, there's no point in looking for logic in the enemy's actions.

In actual fact, no evidence has been produced at all except for the confessions of the accused. But not one of them can provide any specific details about the sabotage—not a thing!

My colleagues are terribly disappointed: the "trial of the century," for which we have all been waiting with baited breath, has turned out to be an utterly pointless affair devoid of any intrigue. Instead, it's like watching prisoners in chains being brutally beaten as they beg for mercy and try to escape the blows raining down on them.

Of all the defendants, there are only two engineers of the old school who behave with dignity, denying all the accusations against them. The others repent tearfully, and when they talk about themselves, they say things like "my capitalist childhood" or "my circle made up entirely of devious counter-revolutionaries" or "being a class enemy in a working-class environment," etc.

It makes me want to look away and stop my ears. No matter how I try, I just can't see these men as conspirators. The whole thing's an absurdity—to talk for an hour about how, by virtue of your class identity, it was inevitable that you would become a saboteur.

I want somebody to explain to me why all the defendants are giving false testimony against one another. Are they being tortured? It doesn't look like it. Are they being pumped with drugs? Apparently not. If they're being threatened, why can't they say so before the assembled court? They will be heard. There are hundreds of people in the room, including representatives of the press. Or have the defendants in the Shakhty Trial been specially selected for their cowardice and spinelessness?

It is all the worse because the German defendants are behaving admirably, and the contrast is striking.

"What did you expect?" Magda asked me indignantly when I confided my woes to her. "Those men know that people in Germany are concerned about their fate. They get letters from their families, and Seibert and the diplomats are visiting them just about every day. You'll see, they'll be exonerated by the USSR in exchange for some trade concessions. But what can the Russian defendants hope to get? Everybody hates and despises them. Even you."

Say what you like, Magda has a way of getting to the heart of the matter.

Every time "my" engineers approach the microphone, I pray that they will stay firm, that they, at least, will not be transformed into cowards, ready to bear false witness against anybody and everybody, including themselves.

For the time being, they have held out.

3

Kitty is still sick. On the days when she feels a little better, she is afraid to turn her head or to bend her neck. She thinks of her pain as something alive, a creature that is punishing her for something.

"Daddy," she says, "why is it back again? Can't you stop it getting in?"

I hold her in my arms until she goes to sleep, sometimes in thirty minutes, sometimes in three hours. There are nightingales singing outside, and I curse them. This is my own personal madness: I think they stop Kitty from sleeping.

The doctor tells me she has some sort of inflammation that should not be allowed to get any worse. Otherwise, things could end badly.

I need to take her south. You can rent rooms in Crimea or in Caucasus through the Resort Department; maybe I can find something for us. Owen has told me I can go as soon as the Shakhty Trial is over, but I have to wait a full month until then.

4

I asked Weinstein to help me sort out a holiday to the south. He was delighted as if this was just what he had been waiting for.

"You can have everything," he said. "Tickets in your own separate railroad compartment and a wonderful hotel in Sochi with full board. All you need to do is write us an article for the *New York Times*. The editors won't take anything straight from us, but you're an official correspondent for a well-respected agency."

He gave me "special materials" from the Shakhty Trial that had been promised to "friendly journalists," but it was nothing but empty claims and abuse directed at the saboteurs.

"You have no proof of any of this—" I began.

"If the *New York Times* publishes this material," Weinstein interrupted me, "that's the best proof we can have. Thousands of specialists on the USSR will quote your article."

He doesn't hide the fact that the Shakhty Trial has nothing to do with justice. His line is as follows: the defendants need to be convicted for the sake of "state business," and if I love my daughter, I must play my part in this business.

5

From the very start of the Shakhty Trial, the engineer named Scorutto has behaved with courage and denied all the accusations that were leveled at him by his colleagues. But yesterday, he came to the microphone and announced in a dull voice, staring into space, that he admitted his guilt and was prepared to testify against his colleagues.

"Kolya, darling, don't lie!" a woman's voice cried out. "You know you're innocent!"

There was a commotion in court, people jumped up from their seats, and the presiding judge was forced to declare a recess. Scorutto was led away, sobbing.

When he appeared again, something quite unprecedented took place.

"Comrades, I have slandered myself and others," he announced to the entire courtroom.

There was a deathly silence.

"Were you threatened?" asked the state procurator in a stern voice.

"No. It's just that my friends betrayed me, so I—I betrayed them too."

Scorutto looked around the court with wild eyes and suddenly cried out, "Don't you understand? I just can't take it anymore!"

He apologized—not for carrying out sabotage as the others had done but for making false accusations of those who had betrayed him. The guards barely managed to pull him away from the microphone.

Seibert cursed under his breath, the French journalists gasped at the bravery of the little engineer. And this is what I was thinking:

Scorutto has no allies left, apart from his wife, who is as small and defenseless as himself. He knows that there is no way he can get out of the trap he is in. Just try standing firm and keeping your personal dignity intact faced with a situation like that! But nonetheless, he didn't give in.

I had been ready to strike a deal with Weinstein, and I was even beginning to regard my own treachery in a heroic light just because it was not in my own interests but for the sake of my daughter's health.

But if I think about it, what can Weinstein do to me? All right, I won't get an all-expenses-paid holiday to

Sochi, but Kitty and I can go south and rent some little beach hut by the sea as thousands of people have always done.

The most important thing is to get train tickets. That might be difficult since all of the tickets are bought up two months in advance, but I'll figure something out.

Even if Weinstein has me fired, it doesn't matter. I have a lot of friends precisely because I can be trusted. I have, up to now, never betrayed or sold anybody. If I need to find a new job or a good doctor for Kitty, my friends will help. But if they find out that I capitulated to Weinstein's demands, everyone would know I can be bought—just name your price.

To cut a long story short, I refused to write the article for Weinstein, and he was furious.

"It's quite impossible to have a normal working relationship with you!" he said. "Do you understand that there will be consequences?"

I answered that there are always consequences and that we choose those that suit us the best.

Kitty, as a matter of fact, is feeling much better as if her health depended on me passing this test with my integrity intact.

I wish I could thank Scorutto for saving me from descending to the level of a swine! I'd like to shake him by the hand and tell him he is not alone and that his battle with the system was an amazing lesson in personal courage. But the professional villains in the OGPU do everything they can to make sure their victims receive no support from outside.

20. CHIMERAS

1

Klim was invited to a banquet in honor of visiting businessmen from the USA and Germany.

"Actually, these gentlemen are here courtesy of the OGPU," explained the all-knowing Seibert. "These days, the OGPU is as much a resource procurement company as it is a police organization. The Soviet authorities are having forests cut down in the north, and they want to dispose of the timber somehow. So, the OGPU have called on Oscar Reich to act as an intermediary between them and the foreigners. Reich sorted it all out: the Germans buy timber for railroad sleepers while the Americans provide credit and underwrite the deal."

At the mention of Oscar Reich's name, Klim resolved not to attend the banquet, but then Seibert said something that made Klim reconsider.

"Mr. Reich is a very clever man. He knows there's no point in talking to the big bosses in the West. Every last one of them is opposed to the USSR. If you want to strike a deal, you need to talk to the seconds-in-command: not the proprietors but the hired managers. Oscar buys these managers off in the old-fashioned way—with jewels and precious metals. You can't slip a bribe to a prominent figure, but if you present him with a fifteenth-century royal goblet, he's unlikely to turn it down. People tend to lose their heads at the sight of real gold rather than figures on paper."

"Where does Oscar get all this gold?" Klim asked.

"From Russian museums and monasteries," said Seibert. "And it's not just gold. He makes gifts of paintings by old masters and ancient sculptures too. All the stuff is sent over to New York and Berlin, and in return, the managers, directors, and board members forget their anti-communist principles for a while. As a plan, it's hard to fault. They get a profitable deal, and their shareholders are happy. What else could you ask for?"

It might be worth going to the banquet after all, thought Klim, just to have a look at this talented Mr. Reich, a man capable of breaking down trade barriers and plundering museum exhibits on an industrial scale.

2

At around nine o'clock, automobiles adorned with the flags of various foreign nations began to converge on Spiridonov Street. Guests mounted the porch in pairs: the men in dinner jackets and top hats and the women in evening dresses. It was difficult to believe all this was taking place in the heart of Red Moscow.

The mansion, previously owned by a wealthy merchant wife, was furnished like a fairytale castle. The walls were lined with peacock-blue silk and panels made of precious woods. There were suits of armor standing in every corner, and the staircase was decorated with wrought iron sculptures.

The Hunting Room had been transformed into a banquet hall. Whole sturgeons were laid out on huge silver platters alongside red lobsters with their tails shelled, grilled lamb ribs with rosemary, thin pancakes with caviar, and fillet of trout in sour cream and chopped dill. There were twenty different types of cheeses and salamis, pyramids of fruit, and a whole array of bottles of wine, brandy, and vodka.

At the head of the table sat Oscar Reich, holding forth passionately about all the things that the USA and the USSR had in common.

"Both our countries," he said, "have to solve the problem of transporting goods and transmitting power over great distances. We both have unevenly distributed populations. But more importantly, we are both nations of dreamers, intrepid and inventive people who can cope with any problems that come our way."

Klim listened attentively to what Nina's husband was saying. He had to admit that Oscar Reich was a born orator. He was arguing that the USSR was like the Wild West of the mid-ninetieth century and that anyone bold enough to investigate the full extent of what the nation had to offer could earn untold riches.

The businessmen cheered on his descriptions of the mighty forests of Northern Russia and the deposits of precious metals in Siberia.

"Gentlemen," said Oscar, raising his glass, "I propose a toast to the great and indomitable Soviet people! Hurray!"

After the champagne, a mound of delicacies was eaten, and a dozen or so foxtrots were danced—also for the sake of the Soviet people.

3

All the guests at the banquet seemed to have been infected by the mood of wild festivity. After a single drink, they were already drunkenly chanting "For He's a Jolly Good Fellow" in English and "Long May He Live" in German: one of the foreigners was celebrating a birthday.

As Klim was walking through the ballroom, a familiar silhouette caught his eye. It was Nina, dancing with a military man. It was an extraordinary sight: a Red Army commander and a young woman in a magnificent dress gliding across the parquet floor to the sound of a jazz band. Nina's partner was smiling at her, enraptured, his hand on her bare back, down the length of which hung a fine jeweled chain.

Klim stood for a moment, spellbound. He had to admit that, deep down, he was hoping to see how his ex-wife fared. But where would that get him anyway?

Seen enough? he scolded himself. *You can go now.*

Opening the glass door, he went out onto the wide balcony, which was adorned by a statue of a chimera. The reflections of the lamps played over the monster's stone body so that it seemed to stir slightly on its pedestal.

At that moment, Oscar Reich came out onto the balcony, holding a glass of brandy. He was drunk; his tie was crooked, and his hair was plastered to his head with sweat.

"Exactly the man I was hoping to see!" Oscar exclaimed, catching sight of Klim. "Have you heard that the Ford Motor Company is planning to help the Russians build an automobile works outside Nizhny Novgorod? Soon, they'll be sending engineers and industrial architects over to check out the area. How would you like to write a couple of features for us about it? We need to cause a stir in the American press and show them that the USSR is a land of opportunity."

Klim shook his head. "As soon as the Shakhty Trial is over, I'm taking a holiday. My daughter is sick, so I'm taking her down south."

The door swung open again, and Nina appeared in the doorway. "Oscar, everybody is looking for you. You promised to play bridge."

"I'm coming." He finished his brandy and left the balcony.

Nina and Klim looked at one another, for all the world like hostile neighbors who had met by chance on the dividing line between their properties.

"What's the matter with Kitty?" asked Nina at last. "Is she sick?"

"Every day is different," answered Klim reluctantly. "Sometimes her arms and legs swell up, and she gets headaches."

"Have you taken her to the doctor?" asked Nina. "What did he say?"

She kept showering Klim with questions, and he began to feel a nagging sense of irritation. Why was Nina suddenly acting the part of the anxious mother?

"Where do you want to take Kitty?" she asked.

"It depends what tickets I find."

"So, you haven't got your rail tickets yet?"

Nina was about to add something, but at that moment, Oscar came back out onto the balcony.

"You came out to tell me to hurry up," he told Nina, "and you're still out here talking to my friend." He threw a meaningful glance at Klim. "I'm starting to get jealous."

"See you again soon," said Nina and left, leaving Klim in the company of the stone chimera.

He squinted at the monster crouched on its pedestal. It had the head of a lion and a crest along its back, and its body was like that of no creature on earth. A chimera was nothing but a chimera, a bad dream, a blend of incongruous parts. And that was exactly what Klim's love had become.

4

Almost every one of the foreign journalists came to the next session of the Shakhty Trial. They all wanted to see the conclusion of the cross-examination of Scorutto.

The judge called the engineer to the microphone, and in quiet, calm tones, Scorutto announced that he fully accepted his guilt.

"I only withdrew my testimony because of my wife," he told the court.

A barely audible sigh of disappointment was heard in the courtroom.

"His wife should never have shouted out to him," whispered Seibert in Klim's ear. "She let the OGPU know that she and her husband loved each other. That was just one more tool in their hands. I expect he was told that his wife would be arrested if he didn't confess."

Klim nodded gloomily. The trial was beginning to resemble the medieval allegory of the "Dance Macabre" in which a grinning skeleton leads people of all ranks and all walks of life into a dance, showing that no matter what a man might do, the force of fate still leads him into the grave.

It was utterly hopeless to resist the Bolsheviks.

5

As soon as Klim came out of the House of Unions, he caught sight of Nina. She came toward him, looking light and elegant in a little straw hat and a white flowered dress.

"Hello," she said. "How's Kitty?"

"She's fine," said Klim without meeting her eye.

Without exchanging a word, they set off in the direction of Okhotny Ryad Street. A stream of people was coming the other way, and as they let them pass, Klim and Nina touched shoulders and then moved apart from one another.

"I know just the place to take Kitty," said Nina. "Elkin wrote to me that he's in Koktebel now; it's a small Bulgarian village in Crimea. His aunt has a house there, and she rents out rooms to holidaymakers. Elkin invited me to go and stay there."

"I can just picture your playboy of a husband in a Crimean village," snorted Klim.

"I'd go to Koktebel without Oscar. He's gone to Germany—he left yesterday."

There was a crash from above the street, and a cloud of lime dust rose into the air. Klim looked around. Behind a fence plastered with theater posters, a group of workmen was demolishing the Church of St. Parascheva. Already, the golden cupolas had gone, and huge holes gaped in the walls, through which could be glimpsed the heads of the workers.

"I know someone who works for the People's Commissariat for Railroads," Nina went on, "and he's booked a rail compartment for me. You and Kitty can come with me to the town of Feodosia, and from there we can take a bus straight to Koktebel."

Klim looked at her in amazement. What was all this about a compartment? She didn't really believe for a moment that he would agree to travel with her?

"My dear girl, you must realize that everything is over between us," he said.

Nina's face contorted as if in pain. "But you said yourself that Kitty needs to go to the south!"

"I refuse to take any charity from you."

"Why not?"

"Because you're sharing Reich's bed!" retorted Klim angrily.

Nina hung her head. "What about you and that Galina?" she whispered. "I don't imagine you're just sitting around playing solitaire."

"Watch out!" came a shout from behind the fence as a beam crashed down from the roof of the church.

"If you'd only listened to me at the start—" said Nina with a catch in her voice. "But I don't know why I'm even interfering. If you want to kill our child out of sheer stupidity—"

"Don't use Kitty to blackmail me!" snapped Klim, but Nina interrupted him.

"I'll be at the Kursk Station on Friday at two o'clock. The train to Feodosia, Car Two, Compartment Four. If you want to come, come."

Then she turned and walked away.

6

Klim arrived home in a state of turmoil. What sort of plan was this of Nina's? It was madness for the two of them to travel together, not to mention in a single compartment. Kitty would realize that her mother had been found, and then what?

But what if I don't manage to find rail tickets in time? Klim thought. His period of leave from work would pass, the summer would be over, and perhaps Kitty would still be sick.

He opened the door to his apartment, and Galina came rushing to meet him. "How was the Shakhty Trial?"

"Fine," he answered, his mind elsewhere.

What if he did decide to go to Koktebel after all? What would he do about Galina? When he had told her he wanted to go south, she had immediately assumed he was taking her, although he had promised nothing.

Klim stared gloomily at Galina's thin legs in their short socks, shrunk from constant washing, and at her coarse cloth dress, creased from long hours of sitting at a typewriter.

Why had he got involved with Galina? For months now, he had been justifying himself by reasoning that it was what *she* wanted, but this charm no longer worked. He had a crime on his conscience: he had allowed Galina to hope for something. Now he faced a choice of either crushing her completely or carrying this pointless and heavy burden around for the rest of his life.

Galina put her arms around his neck and gave him a kiss on the cheek. "Why were you so long? I missed you!"

Any failure to respond to her affectionate advances was to risk bringing forth a torrent of alarmed questions. But to respond was only to wrap a noose tighter around his own neck.

Galina could already see from his face that something had happened. "What's the matter?" she asked anxiously.

Klim blurted out the first thing that came into his mind. "I just saw them demolishing the Church of St. Parascheva. What a shame! That church is more than two hundred years old, you know. It's the same all over the country. I read in the paper that in my hometown of Nizhny Novgorod, the city council has ordered the demolition of the churches on the main square so that they don't get in the way of military parades."

Klim remembered the church in which he and Nina had been married. "The Church of St. George is going to be demolished too," he said. "Those swine don't give a damn for history or tradition."

"Are you from Nizhny Novgorod?" asked Galina, surprised. "You always said you were from Moscow."

Klim cursed himself silently. What a stupid blunder!

"Well…I used to visit Nizhny Novgorod…a long time ago when I was a child…." Just in case, he decided to change the subject. "Do you know what? I think that all those fires and accidents in the Shakhty region were the result not of sabotage but of something far more mundane: worn-out equipment and a failure to observe safety procedures. After all, similar things are happening all over the USSR."

Klim was hoping to draw Galina into an argument so that she would overlook the slip he had just made. But, unusually for her, she did not rise to the bait.

"I've got soup on the stove," she said and went off into the kitchen.

21. THE HOUSE OF GLORY

1

The news of Kitty's illness had alarmed Nina so much that it had driven everything else clean out of her head. She was beside herself with fury at Galina. Nina was convinced that the fool of a woman had failed to keep a proper eye on Kitty.

Taking matters into her own hands, Nina managed to get ahold of rail tickets to Feodosia in two days. Now, fate had given her and Klim a chance. What they needed was to go far away and forget all their previous woes.

"He *has* to come to the station!" Nina kept repeating to herself. But every now and then, a sickening thought would set her heart beating wildly: *What if he doesn't come?*

On the day of the last session of the Shakhty Trial, Nina was on the point of telephoning Klim several times to find out what he had decided but could not bring herself to do so.

Everywhere, it seemed, there was talk of "the verdict." The word was on the lips of market traders and cab drivers and blared from loudspeakers on the street. To distract herself from her own gloomy thoughts, Nina went to the cinema only to find that the main feature was preceded by a newsreel on the Shakhty Trial. Eleven men had been sentenced to be shot while the others had received long sentences in labor camps. The presiding judge of the Supreme Court was shown silently pronouncing sentence while the pianist thumped out a solemn march and the cinema-goers on either side of Nina commented approvingly, "That'll show them!"

That evening, Yefim came to check on Nina. Oscar had asked him to keep an eye on his wife while he was abroad.

"Have you heard the news about the verdict?" Yefim asked. "They let the Germans off in the end. Oscar arranged a swap—their liberty in exchange for a contract for railroad sleepers. But the Russians are of no use to anybody; neither their government nor their people."

Nina buried her face in her hands. She felt that she too was of no earthly use to anybody.

2

Nina arrived at the station early and set off slowly along the empty platform to the second car. She had told Elkin that she would be arriving together with Klim and Kitty, but she no longer had any faith that her plan would work.

What would she do if Klim did not come? Should she go to Crimea alone? *Oh, God,* Nina thought, *anything but that!*

"Mommy!" she heard a child's excited cry. "Daddy, I've found our Mommy!"

Kitty, dressed in a comical, frilled pink sundress, came running up to Nina and hugged her legs.

Nina was overcome by happiness and relief. Her hands shaking, she kissed Kitty, exclaiming over her and hugging her tightly. "Look how much you've grown!"

It was hard to believe that her daughter still recognized her after such a long absence.

"Hello," said Klim, walking up to them.

He was carrying a small suitcase decorated with pictures of flowers cut out from postcards.

Nina looked up at him happily. "I'm so glad to see you both! Where are your things?"

"I'm not coming with you," said Klim.

Nina's heart froze. "But why not?"

Klim took a small folded piece of paper from his pocket and held it out to her. "I got this yesterday evening."

It was a carbon copy of a typewritten text. Nina quickly scanned it:

Dear Comrade Rogov,

You have been selected as a participant in a polar expedition of journalists leaving for Archangelsk this week. Everything has been arranged with your employers in London.

As you will know, the airship *Italia* piloted by General Umberto Nobile has been wrecked somewhere in the Spitzbergen Archipelago. The Soviet government has sent the icebreaker *Krasin* to the aid of the airship, and now, the world is watching our valiant sailors break their way through the ice to the stranded Italian fascists.

You will be taken to the vessel by airplane. There is a radio transmitter onboard which will allow you to send your reports back.

Communist Greetings,

Weinstein

"It's a petty act of revenge by the Press Department," said Klim with a bitter smile. "Weinstein knew I was planning to go south, so he has deliberately sent me north."

"But you don't have to go!" exclaimed Nina. "Why didn't you refuse?"

"Well, for my press agency, this polar expedition is a great scoop. Usually, the Soviets don't send foreign journalists to the north. Would you be able to look after Kitty while I'm away?"

"Of course."

"When will you be coming back home?"

"I've left Reich, so there's nothing to come back to."

Nina had been sure Klim would be pleased to hear this news, but instead, he clutched Kitty to him as if Nina had told him she was planning to kidnap her.

"Promise you won't take Kitty away from me!" he said.

Nina stared at him, nonplussed. "What are you talking about?"

"Anything could happen. Your Oscar would never have a little Chinese girl in the house, but you're a free woman now. You can do whatever you please."

Klim did not seem to realize how hurtful his words were. He had no faith in Nina's good intentions and was asking her not to act even more contemptibly than he had come to expect.

"Promise me you won't take Kitty," he repeated. "I'll come and collect her as soon as I can get away."

Nina was on the point of losing her temper but managed to restrain herself. She took a pencil from her bag and wrote down a few lines on the back of the letter from Weinstein.

"This is Elkin's address. If you don't trust me, send him a telegram and ask him to keep an eye on us."

Klim nodded and put the letter in his pocket.

They went through to the compartment, and Klim explained to Nina what she should do if Kitty became ill again. He showed her where he had packed her medicine and, most importantly of all, her pink rag horse.

Kitty clambered up onto the seat and began fiddling with the light switch on the wall. "Look! You can turn the light on. Daddy, do you remember when we went to Moscow? There wasn't a light in the train then."

Kitty kept turning the light switch this way and that. One second it was bright, and the next, they were plunged into gloom.

The bell rang.

Klim got up and hugged Kitty tightly. "Be a good girl; try not to be too much of a nuisance to Nina."

He had said "Nina" not "Mommy" just as if she were some stranger.

3

The train began to move, and a succession of dreary station outbuildings slid by outside the window.

Kitty sat swinging her legs, chattering to Nina of how she had recently fallen from the porch and got "a re-e-e-ally funny cut on her leg." She wanted very much to make an impression on her mother.

Nina nodded, looking at the tiny scar on Kitty's brown knee.

Why hadn't Klim left Kitty with Galina? she was wondering. Did he trust her even less than Nina? Or perhaps his lover had developed a dislike for the girl?

Nina was quite unprepared for the maternal responsibility that had suddenly fallen to her. Shameful to admit, she and Kitty had been apart from each other for so long that now, neither was sure of how to behave with the other.

They heard a group of children in the neighboring compartment begin to sing the "Internationale" in German. One-third of the railcar was taken up by foreign Young Pioneers, the children of communists from other countries who had been sent to the Soviet Union for summer camp.

Kitty began to pester Nina to take her to meet the foreign children, and when Nina refused, she had a tantrum. All of a sudden, Kitty had realized her father was no longer there, and there was nobody to indulge her every whim.

Things went from bad to worse. The food in the restaurant car was horrible, and the tea was too hot. And what was so bad about putting bread up your nose, anyway, Kitty wanted to know. And if it was so bad, why did people have nostrils? Before long, Kitty was howling, and Nina was desperate.

When the train stopped at the next station, Nina ran out onto the platform and darted about among the peasant women selling home-cooked wares. The engine stood under steam, and every time one of the couplings heaved or gave a shudder, all the passengers would dash back to the cars in a panic. Nina was terrified the train would move off before she could get back on board, taking Kitty with it.

She bought some fried chicken, some boiled potatoes, and a few small cucumbers. Kitty at last consented to eat but was sick almost immediately.

Nina rinsed the pink sundress in the sink in the toilet cubicle. *I've completely forgotten how to look after my own daughter*, she thought with desperation. *What if it turns out to be a serious case of food poisoning?*

But when she got back to the compartment, Kitty was bouncing on the seats as though nothing had happened.

"Let's play fishermen!" she said to Nina. "You can be the fisherman—you cast your line and pull me out of the sea."

She made a great show of pretending to be the biggest fish ever, then a cabdriver's horse, a singing radio loudspeaker, then a variety of sea monsters.

"You have to faint!" she shouted excitedly. "I'm a hideous three-headed diver!"

Again and again, Nina swooned obediently back on the seat.

After it grew dark, they lay in each other's arms while Kitty told Nina how Kapitolina would pray to her "little father God" and how she sewed cloths embroidered with cockerels.

Nina wanted very much to ask about Galina, but she did not dare. It would be too terrible to hear confirmation of what she knew anyway.

Sparks from the engine flew past the window, the wheels clattered, and from the corridor came the sound of women laughing.

"Mommy," said Kitty, "I know a magic spell. Kapitolina taught it to me. You have to say it to the brownie—that's the house spirit—when you've lost something. It goes like this: 'Brownie, Brownie, bring my sack back to me. What was lost will now be found, in the sack, safe and sound.' I did the spell, and I asked the brownie to bring you bac k—and look! It worked!"

Nina kissed Kitty on the top of the head. "Now we need to get Daddy back too."

"All right," murmured Kitty sleepily. "Only I don't know if the brownie will be able to pick Daddy up. He's quite heavy."

"We'll think of something," promised Nina. "Perhaps we can get ahold of a crane."

4

Elkin was on the platform at Feodosia to meet Nina and Kitty, tanned and bearded, his hair a brighter ginger than ever. In his faded red fez and his Russian shirt with the sleeves rolled up, he looked more like a Turkish fisherman than a Moscow engineer.

"Where is Mr. Rogov?" he asked after he had kissed Nina in greeting.

"Daddy stayed in Moscow, and Mommy and I came on our own," said Kitty.

Elkin looked at Nina, bewildered. "What do you mean, 'with Mommy?' Klim told me his wife was dead."

Nina blushed awkwardly. She should have warned Elkin about all this. And now there would be all sorts of questions and explanations.

"Klim and I used to be married," she stammered.

"But what about Kitty? How…?"

"We adopted her."

For a moment, Elkin was lost for words.

"Well, then, let's go," he said at last and, taking the suitcases, led his visitors through the station crowds.

Nina was not sure how Elkin had taken the news about her former marriage. Had he guessed that it was for Klim's sake rather than his that Nina had been coming in to the Moscow Savannah all that winter?

Feodosia was hot, dusty, and marvelously beautiful, and Nina gradually recovered from her feelings of embarrassment. She gazed at the Tatar women in their brightly colored rags, at men with great black mustaches carrying enormous wooden pallets on their heads, and at the jovial traders selling shrimps that they poured, like sunflower seeds, into cones of newspaper.

"This rattletrap here is our ride to Koktebel," said Elkin, indicating an open-top car parked nearby in the shade with odd headlights and a battered chassis but an expensive oriental rug covering the back seat. "It's the car used by the local Party executive committee. I've arranged everything."

The chauffeur, a swarthy young man in a tattered vest with a pair of large motor goggles strung around his neck, stared at Nina and Kitty with interest.

"Shall I start her up?" he asked.

"Yes, get her going!" ordered Elkin, helping the ladies into the car with a great show of chivalry.

Soon, they were racing through the streets, scattering chickens and stray dogs.

Elkin, turning around in his seat to speak to Nina, described how he had managed to restore an abandoned blacksmith's forge in Koktebel and turn it into a workshop.

The local authorities left him alone, even though they had been instructed to "crack down" on private business. Elkin was the only handyman in the whole district, and people brought all sorts of things for him to repair—from prerevolutionary generators to railings for burial plots in cemeteries. The executive committee car was also his own handiwork, cobbled together from the parts of three other cars.

"The only problem here is that people are very poor," said Elkin, holding on to his fez, which kept threatening to blow away. "Sometimes, they'll bring me a donkey to be shod, and they'll pay me with a piece of sheep's cheese wrapped in a cloth. But I need money to pay my taxes. It would be good if Klim could give me the money he owes me for Mashka as soon as possible."

"He'll be coming here soon," replied Nina

"If he doesn't have time, he can wire me the money," said Elkin quickly. It seemed that now he was not keen for Klim to come to Koktebel.

They left town and drove through yellow hills that looked like the folds of a velvet shawl. Surrounded by all this bright, untouched beauty, Nina found it hard to believe that the gloomy city of Moscow still existed somewhere—together with Oscar Reich and the Workers' and Peasants' Inspectorate.

Soon, they caught a glimpse of the sea, sparkling turquoise between the hills.

"That's where we're heading," said Elkin, pointing to a cliff that looked like an enormous slice of halva.

In five minutes, the car stopped at a small stone wall. Two shaggy dogs came hurtling out of the yard and set up a deafening bark.

Elkin jumped out onto the road. "That's enough, you damn pests! This is Softie, and this is Oink," he said, introducing the dogs to the ladies. "Welcome to the House of Glory!"

"Why Glory?" asked Kitty

"It's a joke on my aunt's Bulgarian name, Gloria."

Nina and Kitty thanked the chauffeur and walked up the path to a curious lopsided building with a large terrace and a number of little balconies on which washing had been hung out to dry. There were apricot trees growing in the yard and an enormous kiln next to the wall of the sort used for firing pottery. Beside it was a whole array of ceramic pots painted to look like faces with handles in the form of ears.

On the porch stood a large elderly woman with dark eyebrows, dressed in a long threadbare smock decorated with brightly colored embroidery. Her pointed slippers had upturned toes, and she wore a colorful shawl wrapped around her head like a turban. She was smoking a long pipe mounted in rough silver from which came clouds of a sweet, fragrant smoke.

"So, you've brought them, have you?" she boomed down to Elkin. "All the holidaymakers are down at the beach. Go and call them for dinner."

A large shadow fluttered behind the hostess, and a white cockatoo settled on her shoulder and began to shriek, to Kitty's great delight: "Glory, Glory, Glory! Two rubles a bed!"

"Come on—let's get you settled in," said the old woman as she gestured for Nina and Kitty to follow her.

Inside, the house resembled some luxurious dacha that had not been refurbished for twenty years. The walls were hung with bookshelves, homemade cloth dolls, plates, and the same pots with painted faces. The windows were wide open, and from far away came the sound of waves and children's laughter.

Gloria led her guests to a small room that had only a chair, a chest, and a bed covered with a brightly covered blanket.

"This is great!" shouted Kitty excitedly and threw herself sprawling onto the bed.

Nina looked out of the window. Down below rose up rocky outcrops of the cliff washed by a dazzling sea glittering in the sun.

Gloria explained that she did not have a bathroom. The holidaymakers bathed in the sea, all water had to be drawn from a well, and the lavatory was a wooden hut in the yard between the house and the cliff. There was no lock on the door but a railroad sign at the path, announcing "Track Closed" or "Track Open."

Nina paid for a month in advance, and Gloria tucked the money in behind the wide belt of her pants.

"Are you here for your health?" she asked, looking into Nina's eyes.

"No," answered Nina. "It's Kitty who's ill."

"Your little girl is healthier than all of us put together," said Gloria. "But you look more dead than alive."

"Communications on the left flank are out!" the cockatoo squawked. "Run out a line, damn you!"

The old woman shook her head and shuffled downstairs.

Nina was amazed. Was it really so obvious how broken she felt inside?

5

The other guests had all been coming to the House of Glory for years, and Nina felt at home with them immediately.

Nobody there asked what you did for a living, observed Bolshevik rituals, or showed any curiosity about what was going on in the wider world. For these people, the most important news was that somebody had caught an enormous fish, and the worst fear was that there might be a gale that would interfere with the day's swimming.

There was something delightful about the simplicity and modesty of this life with its lack of worldly cares. At dawn, all the holidaymakers would go to the beach, to the green-blue sea. Nina would stretch a sheet between two rocks and put an old counterpane down on the pebbles to make a comfortable tent.

She and Kitty would sit in this shelter, staring at some wispy cloud in the sky and trying to think what it looked like. They would swim or lie on their stomachs, searching for semi-precious stones in the shingle—orange carnelians, translucent chalcedony, and red jasper.

The guests would all gather on the terrace for lunch around the enormous table scarred with knife cuts. They would pour out the semi-precious stones they had found on the beach, and an avid session of swapping, trading, buying, and selling would begin.

"The field kitchen is here, lads!" the cockatoo would shriek, flying onto the terrace.

Gloria would sweep the stone bartering chips to one side and set the table with enamel bowls, flatbread and mustard, and a large copper pot full of a mess they called "soldier's joy."

Elkin also ate at the House of Glory—his workshop was only a two-minute bicycle ride away. He would bring the holidaymakers little gifts and immediately set about mending something in his aunt's ramshackle house.

He made a swing for Kitty and presented Nina with a small figurine of a giraffe carved from a shell.

"This is to bring you luck," he told her, smiling. "You can put it on a lace and hang it around your neck."

Nina was both touched and embarrassed that Elkin was trying to court her. She predicted that one day he would try to have a serious talk with her, alone, and was already worrying about it. How could she turn down such a good man, break his heart, when he had already gone through so much? But what else could she do? While she felt the warmest affection and the utmost respect for him, she did not and could never feel any passion for him.

After dinner, everybody would rest, and then they would laze on the beach again. Toward evening, Elkin would gather all the guests around a bonfire. They would sing to the guitar, drink strong homemade wine, and make up detective stories.

"A quite unheard-of crime has taken place in the House of Glory," announced Elkin menacingly. "Somebody has run off with the sign 'Track Free,' putting our freedom in grave jeopardy. But we will flush out the criminal. We need to think about who had a motive for this crime. Confess to your weaknesses!"

Obediently, each of them owned up: one guest had a habit of flicking at his teeth with his fingernails, another liked to gnaw chicken bones and suck out the marrow, yet another wrote terrible love stories. Nina admitted that she liked to balance on fallen logs.

"Let's take a note of that," said Elkin. "Our young friend Nina is looking for balance in her life. I think we have a chief suspect. She is the only one of us who needs to be told which way to go."

Then, the missing sign was found in the dogs' kennel, and to general laughter, Elkin wrestled it away from Oink, who had already chewed it half to pieces.

The night air was full of the sound of the cicadas, and now and again, a bird chirruped in one of the apricot trees.

Huddling under a colorful blanket, Nina gazed at the fire and relived the day's most vivid memories: the green line of the surf, the little crabs scuttling away from her shadow, and the water in the rock pools so crystal clear that she could see every grain of sand below.

Opposite Nina sat a young couple from Kiev—fair-haired Alyosha and round-faced Ira. They had recently been married and had come to Koktebel for their honeymoon. It was always a pleasure to see them walking around hand in hand, completely absorbed with one another, young and happy with dazzling white smiles.

But I'll never be like them, thought Nina sadly.

Klim had sent her a cable informing her that he was already in Arkhangelsk. The rescue of the Italian expedition had become the latest big news story, and the Soviet government had announced that all news of the polar explorers would be conveyed free of charge. Klim and Nina were brazenly taking advantage of this to send one another free telegrams.

"How are you getting on in the search for Nobile?" Nina had written. "We are fine. We are swimming and sunbathing."

Klim had answered in a similar tone: "The pilot Chukhnovsky has spotted some people stranded on an ice floe. Do you have enough food? Is Kitty well?"

There was not a trace of affection in these messages. Once, Nina had written to him, "Please come soon! We miss you!" But Klim had just ignored her appeal.

22. NORTH AND SOUTH

1

BOOK OF THE DEAD

For several decades now, the world has been on the lookout for a Superman (or *Übermensch* as the German philosopher Friedrich Nietzsche called him). Industry has reached unprecedented heights, yet human nature has remained the same. Many people dream of how they might improve it to match our technical abilities.

The Superman should lead us by example to the bright feature. But there are so many candidates eager to take the position, that it's not quite clear who to pick: a communist, a fascist, or just a chiseled-chinned civilizer carrying the white man's burden. Only one thing is clear: we need a hero larger than life.

Those who are running for Superman try to prove themselves and climb the highest mountain or fly to the North Pole in an airship. And if you are lucky enough to go a step further and save a life, instead of merely taking a ride over the ice, then your deeds will be lauded to the skies, and your chances of becoming a true hero will be significantly improved. This is why the search for Nobile's expedition is the cause of such excitement.

The stranded victims are just about the last thing on everyone's minds. Every day, thousands upon thousands of people are dying as a result of hunger, wars, epidemics, or industrial accidents, but nobody gives a damn about them. What people care about is the idea of conquering the Arctic—one of the last unexplored places on earth. The rescue of the crew of the *Italia* is simply a particularly striking symbol of the triumph of man over nature.

Weinstein is deluded if he thinks that the world is following the progress of the Soviet icebreaker, the *Krasin*. In fact, it feels as if we're all watching some great international competition, like a tournament in which everybody is cheering for their own team. The victims of the disaster have become a trophy to be won by those who most closely fit the bill of Supermen. After all, the Italians, the Norwegians, the Swedes, and the French, among others, have also sent out search parties.

The race is of particular importance to the Russian communists and the Italian fascists, who are prepared to spend any amount of money and risk any amount of lives in the interests of securing a victory. The People's Commissariat of Foreign Affairs has decided to send us North in order to capture the Soviet Union's moment of triumph.

My fellow journalists and I all pretend to be delighted to join the ranks of the Arctic explorers. The very fact that we are on board the *Krasin* makes us into the heroes deserving of money, fame, and the love of beautiful women. But at the same time, we can't help recalling Admunsen's hydroplane, which was lost without trace in the Barents Sea during the search for Nobile, or the plane of the Swedish pilot, Lundborg, which overturned when he landed on an ice floe. The weather around Spitzbergen Island is harsh—extreme cold, fog, and strong wind—and we feel like soldiers going off to the front, unsure which of us will be coming home again.

When I started to imagine what would happen to Kitty if I perished in the North, I decided that it would be a mistake to leave her in Galina's hands. If I did, she would end up exactly like Tata. It would be better to let Nina take her. At least Mrs. Reich will not turn the child into a brainless propaganda-spouting parrot.

I kept Nina in the dark about my plan though and lied to Galina too, telling her I had sent Kitty off to a summer camp. I don't know if she believed me or not.

2

The commanders have refused point-blank to allow any journalists onto the Soviet ships, so we are sitting in a hotel in Archangelsk, waiting for the People's Commissariat of Foreign Affairs to sort things out with the Commissariat for Military and Naval Affairs.

Our editors beg us to spare their blood pressure and send at least some scrap of news about Nobile's crew, but our only source of information at the time is a loudspeaker opposite my hotel room window.

As soon as we hear the words "And now—news of the *Krasin* icebreaker," my colleagues and I rush to open the top window pane, take out our notebooks, and do our best to catch every word.

The Soviet news agency, TASS, is hardly bombarding us with details, and we need to scrape together something to send back to the editors, and as a result, several correspondents are unable to resist embroidering on the facts.

The other day, Seibert showed me an article he had written about the rescue of two navigators from Nobile's expedition. The loudspeaker had announced that they had been picked up by the *Krasin* and that the third crew member, a meteorologist by the name of Malmgren, had died before he could be rescued.

Seibert couldn't keep from adding some touches of his own. He gave a description of the funeral held for the brilliant scientist with touching valedictory speeches and traditional Russian lamentation chants for the deceased. His report was published in hundreds of papers all over the world, and only later did it come to light that Malmgren had not been buried at all and that he had not been with the navigators.

Now, we are all teasing Seibert mercilessly, telling him it's time he changed profession: he clearly has a talent for composing obituaries.

He is walking about like a thundercloud, promising to get his back on the lot of us, and particularly on me, as I am a "tiresome pest" with "no feeling for the art of writing."

3

Arkhangelsk is home mainly to fishermen, loggers, and political exiles. There are barely any old people here, but a great many children and youngsters.

Following the recent rains, the town is drowning in mud and overgrown with weeds. We can't walk down the streets and instead have to jump between the boards and bricks that deputize for pavements here.

There is not a lot in the way of entertainment: it's a choice between going to the cinema to see the film *The Poet and the Tsar* for the fifth time, admiring the elaborate carved window frames (which are skillfully made hereabouts), or sitting on a bench outside the nursing school and watching the haughty northern girls walk by without a glance in our direction. We foreigners are the object of their undisguised contempt.

The food situation here is far worse than it is in Moscow. There's no sugar in town whatsoever—it's all gone into making icebergs.

Recently, there was a confectioners' competition in our hotel on the subject of "The Rescue of Nobile's Expedition," and now, they have put up a display of cakes decorated with snowy plains, tents built out of biscuits, and marzipan figures signaling for help.

I made a deal with the confectioner and got some sweets for Kitty and Nina. I'm planning to send a parcel via one of the conductors on a train. The post is unreliable to say the least: a packing crate takes several months to get to Feodosia from Archangelsk.

As my death in the polar wastes seems to have been postponed for the moment, I am thinking about what I should do about Nina. I'm sure Kitty became attached to her and will want her mother to play a part in her life.

Seeing Nina for a few minutes is enough to set me back for days. I don't think I could ever get used to meaningless small talks—to "hellos" and "goodbyes" when dropping Kitty off or picking her up.

Unfortunately, I cannot forget Mr. Reich. I go down to the river to watch the huge rafts of logs traveling seawards, hundreds of thousands of them to be sorted, dried, and stacked. As I gaze at all this, all I am thinking is that these are the railroad sleepers that Oscar Reich is sending to Germany.

Back in the hotel, I sit down at the piano in the lobby, open the lid, and run my fingers over the keys. And then I find myself thinking of Mr. Reich's teeth, which are equally white, even, and false.

It's silly of me, but what can I do?

4

Nina received a telegram by Klim telling that he had sent a package with a conductor and asking her to collect it.

Although the bus to Feodosia did not come through Koktebel until twelve o'clock, Nina woke at dawn and wandered aimlessly about the house for some time, too agitated to settle on anything. All her thoughts were of one thing only: Klim would probably have written a letter to go with the parcel. What would it say?

Nina decided to go and have a swim. Taking a towel, she stepped out into the yard, which was bathed in the rays of the early morning sun. Gloria was sitting at her potter's wheel under a canopy. Softie and Oink lay beside her, watching attentively as their owner shaped a pot-bellied vase.

The cockatoo was muttering sleepily on her shoulder, "Sir, we need to bring in the missiles. What are we going to fight with?"

Gloria slapped down some clay with her hand and stared at Nina. "Sit down!" she ordered, rising heavily to her feet from the rickety bench. "I want to have a look at you."

"What for?" Nina asked.

"That's my business. You just shut your eyes and model something with the clay. Whatever you like."

Nina shrugged and sat down at the potter's wheel. Closing her eyes, she took a piece of clay in her fingers and began to shape it.

"Stop!" Gloria said.

She looked at what Nina had made as if it was something extraordinary.

"A man trap!" Gloria muttered. "That's your past…. It's got a tight grip on you. I can feel it."

Nina looked down at the clay in front of her: a flat circle with uneven, jagged edges. Actually, she thought it looked more like a beer-bottle top.

Gloria took out another piece of clay from the barrel. "Shut your eyes and have another go."

It was clear that Gloria was trying to work out what was on Nina's mind. This time, Nina attempted to make the shape of a heart, but she ended up with a strange shape pitted with holes left by her fingers.

"That's a piece of cheese!" exclaimed Gloria. "'At the top of the tree sat Mr. Crow, clutching a piece of cheese in his beak…' Have you heard this fable? You hold onto your prize tight, or a fox might come running past and take it away."

Nina was puzzled. "Are you talking about Galina?" she asked, warily.

Frowning, Gloria squashed the "man-trap" and the "cheese" together in her fist to make a single lump.

"Get up!" she ordered, and sitting back down in Nina's place, she set the wheel turning again with the pedal.

"Daft girl!" she muttered. "Do you have a brain at all behind those curls?"

Nina stood, wiping her fingers with a cloth, waiting for some sort of explanation, but Gloria did not say a word. The wheel turned with a soft hiss, and a new pot began to take shape under the old woman's gnarled fingers.

"I don't know what to do," said Nina timidly. "I don't know if he still loves me or if he still wants—"

The cockatoo bent its head toward Gloria's ear and began to jabber something.

"Mm-hm," nodded the old woman, raising her at Nina.

"You should think about making him feel good *with* you rather than bad *without* you. And now, off with you. I have work to do."

5

All the way to Feodosia, Nina thought about what Gloria had told her.

When was the last time she and Klim had felt good together? It had been several years ago. Their love had become like opium—it gave a short illusion of happiness but was actually destroying them both. Klim had been the first to realize this and decided to put an end to the torment.

Kitty took her spillikins out of Nina's bag. Elkin had made her a whole set of tiny models, each no larger than a child's fingernail. There was a pail with a handle, a samovar, a saw, and a carpenter's plane, a hundred different items in all. The idea of the game was to tip them into a pile and then take them out one by one with a little hook, making sure not to touch anything else.

Kitty had no luck with the spillikins—the bus bounced too much as it drove over the potholes.

Klim and I have no luck sorting our relationship out either, thought Nina gloomily. *But nobody is to blame. It just happened that we have had a rough ride.*

6

The train had arrived early for a change.

Taking Kitty in her arms, Nina ran through the dim station building and onto the sun-drenched platform. Cheerful passengers hurried past them, carrying suitcases, baskets, and butterfly nets.

Nina saw a crowd gathered at the last car and ran toward the back of the train.

"Stop pushing!" the conductor shouted as he handed out parcels and letters. "You'll all get your turn."

He sorted deftly through the packages and envelopes with his wrinkled hands. "Not, this one's not yours, nor this one either."

At last, he handed over a plywood box to Nina.

Kitty jumped up and down beside her impatiently. "Mommy! Open it quickly!"

Having settle down on the bench under a poplar tree, Nina cut open the package with a knife borrowed from a vendor selling watermelons nearby.

"What's inside?" fussed Kitty "Are there any toys?"

There were biscuits, sugar, and chocolate wrapped in paper. At the very bottom, under Norwegian canned goods, there was a letter. Klim wrote that the *Krasin* icebreaker had saved all the crew members of Nobile's expedition and that the foreign journalists had not been allowed anywhere. He promised that he would soon be coming to Feodosia to bring Elkin his money and to collect Kitty from Nina. It seemed that it was a lot easier to buy long-distance train tickets up in Archangelsk.

"Thank you for helping me out in a tight spot," wrote Klim at the end of the letter. "I hope Kitty didn't make too much of a nuisance of herself."

7

Nina felt as if the wind had been taken out of her sails. She had been eagerly awaiting Klim's arrival, but now, she was dreading it. He was planning to take Kitty away and leave her alone.

Elkin saw that Nina was suffering and tried to raise her spirits.

"You and I must definitely go on a tour of the ancient world," he told her. "I'll show you such beautiful sights they'll take your breath away."

Nina agreed to go. She had to take her mind off her gloomy thoughts in some way.

They spent a day wandering through the rocky spurs of the Kara Dag and staring into the mouths of chasms.

"You and I are standing on an extinct volcano," Elkin told Nina. "Can you imagine what it would have been like here in prehistoric times? Boiling lava, and the earth shuddering with earthquakes…. But now, everything is quiet and peaceful."

They climbed a steep cliff and looked down on a breathtaking view.

"It's so beautiful!" Nina said, almost in tears with emotion. "When you can't tell where the sea joins the sky, it feels as if you're on a huge ship floating through the air."

Elkin took a deep breath. "Nina, I've been wanting to say something to you for a while now, and I think now is a good time—"

Nina looked at him in alarm. Had he made up his mind to propose to her? Please, anything but that!

"I have something to say to you too," she said quickly.

For some time, Nina had been aware that there was only one way to save Elkin from a humiliating refusal: to tell him beforehand all about her relations with Klim.

She told him everything: how she had met her exhusband, how they had traveled about Russia during the civil war, and how they had emigrated to China.

Elkin listened for a long time, his face frozen into an expressionless smile. Clearly, he understood that Nina was trying to save his dignity, and he was grateful to her for it.

They sat on the edge of the cliff, watching the clouds over the bay turning pink in the sunset.

"I think both of us appeared on this earth at the wrong place at the wrong time," said Elkin in a thick voice. "I should have been born a hundred years later, and you would have done well in the late eighteenth century. You could have been the ruler of some small, enlightened duchy."

"What would I have done there?" Nina asked him.

"Well, you would have had secret lovers, a beautiful, well-kept capital city, and loyal subjects. Artists would have painted you as a bright angel surrounded by cupids, and poets would have written ingenious madrigals about you. What else could you wish for?"

"And the story would have ended either with a foreign invasion or a palace coup," said Nina, getting to her feet. "It's the same thing in the twentieth century—I was faced with the choice of being sent into exile or put in jail. And there was nothing the greatest intellects could do to help me. It's just my fate, I suppose."

8

They came home after dark. Gloria came out to meet them with the kerosene lamp, her face like thunder.

"Where have you been all this time?" she shouted, taking Nina by the arm and dragging her into the house.

"What happened?" Nina asked in alarm.

Gloria opened the door to Nina's room and showed her Kitty, lying doubled up on the bed in agony. "See for yourself!"

Nina rushed to her daughter. "What's the matter with you?"

Kitty's face had swollen up until her eyes were no more than tiny slits, and a painful rash had broken out all over her cheeks.

"It hurts all over again," she sobbed, flinging her head back.

Nina looked at the child in bewilderment. She had been sure that when Kitty was with *her,* her daughter would not be taken sick.

"Mommy's here…. Mommy will make it better," Nina said, holding Kitty close to her chest. "We'll go to Feodosia and find you a doctor."

"What's the good of getting the girl to a doctor when her fool of a mother feeds her the devil only knows what?" retorted Gloria, pointing to an empty chocolate wrapper on the floor.

"Her father sent it," Nina said. "Kitty loves sweet things…"

Gloria stamped her foot angrily. "If you had any sense, you'd have realized what the problem was long ago!"

Then she swept out, leaving the paraffin lamp on the chest.

Nina sat for a long time on Kitty's bed, shaken to the core. So, this was the cause of Kitty's illness: Klim had been giving her chocolate. Nina had heard that some people had a serious reaction to it.

Soon, however, Nina's train of thought went off on a different tack. Now that she knew the secret of Kitty's illness, she could use it to get Klim away from Galina. Nina could tell him that the child became ill when she was with his new lover, and he would believe it.

Nina heard the door creak and saw Gloria standing on the threshold.

"Here, take this," the old woman said. "I've made a likeness of you." She held out a pot decorated with eyes with handles for ears and curls around the top.

Nina looked inside the pot. There was a tiny mousetrap with a piece of sheep's cheese.

"That's what's in your head at the moment," said Gloria. "If you don't like it, you can put something else inside."

It is true, Nina realized, horrified. All she thought about, regarding Klim, were lures and traps. *I wanted to deceive Klim and at Kitty's expense. What kind of prize I am being a schemer like that?*

Gloria was watching Nina's face with amusement. "Have fun tonight," she said, closing the door behind her.

Nina could not get to sleep. She was itching to do something, to make some momentous decision, and to act completely differently from now on.

She pondered for a long time what she might put into the pot as a symbol of her new life but had still not thought of anything when she began to doze off.

In the morning, she saw that Kitty had filled the pot with her spillikins.

23. THE SOVIET CASINO

1

Ever since Klim had left, Galina had felt weak and listless as if all the life had drained out of her. Something very wrong was going on: Klim had sent Kitty off God knows where with God knows who, and Galina had only received a single telegram from Arkhangelsk: "Away on leave. Will call on return."

She could forget her ideas of a dacha outside Moscow or a trip to the South. And it seemed she had sent her daughter to Leningrad for nothing. Still, Tata was not complaining: she had joined the Young Pioneers and was in seventh heaven.

While "Mr. Prince" was away on his work assignment, Kapitolina had started up an illegal trade in dairy produce, smuggling in butter, cream, and milk from the countryside. Her customers were all close to hand on the ground floor of the building. The League of Time had been evicted, and now, instead of penniless students, respectable members of the organization Proletkult had taken up residence there. Their job was to destroy the old aristocratic and bourgeois culture and create a new, proletarian one. This meant attending art exhibitions and theater performances to ensure that the work on offer reflected the class struggle, collectivism, and solidarity among the laboring masses. The Proletkult employees had plenty of money as the government regarded their work as highly important and funded it lavishly.

Kapitolina was weighing out bags of curd cheese on a spring scale.

"Galina, you'll never guess what!" she said. "I put a love charm on this man I know, a machine operator. I said a special prayer I learned from a wise woman—it's called a 'sticking charm.'"

It turned out that the machine operator had already taken Kapitolina to the cinema twice and once even treated her to sunflower seeds.

"You have to look at a photograph when you say the prayer," Kapitolina instructed Galina. "My Terentiy is on the Wall of Honor right next to the factory entrance, so I went up to it, waited till I heard the church bell chime, and said,

> Dead one, rise upon this hour.
> Give to me your cursed power.
> Let God's servant, Terentiy, be
> now and ever bound to me.
> Neither eat nor sleep shall he,
> Suffer him my face to see.
> This word is the lock that binds,
> And the devil has the key.
> Amen, amen, amen!"

"And you think it worked?" asked Galina doubtfully.

"I'm certain of it. There was another photograph on the Wall of Honor, an old fellow called Arkadiy Ivanovich, a foreman. And now he's started giving me the eye. So, it worked on him too."

When Kapitolina went out, Galina stood for a while in the corridor in a state of indecision. To practice witchcraft was a desperate step, she told herself. But the temptation was too great, and in the end, she went to look for a photograph of Klim.

Kitty had an album in which she kept postcards and photographs. Galina remembered that among them were one or two snapshots of Klim taken for official documents. On opening the album, however, she was thrown into confusion when she discovered a picture of a woman she recognized—the woman who had come to visit Klim and who had gotten a job at Elkin's store afterward.

Galina stared for some time at the stranger. Where had this photograph come from? Why had Kitty put it in her album?

Galina turned the picture over and was still more amazed to see the name "Nina Kupina" scored out and over it, in Klim's handwriting, the words "Mrs. Reich."

So, this was the woman he had tried to find out about. The same woman who had stayed a night with him and seemed to have completely shattered his peace of mind.

Who was she? There was something very familiar about that surname, Reich, but Galina could not remember where she had heard it before.

She took Nina's photograph as well as Klim's so that she could cast a spell on both of them. Having resolved on the sinful course of action, she felt she had nothing to lose.

2

Galina wrapped Nina's picture in paper, and the next time she went in to the Lubyanka, she asked Ibrahim to put it into the pocket of one of the dead prisoners. This was the best way to get rid of a rival—the main thing was for the dead man to take the picture to the grave with him, or if that wasn't possible, to the crematorium.

Ibrahim was only too happy to oblige. He often helped to load dead bodies onto the *meat wagon,* and it was easy for him to carry out Galina's request.

She thanked him and ran off to see Alov.

"Well, is your employer back yet?" he asked and then began to complain of how he and Dunya were fed up of being cooped up in a corner in the room belonging to Valakhov, the Drachenblut's assistant.

Back in the civil war days, Valakhov had managed to secure a large room for himself in the former lawyer's apartment. But he had too many square meters of living space, and during one of the many campaigns against bourgeois values, he had been forced to "consolidate."

He had registered Alov as a tenant, and then Alov had brought along his young wife. The old friends had fallen out so completely that they could no longer stand the sight of one another. Valakhov had no success with women, and it was galling for him to see Alov, old and ill as he was, enjoying a personal life while he did not.

Galina still felt awkward that she had taken the room on Bolshoi Kiselny Lane.

"Maybe you should ask Drachenblut to put you on the housing list?" she suggested, but Alov pulled a face.

"I've asked him a hundred times already."

He took his amber beads out of his sleeve and began to count them off one by one.

"Drachenblut has ordered us to prepare ourselves for a purge," Alov said. "After that, there is bound to be some free living space, so we have to redouble our efforts. Do you have any news?"

Galina shrugged. "I met Seibert the other day. He's just back from Archangelsk, and he asked me to go to the casino with him."

"What did you say?"

"I told him to get lost. I think he's angry with Klim about some article he wrote."

Alov tossed the beads up and caught them. "Pidge, I think you should agree to go out with him."

"Oh, for goodness' sake!" Galina said, taken aback. "It's not *me* he's after. He just has a score to settle with Klim."

Alov looked at her sternly. "Don't go putting on airs! Just do as you're told. Go with him to casino and listen to what he has to say. Maybe you'll find out something useful."

He took a voucher for the OGPU shop from his pocket and handed it to Galina. "Here—take this. You can get Tata some felt boots for the winter. And don't cry! We all have to serve the Revolution in whatever way we can."

On the way back out, Galina met Ibrahim again.

"I did what you asked," he reported. "They just took three of 'em down to the crematorium."

Galina thanked him and hurried off. So, now, the deed was done. All that remained was to read out the prayer for the "sticking charm." But where should she do it? Churches were closing down one after another, and if one stayed open, the priests did their best not to draw attention to it.

Galina skirted the Kremlin and set off along the bank of the Moscow River. The golden dome of the Cathedral of Christ the Savior gleamed far away in the setting sun.

The bells would almost certainly ring there, she thought. After all, it was such a huge cathedral that nobody would ever try to close it, surely.

Galina walked slowly toward the shining dome as if toward her own death. She was ready for hell and endless torment if only Klim would love her!

The chiming of a bell rang out over the river. This was it! Galina took out the piece of paper in which she had wrapped Klim's photograph, and a moment later, she froze in horror.

In her hand was the photograph of Nina Kupina. She had given Klim's photograph to Ibrahim by mistake.

3

Galina met Seibert under the gleaming clock in the square by the Triumphal Arch. It was drizzling, and Seibert held a large umbrella over her head.

"Don't be embarrassed—take my arm," he said. "My dear, your perfume is delightful."

Galina had never worn perfume in her life. The only smell that might have clung to her was that of the boiled cabbage she had made for dinner.

"Have you ever been to a casino?" asked Seibert. "You haven't? Oh, dear me, this won't do! You must try everything life has to offer you while you still can. Especially as gambling houses are being closed down one after the other. A relic of bourgeois society, don't you know!"

They entered an unmarked building, and its once fine lobby was now dilapidated and smelled musty. A worn staircase led up to the floor above, and a dim chandelier with broken strings of crystals hung from the ceiling.

"Comrades, where do you think you're going in your galoshes?" barked the gray-whiskered doorman. "Off the carpet please!"

Seibert put on a puzzled expression and began to say something in German.

"Foreigners…" the doorman muttered with disgust but made no further comment.

The big hall on the floor above was hung with mirrors and political posters. Men in rumpled double-breasted suits and fashionable pointed brogues crowded around the gaming tables.

"Who are they all?" asked Galina in a whisper. "Are they Nepmen?"

Seibert shook his head. "They're mainly foreigners, cashiers on the fiddle, and romantics who believe that one day, they'll get lucky."

There were few women among the clientele, and to Galina, they looked as if they had not come to play but to hunt for customers for the night.

Goodness, how horrible! she thought. The only sight that cheered her up was a group of old women in threadbare silk dresses and old-fashioned hats. They sat at a separate table, deeply engrossed in playing poker, or rather, in playing at "the good old days." Seibert explained that the old ladies used the place as a club and did not bring in any money, but the management tolerated them because they had become something of a local attraction.

As she walked between the tables, Galina noticed that all the gamblers were using cards produced by the League of Militant Atheists: all the kings were priests and wonder-workers, the queens were treacherous looking nuns, and the knaves were deacons with drunken leers.

Seibert took Galina to a roulette table surrounded by a crowd of young men, their faces flushed with drink and excitement.

"Hey there, you great white capitalist shark!" they called out when they saw Seibert. "You've brought along another lady friend, have you?"

"And you still haven't been paid, I see?" answered Seibert.

He explained to Galina that the young men worked in a corporation called Radio Broadcast. Once, they had produced wonderful lectures on subjects like "When Will Life on Earth Come to an End?" and "Hypnosis in the World of Crime." Unfortunately, their work had become so popular that the government had sequestered their business. Now, they no longer produced educational programs but propaganda.

Galina remembered what Klim had told her about theater companies, film studios, and artists' unions. It was the same thing everywhere: bureaucrats were becoming involved in the work of creative professionals, believing that they knew better how things should be done. Artists and performers were forced to follow the new rules whether they liked it or not, but they did so without enthusiasm. After the initial creative explosion of early Soviet culture, art was deteriorating into nothing better than hack work.

The young men pooled their money to buy a stack of gambling chips.

"That's how they earn their supper," said Seibert. "If they win, they eat, but if they don't, they have to tighten their belts."

"Comrades, place your bets!" announced the croupier.

Seibert put a pile of gambling chips into Galina's hand. "You ought to be in for some beginners' luck. Come on. Put it on whatever number you like."

Hesitantly, Galina placed a chip on square number eight.

"*Merci*—no more bets," announced the croupier.

Galina had always thought of herself as unlucky, and she was proved correct now—she did not win so much as a kopeck in half an hour. All she wanted was to go home, but Seibert, however, clearly had plans for a romantic evening.

"Let's go wild and have some drink," he told her.

What a vile man you are! she thought. *After all, Klim is your friend, and you know that there's something between us. Why do you have to stoop to such petty acts of treachery?*

Still, she followed Seibert into the bar room. There, behind an enormous carved counter, was a bored waitress in a starched apron and a lace headpiece pinned to her hair. Behind her stood an array of dusty bottles, and in front of her on the bar, cheese, salami, and cakes languished untouched. Everything, including the soda water, was on sale at extortionate prices.

"A table please, my dear," Seibert told the waitress.

Stern male faces stared down at Galina from all the political posters on the walls.

Be Ready to Serve Your Country!
We Shall Dedicate Ourselves to Socialism!

It seemed to Galina that everybody was demanding something from her.

Seibert poured out two glasses of vodka. "Today, we'll drink to you and to you alone!" he announced and chinked glasses with a resounding chime.

Galina was only too happy to have a drink.

"I've had my eye on you for some time," said Seibert with a sigh. "And I have to say, I feel terribly sorry for you. You're prepared to sacrifice everything for Klim's sake. You'll give him your youth, your time, and your hopes, and what are you hoping to get from him in return?"

"I don't need anything," replied Galina quietly.

"Oh, that's not true! You want to *change* your boss. I can tell that. But I'll tell you something else: you won't do it because you don't know who you're dealing with."

Galina looked up at him with a sullen gaze. "What do you mean?"

But before Seibert had managed to reply, the young men from Radio Broadcast, flushed with success, came piling into the bar.

"Waitress!" they shouted, excitedly. "Six ham sandwiches—and cut them thick!"

"And two bottles of port!"

"And some sardines! And cheese! Let's have some for Seibert and his lady friend too! Let's push the boat out!"

The young men had clearly had a lucky streak at the tables.

At that moment, a woman came running into the bar, her red headscarf knocked awry.

"We've just had a telegram!" she said, panting. "The *Krasin* icebreaker has been damaged and is going to be repaired in Norway. They've sent two steamers out from Murmansk to come to its aid. We need to prepare a special edition!"

The young men immediately forgot their sardines.

"Marusya, bring the food, could you?" shouted one of them as they dashed for the door.

Seibert gazed after them, eyes wide. "Please, Galina, for God's sake, come with me to the Central Telegraph Office!" he said hoarsely. "I have to ring Murmansk and find out what's going on with the *Krasin*."

"Go yourself," muttered Galina. "You can make a call. Why do you need me?"

"But I have a German accent! As soon as the telegraph operator realizes I'm a foreigner, she'll ask if I have permission. You can say you're ringing about something personal."

Galina rose to her feet and found that she could barely stand upright. The drink had already gone to her head.

"I really ought to go home—" she began.

"I'll pay you!" cried Seibert. "How much do you want? Five rubles? Ten?"

It was pathetic to look at him, his forehead puckered and his lower lip trembling.

Galina gave a dismissive wave of her hand. "All right, damn you. I'll come with you."

4

Despite the late hour, the Central Telegraph Office was full of people. Galina found a number for the port of Murmansk in the directory and booked a long distance call.

Seibert, frustrated by the wait, kept looking at his watch.

"Radio Broadcast has probably already produced its special edition," he said. "Never mind. It's too late now, and nobody will listen to it anyway. We still have time to find out the details and send a wire to my editors."

At last, they were called to the telephone booth. "Murmansk on the line for you!"

It was so cramped inside the cabin that Galina and Seibert barely managed to squeeze in together.

"Well, go on then!" begged Seibert.

Galina put the cold receiver to her ear. "Hello. Is that Murmansk port?"

A faint voice could just be heard through the crackle and hiss on the line. "Yes! This is the duty operator. Who's calling?"

"We're calling from Moscow," Galina said, "from the Central Telegraph Office. I am the secretary of Comrade Seibert. There are two ships—"

"Could you say that again, please? I can't hear you!"

"From the Moscow Central Telegraph Office!" Galina shouted. "I'm the secretary! Have you sent two ships to Norway?"

"What?"

The duty operator was astounded when at last he grasped that the call was from Moscow. He clearly had no idea that it was possible to make a telephone call between cities.

With great difficulty, Galina managed to explain that she wanted to find out the details about the damage to the *Krasin* icebreaker.

"Well, what did he say?" prompted Seibert as soon as she hung up.

"He told me to call later. He'll find the commandant and get him to speak to us."

It was after midnight, and Galina wished she had never agreed to help Seibert. Now, he was looking into her eyes, for all the world like a wistful puppy.

"Galina, my dear, couldn't you stay here a little longer? Please?"

They sat in the waiting room for another hour before they were called into the booth again.

"So, what's going on?" Seibert kept asking impatiently.

Galina held the receiver to her ear with her shoulder and took a notebook and pencil from Seibert.

"Hello, Moscow!" shouted the distant voice. "Murmansk has received your message. All hands are on full alert!"

Seibert could tell from Galina's horrified face that something quite unexpected had happened. She threw down the receiver and left the booth without a word.

"Wait!" wailed Seibert. "What did he say?"

But Galina was not listening; she was already heading for the door.

It was dead of night, and the streets were deserted with only the odd horse-driven cab rattling past once in a while.

Seibert clutched at Galina's sleeve. "Could you please just tell me what happened?"

"It was a bad line," she told him. "They misheard me in Murmansk. They thought I had told them that ships were on their way from Norway. They thought the call from Moscow was to warn them of an attack. The whole town is on alert."

Seibert's jaw dropped. "Still," he began slowly, "I think we might be all right. After all, they probably didn't hear my name."

"Your name is on the check," said Galina. "You paid for the telephone call."

"But they heard a woman's voice!"

Seibert took a large handkerchief from his pocket, took off his hat, and mopped his bald head.

"Galina…"

"What?"

"Let's go back to my place. Lieschen isn't at home. She's gone to see her parents, and we can—"

Galina gave a stiff little laugh. "You don't even care to find out whether I like you or whether I have other plans."

Seibert hesitated a moment. "Nobody ever asked you about that sort of thing. Even your oh-so-wonderful Klim Rogov."

"Unlike some, he's not a womanizer or a liar," retorted Galina.

"He lies to you far more than I do," said Seibert. "If you actually listened and thought carefully about what he says, you'd realize that he's no American and has never been to New York in his life."

"Where did you get that idea?"

"Just try asking him what side of the road they drive on in the States—he'll tell you they drive on the left. He calls the New York subway "the underground" like in London, and he can't name two stations if you ask him."

"That doesn't mean a thing!"

"Is that so? Then ask him what were the most popular songs when he lived over there or who were the most famous actresses in the city or who stood for election as governor or president. Go and ask him about all the little things that a person would only know if he'd actually *lived* in New York. Ask him what Ellis Island is! He has no idea that it's a gateway for immigrants coming to New York."

"Do you think he has a fake passport?" Galina asked, trembling inside.

"Of course he does."

"Go to hell!" Galina shouted and went running off.

Her head was spinning. The curse she had put on Klim had already started to take effect.

Could he be a spy? But who was he working for? What was he trying to find out? And why had he made such a poor job of disguising his identity?

Galina collapsed feebly onto some steps and hid her face in her hands. *I don't care why you came to the Soviet Union,* she thought. *I still love you.*

That dirty scoundrel, Seibert! He hadn't been trying to lure Galina away from Klim; instead, he had hoped that she would report what he said to her boss at the OGPU. Klim was beginning to be seen as the top foreign expert on Soviet Russia, and Seibert wanted to get him out of the way.

Galina clenched her fists. "He'll be sorry he ever got me involved in his little schemes!" she said to herself.

In the morning, she came in to the Lubyanka and wrote a report in which she stated that Seibert had put together a network of agents that included the employees of the Radio Broadcast company. They had arranged an act of military sabotage at Murmansk with the aim of creating instability and wasting government resources.

Alov was over the moon and told Galina that she could expect a bonus.

5

Galina was doing the washing. It was high time she boiled the bed linen, which was already gray. The tenants used a primus stove for cooking, but to heat up water in the tub that was big enough to hold sheets, she had to use the range, which used up a stack of coal at a time.

The frugal Mitrofanych had asked to heat up a small panful of soup on the range and offered Galina the use of his washing line in the bathroom in return—as it was his day to dry laundry there.

He took out a loaf wrapped in a cloth and carefully cut off two pieces. Galina thought he was going to treat her to a slice, but after thinking a while, he sighed deeply and put both pieces in his pocket.

"Who'd have thought we'd live to see times like these," he said ruefully. "There was a riot at the labor exchange today—and all because of the Jews."

He began to sing a popular song, which Galina had heard several times before from beggars on the street:

The USSR has got it bad—
There's no flour for our bread,
And there a no yid without a job,
No job without a yid.

"What have the Jews got to do with it?" snapped Galina, annoyed. "The police are rounding up seasonal workers and sending them out of Moscow by the trainload. That's why they're rioting."

"A likely story!" Mitrofanych snorted. "And who put them up to it? I'd like to know. A true Russian never riots—not for anything."

He tested the soup and took his pan from the range.

"Make sure you don't leave any hairs in the tub. Last time, your Tata didn't clear up after herself. It's irresponsible—that's what it is."

Galina looked him up and down gloomily.

I wish I was at <u>home</u> with Klim, she thought for the hundredth time.

But Klim had gone somewhere far away, and without him, the apartment in Chistye Prudy felt like an abandoned nest.

The more Galina thought about what Seibert had told her, the more convinced she became that he was telling the truth. Klim definitely had some secret life of his own. It was the only explanation for his sudden disappearances, for all the things he left unsaid, and for the strange connection with Mrs. Reich.

Galina felt dizzy just thinking about it. She went over everything she knew about Klim. Most of all, she was bothered by what he had once said about his "native town of Nizhny Novgorod." There was something odd there!

Galina rinsed out the sheets, hung up the washing, and, quite worn out, went to her room.

Mitrofanych's door was open. He had already finished his soup and was now deeply engrossed in the paper.

"This is quite a puzzle I've got here," he said when he saw Galina. "'Using just four cuts of the scissors, divide the picture into eight pieces, which, when put together, will make up a picture of the greatest enemy of the working people.' How should I cut it, I wonder."

"Do you have a cigarette?" asked Galina plaintively.

Mitrofanych took out a packet of Kazbek cigarettes and, choosing the most crumpled, held it out to Galina.

"I thought you'd given up smoking," he said.

"I wish I could."

Galina went out onto the landing and stood for some time, drawing in the pungent smoke. All her resolutions were pointless now.

Mitrofanych came out on the landing too.

"Are you lonely?" he asked. "If you like, you can come in to my room, and we can do puzzles together. I was really stumped by one the other day. You had to put the ink blots together to make the silhouette of a Red Army soldier with a gun. But no matter what I did, I got either a toad or a teapot."

Galina looked at his worn slippers, moth-eaten jacket, and pants, which had gone baggy at the knees.

"Do you still work in the archive office?" she asked. "Would it be possible for you to arrange a search for me? I need to find something in the Nizhny Novgorod archive."

Mitrofanych puffed out his chest. "What exactly do you need?"

"I need information about a certain Klim Rogov. His birthday is July 4, 1889. If you can find out anything about him, I'll give you a voucher for felt boots."

Mitrofanych's face brightened at the suggestion. "That's very kind of you. My shoes are falling to pieces. Maybe I can do something else for you?"

Galina thought for a moment. "Yes, you could ask them to look for any mention of Rogov in the St. George Church archive in Nizhny Novgorod."

Back in her room, Galina collapsed onto her bed. She did not know what was worse: to live in ignorance or to find out the truth.

"Whatever will be, will be," she told herself.

She did not dare say a prayer. After her witchcraft, false accusations, and treachery, she felt that any prayers she said would only be heard by the devil himself.

24. HOLIDAY IN CRIMEA

1

After the dark and rainy north, Crimean sun seemed dazzling to Klim. Jumping down from the footboard of the railroad car, he caught sight of Nina and Kitty straight away. They were hurrying to meet him, both in identical flowered muslin dresses and white crocheted berets.

"Daddy's here!" squealed Kitty in delight.

He lifted her up and kissed her. "Well, how are you enjoying yourselves here?"

Kitty immediately began to tell him about how she and Nina had been to the cinema to see a film called *Tip-Top in Moscow*, which featured a little cartoon black boy against a real city backdrop.

Klim peered up at Nina. She was standing beside Kitty, absently fiddling with a small mother-of-pearl giraffe on a string around her neck.

"A present from Elkin?" Klim asked.

Nina blushed and tuck the pendant into her dress. "Well, it's just—"

She and Klim did not even say hello to each other.

"All right. Let's go and find the bus." Klim picked up his suitcases. "Is Kitty better now?"

Nina nodded. "I found out what the problem was. She mustn't eat chocolate."

As they walked to the bus stop, Nina told him how she had made her discovery. Klim tried to think of something to say without success.

Nina was looking at him expectantly.

"Well done," he said at last and immediately felt annoyed at himself. He sounded exactly as if he were thanking Galina for bringing him a press report.

On the way to Feodosia, Klim had decided that he would try to act naturally. The problem was that what felt most natural to him was to shun Nina, and she sensed it.

When they took their seats in the bus—opposite one another, not side by side—Nina put her feet on Klim's suitcase while he moved his knees to one side to avoid accidentally brushing her legs. Nina gave a wry smile as if to say *she* certainly had no desire to touch him.

The bus set off. The wind from the open windows ruffled Nina's hair and made her skirt billow up like a sail. Klim stared around him, careful to look anywhere except in Nina's direction.

Across the aisle, an old man was scolding his wife affectionately, telling her that on no account was she to lift buckets of water because it would hurt her back.

A little fair-haired boy was pestering his mother: "Is Lidia here already? Is she expecting us?"

You wait, thought Klim. *You'll get involved with some Lidia or other, and the next thing, you'll be cursing everything under the sun.*

"Are you playing that game where nobody's allowed to say anything?" piped up Kitty. "I want to play too! One, two, three—and the first to speak is a big fat flea!"

She puffed up her cheeks and covered her mouth with her hands. Klim was very glad of the excuse to stay silent.

The bus bounced over a pothole, and Klim was thrown toward Nina. He barely managed to stay in his seat by grabbing the handrail.

"Damn!" he swore.

"You lost!" crowed Kitty. "You're a big fat flea! Mommy, now he has to do everything we tell him!"

2

When they got to Gloria's House, Nina took Klim to meet the hostess.

Gloria was sitting in the small, smoky kitchen with its whitewashed stove and huge array of shelves holding various pots and dishes. The last rays of the setting sun glowed on the glass jars of jams and preserves, and the smell of toasted sunflower seeds hung in the air.

When she saw Klim, the old woman got to her feet and put her hands on her hips. "What does he want? I don't have any rooms left to rent."

"He can stay in my room—" began Nina, but to her surprise, Gloria became angry.

"Where's he going to sleep, I'd like to ask. You've divorced him—let that be an end to it!"

Klim looked at Nina, confused. Evidently, he was not welcome here.

The cockatoo, which was perched on the window sill, suddenly shrieked in a terrible voice: "Take aim, squadron—and fire! Finish him off, I tell you!"

Nina started to argue with Gloria, explaining that she had already warned her that her husband would be arriving.

Klim smiled to himself. *How about that?* he thought. *I've been promoted to the rank of husband again.*

"It's all right," he said. "I'll go."

"Stop!" cried Nina. "Wait outside. I'll sort everything out."

On the porch, Klim ran into Elkin.

"So, you've arrived, have you?" Elkin muttered grimly.

Klim remembered the mother-of-pearl pendant around Nina's neck. He was starting to realize why he had been given such a cool welcome. Aunt Gloria and her nephew were clearly of one mind.

"Let me give you the money for your car," said Klim.

He handed Elkin a package of ten-ruble notes. Elkin stuffed them into his pockets without bothering to count them.

"So, do you plan to drive Mashka yourself?" he asked, after a pause. "Or will you hire a chauffeur?"

"When I get back, I'll sign up for driving lessons at the Red Army Club," said Klim.

"And when will that be?"

They heard footsteps behind them, and Gloria and Nina came out onto the porch.

"It's too late tonight to do anything," muttered the old woman with a hostile glance at Klim. "You can sleep on the terrace if you want. Tomorrow, go to see Ainur—he's renting some rooms too. He's not here though. He's at Koroneli—on the other side of Feodosia."

Clearly, she wanted to send Klim as far away as possible.

3

Nina had not expected her hostess to put such obstacles in their path.

"Why are you throwing Klim out?" she asked her. "You said you would help me."

"And that's exactly what I *am* doing!" snapped Gloria. "You had a trap somewhere in your past, and you need to rid yourself of it. Your future happiness is walking about under your nose!"

"Elkin, you mean?" asked Nina tentatively.

"Clever girl! At last, you've worked it out for yourself."

The old woman's "fortune-telling" had had nothing to do with Klim after all. Nina had simply read her own story into it.

Klim left his cases in Nina's room and went straight off somewhere with Kitty. Nina went out to look for the two of them on all the nearby beaches but was unable to find them.

When she got back, Elkin announced that it was his birthday. All the holidaymakers were preparing for the celebration with great excitement. Gloria took out some old kerosene lamps from the scullery, and Alyosha and Ira hung them on the apricot trees. The table was laid with bunches of black grapes with a silvery bloom, white cheese made of sheep's milk, and golden smoked mullet. The women had baked unleavened bread, which filled the air with a delicious aroma.

Musicians had come in from the village together with a whole crowd of Elkin's friends and acquaintances. One guest rolled up a bottle of new wine; there were not enough glasses to go around, and people took it in turns to drink from the battered enamel mugs.

Nina kept glancing anxiously toward the path down to the sea. Where on earth had Klim got too? It was already dark, and he did not know the way back. What if he got lost?

At last, she heard the dogs barking, and Kitty's voice rang out, "We're back!"

Gloria pulled Nina's sleeve. "Don't be a fool!" she warned.

But Nina had no chance to "be a fool." Klim took no notice of her whatsoever. He was asked to dance by a young medical student, Oksana, who had recently arrived in Koktebel. Much to Nina's annoyance, he seemed happy to accept, and the two of them whirled about so gracefully to the music of the village band that all the guests applauded.

Elkin sat down on the bench next to Nina, looking flushed and happy.

"Recently, we have witnessed a rise in the number of evenings at which young people do nothing but dance," he said in imitation of a Party member giving a speech. "What benefit is to be had from such events? They achieve nothing except the corruption of the working element! In order to root out this perversion from our society, we must perform dances that reflect the struggle of the working class."

He was trying to make Nina laugh, but she did not even crack a smile. Hot tears stung her eyes. To stop herself from crying, she gazed at the moon, which hung in the sky over the mountains. Nothing was as before: even the moon seemed too small and pale for Nina.

"Shall I bring you out some baked tomatoes?" Elkin suggested.

Nina nodded, and he ran off to the kitchen.

"Do you have the key to the room?" asked Klim, walking past. "Kitty's tired. I'll go and put her to bed."

Nina got to her feet. "You still haven't told me anything. Are you leaving tomorrow?"

He raised an eyebrow quizzically. "Are you suggesting I stay to spite our hostess?"

Nina's heart sank. She had been so hopeful that her new honesty and openness would help her to rebuild her relations with Klim, but he had failed to notice any change in her at all.

4

Kitty was not in the least bit tired and had no desire to go to bed while everyone around was still dancing and laughing. Klim had taken her up to her room because he himself wanted to get away from Nina.

He was in a very morose frame of mind. What should he do? Take Kitty and set off to another village? That was exactly what he had been dreaming of—spending a couple of weeks with his daughter at the seaside and forgetting all his worries for a fortnight or so. But of course, Nina will throw a spanner in the works. He could sense that she was not going to leave him and Kitty alone.

Klim sat down on the bed beside Kitty and listened for some time to the faint sound of laughter and music from the garden.

Perhaps he should throw caution to the wind and indulge in a mad holiday romance? During the bus journey, he had taken care to avert his gaze from Nina. Still, he had notice the line in the collar of her dress where the sun-tanned flesh on public display gave way to a tantalizing glimpse of creamy golden skin—the threshold of the private chamber into which only the chosen one was admitted. Klim was fairly sure that he could count on gaining permission.

Kitty showed no signs of settling down. "There's a girl staying downstairs, and she has a gas mask. She says she can put it on in five seconds. I want one too."

"We'll get you one when we get back to Moscow," Klim said.

"Can you get gas masks for horses?"

"I expect so. Go to sleep now."

"What about giraffes? Elkin made me a giraffe rocking horse. I need to get a gas mask for it too."

Elkin seems to have been getting all sorts of ideas, Klim thought. *Well, I suppose he can dream.*

Klim was already picturing the scenario to himself—the seduction of Mrs. Reich. It would be like the classic plot of a Russian novel. A high society lady dreams of leaving her rich husband, and while touring from city to city in the South, she meets an old acquaintance with whom she has previously been in love. They both know the affair can't last—the holidays will end, and they will go back to their own social circles. But why should they deny themselves the pleasure when fortune is offering them this wonderful opportunity never to be repeated?

Gradually, the voices outside began to die down. The locals were starting to leave for their village and the guests to go off to their bedrooms.

At last, Kitty was asleep. Klim tucked the blanket around her and went out into the corridor. He wandered around the house for some time before he found Nina out on the terrace. She was lying in a hammock between two pillars, rocking herself gently with one foot.

"You can go to your room now," Klim told her.

Nina sat up hurriedly and began to pull out the pins that had worked themselves loose from her hair.

"Yes, just a minute…" she began but then patted the hammock beside her. "Come and sit. We need to talk."

"What about?"

"About us."

The hammock stretched under Klim's weight, forcing Nina closer to him.

This is it, he thought. This was what he would travel to the ends of the earth to feel—the touch of her thigh, the warmth of her body, which he could feel through two layers of clothes.

"Will you let me explain everything to you?" asked Nina.

Klim put his arms around her and pressed his lips to hers. "Tell me later."

Nina wound her arms around Klim's neck, and the giraffe pendant dug painfully into his chest.

"Take this thing off," he said.

Nina pulled the pendant off over her head and threw it to the floor without a glance.

In his mind, Klim was already gathering her skirt in his hands, kissing her voluptuous breasts, gripping her tightly by her slender wrist to hold her completely in his power, to give her no chance to escape.

He pushed her back onto the hammock, which swayed precariously under them.

"We'll fall out of here in a minute," Nina laughed.

Klim bent over her. "If we do, it would be a wonderful illustration of the collapse of contemporary morals."

Suddenly, a ray of light swept over them, and the cockatoo came fluttering overhead.

"Court martial!" it shrieked, landing on the terrace railing.

Klim raised his head to see Gloria in the doorway, a lantern in her hand. Surrounded by wreaths of pipe smoke, she seemed to be emerging from a cloud.

"Why have you left your daughter alone?" Gloria scolded Nina. "Go back to your room this minute!"

Shamefaced, Nina stood up and began to fasten the buttons of her dress. There was a crunching noise under her foot. She looked down and saw that she had stood on the Elkin's giraffe figurine.

Gloria shuffled up to Klim and handed him a telegram envelope.

"Here," she said. "This came yesterday. I forgot to give it to you."

It was a message from Seibert:

Come Moscow immediately stop matter of life and death stop ticket reserved

Nina looked at Klim in alarm.

"What is it?" she asked.

He was silent for a minute, gathering his thoughts.

"Take no prisoners!" the squawk of the cockatoo came out of the dark.

"A friend of mine is in trouble," said Klim. "He needs help, so Kitty and I will have to go back to Moscow tomorrow evening."

5

BOOK OF THE DEAD

Galina once told me I was the only gentleman of her acquaintance. I fear she was badly mistaken.

A true gentleman should be gallant and chivalrous and never abandon a damsel in distress, especially if that distress takes the form of a desperate desire to kiss him.

When I explained to Nina that I had to return to Moscow out of duty to a friend, she tried to talk me out of it. "Stay here! After all, you love me, don't you?"

Then, with unforgivable rudeness, I announced that I love *my* wife—that is the old Nina. Now, she is another man's spouse. It seems she sees marriage rather like a joint stock company: if her husband doesn't put in his share in time, she begins to shift her assets and make investments elsewhere. Alas, that isn't what I want at all.

This made Nina angry.

"You was the one who kissed me first!" she reminded me.

A gentleman in my place would have said something about her charms or about the power of Cupid's arrow or something else appropriate, but instead, I did something outrageous. I told her that I had had a choice: either to hear details of all her infidelities or to pay Oscar back in kind and to cuckold him just as he had cuckolded me. The second course seemed to me the more interesting one.

"But I told you," Nina cried, "I'm not going back to Reich!"

"Well, that's a shame," I said. "Of course, you could stay with Elkin and be the wife of a country blacksmith for a while, but I imagine that wouldn't be a very good deal for you."

Then all hell broke loose. Nina is not only passionate in matters of love; she has a fearsome temper too. She poured such a torrent of abuse at me that I'm afraid I'll never manage to clear my name.

I was listening respectfully to all this when she suddenly stopped mid-flow and announced that in any case, I would not escape her. She would get ahold of a ticket and come back to Moscow after me, sinner that I am.

Now, I am full of curiosity about what she is planning to do. After all, I haven't had the holiday I was hoping for, so I'll have to find my amusement in some other way.

I think I have hit on the right way to handle my relations with Nina. We need less drama, more pragmatism, and a sensible approach to our affairs. We should behave like relatives with shared family concerns. After all, I did want Nina to take a role in bringing up Kitty. If she can get herself settled in Moscow, then we can be on friendly terms.

I am very grateful to Seibert for whisking me away from Koktebel in the nick of time. I came very close to crossing a line I must never cross.

25. THE HOUSING PROBLEM

1

Alov was woken by the rattle of the lid on the coffee pot.

"Dunya, my dear," he heard Valakhov saying on the other side of the dresser, "do you know why it is that only twenty-five percent of the overall membership of the Young Communist League are women? It's because they have to stop taking part in public life after they're married. Look at you, for instance. What are you doing now? Making breakfast for your husband. But you could be using that time to go to a party meeting."

Dunya said nothing. The only sound that came from behind the dresser was the measured tapping of her knife against the breadboard as she cut something.

"Everyday domestic chores will turn even the most principled women into empty-headed housewives," Valakhov continued. "With your talent, you should be acting in movies, and you're wasting the best years making sandwiches and washing dishes."

Alov sat up in bed. *I'll smash his face one of these days, I swear!* he thought for the thousandth time. But he knew it was impossible. Valakhov was the star of the OGPU wrestling team while Alov was unable to manage even a single pull-up on the crossbar.

"Get some portraits done by a photographer and give them to me," Valakhov said eagerly. "One of my friends is a director, and as it happens, he's looking for a girl just like you."

"Don't listen to him!" Alov barked, poking his head around the side of the dresser. "It's all lies!"

Dunya was bustling about in their "kitchen," a small area next to the window sill. On the sill stood two primus stoves and a breadboard with shelves underneath for storing food. The top shelf was for Dunya and Alov, and the bottom shelf for Valakhov.

Dunya thrust a sandwich and an enamel mug of ersatz coffee under her husband's nose. "Here's your breakfast."

Valakhov was lying on the sofa, his muscular white arms flung behind his head. Alov stared at Valakhov's faded underpants with disgust. What kind of man walked about in his underwear in front of another man's wife?

"Good morning to you!" Valakhov waved cheerily to him. "What's the health forecast today then? You were coughing so loudly last night you just about deafened me. Seriously, it was louder than artillery training."

"Knock it off," spat Alov, seething with impotent rage.

Dunya fastened a white headscarf around her head, planted a kiss on Alov's unshaven cheek, and ran off.

Every day, she went out to a theatrical agency looking for work. Sometimes, she would land a role and bring back a fee of five rubles. For children's matinees, she would get three rubles, and for pageants, no more than one and a half.

Valakhov knew that Dunya would do anything for a genuine role and exploited the fact shamelessly. And if Alov made any objection, he would just mock him.

"Dunya, my dear, it looks as if your husband wants to keep you locked away between these four walls—or should I say two walls?"

The dresser between the Alovs' corner and the rest of the room did not count as a genuine wall.

Alov dreamed of one thing above all else—a room of his own. One day, he had been present during the interrogation of a biology professor who had come out with a comment that had left a deep impression on Alov. The professor had argued that the surest way to make people unhappy was to cramp them together and leave them no way out.

"You've packed us into crowded trams and communal apartments," the professor had harangued his interrogators. "And you know what will happen now, don't you? All-out war when neighbor fights against neighbor for living space—the same way as animals fight for their territory."

He's right. That's exactly how it is, Alov had thought. Though it had not stopped him leafing through the professor's personal file, which contained a note of his address. Alov had known that this counter-revolutionary would be sent off to the camps and was wondering who would get their hands on the professor's accommodation.

Alov often dreamed that he and Dunya had got a permit for a room of their own, and he told her of these dreams in which they would pack their belongings into pillowcases, say goodbye to Valakhov, and set off by tram to their new house.

He imagined having a place of his own with tall windows, a stove, and an extra big windowsill. And underneath it, *three* shelves, every one of them belonging to the Alovs.

Listening to him, Dunya always laughed. "Stop your nonsense! It'll never happen."

But Alov's idea to send Galina with Seibert had borne fruit: she had got hold of information that might win him not only a room but also a promotion. Alov was sure his chief would snap up the story and make something big of it.

Once, when they had been drinking, Drachenblut had told Alov about Stalin whom he frequently visited in the Kremlin.

Stalin had never been sociable, but he had now become a complete hermit, surrounded by "courtiers" who brought him information about ill-wishers both within and without his circle. He was obsessed with coded messages and secret files and demanded absolute vigilance from his subordinates.

The craze for exposing enemies had spread like wildfire through the whole of Soviet society. For anyone wishing to gain promotion at work, it was essential to display vigilance. This was what lay behind the mass purges and political repressions—bureaucrats were doing their best to advance through the ranks while at the same time seizing the chance to remove competitors.

As might be expected, these workplace battles were most brutal inside the OGPU. The situation was exacerbated by the fact that the chairman of the organization, Menzhinsky, was constantly ill, and his two deputies, Drachenblut and Yagoda, were engaged in a deadly struggle for the place of his successor.

Yagoda had staked his efforts on unmasking conspiracies within the USSR—he had personally masterminded the Shakhty Trial. Drachenblut, on the other hand, was trying to curry favor through operations abroad, which allowed him to procure not only valuable information but also foreign currency. But he was also obliged to expose opponents to the regime—those who did not report on counter-revolutionary plots could be accused either of trying to cover up for the enemies of the state or simply failing to carry out their work properly.

Alov thought he held a trump card in his hands. But when, on the previous day, he had presented his supervisor with Galina's denunciation (altered slightly so that it would read more convincingly), Drachenblut merely gave it a cursory glance and told Alov to come in again the following day.

Though surprised, Alov decided to think nothing of it. Drachenblut was flesh and blood after all, and he too needed to rest from his duties occasionally.

As for the question of whether Seibert was actually guilty of conspiracy, this did not bother Alov in the slightest. Guilt was determined not by the actions of a given "customer" but by the potential threat he represented. If foreign journalists were given free rein, they would not hesitate to harm the USSR in word and deed. There was no sense in going too soft on them.

2

Drachenblut took off his glasses and looked sharply at Alov.

"You claim that Seibert set up an espionage ring to intercept radio communications?" he asked.

Alov nodded readily. "That's right."

"Nonsense. Any radio enthusiast can 'intercept' messages in just the way you suggest. What else do we have?"

Drachenblut bent his head over the paper, found the place he was looking for, and began to read aloud:

"In order to discredit the USSR, Seibert arranged the dispatch of warships from Murmansk, charging them with the mission of destroying the icebreaker *Krasin* and the Soviet Arctic heroes on board as well as the Italian airmen."

Alov felt an unpleasant gnawing sensation in his chest. Drachenblut did not seem very happy with the report at all. But why not? He had instructed all his subordinates to sniff out some serious case for him in whatever way they could.

"We have been in contact with Murmansk," Alov said hoarsely. "The duty officer received a telegram from

Moscow and thought it came from the Central Committee rather than the Central Telegraph Office. He reported to his superiors, and the port was put on a state of alert—"

"There are no warships in Murmansk," said Drachenblut in an expressionless voice. "During the war, it was used for delivering supplies from the Allies, but now, it is a small commercial port. Who could even be put on a state of alert in Murmansk? The local fishermen?"

Alov began to cough as he always did when agitated. His lungs almost burst with the effort.

Drachenblut poured him some water from a decanter on his desk.

"I understand perfectly what you mean," said Alov as soon as he got his breath back. "But if we don't act on this information, there could be serious consequences for us."

"What consequences?" Drachenblut demanded. "Don't take me for a fool."

"The duty officer from Murmansk will be frightened out of his wits by now. Like as not, he'll go to the local OGPU office to make a confession of guilt. Then they'll question him about the telephone conversations, there will be an investigation, and the case will be sent straight to the top—to Yagoda. When he finds out that Seibert was under our jurisdiction, he will almost certainly ask, 'Why did Comrade Drachenblut not show sufficient vigilance?'"

"Do you think anyone will listen to him?" Drachenblut asked, raising his voice. "Yagoda's a liar! He writes on all his forms that he joined the Bolsheviks in 1907. It's not true! He's nothing more than a common criminal! He only joined us to rob and kill with impunity!"

Alov's shot had hit home. Drachenblut, an idealist prepared to sacrifice his own and everybody else's life for the world revolution, now felt that the old Bolshevik guard was giving way to pressure from cynical careerists like Yagoda.

"We can't arrest Seibert," said Drachenblut with a frown. "He's almost a national hero in Germany, and we have to organize timber shipments to the West."

Alov was still hoping to profit from Galina's report. "We can't let this affair with Seibert go unpunished!"

But Drachenblut was no longer listening to him.

"If we so much as touch a hair on Seibert's head," he said, "there'll be a press scandal, and that might jeopardize our deal. I think we should deport him. As long as he's out of the country, we won't have a problem. And we'll punish those blockheads in Murmansk to show that we were not keeping our powder dry."

Alov drooped. The deportation of a German citizen was not enough to get him an apartment.

"Comrade Drachenblut," he began, "I've already talked to you several times about the situation with my accommodation—"

"It's good for OGPU agents to be cold and hungry," said Drachenblut with a smirk. "It keeps them on their toes. Bring me something worthwhile, and then you'll get a room."

3

It was chaos in the former Neapolitan Café—Seibert was packing together all his Moscow belongings. Lieschen's wails issued from the bedroom. The news that her employer was going and leaving her behind boded no good for her whatsoever.

Seibert was standing on a chair, taking the pictures down from the wall.

"Please, Lieschen, calm down!" he yelled. "Or I'll do something I regret, so help me, God!"

Klim was sitting in an armchair opposite the window, which was already being stripped of its curtains.

"So, you still haven't worked out why they're deporting you?" he asked.

Seibert jumped to the floor and yanked out a drawer from the chest so hard that it came loose from its runners, scattering letters, scissors, and broken pencils all over the carpet.

"In this country, they can deport whomever they like for whatever they like," Seibert said. "I simply had a call from the Commissariat of Foreign Affairs instructing me very politely to leave the Soviet Union." He pointed a finger toward the bedroom. "It's her I feel sorry for!"

Seibert picked up a piece of notepaper from the floor and handed it to Klim.

"I didn't ask you to come here for nothing, you know. These people are in trouble. If you don't help them, they're done for."

"Who?" asked Klim.

"Have you ever heard of the Volga Germans?" Seibert asked. "Back in her day, Catherine the Great invited German peasants who had suffered from the Seven Years' War to come and settle in Russia. In the course of a hundred and fifty years, they grew wealthy, built up a number of villages near Saratov, and even started their own companies."

Seibert told Klim that recently, a group of bearded men in peasants' clothing had come to him and asked in a strange, antiquated German dialect if it was true that this was the house of a famous journalist.

Their priest, who spoke good Russian, had composed a letter, which they wished to be passed to Stalin.

"Just take a look at what they wrote!" said Seibert with a bitter laugh.

Klim began to read:

Dear most esteemed ruler of Russia, Comrade Stalin:

After the revolution, the laborers of our village set to work, thinking that at last the good times were here, and we would see equality and brotherhood. But destruction is underway among us, and in the Volga Region, it is being carried out systematically.

Our canton was given an assignment for grain production, but half our winter rye is ruined. The authorities do not believe this is the case because they have never worked in the fields. The Party people are coming out from the city with revolvers and going around our houses. They declare that any family with wallpaper on the walls are the bourgeoisie. Then they demand a tax of whatever sum the devil puts into their heads. It is quite impossible to give them what they ask for.

Nine families in our village have been robbed, all their possessions handed over to state and cooperative organizations run by these city people. Otto Litke even had his children's swing taken down and carted off. Please look into this, Comrade Stalin. Why was this necessary?

A teacher was sent out to our school to teach the children the way they are taught in Saratov city. But the teacher does not know our language, and the children do not understand anything he says. They have been instructed in this Saratov wisdom for a whole year and have only one line written in their exercise books: "At the first call of the Party, we will all go to the barricades to fight for the dictatorship of the proletariat."

Who will take care of the crops if they all go to the barricades?

Who needs all this? Or perhaps you are all sitting there in the capital without any idea of what is going on in the countryside?

We were close to giving up, so we sold all our possessions. The whole village decided to go to Germany where we heard they were looking for hired hands on farms. We came to Moscow and went straight to the German Embassy, but they told us that we would not get a visa without a special passport for traveling abroad. We went here, there, and everywhere, trying to find these passports, but all the city workers just take our money for nothing and don't do their job. Bishop Meier took pity on us and let us stay in the Church of St. Michael, and our whole village has been living there now for two months like mice in a cellar, and because of this, our children are starting to fall ill.

Please send us a representative to see how we are suffering. And tell the city people not to torment us but let us out of the country without these passports that we do not need. If you do not come to our aid, we will die this winter since we have no money and no way of getting any because nobody will give us work.

Long live Soviet power and a brighter future! Death to those who refuse the workers their freedom!

Goodbye, Comrade Stalin. I am sending you this letter in secret, but if I need to answer for anything, I will do so willingly.

Truly yours,
Thomas Fischer

Beneath the first name were dozens of crooked German signatures.

Klim looked up at Seibert. "They'll all be sent to prison for a letter like this."

"That's exactly what I told them. But they have nowhere to go back to, you see. I wanted to ask the Deputy Commissar of Foreign Affairs, Comrade Babloyan, to help them. He owes me a favor—he has a liver disease, and I organized for him to get treatment in Berlin. But he won't be back in Moscow for another couple of days, and I'm being deported. So, we won't have a chance to meet."

"Would you like me to speak to him?" asked Klim.

Seibert clasped his hands together beseechingly. "Please, speak to him! If you do this for me, you won't regret it."

Seibert's forehead puckered, and the corners of his mouth turned down. "You've no idea how long I've been chasing after this Babloyan," Seibert said with a sigh. "He's a member of the Central Executive Committee and a personal friend of Stalin. I was hoping to arrange an interview through him."

"And you'd pass that connection on to me?" Klim asked, astonished.

"I would die of envy if you pull it off, of course. But you can consider it payment for helping my fellow Germans."

"I'll do what I can."

"Then I'll write you a letter of recommendation. A couple of days from now, you can go to see Babloyan in the sanatorium for the All-Union Organization of Prerevolutionary Political Convicts and Deportees. Babloyan will continue treatment there for his liver complaint."

Klim wrote down the address. "What will you do in Berlin?" he asked.

"I'll get a job with a newspaper," Seibert said. "After all, I have made a name for myself, and I've got plenty of experience. If we manage to get the Volga Germans out of the country, I'll try my hand at politics. It would be a good start for my career."

4

The caste system within the USSR had its untouchables—*lishentsy*—but it also had its Brahmins—members of the All-Union Organization of Prerevolutionary Political Convicts and Deportees. These people were lionized. They enjoyed enormous pensions, private apartments, and countless other privileges.

There were around three thousand members of the organization—several generations of anarchists, nihilists, and revolutionaries. It was calculated that between them, they had spent sixteen thousand years in labor camps and still longer in exile.

These former convicts had their own publishing house, bookshop, and a museum, which displayed documents testifying to the political repression that had taken place in the Russian Empire. But the jewel in the crown of the organization was the former mansion of Count Sheremetev, which had been transformed into a wonderful hospital and sanatorium. As well as former political convicts, members of the Party elite also went there often for treatment.

Klim used his connections with his downstairs neighbors, the Proletkult workers, to get himself a place on an excursion to this sanatorium. The other participants were a group of Young Communist League members.

They left Moscow by bus. The group leader, Vasya, a muscular bronzed young man in a striped shirt and baggy canvas trousers had brought a concertina with him, and all the way he roared out *chastushkas*, humorous folk songs consisting of one couplet.

> See them now, the bourgeois lackeys
> Trembling like jellies;
> Now they have to pay new taxes
> For their big fat bellies!

The girls around him all howled with laughter.

After a long and bumpy ride over country roads, the bus drove into an old-fashioned park with artificial lakes and shady avenues of trees.

The Young Communists were glued to the windows.

"Oh! Just look at those statues!" gasped the girls, pointing to the marble figures in the fountains.

"And look at all the flowers! More than on a May Day Parade!"

They got off the bus and stood, hesitating next to a large building of white stone with pillars and a broad staircase leading up to the porch.

"This is the good life, all right!" said Vasya. In his astonishment, he dropped his concertina, which let out a loud bellow as it fell to the ground.

A small, plump man with dark hair and a bushy mustache came out to meet them.

"Good to see all you fine, young people!" he said, heartily. "Come along, and I'll show you around."

Klim was the only one of the group who recognized Babloyan, although his picture was always in the papers, and his portrait was sold widely in sets of postcards. It would not have occurred to any of the younger people that such an important man could talk to ordinary workers so simply and easily and even show them around.

But Babloyan was clearly fond of consorting with the Young Communists. He laughed together with the young men and jokingly put his arm around the girls' waists.

"Shh—quiet now!" he ordered when they came up to a terrace where old men and women in smart bathrobes were lying about, dozing in comfortable deckchairs.

"This place is like a living museum," breathed Babloyan in awe. "These people sacrificed everything so that you, young people, could witness the dawn of socialism."

The Young Communists tiptoed onto the terrace and, blushing awkwardly, began to thank the old men and women and shake their wrinkled hands, which still bore the scars of shackles.

Babloyan gave them a blow-by-blow account of the activities of the political convicts—which of them had attempted to assassinate generals and which had planted bombs in the official residences of city governors.

The Young Communists had grown up under Soviet rule, and as far as they were concerned, all this had taken place long ago in ancient times. They could hardly believe that the heroes of these historical events were still alive.

They were particularly amazed to be introduced to an eighty-year-old man called Frolenko. He had been one of the ringleaders in the assassination of Alexander II.

"Why did you try to kill the Tsar?" asked Raia, a tiny, dark-eyed girl with a snub nose covered in large freckles. "The country wasn't ready for revolution at that time."

Frolenko sucked in his false teeth. "We didn't have a choice back then," he said. "We had to rouse the Russian people from their hundred-year sleep. We wanted to give a signal that revolutionary forces were alive and well and that all those who oppressed the working people would pay for it."

The Young Communists all applauded.

Babloyan pointed to an old lady with a cane who was standing in the doorway. "And this is the famous Vera Figner. Do you know what her comrades used to say about her? 'There are some natures that will never yield. They can be broken but never bent to the ground.'"

The old lady fixed him with a malign stare. "You'd do better to hold your tongue. We wanted to achieve freedom of speech and freedom of conscience, but your lot have destroyed everything. Russia needs another revolution!"

A nurse came running up to her. "Comrade Figner, it's time for your treatment!" She took the old lady gently by the elbow and led her away.

"Her age is beginning to tell, I'm afraid," Babloyan sighed. "Sometimes, Comrade Figner even forgets that the revolution has happened already."

Next, Babloyan handed the young people over to the director of the sanatorium who took them to see the old hothouses and the poultry yard.

Klim approached Babloyan. "Seibert sent me," he said. "He asked me to give you this letter."

Babloyan's expression changed. "Come with me," he said quietly and gestured for Klim to follow him.

They sat down on a bench surrounded by flowering rose bushes. Babloyan read the letter from Seibert and then took a box of matches out of his pocket and burned the paper immediately.

"It's a shame they've sent Seibert out of the country," Babloyan said. "He was a useful man to know."

"So, what about these Volga Germans?" asked Klim. "They're being told that in order to get passports, they need to bring in permission documents that they can't get ahold of. They would have to go back to Saratov, and they have no money."

Babloyan shrugged. "It's not in our interests to let them out. If the whole village goes over to Germany, the story is bound to leak out to the press, and then we'll see the usual malicious reports about the Soviet Union."

"But you can do something about it," urged Klim.

Babloyan looked Klim up and down quizzically. "Fifty rubles a head," he mouthed, barely audible. "If you care so much about the Germans, you can raise the money needed to pay the 'state duty.' But only in foreign currency, please."

Klim smiled sardonically. Babloyan had full board and lodging, and all his needs were supplied. Why did he want foreign currency? There could be only one answer: he, like many of the Kremlin elite, considered emigration and looked for a way of amassing foreign currency just in case things began to fall apart.

Now and then, the papers would carry an article on the traitors who went abroad on work assignments and refused to return to the USSR. Among them were Stalin's personal secretary and prominent OGPU agents. People were running away like rats from a sinking ship.

All the Party members knew that, at any moment, they could be brought to account not only for their own crimes but also for friendships with people who had fallen out of favor. And there was no knowing who would be on the blacklist from one day to the next.

"Could you please help me to arrange an interview with Stalin?" asked Klim. "I'm sure that in return for copy like that, United Press would help us solve the problem of the Volga Germans."

"The Germans aren't my problem; they're yours," said Babloyan. "I wish you all the best."

In the hierarchy of Bolshevik values, access to Comrade Stalin was worth a lot more than a bunch of Germans. In any case, Babloyan was not willing to enter into any bargain on the subject.

26. THE VOLGA GERMANS

1

BOOK OF THE DEAD

I went on a visit to the church of St. Michael, the oldest Lutheran Church in Russia, founded in the sixteenth century. There have been no services in the church for several months as the Central Aerodynamic Institute is right next door, and the Moscow Soviet has ordered the closure of the church on the grounds that parishioners were "preventing the organization of appropriate security."

In fact, churches, like all other autonomous organizations, are being destroyed as the government wants to get rid of all independent sources of income or social support. The Party alone can now provide material wealth, recognition, and censure; in this way, it controls everyone and everything.

The Moscow Lutherans are trying to save their church, though they have only a slim chance of success. The Bolsheviks have hit on a formula that allows them to close down churches "at the request of the workers." Members of the Young Communist League go from door to door, asking everyone in the district whether they are in favor of combating religious obscurantism. Those who agree are asked to sign a petition. Nobody dares refuse; if anyone breathes a word in support of religious freedom, their bosses will be informed immediately, and the black sheep will be the first in line for the chop during the next workplace purge.

I cannot imagine what will happen to the Volga Germans if they are driven out of the St. Michael church. They are already living in atrocious conditions! Today, I saw crowds of haggard women and little kids as thin as rakes. The children haven't had a proper wash in the bathhouse for months, and their mothers shave their heads to keep away the lice. There were no men or youths to be seen. They are all out working—trying to make money by hauling or loading.

I was immediately reminded of the internment camps for White Russians in China—but those were the result of the civil war. Now, in peacetime, the country has an artificially created refugee problem.

Babloyan asked me for a quite impossible sum. Of course, I wrote to Seibert, telling him how much money he needs to raise, but it's unlikely he'll manage to do anything. The German economy is in bad shape just now.

The whole situation drives me mad. On all sides, Soviet officials are perpetrating a dreadful, senseless orgy of cannibalism. But rather than devouring the flesh of their fellow citizens, they eat up their time and energy—in other words, life itself.

Kitty asks me every day where her mother is. I am teaching her to play the piano, and she is impatient to show Nina what she can do.

She piles music books onto the piano stool, perches on top of the pile, and bangs away enthusiastically at the keys. Her favorite keys are the ones at the top: these produce a delicate tinkling sound, so she has christened them "Mommy's notes." "Daddy's notes," on the other hand, are the deep bass ones at the bottom. I'm sorry to say, they're a lot less popular.

I told Kitty that her mother would be coming soon and that she was bound to write to us, in any case. But the days go by, and our mailbox remains empty except for newspapers and official letters. I'm back in the old routine- work, trivial chores and worries, and never enough time. I have not been in touch with Galina and now have to do everything myself.

2

Whenever my foreign colleagues write about the Soviet people, they dehumanize them whether they mean to or not. I can understand why this happens—if you only scratch the surface, the people here seem like a bunch of madmen who make decision after decision that can only harm themselves.

There are no roads in Arkhangelsk and nothing to eat, and meanwhile, the government is sending money and arms to communists all over the world. Why?

Rather than helping private businesses feed the urban population, it does its best to ensure the Soviet people eat as poor a diet as possible and stand in queues as long as possible so that they grow cold, tired, and sick, and die prematurely as a result.

The state budget is spent on polar expeditions, on sending foreign journalists to the north, and on huge sporting demonstrations. The Bolsheviks have been excluded from the world Olympic movement, so in order to spite the organizers of the Olympics in Holland, the USSR decided to stage an enormous sporting event, the Spartakiad, a thousand times better than anything the bourgeois West had to offer. While the country was in the throes of an economic crisis, the government was building a 25,000-seater stadium for the Dynamo soccer team.

Foreigners find it difficult to understand why, far from being indignant at folly on such a grand scale, the Soviet people actually seem to be enthusiastically in favor of it.

What they don't realize is that man cannot live by bread alone. Everyone in this country wants to be somebody, to have some value in the world, and to enjoy general respect. When people are disenfranchised and demeaned by poverty, their need for *greatness* only increases. The achievements of sporting heroes and polar explorers are looked on as common property, and people truly enjoy reading in the papers about how the USSR has rescued the explorers of Nobile's expedition. In this way, Soviet citizens get to prove that they, as a nation, are strong, intelligent, and brave, and against that backdrop, their day-to-day problems seem less important.

I think I should write a book called *A Dictators' Manual.*

I've already made a chapter outline:
1. Keep a Tight Grip on Power: how to get the money for the army and police in a wretchedly poor country
2. Invent Enemies Both at Home and Abroad: how to give people a plausible explanation for their misfortune
3. Entertainment for the Masses and the Fostering of National Pride: an easy method to quell public discontent
4. Propaganda and the Art of Concealment: how to arrange things so that people don't believe what they see with their own eyes

I'll have ten copies printed, and then I'll sell each one to the tyrants of the world who will have to pay me its weight in gold.

3

The New Economic Policy introduced under Lenin is now being phased out swiftly and stealthily.

You can't see any more signs bearing the names of private firms or shop owners. The Bolsheviks have got rid of the private traders but put nothing in their place, so it looks like this winter will be a hard one.

The country is now gripped by a cult of fervent worship of the Soviet leaders and, above all, Comrade Stalin. The rulers' portraits have clearly taken the place of icons: their faces are pinned up everywhere.

The Party is the fount of all blessings, and therefore, anyone with any talent puts it to use for the glory of the Bolsheviks. Meanwhile, those who have no talent try to move up the ladder by protecting their leaders from all sorts of spurious dangers.

In part, this sycophancy is calculating, and in part, it is driven by our instinctive desire to attach ourselves to strong leaders. For ordinary people, this is the only way to survive when the going gets tough.

I think I should add a new chapter to my book for dictators. "Keeping Control Over Food, Fuel, and Housing: a guaranteed method to win the love of the people."

Nina still hasn't appeared. Not long ago, Kitty and I were reading a book and came upon a riddle about a clock pendulum:

I don't stop all day
And I don't stop all night
I go back and forth
To the left, to the right.

Immediately, Kitty said, "That's you, Daddy!" When I asked her why, she said that I can't make up my mind. First, I go looking for Mommy; next, I say she's never coming back; and now, I'm expecting her to come to see us.

4

I rang all of my friends and told them about the situation in the Church of St. Michael. We have all clubbed together and managed to lay in supplies of flour, drinking water, and anti-lice treatment. Some of the doctors from the embassies have agreed to offer their services free and have given our refugees a basic medical examination.

I don't know why we have suddenly decided to help these people who are not connected to us with any national, social, or religious ties. Perhaps the Volga Germans were simply the first to come our way.

I spoke to some of my fellow journalists. They all feel just what I feel—an oppressive sense of helplessness in the face of a catastrophe that looms ever closer. By coming to the aid of destitute people, we are mounting a personal protest against the forces of violence and falsehood.

I took the Germans to the bathhouse, spending my very last kopeck in the process, and felt an incredible sense of elation. The Bolshevik system demands that I shut up and put up. Is everything all right in your life? Then stay where you are and don't stick your head above the parapet. You won't be able to change anything anyway. And while I nod and agree, I am carrying on doing what I believe is right.

My colleagues are all doing the same thing, and it amazes me to report that we have been joined by employees of the Press Department. Weinstein complained that my article about the Volga Germans was just another case of "mudslinging" and cut it, but the very next minute, he told me that he had a dacha outside Moscow with a shed that he had been meaning for some time to break up for firewood.

"I won't be going there again this year," he said, looking at me pointedly. "You understand what I'm saying? There'll be nobody there."

It's amazing but true: even the most fervent supporters of the Bolshevik regime are prepared to carry out good deeds when they get the chance so long as there is no danger their bosses will catch them displaying a love for their fellow man.

This weekend, Weinstein's neighbors out at his dacha observed a curious sight: a group of foreigners piling out of a couple of embassy cars, flinging off their jackets, and setting to work breaking up the old shed with sledgehammers. The logs and boards were then sawed up and dispatched in a number of consignments to the Lutheran church.

Magda, fresh from a recent trip to Central Asia, has also taken the plight of the Germans to heart. Traveling around Turkestan, she saw so many cases of ill-treated women and children that the "sin of wellbeing" has become unbearable to her.

Now, she goes out to the Church of St. Michael every day, taking Friedrich along too.

He tells us that the residents of the Comintern hostel are out of their minds with fear. If you knock on somebody's door, a strange voice will shout out, "He's sick!" If you ask, "When will he be better?" the answer will be "Never!" Everybody is keeping themselves to themselves, burning their personal documents and drinking vodka to help themselves sleep.

Friedrich says he has had enough of all this hole-in-corner business. He has decided to help the refugees, "consequences be damned."

He has friends who receive vouchers for horse meat because they breed guard dogs for the Soviet border patrol. Friedrich gives them cigarettes in return for the meat, so now our displaced Germans are able to make hot broth to feed their sick children.

None of us has any idea how this adventure of ours will turn out. When Friedrich was in Berlin, he met Seibert, who told him that the German government does not intend to give any money to the refugees.

As I expected, we have not found any benefactors willing to take on a whole village. Worst still, Seibert has no time to search for a Good Samaritan for us. So far, he hasn't managed to find a job and has had to go freelance. Of course, the national papers are happy to buy up his articles, but they pay badly. Seibert spends all his time in the quest for the money.

Well, I suppose we'll keep dashing to and fro so long as we have the strength. No harm in trying after all.

27. THE PIONEER GIRL AND THE CROSS

1

Alov was furious with Galina.

"You told me Rogov was on holiday!" he scolded her. "But he's been back in Moscow for ages! I had a call from the Central Aerodynamic Institute: there's a church on their territory, and Rogov has set up a shelter for vagrants there. What's more, he's inciting foreigners to help him."

"I didn't know anything about it," said Galina, flustered.

Her eyelids burned, and she had a lump in her throat. Why hadn't Klim rung her? Why hadn't he told her he was back?

"There's something fishy about all this," Alov kept saying, wagging a crooked yellow finger. "I want you to go to see Rogov, and I want you to bring me back a *thorough* report."

Dazed, Galina made her way to Chistye Prudy.

"Just look who it is!" cried Kapitolina, opening the door to Galina. "You'll never guess who's dropped in to see us, sir!"

Galina shivered at the thought that she was now no more than a guest who "dropped in."

Klim was sitting at his Underwood typewriter, typing out an article—*without her help*.

"Wait a second," he said. "I have to finish up here."

He thumbed through a dictionary and wrote in his notebook while she sat opposite him, pulling at the cloth strap on her bag, which eventually came loose.

I'm a complete stranger to him, she thought, gazing at Klim, who was working with an expression of intense concentration.

"The OGPU know what you're doing in the Lutheran church," she said.

Finally, Klim looked up from his papers. "What business is it of theirs? It's a private charity. That's all."

"There are no charities in the USSR!" Galina cried. "The state helps everyone who needs it." Forgetting herself, she sprang to her feet. "What I want to know is why are you helping Germans? They killed so many of our people during the Great War!"

"These Germans are Soviet citizens. They didn't kill anyone."

"I don't care! How can you help them when there are Russians in need of help?"

Klim folded his arms across his chest. "So, you're jealous? Is that it?"

"Yes, I'm jealous!" replied Galina hotly. "You go off somewhere without a word, and then it turns out—" She pressed her hand to her mouth to stop herself from dissolving into tears.

Klim frowned. "I didn't want your real bosses to find out about it all."

"Is that why you kept me out of everything?"

He nodded.

"Then I'll resign from the OGPU!" exclaimed Galina passionately. "Just say the word! I don't need their vouchers or their salary. I don't need anything from them at all. I would never betray you!"

Klim looked at her reproachfully. "Well, it's a fine sentiment…but if you resign, you'll be in trouble."

"I don't care! I love you."

Galina waited for Klim to answer, but when he spoke, he said something quite different from what she had been hoping to hear.

"Make sure Kitty doesn't eat chocolate. That's what's been making her ill."

"Should I come in to work tomorrow?" Galina asked after a pause.

"Yes," Klim pointed to a pile of envelopes on the table. "All these have to be delivered."

2

On the way home, Galina hatched a new plan. She would resign from the OGPU. Soon, Kapitolina would be getting married, her little cubbyhole would be free, and Galina could move in with Klim.

I'll become his servant if I have to, she thought selflessly, and this idea seemed to be the answer to all her worries.

When she got home, she saw that the door to her room was open, and a note in Tata's handwriting was lying on the table.

To my deer Mommy and Comrades,

Let my deth be a wepon in the war against semeteries and religious superstishion as graves use up lots of land and are no use to anyone. Instead of semeteries, we should have parks with sports grounds so peeple can play volleyball.

Long Live the Great Lenin!

Tata Dorina

Galina looked at the note, bewildered. Where had it come from? Where was Tata? What had happened to her?

Then she heard a quiet sniffing from inside the wardrobe and threw open the doors.

Tata was lying on her mattress, her hands behind her head.

"How did you get here?" Galina gasped.

"I stowed away on suburban trains," said Tata in a small voice.

"What? You ran away from school? Why?"

"They told me they'd throw me out of the Young Pioneers."

"What for?"

"Because of my cross." Tata's face screwed up, and she began to wail. "I told them my daddy was a commissar and that he only left me two things, an ashtray and this cross, and that's why I wear it. But they didn't believe me. They said I was making up stories about my father to hide the fact that I was religious. I won't let them throw me out of the Pioneers—I'd rather die! Only I want you to send my body to the new crematorium, the one where the church of Serafim of Sarov used to be. They have new ovens in there now from Germany. After two hours, all that's left of you is a kilogram of calcium phosphate. That's what the lecturer from Friends of Cremation Society told us."

Galina sank down wearily onto her bench. The story about the cross had been her own invention. Otherwise, Tata would have refused to wear it.

It was quite impossible to move into Klim's house now.

"Well, it's a good thing you're back," Galina said in a dull voice. "I've missed you terribly."

Tata was so astonished that she sat up on her mattress and got her head tangled up in the clothes hanging in the wardrobe.

"So, you're not angry with me at all?" she asked. Moving aside the hems of the dresses, she climbed out and went to sit with her mother on the bench.

The two of them sat for some time, hugging one another and crying.

"I thought you were going to get married to Uncle Klim," sobbed Tata. "I didn't want to get in your way."

"You silly thing," said Galina. "We never spoke about that, did we?"

"I'm glad you've realized what a rotten capitalist he is. We need to fight his sort! And we have to get Kitty away from him. How do you think we can do it? Why don't we write to the authorities and ask to be allowed to adopt her?"

Tata was incorrigible.

What on earth shall I do now? Galina wondered. She would have to sacrifice either her own life or that of her child. If she sent Tata back to the school, the cruel Pioneers would make her life a misery. On the other hand, if she let her daughter stay in Moscow, she could forget about having any personal relationship.

There was a knock at the door.

"Galina!" came the voice of Mitrofanych. "Some work for you. This letter came from the Nizhny Novgorod archive today." And he thrust a large, battered envelope under the door.

3

Galina went to the bathroom and lit the boiler but did not run a bath. She sat on the floor under the hot pipe, which was hung with drying clothes, and pored through the documents from the archive, sobbing bitterly.

The man she loved more than her life had been lying to her all along. Born into the family of a public procurator, he was a member of the nobility and heir to a large fortune. In 1917, he had come to Nizhny Novgorod, and at that time, he had been an Argentinian citizen, not an American. There was a document to prove it from the police station where he had registered his arrival. In 1919, he had worked on a paper called the *Nizhny Novgorod Commune*—among the documents was a record of his union fees payment.

And here was a certificate of marriage to Nina Vasilievna Kupina dated December 1918. They had been married in the Church of St. George, and that was why Klim had mourned the loss of it.

There was another document showing that at the height of the White Army offensive, Comrade Rogov had left for the front, heading up a team of Red political agitators. Then the trail went cold.

This could only mean one thing. Klim had gone over to the Whites, emigrated, and then came back to the USSR to look for his wife, but she had turned him down. That explained the events of Christmas Eve and everything that had happened after.

Now, it was clear that Kitty was Klim and Nina's adoptive daughter.

Galina's first thought was to run to Alov and hand him Klim's head on a platter. The papers in her hands were enough to doom Mr. Rogov even if he had had no connection with any White Army organizations.

The image of Ibrahim cheerfully hosing down the blood-stained Black Maria floated into Galina's mind.

Alov would be delighted, she thought. He would probably give her a voucher for a couple of pounds of jam or a length of good cloth, and Tata would be happy.

Galina got to her feet, opened the door in the side of the boiler, and began to thrust papers into the burning coals. The flames leaped up, and the smell of burning paper hit her in the face.

Her neighbor, Natasha, knocked on the door. "What are you doing in there? The whole corridor stinks of smoke!"

"Just a minute…just a minute," Galina kept repeating in a daze.

She did not care if Klim was a member of the White Army conspirators. He could be a terrorist for all she cared. She could not live without him.

4

BOOK OF THE DEAD

It seems I'm in a real quandary now. I can't dismiss Galina, or she will end up on the streets, literally. She will be thrown out of the OGPU house for failing to do her job properly, and if she comes to live with me on Chistye Prudy, I will end up on the streets myself because it will be the only way to get away from her meddling.

She has taken to looking at me in a new way as if she was afraid of something, and each time, I remember Seibert saying just before he left, "Watch out for Galina!"

What did he mean? Was he hinting that unrequited love can turn a woman into a monster? The same could be said of men too. I know from my own experience.

I'm trying to make sure Galina spends as little time with my daughter as possible. God forbid Kitty should blurt out something to her about my trip to Crimea!

Fortunately for me, a new library has opened near my house with lots of activities for children. Kapitolina takes Kitty there, and she can play with other kids a little.

Of course, the library isn't offering anything even remotely resembling a proper education. The teachers keep asking Kitty, quite seriously, to tell everyone how she has been oppressed by evil imperialists. They have also taught her a poem by a certain Agniya Barto, "Li, the Little Chinese Boy":

Li had heard of a land far away
Where everything was as bright as day,
Where a magician, great and wise,
Has raised a red flag up to the skies.
And secretly Li dreamed and planned
To walk all the way to that magic land.

Kitty happily reads out this doggerel to a delighted audience, and I have decided to overlook their patronizing racism. So long as Kitty's happy, that's all that mattered.

Magda, Friedrich, and I have been thinking how we can buy some time for our Germans. I have put up a huge sign over the entrance to the Church of St. Michael, "School for the Study of the Lenin's Works." There are quite a few books of his writings left over from Elkin's shop, and I have given them to our refugees. Now, if one of the boys on sentry duty signals that a stranger is approaching, the Germans grab books and try to look studious.

So far, they have not been evicted—nobody dares to close the Lenin school. But all our cleverness has not solved the basic problem that the refugees have nothing to live on.

Seibert sent me an indignant letter, and I can't quite face showing it to Father Thomas just yet. Apparently, the government in Berlin has refused to take in any Russian Germans. In Europe, everyone fears Bolsheviks like the plague, and nobody cares to find out whether refugees from the USSR are communists or poverty-stricken peasants. It's far simpler to refuse them all a visa.

5

I have signed up for driving lessons in the old Catherine Institute for Noble Maidens, which is now the Red Army Club.

The kind old lady in the reception turned out to be a graduate of the school. Recognizing immediately that I was a "gentleman," she took me on a tour of the recently refurbished classrooms.

The Red Army has done very well for itself indeed. It's quite something: precious parquet floors and marble staircases. Apart from this, there is an ancient park behind the building with ponds and bicycle tracks.

In the club, efforts were being made on all sides to raise the cultural level of soldiers and commanders of the Red Army and the members of their families. From the classrooms, we could hear the sounds of choirs singing, accordion music, and the hum of fretsaws. Muffled shots came from the cellar where they were holding military training classes, and in the lecture hall, a gray-haired professor was giving a lecture on "Chemical Warfare and How to Combat It."

I have already made a mental list of the courses I will sign up for when I have finished my driving lessons. I would far rather build birdhouses or dance Russian dances than have to look at Galina's crushed expression.

28. THE DRIVING LESSONS

1

All day, Klim had been traveling around the Moscow markets, conducting research for an article about the economic situation in the capital.

He got talking to a peasant who was selling horses' tails for making soft furnishings.

"How does a horse manage without its tail?" asked Klim in amazement. "The flies must eat it alive."

But the peasant only shrugged his shoulders. "Horses these days are all being sent off for slaughter. If you have a horse, you're made to pay extra tax. But if you haven't even a shirt on your back, you can join the collective farm next year and get a tractor."

The man did not seem to know what this "collective farm" was and did not seem to want to know.

"We'll get by," he said. "We haven't seen the end of Mother Russia yet."

But I wonder how much longer she can hold out? thought Klim.

Russia was dying in instalments. In the Great War, more than eight hundred thousand people had perished; in the civil war—ten million, and during the famine of 1920–21—another five million. That was as many as the population of a country as big as Romania.

And it was frightening to think what awaited Russia now. The threat of famine and terrible privations was becoming more real every day.

2

Klim arrived for his driving lesson in a deeply gloomy state of mind. The lessons had not begun yet, and a crowd of would-be drivers—young men in work overalls—were crowding together next to the locked classroom door.

Klim approached the group and froze.

"The fire in the samovar went out," he heard Nina's voice, "so my daughter decided to 'help it along.' She took some paraffin and put it into the water, not the pipe. The landlady arrived and poured herself a cup of tea, and it stank to high heaven!"

The young men laughed.

Nina was wearing a sky-blue dress and a lacy shawl with a long fringe. With her simple outfit, her golden tan, and her seductive girlish smile, it was no wonder the driving students could not take their eyes off her.

When she caught sight of Klim, Nina gave a barely perceptible nod and continued with her story. "The landlady ran to the neighbors to ask them if they could smell paraffin, and Kitty was afraid that she would get into trouble. So, she tried to fix things by pouring a bottle of cologne into the samovar."

Klim could not help smiling. *So, she's come back after all,* he thought. *Well, I wonder what she'll get up to now?*

The instructor appeared, a droll little old man with a fat belly and a mustache twisted up at the ends. He opened the door, and the students entered the classroom. Nina sat at the front next to a loutish-looking fellow with fair hair who hadn't even bothered to remove his cap indoors. Klim made his way to the "dunce's bench" at the back of the class.

The instructor put up a diagram of a Ford Model T on the blackboard.

"Today, we'll be studying the construction of a modern passenger car with a four-cylinder engine," he announced. "This car has a twenty-horsepower engine, and it can achieve breakneck speeds of seventy kilometers an hour."

Klim did not take his eyes off the back of Nina's head, but she never once looked around. She seemed to be genuinely interested in the location of the car's fuel tank and how to measure the level of petrol using a special gauge stick.

During recess, Nina once again gathered her crowd of admirers around her and began to tell anecdotes about the time she had spent in Crimea. Klim stood a little way off, listening, growing gloomier with every minute.

A small Red Army soldier with protruding ears came up to him. "She's a bit of all right, isn't she?" he said. "I guess there's some lucky guy out there enjoying all that, eh? Gotta be."

Klim could barely restrain himself from breaking the man's nose.

After the class, Nina said goodbye to her new friends and left.

All Klim had to show in the way of personal triumphs that day was a single nod of her head.

3

Klim was sure that Nina had only signed up for driving lessons because he would be on the course, but she paid no attention to him. During recess, a crowd would always gather around her, and the only time Klim found a way to speak to Nina was when they were instructed to crawl under an old Ford car together.

"Have you found the coil spring?" asked the instructor.

"Yes, I've got it," answered Nina.

"If the car should break down on the road, you'll need to fix it on your own. Go on then. As for you, Comrade Rogov, keep an eye out and help the young lady if she needs it."

The screw nut was worn, and no matter how hard Nina tried to undo it, she could not get it to budge.

"Let me help," suggested Klim, but she motioned him away with an irritable jerk of her shoulder.

"There's no need."

"You don't have the strength."

"Maybe not, but when I make up my mind to do something, I generally do it."

It was difficult for Klim to argue with that.

Eventually, Nina managed to release the screw nut. There were cheers from the other students as she handed it to the instructor.

"You see, we can achieve anything with patience and hard work," he said, shaking her by the hand.

After class, Klim went up to speak to Nina.

"You haven't once asked me about Kitty," he said. "Don't you want to know how she is?"

"I already know," she said coolly. "Kapitolina takes her to classes at the children's library, and I see her there."

Klim did not know what to say at this.

"How's Elkin doing?" he asked.

"He stayed behind in Crimea," Nina said. "He proposed to me, but I told him it would never work."

"Why not?"

"I'll give you three guesses," laughed Nina and, swinging her bag, she set off down the path to the park.

4

Kitty admitted to Klim that she really had been meeting her mother. Kapitolina remembered Nina from her time in Elkin's store and decided that she must have got a new job in the children's library. Kapitolina had simply been leaving Kitty with Nina and going off about her own business.

"Why didn't you tell me?" Klim asked Kitty sternly.

"Because you already took Tata away from me!"

It was painful to look at Kitty. She was convinced her father would forbid her to see Nina, and she already had tears in her eyes.

Klim pretended that he did not care about their secret meetings. He himself was seeing Nina three times a week. But that was all he was doing—seeing her. She spoke more to the cloakroom attendant than she did to Klim.

Nina was close but at the same time quite out of reach. She was doing everything she could to make herself into a valuable prize and was always surrounded by a throng of admirers. She was insinuating herself into Klim's thoughts, making him wonder where she was living, how she was earning a living, and what plans she was making. There was some air of *mystery* about her.

It was a strange feeling, thought Klim: to know that you were being shamelessly seduced, to be indignant about it, and at the same time to wait impatiently for the next session of emotional torment.

Klim noticed that after class, Nina did not go with everybody else to the bus stop but hurried to the park. It happened time and again, and it could only mean one thing: she was meeting somebody there.

Naturally, this was too much for Klim to bear, and one day, he set off after her.

The evening sky was soft and clear, and little butterflies were fluttering over the late-blooming flowers.

Klim followed Nina at a distance, annoyed at the cyclists who kept hurtling toward him, shouting at him to watch out. God forbid Nina should turn around and see him!

She disappeared around a corner, and Klim began to walk faster. He already imagined finding some Red Army officer waiting for Nina on a park bench, but when he rounded the corner, he saw her in the company of a large gray goose. She was standing on the bank of a pond, feeding it from her palm.

Spotting Klim, the goose shook itself, spread out its wings, and set off toward the stranger, hissing.

Nina laughed. "Hey! He's a friend! Stop that this instant!"

She threw the goose a crust of bread, and it immediately forgot about its rival.

The ground was damp after the rain the day before, and as Nina tried to climb up the bank from the pond, she kept slipping on the wet clay.

Klim held out a hand to her. "Here—let me pull you up."

This time, Nina accepted his help and even allowed him to hold her by the elbow while she cleaned off the mud from her shoes with a stick.

Klim had imagined she would ask him why he had been following her and was trying to think up an acceptable excuse, but Nina, acting as if nothing had happened, began to tell him about the goose.

"The rest of its clan have been caught and eaten long ago," she said, "but it's been hiding in the rushes all this time. I come here to feed it."

They walked along the path together, followed by the goose. From time to time, it gave an angry honk and flapped its wings noisily. It seemed to regard Nina as its own property.

Klim was no longer trying to think about anything. He just walked along beside Nina, breathing in the heady scent of the autumn leaves and feeling amazed at how neatly she had forced him to make the first move.

Nina, it appeared, now lived in Saltykovka, in the house of Count Belov, and traveled to the capital every day on the suburban train.

"To see Kitty?" asked Klim.

"To see both of you. Also, Belov and I have started up a soap-making business. Once, I translated a brochure for Magda about it, so we use the technology she had described. But I have to go around Moscow all the time to find our supplies."

"But how do you sell your products?" asked Klim, amazed. "I don't suppose you have a patent, do you?"

"No, but I have a head on my shoulders," said Nina, laughing.

From what she told him, it was clear that private enterprise had not disappeared but had been pushed underground by the draconian measures of the government.

Nina had spent all that remained of her money on buying raw materials and equipment. In the suburbs, there were whole colonies of *lishentsy* who had been driven out from the capital. They were prepared to take any job they were offered.

"We found a young chemist," said Nina. "He was expelled from the university because he came from an aristocratic family, and he's thought up a cheap method of creating lye for us."

Nina's soap was being peddled around various markets and stations, but most of her profit came from government organizations. Nina was coming to agreements with the directors of laundries, hospitals, and schools to supply them with soap, given the current shortage.

"The state demands that institutions comply with standards of hygiene," Nina told Klim, "but there are no soap supplies left. Nowadays, every company has two sets of accounts. The first books are the official ones, for the government officials, and the second are the work accounts. They include a completely different list of goods and completely different figures."

Klim remembered what Elkin had told him about translating Swedish manuals.

"So, you're telling me that all manufacturers are breaking the law and that they're criminals by definition?" he asked.

"The whole population is engaged in criminal activities these days," said Nina. "Some people are trading illegally; others are evading taxes or getting their salary paid cash-in-hand. And all the officials take bribes. We're all in it together."

They arrived at the gate, and the goose, deciding not to go any farther, flew back to its pond.

"Where are you going—to the station?" asked Klim.

Nina nodded, and he hailed her a cab.

"See you tomorrow," she said, shaking his hand as if they were just friends.

5

BOOK OF THE DEAD

Nina has had an idea about what to do with the Volga Germans. She has advised us to find people who have connections with the Canadian Railroad Company. The population of Canada is very small, no more than nine million people, and they don't have anyone to service the railroads that run through the forested areas. Nina has heard that the government in Ottawa is prepared to help immigrants who are willing to settle in these remote areas. They will be given land, equipment, and interest-free loans. Magda has made contact with the Canadians and found out that they are indeed ready to take our refugees, and the German embassy in Moscow has agreed to give the Germans transit visas on condition that they go to Hamburg beforehand and charter a steamer from there to take them to Quebec.

Once again, it all comes down to foreign passports and money. We're all hoping that Seibert will manage to raise the necessary funds, but so far, he hasn't had any success.

Nina has also thought up a way for the Germans to earn some cash in the meantime. She has suggested that they gather up old flags and banners left after political demonstrations and make them into various items, from shopping bags to children's clothes. Friedrich has brought several crates of thread and sewing materials from Germany, and production is already underway.

What's happening at the moment between Nina and me? There is not a great deal to report. We've found common cause caring for other people who are connected to us only because they are fellow human beings. Nina and I have taken to wandering in the park by the Red Army Club, and instead of talking about our own affairs, we discuss our plans to rescue the Germans.

During one of these walks, we found a mysterious fence and discovered behind it a whole store of prerevolutionary statues commemorating subjects that are no longer in favor. All the bronze sculptures have long since been taken to be melted down, but the marble figures of emperors and generals are all still there, gradually becoming overgrown with moss and begrimed with soot.

During recess, we go to visit these vanquished heroes. Nina spreads out a cloth on a pedestal supporting some general and treats me to her own homemade bread.

I don't always come empty-handed either. A couple of days ago, I managed to get a bottle of champagne from the canteen at the People's Commissariat of Foreign Affairs. I'll never forget how we cracked it open and drank champagne straight from the bottle.

When our classes are over, we go to visit the goose—he's still alive for the moment. Then I walk Nina some of the way home. Our evening strolls around Moscow are becoming longer and longer. At first, we would say goodbye on Tsvetnoy Boulevard, but now I take her as far as the station and then go home…to Galina.

Tata is now back at her old school. No sooner did she get there than she created a scene: the Young Pioneers were playing the traditional skittle game, *gorodki*, where you knock apart formations of wooden pegs. The Pioneer leader had suggested that instead of the traditional shapes like cannons and forks, they lay out the pegs in the shape of granaries and factories—then their game would be more in tune with the spirit of the age.

This sent Tata into a frenzy of righteous indignation. She wrote a denunciation to the headmaster complaining that the Pioneer leader was guilty of encouraging sabotage and was planning to destroy Soviet enterprises by knocking them apart with sticks.

Galina told me the whole thing as if it were a joke. The headmaster turned out to have a head on his shoulders and told Tata not to be a fool, and the Pioneer leader didn't get into trouble. But I was stunned to hear the story. It seems that Galina has no idea what a little monster she has raised.

I can't bear to be around Galina now. Her eyes, which I once thought of as honey-colored, now seem to me the color of engine oil. But I still don't have the heart to dismiss her. She has always shown kindness to me, and I couldn't repay this kindness with rank ingratitude.

All my castles in the air have come tumbling down, my life is in disarray, and I am living each day as it comes. My contract with United Press is coming to an end, I have no money saved up, I have not managed to get an interview with Stalin, and I have no idea what will happen to me next.

I know only one thing: I live from one driving lesson to the next. I'm prepared to spend hours rummaging under a radiator hood or steering a car between empty buckets or even pushing the Ford we use for training when it gets bogged down in the autumn mud. All this just to be next to Nina, to gallantly offer her a screwdriver or go trailing behind her with a spare wheel.

29. EXPOSURE

1

Galina knew that Klim had begun seeing somebody. He now did his best to avoid her and clearly disliked it when she tried to kiss him. There had been no question of them going to bed together for some time.

In the middle of dictating an article, he might stop mid-sentence and point at the typewriter with a smile. "Here's an interesting puzzle. Look at the keys on the top row of the typewriter: Y-U-I-O. Can you make them into words that fit?"

Galina stared back at him, bewildered. "What words?"

"Look. It's the words 'You' and 'I' mixed up together. Don't you see it?"

Gazing at the black Underwood, Galina found her eye drawn to something else completely: the key of the space bar denoting nothing but emptiness.

However hard she tried to avoid facing the truth, it was no good. Recently, Klim had, by some miracle, brought back a pineapple and then taken it off to his driving lessons. What was he thinking of? Was he going to offer some to the other students instead of eating such a rare delicacy at home?

So, when Klim asked her to collect some statistical reports from the Moscow Tuberculosis Institute, Galina could not resist calling in at the Red Army Club, which was right next door.

She marched up to the receptionist and, in a stern voice, demanded to see the student register.

At first, the old lady was reluctant to bring out the list, but Galina's OGPU card made her change her mind.

"Everything is in perfect order," she assured Galina in a flustered voice. "We always check the papers of everyone who comes here."

There were twenty men and a single woman signed up for driving lessons. Galina ran her finger down the list of names. Here was Klim's name, and here, sure enough, was Nina's. An address was written beside Nina's name, copied out from her documents: 8 Petrovsky Lane.

Where is that? Galina wondered. Wasn't it opposite the Korsh Theater? And why was there no apartment number?

All of a sudden, she remembered where she had heard the surname "Reich" before: that was the name of the famous American businessman who had been granted all those Soviet concessions. She had heard Alov mention him more than once, invariably with a sense of outrage that this bourgeois had his own *house* while honest workers like himself had to put up with four square meters of living space behind the dresser.

Now she understood it all: Klim's wife had left him for a millionaire, but she hadn't enjoyed living with her new husband and had started meeting her ex-husband again.

Galina wondered if Mr. Reich knew Klim Rogov was bringing pineapples to his wife?

When she got home, Galina went straight to see her neighbor, Mitrofanych.

"I need everything you have in the archives on Nina Reich," she said. "Nina Kupina and Nina Reich are the same person."

Mitrofanych brightened up at her words. "And what do I get in return?"

After a pause, Galina began to undo the buttons of her blouse.

2

Drachenblut placed a pile of sealed packages of banknotes before Oscar.

"There are ten thousand dollars here, and all the numbers have been recorded. Pass this money to Seibert when you're in Berlin."

"So, Seibert has decided to work for the OGPU?" Oscar asked in surprise, putting the notes away in his briefcase.

"Seibert is desperate—he's completely high and dry. He'll be working in secret, picking out journalists for us who will write encouraging articles about the USSR. We need to have positive press coverage. The Canadians are doing everything they can to disrupt our consignments to Germany. They want to sell timber to the Germans themselves, but their transport costs are higher than ours. So, they're pushing the idea that it's risky and unethical to do business with us. But with a bit of help from Seibert, we'll get the better of them in no time."

"Whatever you say." Oscar found it amusing that Drachenblut claimed to be waging war on capitalism, but that when it came down to business, he behaved like a hard-nosed trader trying to cut himself a fat profit.

When he got home, Oscar saw a pale-faced woman with auburn hair waiting at his gate.

"Ask that woman what she wants," he instructed his chauffeur.

The driver lowered the window, but without waiting, the woman ran up to the car and began to speak in perfect English.

"Mr. Reich, I have something to tell you about your wife."

Oscar flinched. Nina had run away while he had been out of the country, and all his efforts to trace her had come to nothing. He had found it hard to accept that the fortune of Baron Bremer, which had been almost within his reach, had eluded him. But what could he do?

He asked the strange woman into his car while he made his chauffeur wait outside.

"Do you know where my wife is?" he asked.

The woman nodded and took a pile of papers from a carrier bag.

"Look at this," she said. "This is the certificate from the civil registration office where you and Nina Bremer were married. And this here is a note from the police archives which states that Nina Bremer is receiving compulsory treatment at the Kashchenko psychiatric clinic."

Oscar stared at the piece of paper. On it was a stamp that read "Certified to be a true and correct copy." According to the document, Nina Bremer had been admitted to the hospital in January 1928.

"But that's impossible," he said, bewildered. "Nina was with me all that time."

"The woman who was with you was a commoner from Nizhny Novgorod by the name of Nina Vasilievna Kupina. Here's a photograph of her."

The woman showed Oscar a picture. On the back of it was a scored-out inscription "Nina Kupina," and below that, somebody had written "Mrs. Reich."

"This young lady has been using somebody else's name," the woman said.

"Do you know where she is now?" asked Oscar.

"She's taking driving lessons at the Red Army Club."

Long after the woman had left, Oscar sat, motionless, staring at the leather back of the seat in front of him.

"Mr. Reich, are we going somewhere else?" asked the chauffeur,

Oscar looked at him vaguely. "Do you know the way to the Red Army Club?"

3

Kapitolina had had a fight with her machine operator, and for two days now, she had been sitting sobbing in the kitchen.

"I told him we need pillows with feathers. How are we supposed to sleep with no pillows? And he says to me, 'If that's the kind of thing you're wanting, you can go marry Rockefella.'" Kapitolina looked up at Klim, her eyes brimming with tears. "What do you think, sir? How can I get to know this Rockefella? I don't suppose he'd make a fuss over a couple of pillows, would he?"

Klim poured Kapitolina glass after glass of milk and tried to reassure her that the pillow crisis would soon be over.

He was late for his lesson that day. There was a raid on black market traders, and there were roadblocks on all the surrounding roads manned by army trainees.

When Klim got to the Red Army Club, he saw a crowd of curious onlookers gathered around an ambulance. As he watched, two medical orderlies took a body covered with a sheet on board and pulled the doors shut.

"You just missed a domestic scene that turned nasty," one of the driving students told Klim. "We were all in the garage, and all of a sudden, Nina's husband came in, demanding to talk to her."

"She just went for him with a crank handle," piped up Andrei, who shared a desk with Nina in class. "Then we heard yelling."

Klim looked toward the ambulance. "Did he kill her?"

"No. It was *her* who knocked him over the head. We come running, and there he was lying there all covered in blood with the crank handle next to him. Reckon he's lucky to be alive."

"And where's Nina?"

"She ran off. She wasn't going to hang around to get arrested."

A policeman appeared on the porch, leading an enormous Alsatian.

"Go find it, Dinah. Go find it!" he urged, thrusting Nina's white shawl under the dog's nose.

The Alsatian made a sudden rush at Klim, who jumped back.

"What are you doing, Dinah?" the policeman cried, dragging the dog away. "It's a woman we're after!"

Klim walked away. So, Reich had tracked down Nina, and now the entire Moscow criminal investigation department was on her trail.

4

"Can I come in for a minute?" Zharkov put his head around the door of Alov's office.

Alov sighed. He knew what was coming next. Zharkov would start tempting him with all sorts of foreign rubbish, and he would not be able to resist. He always bought something for Dunya.

Zharkov closed the door behind him.

"I've just come from the personnel department," he said. "You know what I saw on the desk? Your work chart. And next to your name was a note: 'From nobility.'"

Alov felt a familiar spasm in his lungs. "But many of our top brass are from the nobility…and that means—"

"Don't argue with me and listen!" Zharkov cut him short. "Haven't you read the latest directive? All the departmental bosses have been told to cut staff and get rid of idlers. We're all on an economy drive right now, so you'd do well to weed out some of your coworkers. If not, they'll give you hell for setting up a 'nest of gentlefolk.'"

Alov was racked by an uncontrollable fit of coughing. Zharkov rummaged in the pockets of his voluminous trousers and brought out a small candy tin. "Here. Have a mint drop."

Alov shook his head. "Don't worry. I'll be fine…."

He folded his arms on the desk and put his head down on them. He felt a little better in that position.

Zharkov clapped him on the back sympathetically. "This purge has got me running scared too, you know. I asked Drachenblut to send me off to Europe while it's going on, but he won't hear of it. 'The OGPU is founded on the principle of equality,' he told me. 'The purge has the potential to affect every one of us.'"

Alov, his head still hidden, smiled bitterly. There was no equality to speak of in the OGPU. Some stayed in their jobs, even though they were from the nobility while others lost their livelihoods for the same reason. Some worked like dogs while others were sent off to live abroad with full board and lodging and a salary of two hundred and fifty dollars a month. No endless meetings for them or "voluntary donations" to the aviation society, and no purges either.

"How about we have a drink in the canteen?" suggested Zharkov. "My treat."

Alov nodded. He was not fool enough to refuse such a generous offer. The price of vodka had just gone up by 60 kopecks.

5

On his return from the canteen, Alov sat for some time at his desk, trying to gather his thoughts.

The purge was to take place on November 12th, and he had very little time left. Everyone would ask him about his achievements. What could he tell them?

Zharkov was right. Alov's aristocratic roots might turn out very badly for him. He was bound to be accused of class-based cronyism and of trying to protect "socially similar elements."

But which employees could he get rid of? All the staff members in his department were vital. Alov called Diana Mikhailovna into his office and asked her what members of staff she thought he should dismiss. She became agitated, talking about Anya the translator who had a young child and about Nikolai Petrovich who had bad knees.

"If he loses his job, it will be the end of him," she fretted.

At that point, the telephone rang. "Off you go now," said Alov, waving Diana Mikhailovna out of the room, but she refused to budge.

"Comrade Alov," she said in a pitiful voice, "you're not going to dismiss me, are you? I have children too."

"If it was up to me, I wouldn't get rid of anyone," he told her. "You're all too valuable to the organization for that."

Diana Mikhailovna beamed. "Thank you!" she said and ran from the room.

Alov picked up the receiver. "Hello!"

It was Galina.

"I need to tell you something," she said. "I'm not working for Klim Rogov anymore."

"Did he throw you out?"

"No. It's me. I don't want to work for him."

Alov was dumbstruck for a moment, amazed at Galina's nerve.

"Listen, Pidge, you and I have got a job to do. What does it matter what you *want* or *don't want*? You have your orders, and you follow them."

But Galina did not seem to be listening. "If anything were to happen to me, would you look after Tata?"

"Are you out of your mind?"

"Why are you so jumpy? You know yourself anything could happen. I could be run over by a cab on the street tomorrow. I just want to know if you'd look after my child."

"But Tata's at boarding school now!"

"She didn't like it there, and she came back."

"You know as well as I do that I haven't got space to put Tata up in my home."

"Then she'll have to go to an orphanage," said Galina thoughtfully. "Just as I thought."

"You're fired!" Alov found himself blurting out to his own surprise. He slammed down the mouthpiece, not wishing to hear or say another word.

He was seething with rage. The cheek of it! A fine pair of princesses he had on his hands! One wouldn't do her job, and the other thought she was too good for boarding school.

He called Diana Mikhailovna again.

"I've given the order for Comrade Dorina to be dismissed from her duties," he told Diana Mikhailovna as she entered his office. "Take care of it for me, please, and ring the duty officers to let them know Dorina's pass is no longer valid."

Diana Mikhailovna gazed at Alov in wonder. She knew that Galina had once been his lover.

"So, you're sacrificing her for our sake?"

Alov frowned. "I'm not sacrificing anybody. Off you go! Why are you breathing down my neck? Actually, wait a minute…. You don't have a cigarette, do you?"

Diana Mikhailovna brought him a couple of her hand-rolled cigarettes, which she made herself using "medicinal" herbs.

Lighting one up, Alov immediately choked on the sweet, unfamiliar smoke.

He really had been a swine to dismiss Galina like that. But then again, he reasoned, she would have lost her job anyway on the 12th of November not only because of her gentry background and her nonpayment of trade union subscription fees but also because she was completely unfit for the job.

He remembered Drachenblut once telling him that by showing pity to weak people, you only encouraged degradation and social deterioration.

I've done what I can for Galina, he tried to reassure himself. *It's not my fault she's so hopeless. And Tata can go back to the boarding school. What is this new fashion, anyway, of only doing what you want? If we all did as we liked, we'd never create socialism in this country.*

6

Drachenblut summoned Alov to come to his office without delay.

He was sitting at his desk and kept putting his hands to his face as if checking to make sure everything was still in place. In front of him was a saucer piled with cigarette butts, a horrible travesty of a dinner plate.

"Today, we gave Oscar Reich ten thousand dollars expenses," said Drachenblut in a queer voice. "And his wife has stolen the money and gone into hiding. What's more, she smashed him over the head so hard that he ended up in hospital."

Alov gasped. "Who is this woman?"

Drachenblut clenched his small, yellow fists. "That's the point. Reich was fool enough to marry some imposter. He thought she was Baroness Bremer, but today, he found out that her name is actually Nina Kupina."

"I know her!" cried Alov.

Drachenblut pointed at a folder on the desk in front of him. "I've been reading the file you started on her. Everything I'm telling you is a state secret, do you understand? If Yagoda knows we've lost a huge sum of money, he'll eat us for breakfast. I asked you to come here because you know Kupina, and you've been keeping tabs on Klim Rogov, the only person who might have an idea where Kupina is. The police inspector spoke to a group of driving students who told him that Rogov and Kupina have been keeping very close company lately."

Alov looked at his boss with a dazed expression. "So, what do you want me to do?"

"I want you to find Kupina. We can't let our agents in on it. They're all accountable to Yagoda, so we'll have to do it ourselves. If we manage to get back that money she stole from Reich, then you've got yourself a room."

"Who exposed Kupina, anyway?" Alov asked.

Drakhenblut sighed heavily. "Some woman. Reich met her on the street and didn't even think to find out her name. If we could have found her, it would all have been a lot easier."

Alov went out of the office, clutching the folder to his chest. *I'm no detective*, he thought. *That isn't my line at all.*

But what if this really was his chance to get a room of his own? After all, miracles could happen. You wished passionately for something, and then some higher power came to meet you halfway.

He had to work out a plan of action. The first thing was to meet up with Klim Rogov, get him under surveillance again, and find out where he went and whom he met.

Alov was already regretting dismissing Galina. She might have come in useful after all.

Back in his office, he called her and asked her what she knew about Rogov's relationship with Kupina.

"I told you back in the winter that Klim was interested in her," she said in a dull voice.

"And that's all?"

"Yes. Leave me alone now, could you? Please?"

It was no good relying on Galina, thought Alov. The fool of a woman really did not have what it took to work for the OGPU.

30. HIDDEN RUSSIA

1

On the off chance, Klim decided to go out to Saltykovka. He prayed the Belovs might have some idea where Nina was hiding. But what if she had been arrested already?

The suburban train was packed with people traveling back out to their dachas outside Moscow. Jobbing laborers stood shoulder to shoulder with dairy women, rag merchants, and street peddlers. Above their heads bristled an array of implements: mops, shovels, and carrying poles.

Klim had to stand in the vestibule at the end of the car. He was next to a crowd of musicians who were traveling back from a wedding. They had had a couple of drinks and were delighted the train was too full to admit ticket inspectors.

"I'd like to give you all a tune on the fiddle," said one of the musicians, a rough-looking man with blue eyes and a paper carnation stuck behind his ear. "But I'd only elbow someone in the face. Still, you got to admit, a tune helps a journey go quicker."

"Give us a song then!" somebody shouted, and the fiddler began to croon in a thin voice:

"All I need to soothe my soul
Is some rubbing alcohol!
Ma and Pa, they both agree
Meths is what my body needs!"

The crowd roared with laughter.

It seemed to Klim that the train was hardly moving. He stood up on his tiptoes to see past the musicians' heads and out of the window, but outside, it was raining hard. He could see nothing beyond the drops on the glass.

A moment later, the train drew to a halt.

"That'll be on account of the Nizhny Novgorod express, the *Blue Arrow*," the fiddler said. "We all have to wait while the top brass goes past."

The tired crowd cursed the passengers on the *Blue Arrow*. It was generally agreed that shooting was too good for them.

The delay lasted one and a half hours, and by the time Klim reached Saltykovka, it was already dark.

An old man, who had traveled into the city to sell mushrooms, showed Klim the way to the Belovs' dacha.

"Watch how you go though," he said. "There are no walkways or street lights. Time was, we had wooden walkways, but they took 'em for firewood when the Executive Committee passed a law against cutting down trees. And there's been no paraffin for a year now."

The warning was a timely one: as it was, Klim almost broke his neck crossing the deep ruts and potholes on the road.

Nina had told Klim that the Belovs had a special knock to the rhythm of the prerevolutionary anthem, "God Save the Tsar," but Klim was so anxious that he forgot all about it.

There was no answer for a long time.

"Who's there?" a woman's voice asked warily from behind the gate.

"It's me," said Klim, and the gate flew open at once.

Nina came running out of the darkness and threw her arms around his neck. "So, you came! We thought it was the OGPU."

Klim felt an incredible rush of relief. It was all too simple and miraculous to be true. He held Nina tightly in his arms and kissed her hair and her cheeks, murmuring over and over again the first thing that came into his head: "I thought I'd never find you…I didn't know if you—"

Nina put her finger to her lips, and Klim realized that she had not told her hosts about the incident in the Red Army Club.

She introduced Klim to Countess Belov, a blonde, rather plump woman in a neat dress with a woolen shawl over her shoulders.

"It's wonderful you're here," the countess said. "Come in and have some tea."

The house turned out to be full of people. Besides the Belov family, their neighbors from nearby dachas were gathered around the samovar. Klim found himself in a world quite unlike Soviet Moscow. Here, the men were polite and chivalrous to the women, the young girls laughed and put their arms around each other's waists, and the children were as excited about the new visitor as if he had been Santa Claus.

There were not enough chairs to go around, so Klim was invited to sit beside Nina on a large linen basket, which creaked ominously under their weight.

Nina's shoulder pressed lightly against Klim's own, and when she turned her head, her hair tickled his neck. She was warm and familiar, and he ached with love for her. He stroked her knee beneath the tablecloth so that nobody would notice, and Nina answered with a squeeze of her hand. It felt as if everything would be as it had been in the days before they had made such a mess of their marriage.

The Belovs were living in dire poverty. Their dacha was dilapidated and smelled of dried mushrooms and apples.

And yet there was a spirit of youthful energy in the house: the walls were covered with children's drawings, an array of chemical flasks and test tubes stood on the windowsill, and a half-dismantled diesel engine sat in the corner.

Klim was showered with questions about Moscow and did his best to reply. He was amazed to observe these people who had offered to shelter Nina. Their intelligent faces shone with kindness, their clothes, though worn and old, were neat and tasteful, and they peppered their speech with foreign expressions, which nobody had any trouble understanding.

The youngest of the family, a twelve-year-old boy, whom everyone addressed respectfully as Georgy Vladimirovich, even made jokes in Latin.

"He's interested in ancient Rome," said Count Belov, ruffling his son's hair. "But I don't know how we're going to teach him. He won't be accepted into university with his family background."

"I can teach myself," answered Georgy Vladimirovich with dignity.

Klim could only feel astonishment that people like the Belovs were now treated as worthless rubbish that had no place in the Soviet society. After all, these were the finest people the nation had to offer.

There was dancing after dinner. The table was carried out of the room, and the countess brought in some sheet music and propped up the lid of the old piano.

Count Belov stood in the middle of the room and made an announcement. "Young men, please take your partners for the first dance!"

Klim bowed to Nina. "Madame?"

She curtseyed as she had been taught back in her school days and held out her hand.

The floors shook, and the curtains jumped in the windows as everybody took part in the dance. Couples whirled to and fro, bumping into each other, pirouetting, laughing, and shrieking. Ladies sank down exhausted onto chairs at the side of the room and fanned themselves with their handkerchiefs.

"Play another, Mamma, please!" the girls shouted, and once again, music shook the house.

It all seemed like a fantastic dream to Klim. Here he and Nina were hiding from the world among strangers, their lives full of fear with no certainty and no hope of planning for the future. And yet right now, his wife was gazing at him with eyes full of love, and he was ready to give up everything for the sake of this dazzling moment.

2

After the dance, Klim followed Nina into the kitchen to help her wash her face before bed. Simply pouring water onto her hands from a mug filled him with indescribable joy.

"Look. This is our product," Nina said proudly, showing him a cake of soap in the shape of a rooster. "We use old molds for making biscuits and sweets. It looks good, don't you think?"

Klim nodded. "Very nice."

The water rushed noisily into the enamel pail. Nina shivered from the cold and wiped her face dry with a towel so old it was almost transparent. Then it was Nina's turn to pour the water for Klim.

My God, I'm about to get into bed with my wife! he thought, and his heart swooned at the thought.

A bed had been made up for them on the floor of Belov's study, a little wooden cubbyhole full of books and sacks of dried apples, the walls hung with portraits of great writers.

The count had unscrewed the only electric light bulb from the chandelier in the living room and offered it to his guests, but Nina had assured him that she and Klim could make do with a church candle.

They put the flimsy door on the latch, placed the candle into a glass jar like a flower in the vase, and sat down on the patchwork blanket, stealing glances at one another.

Nina lay down on her back, and her hair spread out around her head like the wavy rays of a sun on a child's drawing. Klim ran his fingers gently along one ray and then another.

He knew he needed to speak to Nina about Oscar Reich, but he was reluctant to come down to earth from the clouds.

"I think that I've found *my* Russia right here in Saltykovka," said Nina. "This dacha, these people, making soap in these old molds—I could stay here forever."

Klim nodded. "I feel the same. But what if Oscar—"

"Please, let's not talk about that now."

She pulled on Klim's hand, but out of mischief, he resisted. Even using all her weight, she could not manage to get his hand away from him.

"You're not playing fair!" Nina said, laughing. "That being the case, I'm going to my den."

She grabbed a sofa cushion in an oversized pillowcase of flowery calico and pulled the end of the case over her head.

"Wow! It's not a den here," Nina said. "This is the Garden of Eden. Do you want to come and see me in here?"

How could he refuse?

It felt wonderful to play together like children, kissing under the pillowcase and looking up at the light through the colored flowers printed on calico.

Klim ran his hand over Nina's waist, then lower, over the steep curve of her hip, and lower still, down the more gentle, gradual line of her thigh. He wanted to take his time, to absorb as many tiny details as he could. The faint trace of warmth on the sheet where Nina had been lying;

the nub of her wrist bone through her skin; the tiny golden hairs on her arm.

It was more than any human heart could bear. Klim crushed her tightly to him and realized all at once that they were breathing as one.

3

"Do you think we made too much noise?" Nina whispered afterward, pulling the sheet up to cover her shoulders. "Now the Belovs will make us leave in disgrace."

"Not only that; we've disgraced ourselves in front of all these literary masters," said Klim, pointing to the portraits of Tolstoy and Dostoevsky.

The great men were staring down from the wall with expressions of evident disapproval.

The candle had burned down, and now, it went out, giving off a sharp smell of burning and releasing a thin stream of blue-gray smoke into the air.

"Oscar somehow found out that I was going to the driving classes," said Nina in a whisper. "He told me that he had documents in his briefcase that would expose me, and I was afraid he was going to turn me in to the OGPU."

Klim laced his fingers with Nina's and squeezed her hand.

"Oscar tried to choke me," she continued, "so I hit him hard with the crank handle and grabbed the briefcase. I was expecting to find the documents inside, but I found something else."

"What?"

"Ten thousand American dollars in hundred-dollar notes."

Klim propped himself up on his elbow. "No kidding?"

Nina pressed in close to him and began to cry. "I can't stay with the Belovs—their position is already so dangerous. And what will happen if I'm caught?"

Klim suddenly had an idea. "I know what to do. We'll get you some false papers. You can be a German peasant girl who has never had any official documents apart from certificates from the village council. We'll use Oscar's money to bribe Babloyan. He'll get you a foreign passport, and then we'll send you out to Hamburg to charter a ship. You can stay in Germany, and Kitty and I will come out to join you. My contract expires soon in any case."

"We're crooks, you and I," Nina said, still sobbing. "The Belovs would never use stolen money."

"That may be so, but we're two of a kind," said Klim. "We were made for one another."

4

Galina rang Klim and, without any explanation, told him that she would not be coming back to the house on Chistye Prudy. Klim breathed a sigh of relief, but no sooner had one problem been solved than another appeared in its place. He was being shadowed. Every time he looked out, he could see an observer standing on the street opposite his house.

Klim tried to tell himself that it was no big deal to be accompanied everywhere by the snoops. After all, they never attacked him and generally left him alone. But despite this, he felt a keen sense of loss—the loss of a little thing called freedom. He could no longer go anywhere he chose or meet anyone he liked.

On the bright side, he had passed his driving exam and was now qualified as a driver, which meant he could get away from the snoops who were shadowing him. Even when the OGPU came with cars, they could not keep up with Mashka.

Several times, taking great precautions not to be followed, Klim had gone out to Saltykovka. What bliss it had been to visit Nina and walk with her in the golden birch woods, making crazy plans for the future!

Father Thomas had agreed to register Nina as one of his fellow villagers by the name of Hilda Schultz.

Klim began to count up all the surnames Nina had had in her life: "You were born Kupina. Odintzova was your first married name; then you took the false name Bremer. Reich was your false married name, and Schultz is your official name according to your documents."

Nina laughed. "But my real name is Mrs. Rogov."

When they came home, they would go up to Belov's study and leaf through the atlas.

"All we need to be completely happy is good food, suitable clothes, and a roof over our heads," said Klim. "All that might be very expensive in London, but it would be very cheap in some places with very beautiful sunsets. What do you think of going to live in British Honduras?"

Nina studied the article in the atlas for a moment and then frowned. "No, that won't do. They have hurricanes and flooding there."

"What about Japan then? We'll find a pretty village up in the mountains. There will be maple trees, pagodas, and waterfalls. What's not to like? We'll teach in the local schools, and when we get bored, we can go to the Italian Alps or to Hawaii."

They both knew that rural idylls were one thing on picture postcards and another in life. The farther they went from the vices of civilization, the more likely they would be to encounter extreme poverty, epidemics, and religious fanaticism. But Klim and Nina loved playing this game in which they dreamed about another world where there was no politics, no passports, and no constant worry about how to make money.

"The main thing now is to meet with Babloyan," said Klim, "get him to arrange a foreign passport for you, and send you to Germany."

"But how will I take the dollars out of the country?" asked Nina. "They always search anyone crossing the border, and if they find such a large sum of money on me, I won't be able to explain how I got it."

Klim asked Friedrich to take the money to Germany for them, but he refused. It was too big a risk. Not long before, one of the pilots had been caught smuggling foreign currency, and the poor wretch had been accused of financing the counter-revolution and was shot.

5

A special performance by the Blue Blouse theater company was to take place in the Elektrozavod Club to commemorate the opening of a new factory facility.

When Klim arrived, a folk orchestra was playing in the foyer. While some people danced, others crowded around the counter where bread and ham sandwiches were being sold as a special treat in honor of the celebration.

Klim spotted Babloyan from a distance. He was having his photograph taken with the factory directors against the backdrop of the slogan "Long Live the Bolshevik Party!"

"Comrade journalist!" Babloyan cried, waving to Klim. "So, you've come to report on our theatrical performance? That's grand!"

He suggested that Klim sit next to him in the front row so that he could get a good view.

"I'm very interested in theater," said Babloyan as he lowered himself into a chair. "Have you heard of the Blue Blouse company? It's something like a live newspaper. About half of our workers can't read and write, and we're short on radios. But we need to explain to people what's going on in the world. So, the Blue Blouse company goes around factories and other workplaces putting on performances."

The show did indeed turn out to be a curious one. The host asked the crowd to welcome the "Pillars of Soviet Economic Might," and six young men and women ran onto the stage, armed with shields on which were emblazoned the words "Industrialization," "Electrification," "Rationalization," "Fordism," "Standardization," and "Militarization."

The orchestra struck up a tune, and the "pillars" began to demonstrate the work of the machines in the new facility.

Babloyan nudged Klim. "What about that Fordism, eh? Quite a looker, isn't she? I already found out her name. She's called Dunya Odesskaya."

Klim made a note in his reporter's book:

Fordism, Henry Ford's concept of mechanized mass production, had already become an object of mockery overseas by everybody from Charlie Chaplin to street beggars, who would put on a show of repeating the same movement again and again as if unable to stop.

But in the USSR, the philosophy is welcomed. The ideal Soviet man is not an individual but a new and efficient piece of a general mechanism.

Dunya Odesskaya began to declaim a poem by a famous Soviet poet, Vladimir Mayakovsky:

"What is 'one'?
It's no good at all!
It's voice is as small
as the squeak of a mouse
heard by none
but your wife! (so long
as she's not
on the market square

but right there
in the house).

But the Party
brings all 'ones'
together as one,
small voices compressed
 into a great storm.
And our enemies' defenses will burst
when it comes,
just as eardrums burst at
the roar of guns."

This was the new proletariat art, an art without poetry, without intimacy. It did not concern itself with the trivial experiences of worthless individuals but with the aesthetics of organized crowds.

Nevertheless, the Blue Blouse company did touch on the subject of love. Dunya Odesskaya donned a leather jacket, mounted a podium, and began to pretend to give a political speech.

One of the male actors addressed the audience with feeling. "That comrade is one *red-hot* mama! She's got me properly *agitated* with her agitprop."

The audience clapped delightedly.

"Take a look at that!" exclaimed Babloyan, his eyes fixed on Dunya. "That skirt barely covers her backside, but if you tell her it's indecent, I bet she'd say she can't afford any more material."

"And now," the host announced, "we'd like to welcome Comrade Babloyan on stage to say a few words."

There was wild applause, and Babloyan was almost too touched to speak.

"At this time," he began, "when our country is threatened by the blockade imposed by the bourgeois countries of the West, we can hold our heads up high and boldly show everyone…this…hmm…. What I mean is, the power of art to change society will win through!"

All anyone understood from his speech that followed was that Soviet girls, such as Dunya Odesskaya, were the most beautiful girls in the world. Nobody was interested in the ideological content, anyway. The most important thing was that Babloyan came across to them as "one of us," a regular guy, representing the Party that cared about working people.

"Pretty soon," he said, "every working man will receive a cartload of firewood for the winter. And don't worry about paraffin! The Soviet authorities will bring electricity into every home, even the humblest worker's cabin."

After lengthy and noisy applause, Babloyan bowed and set off toward the exit with his entourage.

On stage, the amateur concert resumed.

Klim barely managed to catch up with Babloyan in the corridor.

"I wanted to ask you a small favor, sir. Do you remember our conversation about the Volga Germans?"

Babloyan glanced meaningfully toward the lavatories and then announced to his henchmen, "Wait here. I won't be a moment."

In the men's lavatories, a tap was dripping, and the walls echoed with the sound of water trickling into the enamel basin. A dim light filtered in through the window, which had been half painted over.

"We now have enough money to sort out the passports and the cost of freight," Klim spoke in a low voice.

He told Babloyan about the Canada plan and about Hilda Schultz.

Babloyan considered his words, frowning.

"All right," he said at last. "Bring me the money and a list of the names of all your Germans."

"What about an interview with Stalin?" Klim added. "Do you think it might still be possible to organize?"

Babloyan looked at Klim uncomprehendingly. "Why do you want an interview with Stalin?"

"Our readers want to know what's happening in the USSR."

"Then they should read *Pravda*. It's all there in black and white," said Babloyan curtly, and then he left.

6

Alov had come to the Elektrozavod Club before the concert began. During the performance, he had been standing beside Klim Rogov, inconspicuous in his peaked cap and standard-issue jacket and trousers from the Moscow state clothing factory.

He was intrigued to see Rogov sit down next to Comrade Babloyan. What, he wondered, was the connection between the two of them?

But soon, Alov saw something that distracted him completely from thoughts of work. Dunya, his Dunya, was up on stage, behaving in the most shameless manner.

For some time now, Alov had not been going to watch his wife perform. He had always said that he trusted her implicitly, but now, he felt that this had been a mistake. In the first place, some young fellow was carrying her about on his shoulders, which meant that a certain part of her anatomy was coming into contact with the man's neck. Besides this, Dunya had performed some "Dance of the Conveyor Belt," which had involved high kicks and a run out on stage in some makeshift sort of toga that looked as if it might fall off at any moment. The very idea was enough to make Alov die of shame.

But the worst was yet to come. The next moment, Comrade Babloyan had got up on stage and begun to praise Dunya's good looks in front of everyone. Alov knew very well that Babloyan was a notorious womanizer. Did he have his eye on Dunya?

When Rogov and Babloyan left the hall, Alov hurried after them and saw them turn off the corridor into the lavatories.

Babloyan's henchmen waited patiently for him. At last, he emerged, and they set off toward the lobby. Alov stared after him furiously. There wasn't much even an OGPU agent could do against a member of the Central Committee. Such people existed outside the law and outside any moral codes; they simply took whatever they wanted.

Soon, Rogov came out into the corridor too. Alov darted up to him and showed him his OGPU identity card.

"What were you just talking about with Babloyan?" he demanded.

The two of them stood glaring stiffly at one another.

"My bosses are insisting that I arrange an interview with Stalin," said Rogov at last. "So, I asked Comrade Babloyan to help. But he told me there's nothing he can do."

"Is that all you talked about?" asked Alov, his voice thick with mistrust.

"Well, no. We talked about actresses too."

"Which actresses?"

"The ones who just performed; the girls from the Blue Blouse. Dunya Odesskaya has made quite an impression on Comrade Babloyan, it seems."

Alov pulled his amber beads from under his cuff and began to click them rapidly to and fro. He was smarting with fury. Just think, this sleek, pampered bourgeois prig thought he had the right to discuss any woman he chose and to demand an interview with Stalin himself!

"Excuse me," said Rogov, "but I have to go."

The upstart did not even feel the slightest alarm at being faced by an OGPU agent. It seemed he had no idea that Alov could have him deported and his visa annulled with no more than a snap of his fingers.

With great effort, Alov forced himself to speak politely and calmly. "We're interested in talking to a woman by the name of Nina Kupina," he said. "You don't happen to know where she is?"

Rogov shrugged. "No idea. We met on a driving course."

"Don't lie to me!" Alov said. "A few months ago, you were interested in the whereabouts of this same individual."

It was clear from Rogov's face that he had not expected the OGPU to be so well-informed.

"So, what do you say?" Alov asked in an insinuating tone.

Rogov winced like some businessman pestered by a street beggar. "Is this an interrogation?"

"No, it's an offer," said Alov. "I'd like you to cooperate with us. Who knows when you might need a connection in the OGPU?"

"Good evening." Rogov left without even holding out his hand.

Just you watch out! thought Alov. *I've got my eye on you.*

If there was one thing Alov could not bear, it was when other people failed to treat him with respect.

31. THE SOLOVKI PRISON CAMP

1

As soon as the passport made out in the name of Hilda Schultz was ready, Klim went to buy Nina's ticket to Berlin. Fortunately, there were no queues for international trains.

On the way to Saltykovka, he pictured how Nina would meet him at the gate and ply him with impatient questions. "Well?" she would ask him. "How did it go with the ticket?" Then he would pull a sad face just to tease her before producing his prize.

Whenever Nina heard good news, she reacted with girlish delight, gasping excitedly and dancing in celebration, and Klim could not wait to make her happy.

But this time, it was not Nina who opened the gate to Klim but Countess Belov. Her face wore an anxious expression, her eyebrows set in a tragic arch.

Klim felt his blood run cold. "What is it?"

"Elkin's here," the countess answered in a dreadful whisper.

Klim followed her into the small kitchen, which was hung with garlands of dried mushrooms, and stopped still, staring at the man sitting by the window.

The man was so thin that his bony shoulders protruded from his dirty military-style tunic. His crew-cut hair had gone completely gray, and his face was deeply lined. He still resembled the Elkin of old, yet at the same time, he looked quite different. It was unbelievable that a man could age so much in two months.

"What happened to you?" asked Klim, stunned.

Elkin smiled. All the teeth on the left-hand side of his mouth were missing.

"I was sent to the Solovki prison camp," he said, "but I managed to run away."

Nina came in to the kitchen carrying two pails of water on a carrying pole and put them down on the floor.

"Now, we'll heat up some water," said Countess Belov, turning to Elkin, "and you shall have a proper wash."

Nina nodded briefly in Klim's direction and began helping their hostess to light the stove. Not a word of greeting. It was as if she was afraid of insulting their guest by showing Klim any particular attention.

"Why did they arrest you?" Klim asked Elkin.

"The Feodosia authorities got an order to find and detain any Nepmen, bourgeois, and other undesirable elements. They knew me personally—I fixed their cars for them, so they didn't have to go very far to find me."

"Did they formally accuse you of anything?"

"They don't give a damn about formal accusations!" Nina snapped out. "The Bolsheviks need free labor. They don't understand anything about efficient production, and their outgoing costs are so high that they don't have enough money to pay the workforce. So, they need slaves to cut down timber in Solovki and work in the mines for nothing."

Putting an iron pot of water inside the big masonry oven, Nina slammed its shutter. Her movements were abrupt and violent. It seemed she was on the point of grabbing something and smashing it to smithereens.

"How on earth did you escape?" Klim asked Elkin. "I've heard it's impossible—Solovki is on some island in the White Sea."

"I didn't get that far," said Elkin gloomily. "I ran away from a transit camp on the mainland."

Klim felt a chill run down his spine. Everybody in the USSR had heard rumors of the camps in the north, but there was no reliable information about them.

"Perhaps you'd let me interview you?" he asked. "I'm sure United Press would be interested in your story."

Elkin looked Klim up and down, scornfully. "So, you're already thinking how to make a fast buck, are you?"

"I'd just like to know—"

"Mr. Rogov, I have nothing left but my story, and I intend to sell it to the highest bidder. I need to get out of this blessed country of ours, and it costs three hundred rubles to organize an illegal passage across the border to Poland."

"We'll give you the money!" Nina exclaimed, her voice full of emotion.

Neither she nor the countess seemed in the slightest bit concerned that Elkin had accused Klim of seeking to profit from another's misfortune.

Countess Belov glanced at the clock on the wall. "We should put the potatoes on to boil," she said. "The children will be back from school soon."

Nina ran out to the yard to the cold cellar, and Klim set off after her.

She opened the hatch and was about to go down the cellar steps when he reached her.

"You never even asked me about the passport," he said. "I've brought you everything."

She turned and stared at him blankly. "Yes, thank you."

There was no celebratory dance. Klim stood next to the open mouth of the cellar, breathing in the damp smell of earth and decay.

"It's fine," he said. "You don't have to thank me."

Nina came out again with a pipkin of small, sprouting potatoes.

"I know Elkin's your friend," said Klim. "I just want you to know that once you've chartered that boat for the German refugees, we won't have any money left to live on. I don't speak German, and it'll be some time before I can find work. My friend Seibert is a famous journalist in Germany, and he's barely scraping a living publishing articles here and there…. I hope you don't mind me speaking honestly?"

"Of course not," Nina nodded. Her face was wan and miserable. A curl had escaped her comb and hung down beside her cheek.

"I'll do whatever I can to fix things for us," said Klim. "But all of a sudden, you come up with some plan of your own like getting Elkin across the border to Poland—"

Nina looked down at the ground.

"I want to help him because it's so easy to imagine myself in his place. The Bolsheviks are just like the Mongol army back in the middle ages. They ambush peaceful civilians and make them into slaves. If you're set to work logging or building one of their mines or plants—then that's it. You'll end up a cripple, physically and morally…. I was just imagining what would happen to me if they got their hands on me. And it could happen at any minute! What would I do? I would have to rely on the kindness of others—and that's all Elkin has to rely on."

Nina took a deep, shuddering breath and put her arm around Klim. "You may not understand what I'm doing, but it won't come between us, I promise you. Just trust me!"

Klim clasped Nina to him. The problem was he could not just trust her. The paradise they were building was too fragile. One false movement, one strong gust of wind, and the whole thing would collapse. What awaited them then? No waterfalls and sunsets; only jealousy and suspicion.

"It will be better for everyone," said Nina, "if I give Elkin the money to get him over the border. He can take our dollars out of the country, and I'll meet him in Berlin. And then we can pay for the ship."

Klim sighed. "You do as you see fit." He took the "Book of the Dead" from his pocket and handed it to her. "Here. This is my diary. Read it and then burn it. I can't take it with me to Germany in any case. All printed material and manuscripts have to pass the censor if I want to take them across the border."

"So, you'd let me into your innermost secrets?"

"I think we need to learn how to understand each other. Even if it means sharing some painful things."

"Would you like me to tell you about Oscar too?" asked Nina.

Klim shook his head. "I'm prepared to postpone that particular pleasure until 1976. When you're eighty years old, I'll stop worrying that you're about to leave me, and I'll be ready to hear your confessions."

2

BOOK OF THE DEAD

Entry written by Nina

I'm sorry, but I can't destroy your notebook. So, I will try to smuggle it into Germany. I will read it to you when I am eighty, and you are scolding me about Oscar Reich. Your diary will be proof that we are both as bad as each other.

3

BOOK OF THE DEAD

Entry written by Nina on a separate page inserted into the diary.

Tomorrow, Elkin is leaving for Minsk. In the end, he decided to tell me the whole story of his escape from the camp by way of thanking me for paying for his journey.

I will try to record it to the best of my abilities.

Elkin was sentenced to ten years of hard labor and sent off to the north.

The OGPU have the whole system working smoothly now: new prisoners are brought in on trains to the station in Kem town, and from there, they are driven like cattle to the transit camp beside the White Sea. They are referred to as "reinforcements" like soldiers at the front. Nobody hides the fact that they are meant to take the place of prisoners who have died.

The transit camp is a plot of land surrounded by a fence and barbed wire with a couple dozen wooden huts. These huts will house about fifteen hundred people at any one time, all living in atrociously cramped conditions and sleeping on long wooden platforms made of boards. At the end of each hut, there is a space partitioned off for the guards. The guards are prisoners too. They are former OGPU employees who have been sent north after being found guilty of professional misconduct. The only free men among the camp supervisors are the camp commander and his two assistants.

The Soviet camp system is organized as follows: prisoners fight for privileges because this seems simpler to them than fighting for freedom. This explains why none of the guards ever tries to run away or ever turns his weapon on his oppressors.

If you go to a labor camp as a prison guard, you sleep on a separate platform and eat from a special pot. You may even be given a fur coat. You won't be kept outside in the wind for hours during inspections or sent down to the sea to retrieve the logs driven across the water from Solovki.

Discipline in the camps is maintained through fear: the fear of being deprived of warmth, food, rest, or the modicum of physical safety you enjoy.

Elkin arrived in the camp in August and realized straight away that if he was sent on to the islands to work at logging or peat cutting, he would never get out alive. There are no roads there and no horses, and all heavy loads are hauled on foot by prisoners who are said to be "temporarily carrying out the work of horses."

On Solovki, a human life is valued no higher than the life of an insect. All the same, before they die of disease or exhaustion, all prisoners must do their bit for the Soviets and earn a few German marks or a couple of French francs with their own sweat and blood.

Elkin told me that several times he saw messages written in blood on logs right next to the official brand of "Timber for Export": "They are killing us here." Could there be anything more desperate than these communications scrawled in Russian and addressed to unknown sawmill workers in Germany or France? Who could ever decipher the impenetrable Cyrillic letters? And even if someone could understand them, what can the Germans or French do to help these modern-day Soviet slaves?

For breakfast, the prisoners are given hot water with bread, lunch consists of a broth of over-boiled vegetables, and supper is gruel. All the prisoners, without exception, are riddled with lice. Half are sick with anything from scurvy to complete mental derangement. The only hope is to get a job working in the office, the bathhouse, or the kitchen, but prisoners fight to the death for these positions. And of course, the political prisoners, the cultured men like Elkin, are never successful.

Every day, the camp supervisors do a little more to corrupt the prisoners and destroy their integrity. Snitch on your bunkmate, and you get an extra piece of bread. Volunteer to be an executioner, and you can avoid being sent out logging. Turn traitor, and you may even get yourself a pair of felt boots.

Without warm clothes, prisoners will fall victim to frostbite on their feet and hands as early as November. And that means death from gangrene because nobody in the camp can perform an amputation.

All prisoners, without exception, are beaten in the transit camp to show them what awaits them if they disobey orders. Many die from the beatings alone, from broken ribs or internal injury. Elkin was lucky that he only lost half his teeth.

Realizing that he needed to escape without delay before the winter cold set in, Elkin managed to persuade another prisoner—a young, strong fellow—to join him.

When they were sent out to the forest with a team to collect wood for brooms, they attacked the guard, tied him to a tree, and took his uniform and his gun.

Then they spent thirty days wandering about beside the railroad line. They couldn't bring themselves to approach any settlements because they knew the peasants would not hesitate to hand them over to the authorities. The reward for capturing escapees was too tempting: they would receive a sackful of grain.

Before long, the cultured Elkin was forced, like it or not, to become a bandit. He and his companion had to eat, so they went into the first village they found and announced that they were going to carry out a search and confiscate any surplus grain. The chairman of the village Soviet brought them off with a bribe, a sack of food, and the fugitives ran back into the forest.

They did this several times until one day, they had the luck to rob an official carrying cash. They split the money and went their separate ways. Elkin set off for Moscow, and his companion decided to try to get to Finland.

A few days later, Elkin had read in the paper that his companion had been captured and shot.

4

Nina sewed the money to pay for the ship into Elkin's coat, and the Belovs gave him a bundle of food for the journey.

Only Nina went to the railroad to see him off so as not to attract unwanted attention.

"I'm leaving tomorrow," she told him, "and I'll probably get to Berlin a few days before you since you still have to think how to get from Poland to Germany. From the sixth of November on, I'll come to the station every day at midday and wait for you under the main departures board."

Everything was going much better than Elkin could have hoped. Thanks to Nina, he had almost immediately got ahold of money and a train ticket to Minsk, but he sensed that everybody was glad to see him leave. The Belovs were afraid he might get them arrested, and Nina was anxious not to annoy Mr. Rogov.

Elkin had never felt so lonely before in his life.

Nina felt ashamed in his company and kept talking about the great future awaiting him in Germany.

"You'll soon find your feet," she said, "and then you can rebuild Mashka. A man with your talent will be worth his weight in gold in Europe."

But Elkin did not feel like doing anything. Ever since that first robbery, when a small, bearded Finn had fallen at his feet with a plaintive cry, "Have mercy on us!" something inside him had been destroyed.

Nobody commits evil for the sake of evil, he thought, *except for out-and-out psychopaths.* People always had their reasons for wrongdoing. They committed crimes to survive both in the camps and outside. And everybody fell into the same trap, even Nina, who had got hold of an enormous sum of money from somewhere and now seemed to be in hiding from the police.

So, which of us is responsible for evil? Elkin wondered. *Every one of us, I suppose, in our own small way.*

He and Nina walked along past boarded-up dachas. Overhead, the sky was overcast. Alongside the fence, the grass was reddish brown, and at the bend in the road stood a rusty sign announcing, "Danger! Beware Trains!"

"Who's helping you cross the border?" Nina asked, jumping over a huge puddle that covered the whole path. "Are they smugglers? Do you know them well?"

"We did business together once," Elkin said. "I ordered them one or two things for Moscow Savannah, but they weren't very happy about it. Books are heavy things and less profitable than powders and perfumes."

The train only stopped at the platform for a couple of minutes.

"Goodbye and God bless," said Nina. "Don't give up! Everything will turn out all right for us, you'll see."

She really is an extraordinary woman, thought Elkin with affectionate sadness. No matter what fate threw at her, she always landed on her feet and expected others to do the same.

And that was the spirit of Russia itself. The country had an incredible capacity for survival, an ability to adapt to anything on earth.

Elkin gazed into Nina's face, flushed with emotion as if for the last time, and held her hand, unable to release it from his hard, calloused palm.

The whistle blew, and the train began to move. A song carried from the open window:

All around us lies the steppe,
The road stretches far away.

"Goodbye," said Elkin, and grabbing hold of the handle, he mounted the footboard.

Clattering over the rails, the train passed gloomy huts, sparse coppices, and endless fields.

There's no need for regret, thought Elkin. Everything was as it had always been. Russia was a steppe. Once in several decades, it produced a layer of fertile soil, but then the whirlwinds descended, crushed it into dust, and carried it away to the four corners of the earth. That was the purpose of the steppe: to bring forth fresh winds and the seeds of new growth.

5

Elkin was struck by the sheer quantity of well-dressed people in the streets of Minsk. Here and there among the crowd, he could see colorful shawls, new fur coats, and sometimes even the odd fedora. It was clear that the border was close by and trade was brisk.

The fresh snow was pitted with the marks of women's high heeled shoes. Elkin stared at them lovingly. How many years had it been since he had seen such a thing in Moscow?

All around, people were shouting Russian, Belarusian, and Polish. The houses here were wooden like the houses in Russia, but their roofs were covered in red and black slates in the Polish style. Soviet banners, prepared for the latest anniversary of the revolution, fluttered in the breeze. On a nearby bench, Red Army soldiers sat beside fine-looking Jewish men with side locks.

After wandering for a while, Elkin found his way to Nemiga, a narrow street lined with low buildings with cluttered stores on the ground floor and living quarters up above.

Elkin found the house he was looking for and knocked at the padded door. A young man with closely cropped hair, dark eyes, and a crooked chin came out.

"What do you want?" he asked in Belarusian.

"I'm here to see Rygor," replied Elkin.

The young man glanced to each side and then took Elkin through into a room piled high with packing cases full of goods.

"Stay here," he said and disappeared into the back room.

Elkin waited for more than an hour. Eventually, he could stand it no more and went out into the corridor.

A narrow metal staircase led up to the floor above, and up above, he could hear voices speaking in Polish.

"They're running out of confiscated goods. So, what have we got right now?"

"Ribbed tricot, French marquisette, velveteen—with and without silk—wool broadcloth…"

The Poles were cashing in on all sides on the Bolshevik economic experiment. As soon as certain goods began to disappear from the USSR, there was a tremendous surge in contraband items. In the villages on the Polish border, people were hard at work concocting mascara, making brassieres from poor-quality imitation silk, and even printing false consignment documents for all sorts of institutions. Nobody was concerned by the poor quality of these goods; they were still better than what was available in the USSR.

At last, there was a clatter of boots on the staircase, and Rygor, a plump man with a curly beard, came down from the floor above.

"Well, just look who it is!" he exclaimed in Russian on seeing Elkin. "So, what brings you here?"

Elkin explained he needed to get to Poland without delay.

Rygor scratched his head thoughtfully. "Well, you *could* set off tonight if you like. But I have to warn you, there's shooting on the border at the moment."

"What? Why?" asked Elkin in alarm.

"Russkies behaving like beasts, that's what. Now, they're waging war on well-off peasants. Our men don't want to give up their produce, so they're hiding in the forest. Folk around here are desperate and still armed to the teeth after the war. So, partisans are killing Red Army soldiers like pigs and then running across to Poland to escape arrest. My friend, Piatrus Kamchatka, is setting out to the border today, and he can take you with him."

According to Rygor, Piatrus was an experienced smuggler. "For three years now, he's been taking gold and artworks over to Poland. He brings all sorts of things back in to the country, from microscopes to toilet paper. He's as strong as an ox. One time, he was asked to take a crippled old woman across the border. And what do you think he did? Took her over on his own back!"

Rygor asked for a hundred rubles for putting Elkin in contact with his friend.

"For God's sake, I can't give you that much!" said Elkin.

Rygor shrugged. "Well, so long as you're no bourgeois, you can stay here, can't you?"

With a heavy heart, Elkin handed over the money. Now, he might not have enough to pay a guide from the sum allocated by Nina for his passage across the border.

"Anyone with any sense is selling their possessions and getting out of the land of the Soviets," said Rygor, putting the money in his pocket. "Piatrus can take you as far as Rakov—it's what you might call the smugglers' capital. I'll be going there myself in three weeks. It's a good little town, Rakov. For a population of seven thousand, it has one hundred and thirty-four shops, nighty-six restaurants, and four official brothels."

6

Ales, the young man with the crooked chin who had opened the door to Elkin, took him to a village on the border.

They traveled for a long time along bad roads. It was a frosty night, and the cart jolted them mercilessly as it went over the frozen ruts.

Eklin tried to ask Ales about the smugglers and about the situation at the border, but the young man merely pulled a face and spat on the ground.

"Ask Piatrus," he said.

All the way, he sang songs about the "Russkies" who had drawn up their borders without consulting the local peasants and about the wrath of the people, which was bound, sooner or later, to overtake the interlopers. The Belorussians had lived for many years between the devil and the deep blue sea, suffering all sorts of misery from both the Poles and the Russians, who kept sending armies sweeping through their land.

Elkin sensed that Ales saw him as an enemy too, as one of the "Russkies." He found it hard to believe how he could be considered guilty of crimes of which he had no knowledge. But as far as Ales was concerned, ignorance of the plight of Belorussia was tantamount to approval of the injustices being done to his country.

Dusk was falling by the time they reached the village.

With trepidation, Elkin gazed at the clapboard houses with their dark blue window frames. Snow lay on their thatched roofs, and columns of smoke drifted from their chimneys.

Ales led the horse into a yard surrounded by a pole fence.

"Out you get!" he commanded to Elkin.

Clenching his body against the cold, Elkin jumped down. The icy puddles crunched beneath his feet.

An old woman wearing a checked dress and a padded jacket came out to meet them. She spoke to Ales rapidly in Belorussian. All Elkin could understand of their conversation was that Ales was going on farther while Elkin was to wait for Piatrus there.

The old woman took him inside the house where it was hot and smoky. Several hens were settling down to roost before an enormous stove.

"Won't you take off your coat?" asked the old woman as Elkin sank, exhausted, onto a bench.

"I'm cold," he told her. "I can't seem to get warm."

After the conversation with Ales, he was haunted by a sense of foreboding. Where had he ended up now? Who were these people? Could he trust them?

Fortunately, the old woman turned out to be good-natured and friendly. She even offered Elkin some bread.

Unlike Ales, she was more worried about the Poles than the "Russkies." Sighing, she told him that when the Germans had come during the Great War, they hadn't touched a thing, but with the Poles, it had been a different story. They stole animals, and any peasant who protested would be whipped with switches.

So, this is life on the border, thought Elkin. On the one hand, there's no shortage of opportunities for trade, but on the other hand, everyone is out to get a piece of what was yours.

He soon felt drowsy from the food and the warmth and kept rubbing his eyes to keep himself awake.

"So, where's Piatrus?" he asked at last.

There was a sound from the shelf above the stove, and the next minute, a great strong boy dressed in a faded soldier's tunic without a belt jumped down to the ground. He stretched, yawned, and, turning to the icon in the corner of the hut, crossed himself.

"Have you got some money for me?" he asked Elkin.

Like Rygor, Piatrus was not prepared to bargain. He would settle for no less than three hundred rubles, and Elkin was forced to get the shortfall from the sum Nina had asked him to take across the border. He cut open the lining of his coat and took out a hundred-dollar note.

"So, you're carrying American money?" Piatrus asked, looking at Elkin's coat with a great interest. "Well, we can be on our way soon. We'll be in Rakov by morning."

7

Elkin had not expected the journey through the forest at night to be such a nightmare. But the memory of his wanderings after escaping the camp was still fresh in his mind, and every fiber of his being revolted.

I don't suppose I'll ever be able to walk in the forest again without being afraid, he thought desperately.

And yet, he had to keep moving, clambering over fallen logs, descending into shallow ravines, and skirting impenetrable thickets of spruce trees.

He had no idea how Piatrus managed to find his way in the pitch dark. The sky was cloudy, and Elkin could barely make out the dim silhouette of his guide up ahead. The bushes rustled, and now and then, some night birds gave a hollow cry. And all the while, heavy drops of water fell from branches onto his cap and his shoulders.

Several times, Elkin slipped and fell in the muddy slush underfoot. Piatrus would curse in a whisper. They had to try to get as far as possible before the changeover of the guards at the border post.

Back in Crimea, Elkin had been able to walk for hours in the mountains without stopping. Now, he already had a stitch in his side, his knee joints were cracking, and there was a dull roar in his ears.

What if I don't make it? he thought. *What if my strength gives out and I just collapse?*

From time to time, he fingered the money hidden under the lining of his coat. Piatrus had told him that if the border guards caught someone with goods, he might be released in return for a bribe. The guards were badly fed and were always glad to get their hands on a smuggler. But if they caught anyone carrying weapons or money, it meant certain death because anyone doing so would be considered an anti-government rebel.

Elkin tripped over a root and fell sprawling to the ground. For some time, he lay there, overwhelmed by an agonizing pain in his arm. Had he broken a bone or just wounded himself on a sharp stump?

Getting up on all fours, Elkin listened. It was deadly quiet all around. Only the hundred-year-old pines rustled and murmured high above him.

"Piatrus?" he called out quietly. "Where are you?"

There was no answer.

Elkin panicked. Where could he go? Where was he? Was he still on the Soviet side of the border or already on the Polish side?

A moment later, he felt a heavy blow to his temple and fell to the ground.

32. JOURNEY TO BERLIN

1

The train from Moscow to Berlin only went as far as the border station of Negoreloye, where passengers had to change trains. Soviet and European railroads ran on tracks of different gauges. This had been a deliberate strategy of the Tsarist regime, intended to hamper enemy supplies in case of an attack from abroad.

Beyond the station lay *terra incognita*, unknown territory to the ordinary Soviet citizen. It was nothing short of a miracle even to be on board this train. Only a chosen, lucky few could sit in these clean railroad cars, full of excitement, making plans, hearts beating fast as they counted down the hours to the cherished border.

Nina's baggage consisted of a single basket containing a change of linen and a clean bag of toiletries. Next to this bag stood a pot decorated with eyes and handles for ears and curls around the top. It was a present from Gloria, containing ashes from the Belovs' stove. Nina was planning to tell the customs officers that these were her grandmother's ashes, which she was taking to Germany to scatter there, according to the old woman's wishes. Nina's most valuable possession, Klim's diary, was hidden inside the lid of the pot, which Nina had sculpted with her own hands.

All the way to Negoreloye, Nina's heart was in her mouth. What if some sharp-eyed official noticed that the lid did not match the pot? Now, Nina was regretting the sentiment that had led her to expose herself to danger for the sake of a foolish notebook. But she could not bring herself to part with the "Book of the Dead." It was the only tangible thread linking her to Klim.

When he had come out to Saltykovka for the last time, the two of them had sat together in Belov's study for a long time, their arms around each other.

"I've decided how things are going to be," Klim had said, kissing Nina on the side of her head. "If we save our Germans, our sins will be forgiven, and everything will be all right."

There were times when Nina thought this impossible. People for whom "everything was all right" were not like them at all. She had had the opportunity to encounter several examples as she passed through the train: a Danish engineer on his way back from a work assignment, a young woman taking her children to see her husband who worked in the embassy in Berlin, and a noisy group of American tourists who had seen what the USSR had to offer and were now setting off to Czechoslovakia.

Nina shared a compartment with a group of artists who were on their way to an international exhibition of proletarian art. They downed one beer after another and talked about their trade.

"I've got a portrait of a woman in oils," a young bearded artist said. "I wanted to sell it to the People's Commissariat for Education, but they wouldn't take it because it didn't have an ideological title. It's a nice picture, and I wouldn't want it to go to waste. Breasts out to here!" he said, holding his hands out from his chest.

All speaking at once, his fellow artists began to suggest suitably ideological titles.

"You could call it 'Proletarian Woman' or 'Worker's Daughter.'"

"No, those won't do. How about 'The Flame of Communism Burns Inside Her Breast'?"

"But that's just it—there's no communism in the picture," sighed the bearded artist.

"Well, you can't see it, can you? It's inside her breast!"

The artists all laughed.

These people have hopes and a future, thought Nina, looking at them from her upper berth.

The artists discussed how the famous painter, Isaac Brodsky, had received an order for sixty copies of his painting "The Execution of the Baku Commissars" for the government offices. Each of the artists dreamed of a similar stroke of unbelievably good fortune.

As for Nina, her own dreams were humbler and less realistic than that. She prayed only that she and Klim would avoid being arrested or killed.

2

For the entire eighteen-hour journey, Nina lay on the upper berth, watching the trunks of pine trees flash by the window like armies of giant yellow pencils. Patches of snow still lay in the gullies. Dark green forests, gray roofs, black kitchen gardens, and yet more forests.

At last, at five o'clock in the afternoon, the train arrived at Negoreloye. The passengers began to gather their belongings, but they had a long wait before their passports were checked by border control officers and they were allowed to leave the train and go to the station.

As the rules required, the passengers laid their baggage out on a horseshoe-shaped bench in the center of the waiting room, and grim-faced customs officers began the inspection.

They rummaged around in suitcases as if they were tossing salad. Every now and again, they pulled something out, yelling, "Contraband!"

This was the signal for a group of young men with scales and official ledgers to descend and begin weighing, measuring, and assessing the value of the contraband item. Then the dumbstruck passengers would be presented with a fine. They could choose to pay up or to jettison the dubious souvenir—to the delight of the customs officers. It was clear from their well-fed faces that nothing here went to waste.

Nina was trembling all over. *Stop!* she told herself. *You'll give yourself away!* But in fact, all the other passengers were just as nervous as she was. Nobody was safe from the insolent, indiscriminate tyranny of the customs officers, and nobody breathed a word of complaint, not wishing to attract unwanted attention.

Anyone carrying foreign currency had to present a stamped form from an exchange bureau. Anyone taking cameras, typewriters, fur coats, watches, or other valuables across the border had to fill out a declaration.

A porter in a white apron wheeled in a trolley laden with neat packages and began calling out the names of the passengers, asking them to collect their property. In the packages were books, magazines, posters, and handwritten material that the censor had allowed to cross the border. A few weeks before their departure, passengers had handed all this over for the censors to read, rubber-stamp, and mail on to Negoreloye.

When the officers reached Nina's basket, she was half-fainting with fear. The customs official, a great hulking lad, rummaged with distaste through her belongings and then pulled out the pot from the basket.

"What's this?" he asked, peering inside.

"My grandmother's ashes," said Nina in a weak voice.

The lad put his hand into the pot and began fumbling about to check there was nothing hidden inside.

"Damn!" he swore suddenly. His great paw had become stuck inside the pot, and he was unable to pull it out.

Amused by the incident, passengers glanced meaningfully in his direction.

He ran to his colleagues. "Hey, men, help me get this thing off!"

Each officer, in turn, tried to pull the pot off his hand but without success. Meanwhile, the ashes of "Nina's grandmother" were scattered in all directions.

The crowd did not know whether to laugh or to be indignant at the mess that was being made of their baggage.

"To hell with it!" the officer shouted. He brought the pot hard down onto the bench with a crash, smashing it into a hundred pieces.

Nina gasped.

"You're free to go!" he barked. "Next time, use a bigger pot."

Nina took the basket and the pot lid and went out to the platform where the Berlin train was waiting.

When I die, she thought, *I think they should scatter my ashes around some waiting room too. It would be a perfect metaphor for my life.*

3

Eastern Poland looked much the same as Belorussia: the same little towns, the same fields of black earth, and the same poor country roads with puddles of rainwater in the ruts.

There were few people about; only a couple of peasants waiting with their wagon at the level crossings for the train to pass.

Now and again, Nina saw rows of old trenches and forests of dead trees with peeling bark and twisted stumps for branches. These were areas in which chemical weapons had been used during the Great War.

The train arrived in Warsaw at night, and Nina slept the whole way through western Poland. And when they arrived in Germany, everything outside the train looked different.

"Good god, take a look at that!" gasped the artists, pressing in close to the windows.

Vast building sites, factory chimneys, and the small, neat houses of workers' districts slid by outside. Even in the smaller towns, the station buildings were as large and fine as cathedrals, and beyond them, elegant, red-tiled turrets clustered beside the green spires of town halls.

"Holy shit!" the artists swore in amazement. "Look at that signalman with the peaked cap! He looks like an army general."

"Look at that cart! It has *tires* like a motor car!"

The bearded artist was already making hasty sketches in a book with an oil-cloth cover, a third of which was already filled with landscapes, portraits, and notes in the margin.

Nina watched the scene outside the window with mixed emotions. She knew from the papers that the last ten years had not been easy for the Germans, yet there had been no talk of an economic slump. It looked as if Germany had managed to recover after the war. Russia, on the other hand, had suffered from "complications" in the shape of the Soviet regime. Good god, how unfair it all was!

The sun came out for a moment, lighting up sidings, railcars, depots, and signs written in an incomprehensible Gothic script.

"Next stop, Berlin!" sung out the attendant.

The train was slowing down now as it passed through the city. For a moment, the sunlight vanished in the shadow of a viaduct, and then they entered the station building.

Nina was the last to get out on the platform. Berlin swallowed her up immediately, a little foreigner in a quaint peasant's sheepskin coat and a headscarf.

Here, all the colors seemed brighter and the sounds louder. She was stunned by the sight of the crowd; there were so many well-dressed men and women in elegant coats! And they had *umbrellas!*

A group of workers went by carrying a large pipe, and every one of them looked smart and well-fed. Even a crippled beggar in the station was wearing a freshly ironed uniform with a medal.

Nina looked around at all the splendor in confusion, overwhelmed with an acute sense of loneliness and alienation. Nobody was waiting for her in Berlin.

"Hilda Schultz?" she heard a voice behind her.

Nina turned and saw a small, broad-shouldered gentleman in a bowler hat. It was Heinrich Seibert.

4

Seibert was doing his best to give the impression that fortune had favored him no worse in his own country than in Moscow. But in fact, he was deeply unhappy.

On the surface of it, he had little reason to be dissatisfied. Germany was a much better developed country than the USSR. Since the Emperor had abdicated and new, far more liberal laws had been passed, Berlin had become the creative capital of Europe. However, the stylish cabarets and shops full of incredible products did nothing to lift Seibert's mood. In Moscow, he had been at the top of the heap thanks to his German citizenship and his position in society; in Berlin, he was just another struggling journalist.

Seibert could not afford to live in the center of town, so he was renting an apartment near the end of the metro line at Thielplatz and had bought a stylish little Mercedes car on credit for extra kudos.

His debts were mounting up, and it looked as if he would soon be forced to sell some of the icons and paintings he had brought back from Russia. The idea was unthinkable to Seibert, and this was why he had decided to do a secret deal with the OGPU—he felt it was the only way out of his situation. But Oscar Reich had not come to Berlin as expected, and Seibert had never received the money he had been promised.

As a last resort, Seibert was banking on getting a sensational interview with a young woman called Hilda Schultz who had escaped from the clutches of Soviet satraps. Here, too, however, he was destined to be disappointed. Instead of the German heroine Seibert had been expecting, Klim had sent a Russian woman, Nina Kupina, who did not know a word of German.

"Have you brought the money to charter the ship?" Seibert asked. He was thinking that he could borrow some to cover his debts.

"Elkin has the money," said Nina with a charming smile. "You know him, don't you? He's coming to Berlin in the next few days. We have to meet up with him."

Seibert gazed at her as if she had lost her mind. "I think that your Elkin is probably drinking cocktails on the Cote d'Azur as we speak," said Seibert gloomily.

Lieschen had had a good expression for people like Klim and this girlfriend of his, thought Seibert. She used to say, "Get a fool to do a job, and he'll make double the work."

"Elkin is an honest man—" Nina began.

But Seibert interrupted her. "Do you have a place to stay?"

"No. It's my first time in Berlin, and I—"

"All right then," said Seibert with a sigh. "Let's go back to my place."

I'll wring Klim's neck when he arrives, he thought. How could he have made such a mess of everything?

33. THE FESTIVAL

1

On the 7th of November, Alov was meant to go on the demonstration to commemorate the anniversary of the Bolshevik Revolution, but all morning, he had been feeling unwell.

"So, there's something going on between your wife and Babloyan?" Valakhov said to Alov while Dunya was out getting water for the tea. "Well, don't say I didn't warn you. These actresses are all tramps. Still, it's a bit late now to be crying into your porridge."

Alov froze in the center of the room, his eyes staring out of his head and his body trembling all over.

"Don't get yourself so worked up," Valakhov said good-naturedly. "Babloyan has no interest in stealing women. He'll have his fun, and then he'll drop her. And you never know. The whole thing might be to your advantage."

Alov threw his greatcoat over his shoulders and headed for the door. "See you at the demonstration."

A moment later, Dunya came back.

"What's going on between you and Babloyan?" demanded Alov, his teeth chattering like an old dog's.

Dunya took him by the shoulders. "Oh, Lord…you're having one of your turns again! Sit down! Sit!"

Alov tried to hit her, but he had no strength left. His fist merely glanced off her cheekbone.

"Have you lost your mind?" squealed Dunya, clapping a hand to her face. "I have a performance today!"

"I'll show you a performance!" wheezed Alov, but he was immediately overcome by a frenzied bout of coughing.

Swearing, Dunya pulled him over to the bed. "Lie down, you jerk! Lie down, I tell you!"

Alov was racked by coughing until he was almost sick. At long last, as the agonizing spasms subsided, he burst into sobs, crushed by humiliation, weakness, and the fear that Dunya would take it into her head to leave him.

She sat down beside him, her hands clasped between her knees.

"There's nothing between me and Babloyan," she said. "And don't worry—there won't be. The girls told me he had a dose of venereal disease when he was young, and he's impotent as a result. He doesn't even sleep with his wife. Why do you think he's always surrounded by women? He's hoping somebody will 'cure' him."

"What bitches you actresses are," Alov whispered, "gossiping about things like that among yourselves!"

"Anyway, he liked my dancing, and he promised to get me work at one of the big state movie studios," said Dunya.

"I forbid it!" howled Alov. "I will not allow you to disgrace me!"

Dunya looked at him with narrowed eyes. "Have you ever thought about the fact that you disgrace me? I'm ashamed to admit I'm married to a man who works for the OGPU. I don't want everybody avoiding me like the plague."

She went up to the mirror and made a great show of inspecting her cheekbone to see if there was a bruise.

"You rat!" she shook her fist at Alov. "You raise a hand to me again, and I'll hit you over the head with the iron. I hope they fire you from your lousy job—maybe then you'll have some chance of becoming a decent man."

She went out, slamming the door behind her. Alov lay for some time on the bed, too weak to pull himself up.

2

On the way to Red Square, Alov felt so bad he decided not to go to the demonstration, and instead, he set off to Lubyanka.

As soon as he reached his office, Alov put three chairs together and lay down to try to get some rest, but he slept fitfully and felt no better. From time to time, he was racked with fits of coughing and eventually developed a terrible migraine into the bargain. It was as if a metal ball was rolling around inside his skull.

In his pocket, wrapped in a piece of paper, Alov had a pill from Denmark, which, he knew, could relieve his symptoms for a while. Zharkov had once brought a whole packet back for him, and Alov had done his best to make them last.

Should I take the pill now, he wondered, *or keep it for when the purge begins?*

Alov smoked two cigarettes one after the other and then set to work clearing his desk. There were all sorts of stupid letters, reports, and nonsense of all sorts. Last in the pile was an unsealed envelope from Minsk. "Urgent. For immediate attention," was written on it in Drachenblut's handwriting.

It was a report of the interrogation of a man by the name of Elkin. He had tried to cross the Soviet border and had been attacked and robbed by his guide. A border patrol had discovered Elkin the next morning and dispatched the offender to the Minsk OGPU where certain facts had come to light during his interrogation.

Elkin had said that he had been sent across the border by Klim Rogov who claimed to be a correspondent for the United Press but was actually working for Chinese intelligence. Having heard it, the Belorussians had contacted Moscow at once.

As he read the document, Alov felt a shiver run down his spine. Good grief. He had found out about this business in the nick of time: Klim Rogov was planning to leave Moscow tomorrow. Luckily, Drachenblut had gone off to the celebration of the Bolshevik Revolution, so today, he would not summon Alov to come to him with the report on the situation. A failure in such an important case as this could have warranted immediate dismissal from the OGPU.

Grabbing the receiver, Alov contacted the duty officer.

3

Mr. Owen himself arrived for the celebrations of the eleventh anniversary of the Bolshevik Revolution, and Klim handed over the documents and keys for Mashka to him. The new correspondent for the United Press was due to arrive in Moscow in two weeks' time.

Klim arranged a farewell party for his journalist friends, went to see Weinstein and the censors, and looked in on the Volga Germans to tell Father Thomas that he could expect some good news in the near future.

Although he still had a whole day left in the city, Klim had already packed up all his possessions. His apartment was almost empty with most of the furniture taken away. A few upholstery tacks lay scattered on the floor, and there were empty medicine vials and wire coat hangers on the window sill in the living room. Kapitolina was going to sell them to a rag merchant for a few kopecks.

Klim had given Kapitolina all his linen and tableware.

"My precious angel!" she cried, dashing about from room to room. "I'll be a rich woman now! Rockefella will have nothing on me!"

Suddenly, she stood stock still. "Oh! I've just thought.

I'll have to give something to Galina. Should I give her a boot brush?"

"I'll think of something," said Klim.

Several times, he had begun composing a farewell letter to Galina—a ridiculous missive full of pointless wishes for good luck, good health, and all good things in the future. He wondered what, in fact, the future held in store for her. It seemed unlikely she would marry again—too many men of her age had been killed in the war. What "good things" could she hope for then? A jar of jam or a tin of meat bought on some special occasion? A free ride on a tram?

Damn it all, it would be far easier not to think about it!

But Klim could not stop thinking about it. In the end, he picked up the phone and gave the operator the number for Galina's apartment.

A minute later, he heard her say, "Hello. Who is it?"

Klim flinched at the sound of her voice, which was hoarse and dull as if she were very sick.

"Galina," he said, "I want to say goodbye. I'm going abroad tomorrow."

"And you're never coming back?"

"No."

A second past in silence, then another, and another. Then, without saying a word, Galina hung up.

Klim pulled out two hundred-dollar bills, all that he had left, and put them in an envelope. That evening he had to go to the Bolshoi Theater for a political event in honor of the anniversary of the Revolution. After that, he decided, he would call in on Galina and leave the money in her mailbox.

4

All six tiers of the Bolshoi Theater were decorated with scarlet banners. On stage, under an enormous portrait of Lenin, a long table had been set up for leaders of the Bolshevik party.

On the podium, Comrade Babloyan, his voice trembling with heartfelt emotion, was reading out greetings from workers: "We hope that before long, a wave of proletarian revolution will sweep Europe and that the twentieth anniversary will be celebrated not only in our country but also throughout a European Union of Soviet Socialist Republics."

Magda, Klim, and Owen sat in the box reserved for foreign guests, observing the spectators in the stalls through opera glasses.

"There's a whole sea of Party bigwigs down there," Magda whispered, gesturing toward the crowd of officials in service jackets and tunics.

"Not a sea—a swamp," said Klim. "They're all wearing swamp-green, at any rate."

Magda eyed his dinner jacket and his starched shirt front. "Well, hark at you, Mr. Black-and-White."

The next to mount the podium was the chairman of the state planning department, Gosplan.

"In the next five years," he said, "we will put an end to unemployment and overcome all the economic challenges that face us. Workers' wages will increase by sixty-six percent. Manual workers will eat twenty-seven percent more meat, seventy-two percent more eggs, and fifty-five percent more milk products."

Klim translated the words of the speaker for Owen's benefit.

"I wonder," Owen said in a puzzled voice, "where the Bolsheviks will get all these percentages from."

"They don't care about the result," said Klim. "It's the ritual that matters. You and I are witnessing a prophecy. Do you remember the words from the Revelation of St. John the Divine? 'And God shall wipe away all tears from their eyes; and there shall be no more death, neither sorrow, nor crying, neither shall there be any more pain: for the former things are passed away.'"

Owen nodded. "Yes, I see what you mean."

"The Bolsheviks began as materialists," Klim said, "but without even realizing it, they've turned into a sect. They have taken all the old teachings about the end of the world and changed the names. The World Revolution is the Apocalypse; Marx and Engels are the Old Testament Prophets, Lenin is the savior who gave his life for the people, and Stalin is the high priest. Those who believe will be saved, and those who don't will be punished as heretics."

Owen put down his opera glasses. "So, you think that Soviet Russia is in the grip of some new type of Christian sectarianism?"

"It's the natural reaction of a society at the dawn of a new epoch," said Klim. "At times like these, people want to cling on to old teachings even while they're in the process of changing everything else. They need an infallible leader too, endowed with some mysterious power; someone who will lead them fearlessly into the 'bright future.' It's a classic example of a 'reformation'— this is what happens when an uneducated people, with more faith in seductive promises and devils than in science, starts seeking a new path in life."

"And how will it all end?" asked Owen.

Klim sighed. "I think it will end in the same way as the Taiping rebellion in China in the 1850s. There, a group of Christians created an independent state and began carrying out 'fair economic reforms.' After that, it was the same old story: battles against enemies within and without, redistribution of wealth, a god-like leader, and, as a result—wholesale devastation and millions dead."

"Surely things can't be that bad?"

Klim gestured toward the worker who had just got up on stage. In his hands, the man held a model broom made of metallic blades.

"That's a delegate from the factory committee," Klim said. "Do you know what he's proposing to the leaders of the country? To sweep away all their enemies with that broom. It looks as if there's bound to be huge bloodshed in the future."

5

When the speeches were over, Owen went to a banquet at the People's Commissariat for Foreign Affairs while Klim walked Magda to the cab rank.

The damp paving glittered in the light of the streetlamps, and the air was thick with the sharp smell of horses.

"Send me a cable when you get to Berlin," Magda told Klim. "Friedrich and I are coming to Berlin soon, I think. We just have to get our Germans safely on their way to Canada."

"Is Friedrich planning to defect?" Klim asked in amazement.

"He thinks that there's been a counter-revolution in the USSR," said Magda, "but nobody has noticed. The state has gone back to the same sort of abuses of power and bureaucracy the Russians had under the Tsarist regime. If the Tsar had never been deposed, they'd have just the same situation, only under a different banner. Friedrich thinks the revolution would have fared better in another country—one without such strong traditions of monarchy."

"You mean he wants to start all over again?"

"I don't know. We'll see when we get there, I suppose."

They embraced in parting, and Magda set off to find a cab.

Klim decided to go to Galina's apartment on foot. He wanted to say goodbye to Moscow.

The city felt restless, like an animal about to settle down for the night, tired, weary and shivering slightly under the first snow, which melted as soon as it fell.

Klim could not believe that in a couple of days, he would be in a completely different world. Living in the

USSR sometimes felt like looking the wrong way down a pair of binoculars. The "bright future" seemed close at hand while neighboring Poland seemed as distant as Mars.

Klim stopped beside a shop window made of reflective glass to see if he was still being shadowed or if his spies had gone home for the night.

No, they were still on his tail. On the other side of the street, there was a tall young man in a coat with the collar turned up, and a broad-shouldered fellow was pretending to read a poster fixed to a gate.

Klim was about to wave to them when a covered truck stopped in front of him. A man in an unbuttoned greatcoat jumped out of the back of the truck, taking his red OGPU ID out of his pocket.

"Come with me, citizen!" he said.

"Where to?" asked Klim, bewildered.

A cabbie's horse passing them by shied away as if sensing the smell of carrion.

Two more men came out of the truck and took Klim under the arms. "Get in the truck!"

From that moment on, Klim was no longer a human being: he had become an object that can be packed away at will, transported from place to place, and kept until required.

6

Tata could see that something was wrong with her mother. Before, her mother would go off to work for days on end; now, she sat about at home and ate almost nothing. She didn't even scold Tata if she forgot to wash her plate after meals.

"Would you like some tea, Mommy?" Tata fussed around her mother.

"No thanks."

"What can I get you?"

"Nothing."

Her mother turned her face to the wall and told Tata to leave her alone.

Nowadays, they had no money, and Tata had noticed that things kept disappearing from their room. She guessed that her mother was selling them to the used-goods store to buy bread.

As soon as she came home, Tata would feel overwhelmed by melancholy and inertia, so she would stay late at school drawing posters and wall-newspapers even at weekends and on holidays.

Recently, she had read about a young worker who had composed a portrait of Lenin using grains of wheat and oats and had immediately been accepted into the Higher Art and Technical Institute.

Wouldn't it be grand to do a portrait of Comrade Stalin from some material that had particular significance for society? Tata thought. For instance, she could make a huge picture out of screws and cogwheels and name it "Stalin's factory." Look closer, and you would see the workings of a complex mechanism, but from a distance, you would see a portrait of the smiling leader. And imagine if she could get the parts to move!

Tata had even made some sketches for this future masterpiece, but so far, she was having no luck with Comrade Stalin: every picture she drew looked like some iron monster with whiskers.

But Tata would not give up. She had to show everyone, and particularly the children from the boarding school, that she was capable of great feats for the glory of the working classes.

7

When Tata came home, it was already dark. She did not have a key and rang their bell again and again, but her mother did not come to the door.

At last, the door flew open.

"Listen now, just don't start blubbing, all right?" Mitrofanych muttered as he let Tata into the apartment.

She looked at him bewildered. "Why would I start blubbing?"

"It's your mother…she swallowed a whole lot of pills. I looked in on her to ask her for some tea and found her lying on the floor."

"Tea?"

"Do you understand what I'm telling you?" Mitrofanych knocked with his knuckles on his head. "Your mother has tried to poison herself! If I hadn't run out of tea, I don't know what would have happened."

Tata felt as if the walls of the apartment were caving in on her. She ran into their room, but there was nobody there. Only a piece of paper on the table in her mother's handwriting:

Dearest daughter,
I feel that I am losing my mind, and I do not want to drag you down with me. I have been fired from my job and have no way of supporting you and cannot find work anywhere else.
You have talent, and it will help you make your way in the world. The Soviet state will look after you a lot better than I can. Please forgive me, and may God preserve you.

Love,
Mom

"Where's my mother?" howled Tata.

Natasha came running at the sound of her wails. "She's been taken to a hospital."

"Which one?"

"I don't know. Nobody told us anything."

Tata slammed the door shut. Without taking off her coat and hat, she fell on her knees before her mother's icon and began to pray. "Dear God, I was lying when I said I didn't believe in you. I know you exist. I'll go to church every day of my life and stop wearing my Pioneer neckerchief. Please just don't let my mother die!"

Tata fell to the floor and lay there for some time, her arms flung out as if she herself had just been killed.

34. THE LUBYANKA

1

A call came for Alov from the duty room to tell him that Rogov had been arrested.

Struggling with a dreadful migraine, Alov set off downstairs to the building where arrestees were taken.

He was shown a box containing the items confiscated from Rogov on his arrest: his passport, watch, fountain pen, and two train tickets. In his wallet, apart from some loose change, there were two gold ten-ruble coins, thirty German marks, and a separate envelope containing two brand new hundred-dollar bills.

"Where's your internal telephone?" Alov asked the duty officer.

The officer showed him an ancient wooden apparatus fixed to the wall. Alov picked up the receiver and asked for Diana Mikhailovna.

"Could you write down the numbers of some banknotes for me?" he asked her. "I want you to check them against the numbers of the notes that were stolen from Oscar Reich."

He hung up and decided to take the pill after all. It was impossible to work with such a headache.

The duty officer took him to the cell where Rogov was being held. The spy hole on the door was low, and Alov had to lean down to look through it.

The small room, painted a dull yellow, was lit up by a light bulb protected by a metal guard. A table and two chairs were in the middle of the room, all bolted to the floor. Rogov's coat lay on one chair, and Rogov himself, still in his hat, evening dress, and bow tie, was pacing from corner to corner.

There he is, my lucky number, thought Alov. *Thanks to him, I'll get myself a room of my own.*

He always found it interesting to see how people reacted when they were arrested unexpectedly. Suddenly, all their plans for the future were changed dramatically, and the landscape of their lives altered. At this point, most people still had no idea why they had been brought in and how serious it was. Some would begin to weep from fear while others would hammer at the door with their fists and demand to see whoever was in charge. Rogov, on the other hand, did not seem particularly frightened. The only emotion visible on his face was that of extreme annoyance.

Alov remembered how Rogov had once refused to cooperate with him. *Let's see what you have to say for yourself now,* Alov thought.

He turned to the duty officer. "I want a full search," he said quietly.

A few minutes later, two heavies—professional boxers—came into the cell.

A full search was the first step in breaking the spirit of a detainee. First, he would be made to undress completely; then the heavies would make a great show of examining the clothes, fingering every crease in the cloth. Then, they would subject the "client" himself to a long, unhurried examination, like a medical, peering and prodding at every inch of his body.

Alov remained glued to the spy hole. Rogov made no move to resist. He merely sneered derisively as if he were above everything that was going on. The heavies confiscated his scarf, cuff links, shoelaces, and suspenders. Then they left him on his own to get dressed.

After leaving Rogov alone for a while so that his panic would escalate, Alov entered the room and sat down sideways on one of the chairs.

"Do you remember how I once asked if you would cooperate with us?" he said. "And how you said you would have nothing to do with us? I was disappointed to hear that."

"I hope you're not keeping me in this establishment of yours overnight," grumbled Rogov. "I have a train to catch tomorrow."

"Oh, yes, believe me, I understand your concern," smiled Alov.

"Could you at least tell me what I'm accused of?"

"Of being a spy."

"If you don't release me this instant, I can assure you that you'll be facing an international scandal."

"And just who do you think will tell your patrons and protectors that Klim Rogov has disappeared? You've told everyone you're leaving, so nobody will be looking for you."

There was silence.

"You can make things better for yourself," said Alov, "if you tell us where Nina Kupina is. I know she's your wife, but as you pimped her to Oscar Reich, I don't suppose there's much love lost between you."

"I refuse to talk to you unless you bring in Mr. Owen. He'll let my employers know what's happened, and the matter will be settled at a diplomatic level."

"Well, as you like. If you don't want to cooperate, we have other methods."

Alov got to his feet and put his head outside the door. "Bring Mr. Rogov's daughter here!"

The prisoner's face fell at the words. "You have no right to touch the child!"

"The fate of your little Chinese girl depends entirely on you," said Alov curtly. "We can arrange for her to be sent to a good orphanage, or we can send her to one full of TB sufferers."

He took a piece of paper and a pencil out of his pocket and put them on the table. "Here. Write out a voluntary confession. I need everything from the beginning: where you were born, what you did before the revolution, when you met Kupina and under what circumstances. I want to know who hired you and who briefed you. Don't mess with us, or you know what will happen."

Rogov stared at him, dumbstruck. "You mean torture?"

"What sort of a word is that to use—'torture'?" Alov said, shaking his head reproachfully. "It's you in the bourgeois world that torture people and execute them. We use 'socialist defense measures.'"

2

Alov left feeling extremely pleased with himself now that he had put the fear of God into his "client." *Well,* he thought, *let him stew for a while in his own juice.*

He rang Diana Mikhailovna again. "Did you find out about the numbers?"

"Yes—they all match," she replied. "They're our banknotes."

Alov beamed at the news. If Rogov had got his hands on some of the money stolen from Reich, he probably had an idea what had happened to the rest.

Unfortunately, the team sent off to Rogov's apartment in Chistye Prudy had come back with nothing. Neither Rogov's child nor his servant had been at home.

Agitated at this setback, Alov could sense an agonizing tightness growing in his chest. For God's sake, when would all this torment end? There had to be some sort of medicine that could help cure his sick lungs!

In desperation, he attacked the OGPU agents who had just returned from Rogov's house. "What's the matter with you? Couldn't you have spoken to his neighbors? Isn't there some sort of housing officer or yard keeper there?"

They replied that the yard keeper had been in a drunken stupor while the office on the ground floor had been shut for the anniversary celebrations.

It was eleven o'clock at night.

Once again, Alov peered through the spy hole into the cell. Rogov was sitting quite still, staring down at a blank sheet of paper. His fringe, slicked back with brilliantine that morning, now hung forward into his eyes, and the cuffs of his shirt, bare of cuff links, protruded comically from the sleeves of his dinner jacket.

Alov made an effort to gather his thoughts. It would have been far simpler to have the information he needed from his "client" with the help of the little Chinese girl, but they didn't have her. An ordinary interrogation could drag on for hours, but if he called in *specialists*, there would be screams and hysterics. Alov felt quite bad enough already without that.

He was racked by a fresh fit of coughing.

"Do you need a drink of water?" asked the duty officer with sympathy.

Alov shook his head and made his way to the exit, holding on to the wall.

He did not have the strength to handle Rogov's case, but he could not hand it over to one of his colleagues; then the reward for bringing the affair to light would go to somebody else.

I still have time to lie down for a bit, thought Alov. Right now, Drachenblut was out at the dacha of the People's Commissar for Defense drinking. Afterward, he would be sleeping it off for a while. So, in any case, there was nobody to report to at the moment.

"Transfer Rogov to a general cell," he told the duty officer. "I'll deal with him later."

3

Klim was taken by prison guards along a dimly lit corridor. All his emotions were dulled. It was as if he had been drugged with something foul and could not wake up from a nightmare.

But still, Kitty had not been brought in. Did that mean she had escaped the OGPU? And if so, how? Where could she have gone?

The rasp of locks and bolts behind him was like the gnashing of iron teeth.

It must have been Galina who had reported me to the OGPU, thought Klim.

How much did they know about him? Just about everything, he supposed. Galina must have noted down every careless word he had let slip.

They reached a cell with a small barred window in the door, and the guards told Klim to stop.

One of them turned the light switch and opened the door. "In you go."

The cell was fiercely heated. A broad platform ran around the room, and on it, prisoners in underwear were lying with their feet to the center of the room. There were two small barred windows close to the ceiling, a basin, and a galvanized bucket with a lid next to the door.

One of the prisoners raised a bald head. "Look—fresh meat!"

The guard shoved Klim in the back. "Lie down and go to sleep. This instant!"

The door slammed shut, and the light went out. Klim stood in the middle of the cell, dazed and uncertain.

"What's with the fancy dress?" asked the bald prisoner. "Are you some sort of a magician? What are you in for then?"

"I don't know," said Klim.

"Well, if you don't know, you must be a counter-revolutionary," said another man with a laugh. "Ten years of hard labor—or a bullet in the basement."

The prisoners began to stir and complain.

"Keep the noise down!"

"Shut up!"

"Go to hell!"

"Over here, Mister Magician," Klim heard a man calling with a strong Caucasus accent. "Lie down here."

Klim moved forward, felt with his hand for the edge of the platform, and sat down.

The atmosphere of the prison—the heat, the stench, the snoring of the men all cramped together—closed over Klim's head like the black water of a murky millpond.

"You have nothing with you?" asked his neighbor. "What will you sleep on? Do you have a spoon or a bowl?"

"I was arrested on the street," said Klim.

He spread his coat on the platform and lay down, appalled by the feel of bodies on either side of him.

Only recently, looking at the emaciated and tormented figure of Elkin, Klim could not have imagined for a moment that he would end up in his place. He was used to thinking of himself as an observer, not a participant. Klim Rogov could not be arrested or frightened, still less tortured. He was sacred and inviolable.

And now he had joined another category of people—those whose lives meant next to nothing. Slaves to be sent to their death, felling trees or working in mines.

Klim pictured himself as a camp inmate in a padded jacket and felt his hair stand on end.

"Hey, Mister Magician!" he heard the man from Caucasus call out again. "In this cell, you can't be a coward for more than twenty minutes, and you've already used up ten."

Klim shuddered. "Who are you?" he asked.

"My name is Ahmed. Now, you listen. You start feeling sorry for yourself in here, and it's the end. Have you been in battle? I have. In a war, you know you can be killed, but you just keep galloping forward and don't think about it—you attack. You make decisions! It's the same in prison. You say to yourself, 'Only I can decide whether to be afraid.'"

Klim was not in any state to hear mantras for survival. "What if they torture me?" he hissed through his teeth.

"Then you don't think of it as pain. I got a bullet in my chest in the war. I ran about for half a day without even noticing. So long as a man does not dig his own grave, he can survive anything."

"Don't listen to him," said an older man's voice. "You should see Ahmed—he had his nose broken with a rifle butt. His eyes stare in different directions, and he's soft in the head. There's no sense living in a fool's paradise. We all are doomed here. I was an infantry general, and I spent five years mucking out the latrines in a Bolshevik camp. They let me go and then arrested me again a week later. I've written to all their departments to ask them to stop tormenting me. 'Shoot me and have done with it!' I say, but they tell me it's their business who'll be shot and who'll be 'reeducated.'"

"Why are you lying to Mister Magician?" Ahmed became angry. "Neither you nor I know what will happen to him. Only Allah himself knows, and he won't tell us."

The light flared under the ceiling, and the face of the guard appeared in the window in the door. He cast an eye around the cell to check all was quiet. Then, once again, the cell was plunged into darkness.

4

Seibert stood at the stove frying eggs for *himself*. He was not going to cook Nina's breakfast for her.

The crazy Russian woman gave him no peace and was always bothering him about something. One minute, she would ask where she could get some decent clothes, and the next minute, she was asking him to drive her to the station to wait for Elkin. Of course, Elkin never showed up, so the whole thing was a waste of time.

Seibert's life was enormously complicated by Nina's presence. He wanted to sleep in his own bed, not on the couch in the living room. He was used to walking about the apartment in his underwear with his bathrobe open, and now he had to be constantly on parade.

Most maddening of all, Frau Hauswald, a very nice woman who lived across the street, had decided that Nina was Seibert's lover. Now, when she saw Seibert, she pursed her lips and exchanged a chilly "Good morning." And that was instead of stopping to discuss the Christmas committee and plans for festive lights on the balconies.

It was all like some cheap circus act. Seibert was not so rude or unkind as to throw Nina out on the street, but how long could this mess continue?

He told himself time and time again that he should ask her to leave, but then he kept postponing the conversation. Seibert enjoyed the company of docile women like Lieschen and Galina. Nina's presence discomfited him—he felt as if he were being stifled.

No sooner had Seibert sat down to eat his eggs than Nina herself came into the dining room.

"Heinrich, let's send another telegram to Moscow. I need to know what's happened to Klim."

Seibert threw down his fork and fixed Nina with an indignant stare. "You know what? I'm tired…. I don't need any of this—I have my own life to live!"

He realized he was behaving rudely, and this made him still more furious.

"You promised to help me with the Volga Germans," he ranted. "And what happened? You didn't bring the money for transport. You deceived me by passing yourself off as Hilda Schultz…. I wanted to interview her and introduce her to some of the benefactors from our religious community. But what am I supposed to do with you?"

"You don't have to help me, I know—" began Nina, but Seibert cut her short.

"Fine! That's excellent! Then you can go to Charlottenburg—it's full of Russian immigrants. Get yourself a paper with small ads and find work as a waitress or something. Excuse me, but I've had enough of visitors."

But Nina did not seem to be listening. She went up to Seibert, took him by the shoulders, and looked him in the eye.

"Klim was your friend," she said. "Help me to find out what's happened to him! I don't have anyone else to turn to."

Seibert groaned. There she went again, putting pressure on him.

"What do I have to do," she said, "to get you to come to the telegraph office with me?"

"Leave me alone!" Seibert almost howled.

"I have some notes about what happened to Elkin in the prison camp," said Nina. "I was going to give them to Klim, but perhaps you could make use of them?"

She ran to the bedroom and brought in some pages torn from a notebook covered in small handwriting.

Seibert began to read. Well, well…logging, labor camps…. He felt his mood brighten at once.

"All right. We'll send one more telegram," he muttered grudgingly. "But we'll address it to Magda. She should know what's going on."

These memoirs of Elkin's might bring in some money, Seibert thought. He had long suspected that the timber Oscar Reich was planning to sell to Germany came from Soviet labor camps. If the *Berliner Tageblatt* carried an article about the dubious provenance of Soviet timber, it might blow up into a top-notch scandal.

He would remind readers of the crimes of Belgian King Leopold II, who had made himself a huge fortune exploiting the inhabitants of the Congo Free State. He had enslaved them and forced them to work in rubber plantations, having them mutilated or killed for the slightest misdemeanor. The story was still fresh in people's memories. Readers would grasp immediately that something similar was happening in the Soviet Union.

The article would have to be published under a pseudonym, Seibert decided. Then he could hint to Oscar Reich that if he did not want his patrons in Moscow to gain a reputation like that of the butchers of King Leopold, he would have to put some of his money into counter-propaganda.

35. HUMAN ORE

1

The prisoners were brought food three times a day: boiled water and bread in the morning, watery soup and mush in the afternoon, and the same mush in the evening, reheated. Once a day, the detainees were taken out across the ice-covered yard to the latrines.

They were not allowed to lie on the sleeping platform in the day, but at night, Klim found it hard to sleep.

It was pitch dark, and the noise of footsteps and the metal clang of doors could be heard on the other side of the wall. Now and again, the guards would come and take somebody outside or push a prisoner back into the cell. Every ten minutes, the warden would turn the light switch on to check that everything was in order.

If Klim did manage to drop off to sleep, he would immediately find himself in a horrible nightmare in which he was the only surviving crew member on board an ice-bound ship. The nightmare combined all the worst human fears: an endless, dark, polar night, bitter frost, and utter loneliness. But this was not all. In his dream, Klim had nothing to eat besides the bodies of his comrades who had frozen to death. In order to survive, he had to become a cannibal.

It would have been difficult to find a more fitting allegory for his present predicament, and now, Klim started to realize what the accused in the Shakhty Trial had gone through.

He vowed that he would never stoop so low as to make false accusations to save his own skin, no matter how he was threatened. He imagined the most difficult questions an interrogator might put to him and mentally rehearsed his answers. But several days passed, and still, he had not been summoned. Alov seemed to have forgotten him.

"You're lucky they're not dragging you out for questioning," Ahmed told Klim. "You take my word for it; no news is good news here."

The guards kept bringing more people into the cell, and the prisoners had to squeeze closer together on the sleeping platform to make space for them.

How aggravating it was to be constantly in the company of thirty other people! You were forced to watch every little thing they did, scratching, picking their teeth, using the toilet bucket, crying, sniffing, or biting their nails. And they too became witnesses to your every action.

The bald prisoner named Billiard, who seemed to be top dog among the inmates, had given everyone nicknames. He had christened one dumpy, dark-haired official "Penguin;" a trainee pilot "Propeller," and a jockey from the hippodrome "Giddy-Up." He had called Klim "Magician," and the name had stuck.

More detainees were brought in; among them were several priests, a shop assistant, an engineer, and a pianist. The pianist seemed the least oppressed by his predicament: he sat with his eyes closed and a smile playing over his lips, apparently improvising jazz solos in his head.

Klim too did his best to escape into a fantasy world of his own.

He would take a deep breath, fling his shoulders back, hold his arms slightly away from his body, palms upward. Then he would try to imagine he was growing to fill the space around him, rising above the earth.

Privacy and freedom meant happiness while prison signified the opposite. In prison, you were under pressure from all sides, physically and emotionally. As a result, your body began to respond instinctively: you frowned, hunched your shoulders, and clenched your fists; your whole body huddled in on itself, dying a slow death.

Klim kept assuring himself that Nina was already in Berlin and that Kitty was being looked after by kind people. These thoughts were all that kept him from despair.

2

"Rogov, leave your things and come out here!" the guard barked.

Klim sat up.

The prisoners fell silent and stared at him in alarm.

"Off for questioning?" asked Billiard. "Well, best of luck to you."

Klim went outside into the corridor.

The guard eyed his creased suit with a smirk. "That's enough lounging about, your lordship. Time to get down to work."

Klim let out a sigh with relief. Apparently, they were not going to torture him just yet.

The guard took him down into a cellar, into a room lined with shelves of brown dossiers. A small officer with a mustache sat at a desk, reading the comic paper by the light of a green lamp.

When he saw Klim, the officer got to his feet and handed him a bucket and dried-out cloth. "Clean up in here."

It was a blessing, not a punishment, to be set to work like this. At last, Klim could move about and stretch his legs.

He walked off to the far corner of the room and began to dust the shelves but brushed against some dossiers by accident, knocking them to the floor.

"What are you doing?" shouted the officer. "Pick those up at once!"

One of the dossiers had fallen open. Klim could see a blue stamp on the document inside that read, "Sentence carried out." The other two folders contained similar documents.

The officer put down his paper. "Keep your nose out!" he snapped. "Do you want me to send you to the lockup?"

Klim returned the documents to the shelf. It was beginning to dawn on him just where he was: this room was a graveyard of personal files, every one of them representing a human life. There were thousands upon thousands of them here—the sum total of everything achieved under ten years of Soviet power. All these lives had been crushed to extract something of value to the country—just as ore is crushed and smelted to make metal. And in some cases, those people had suffered for nothing; they had been no more than dross to be discarded.

The door creaked, and a stooped figure holding a mop appeared in the doorway.

"In here!" barked the officer.

The old man entered the room and began to wash the floor.

An oppressive silence set in, broken only by the clink of the handle against the pail as the old man shifted it about and the rustle of pages of the officer's paper.

The old man kept backing toward Klim as he mopped, getting closer and closer. Then he turned—and Klim saw it was Elkin.

His face was dark with half-healed cuts, and his body moved strangely and awkwardly as if his every joint had been broken.

"Listen," Elkin hissed in a barely audible voice. "After lockdown tonight, hang yourself. You can tie the leg of your pants to the window bars. The bars are strong enough to take your weight."

"What?" Klim asked, bewildered.

Elkin's face twisted into a pained grimace. "Don't wait till they start to torture you. They haven't laid a finger on you yet, have they?"

As he looked Klim up and down, tears appeared in his eyes, and his teeth began to chatter.

"They'll slam you down onto the concrete floor until your mouth and nose are bleeding," Elkin said. "Or tie you up and kick you. But the worst of all is when they shut you up in a metal crate and start to beat it with crowbars—for hours on end. You won't be able to stand it. You'll betray all your friends, and then they'll be arrested too."

The officer put down his paper again. "Do you two think you've come here for a chat? Is that it?"

Elkin shuddered. Then he bent down and began to swab at the floor with his cloth. His face wore a strange, forced smile.

"Pay no attention," he whispered. "They brought me in here specially to speak to you. They want me to persuade you to give Nina up to them. I'm sorry I gave away your name to them. I held out for a long time, a really long time. Back in Crimea, Nina and I used to go on walks and talk about you. So, now the OGPU knows who you are."

Klim looked at him in horror. Not too long ago, Elkin had been in the prime of life, smart and self-assured; now, he was a broken man. Even if he got out of prison, he would never recover.

"What do they want from Nina?" asked Klim.

"They want the money she stole from Reich. I told them that I was trying to take it over the border when I was robbed. They don't believe me though. They know Nina's in Berlin. Tonight, they'll take you for questioning and torture you."

Elkin held up one of his fingers: at the end, instead of a fingernail, there was a wrinkled hollow.

"Don't make the same mistake I did," he said. "String yourself up while you still have a chance. It's the only way to save Nina. I'm planning to get away too—to escape to the next world. I'll be safe from them all there."

3

"Lights out!" shouted the guard, turning the switch and plunging the cell into darkness.

Klim lay on his back, gazing into the dark with unseeing eyes. He ran the tip of a finger over his cheekbones, his collarbone, and his wrist. *Say goodbye, Mr. Rogov,* he thought. *Goodbye to yourself as you are now: healthy, strong, and in your right mind. Today, you'll either be beaten or maimed. By the time they drag you back in here, your teeth will have been shattered and your kidneys kicked to a pulp. And no matter how brave you are, it won't help.*

Thank goodness Galina had not been the one to betray him. If it had been Galina, Klim would never have seen Elkin. Still, that was cold comfort in the circumstances.

Klim bit his lips as he struggled not to give in to panic or to sickening, desperate misery. Perhaps, he really should try to kill himself.

Screwing up his eyes and squeezing his fingers together until they hurt, he prayed deliriously for a miracle. Now, looking back, all those quarrels with Nina and the jealous games he had played seemed ridiculous. He should have lived his life to the full and been glad of what he had. But now, it was too late.

Could he find within him the strength not to betray Nina? If Soviet intelligence found out she was staying with

Seibert, they would hunt her down and kill her. There were any number of Soviet secret agents in Germany.

Klim remembered their house in Shanghai and the bathroom with the blue tiles. He pictured Nina emerging from the shower, shivering with cold, her dark curls dripping water. She threw on a white dressing gown and wrapped a towel around her head so tightly that it made her eyes slant upward. He said that it made her look Chinese, like Kitty, and Nina readily agreed.

The electric light flared on, and a hefty, clean-shaven guard with a fat, freckled face came into the cell.

"Rogov!" he shouted out, checking his list.

So, this was it. They had come for him.

Klim sat up slowly.

"Name and patronymic?" asked the guard.

"I'm a citizen of the United States," Klim reminded quietly. "We don't have patronymics on American documents."

"Shut your mouth, scum! Leave your stuff and come out now."

Klim's heart was hammering in his chest. He felt as if he were about to have a heart attack. He put on his shoes and, for some reason, buttoned his shirt collar.

The freckle-faced guard shoved him in the back. "Hurry up!"

They went out into the corridor lined with rows of doors. A dim light filtered from the lightbulbs overhead, throwing crisscross shadows on the floor.

The guard gave curt instructions. "Straight ahead. Right. Right again." Then suddenly he shouted, "Halt! Face to the wall."

Two other guards dragged along a man, bloodstained and struggling. He had a rubber bulb in his mouth and kept bellowing something indistinctly.

"Come on now!" said Klim's guard. "Straight ahead."

Should I attack him? Klim wondered. It would surely be better to be killed for resisting the authorities than to endure hours of "socialist defense measures."

"Halt!" shouted the guard.

They stopped outside a brown door.

"Knock."

Klim closed his eyes for a moment.

"Knock, you bastard!"

This time, Klim knocked on the door.

"Yes?" came a male voice from inside.

"In you go," the guard ordered.

As Klim entered the interrogation room, he saw Alov and felt himself grow weak with relief. This man would never torture him. Alov might be a fanatic and a scoundrel, but he was no cold-blooded killer.

There was also a typist in the room, sitting under a large portrait of Lenin—a plain, aging woman with a prominent forehead and a mouth that turned down at the corners. She looked at Klim with a weary, disinterested gaze and then adjusted the paper in her typewriter.

No, thought Klim, nothing terrible would happen to him here. They would never beat him in the presence of a woman, surely.

Alov blew his nose loudly into a handkerchief and gestured to a chair in the middle of the room. "Sit down."

The chair was screwed to the floor, which was covered with battered yellow linoleum. *Still,* Klim said to himself, *that doesn't mean anything.* It was the usual setup for an interrogation room.

Alov looked sick. His eyes were red-rimmed, and the skin under his nose raw. He patted at his pockets and then began opening each one of the desk drawers in turn. At last, he had found what he was looking for—a crumpled packet of filter-less cigarettes.

"Smoke?" he asked, holding the packet out to Klim. "No? Your loss. Now then, let's try to wind up this business as quickly as we can so that we can all get home."

The typist began to bang away at the typewriter. With a loud *ding*, the carriage of the typewriter shot back.

Alov set an envelope on the table. The address was in Klim's handwriting. "London Central Post Office, for collection by Mr. Smith." Judging by the stamp, the letter had been sent from Warsaw almost a year ago.

"Do you recognize this?"

Klim shrugged. "I don't remember what it is."

"The addressee of that letter never picked it up, so it was returned to the sender, Klim Rogov," Alov said. "The letter was opened at the Soviet border, and what do you think was inside?"

Alov put his cigarette down on the edge of the ashtray, drew out several postcards from the envelope, and fanned them out. The cards all had holes punched right through them. One bore a portrait of Stalin with a hole straight through his forehead.

At last, Klim remembered. These were the postcards Kitty had been planning to hang on the tree as decorations. Last Christmas, without thinking, Klim had shoved them into an envelope and handed it to Oscar Reich.

"So, what do we have here?" asked Alov. "A former member of the White Guard, Klim Rogov, and his wife, Nina Kupina, were recruited by Chinese intelligence to carry out espionage and sabotage in the Soviet Union. They were given orders to assassinate Comrade Stalin, and we have this on irrefutable evidence."

"That's a lie!" Klim interrupted but stopped himself immediately. Here, nobody cared what was a lie and what was the truth. Alov knew quite well it was all nonsense. He was just showing Klim that he was in deep trouble and in it for the long haul.

"You know," said Alov. "I have a neighbor who's an expert in preparing skeletons for display. There are maybe ten people in the whole of the USSR with that level of knowledge. It's quite a skill. First, you have to soak the body for a year to get the flesh off the bones. Then you use chlorine to bleach the bones and dry them out in the sun. And only then can you put the skeleton together, bone by bone. Would you like us to make you into a skeleton for the biology class? I shall make sure you're put into the school at the orphanage—the one in which your Kitty will be sent. That might even be rather fun! Just think: your little girl will come into the classroom and see her father smiling at her."

The typist gave a faint snort of laughter.

"Still, if Mr. Rogov will cooperate with us, there'll be no need for skeletons," said Alov amiably. "Let's begin at the beginning. Who sent you to the Soviet Union?"

"I won't say a thing until you call for Mr. Owen," retorted Klim.

Alov looked at him for a long time with his blood-shot eyes before dissolving in a furious fit of coughing

"Damn it!" he shouted when he got his breath back. "Do you think I've nothing better to do than run around after you, you bastard? Guards!"

Two hefty men came into the room.

Klim tried to get up, but they twisted his arms and handcuffed them to the back of the chair.

Alov blew his nose again into his drenched handkerchief and turned to the typist. "Take this down please, Olga Rustemovna: Record of interrogation of a suspect—"

The carriage bell rang out again, and one by one, the metal letters stamped into the paper.

4

Whatever Galina tried to do, she never seemed to succeed. She had not even managed to commit suicide successfully.

She had been taken to the hospital to have her stomach pumped, and now, she lay for days on end in the general ward, recovering.

With her face to the wall, Galina tried not to think of anything, but the wretched thought kept coming back to haunt her. How was Klim and his Nina? How was Tata? Was anybody even feeding her?

At first, the other women on the ward had tried to speak to Galina, but soon, they gave up and left her in peace.

"She's not quite right in the head, that one," the patients explained to the young woman doctor who came to do the rounds of the ward.

"Now, now, what's all this?" said the doctor reprovingly. "How are we feeling today?"

"Abandoned," said Galina and immediately regretted it.

Hearing this, the young doctor called the ward sister and scolded her for neglecting her patients.

Alov came to see Galina only on her fifth day in the hospital. No sooner had he entered the ward than he began to yell at her, calling her a hysterical fool. "Was it because of me you took it into your head to take an overdose?"

The other patients listened with baited breath, intrigued.

Alov grabbed Galina by the arm. "I need you right away. The doctor has told me you're quite capable of getting up on your feet. We're off to the Lubyanka."

Alov glanced around at the other patients and leaned in to whisper in Galina's ear. "We're questioning your Rogov, and he won't admit to anything. Do you think you can help us break him?"

Galina stared at Alov, dumbstruck. Klim had been arrested? But he was supposed to have left the country!

Alov pulled the blanket off her bed. "Come on. Get dressed! We're expecting a purge any minute. It would be good to have some positive results before it starts."

They got into the waiting OGPU car. As it drove off, Alov explained that for forty-eight hours now, Rogov had been "on the conveyer belt"—this was the name for constant questioning during which a "client" was passed between interrogating officers without being given space to breathe or gather his thoughts.

"The bastard's digging in his heels," cried Alov with feeling. "What we need you to do is to squeeze out Nina Kupina's address from him. You're on good terms with him, aren't you? Right now, the Mincing Machine is working on him. Then, you can come in and explain in a nice voice that things will be better for him if he gives us an honest confession."

The Mincing Machine was the nickname of a pale, shapeless woman who worked in the OGPU. She had a habit of talking about lofty subjects, knew many poems by heart, and even lavished care on her appearance—plucking her eyebrows and dying her hair with henna. From time to time, she was brought down into the OGPU cells. Nobody was as efficient as she at unmasking enemies of the state.

"Is Rogov being beaten?" asked Galina in a quiet voice.

Alov shook his head. "No, not really. I decided against it for now. We might need him for a show trial."

Galina looked at her reflection in the window. That small, hazy ghost was all that remained of her. She had long since died, and now, she was being carried back on the wind to the places she had haunted in her lifetime.

Alov was talking about the coming purge and of how he had been in bed sick with a temperature for several days and was without time to memorize the *History of the Soviet Communist Party*.

He too was like a ghost, thought Galina. A ball of dull, pulsing energy. In order not to fade away altogether, he needed to take energy from other people, and just now, he was sucking it from Klim and Galina.

Alov was overcome by another fit of coughing.

"Just look at me," he muttered as he wiped away the tears. "I feel as if I'm being turned inside out, and I don't have a single pill left. Listen, Pidge. If you talk Rogov around for us, I'll ask Drachenblut to get you your job back. What do you say?"

Galina nodded indifferently.

The car drove into the inner courtyard and stopped outside the OGPU prison. Alov jumped down into the snow.

"Come on. Quickly!" he called to Galina. "I still need to look through the materials from the fifteenth Party Congress after this. My head's like a sieve these days—I can't remember anything."

They walked through the yard and down into the cellar. The warden, a snub-nosed young man in an outsized peaked cap, followed after them.

"How's the Mincing Machine doing?" asked Alov.

"She's doing her best, the old battle-ax," grinned the warden.

They turned into a side corridor. Now, Galina could hear the sound of a woman screaming out a torrent of shrill abuse.

Alov looked at Galina with consternation. "What's got into you, Pidge? You're shaking all over. Are you sick?"

The warden stopped outside the room from which the screams were issuing and opened the door.

"Could you bring some hot tea for Galina, here?" Alov asked him. "She's out of sorts."

The warden nodded. "I'll see to it."

Alov patted Galina on the shoulder. "All right, I'm off. Let me know if you have any luck."

5

Alov set off to the canteen, which was already full of employees from the Foreign Department.

They were all tearing their hair out, trying to guess what was going to happen. They had heard that the purge was to be led by Ivanov, an elderly martinet from the Central Control Commission, and Drachenblut had been appointed as second in command. Nobody knew the name of the last of the *troika*, a commission of three. Those who worked in the Foreign Department were praying it would not be somebody from Yagoda's camp.

Alov sat down at the table and took out his chit sheet—a card folded in quarters. So, here were directives on the development of the first five-year-plan...and the plan for collectivization...and the fight with Trotskyism...

Good grief, who needed all this? he wondered. *Why couldn't they let people work in peace?*

Alov looked at the clock on the wall. Would Galina manage to get the information they needed in time? Drachenblut was sure to ask about Rogov.

I ought to tell the Mincing Machine to use all the means at her disposal, Alov thought. *To hell with sentiment! I have to save my own skin.*

Just as he had got up to go back down to the prison, Eteri Bagratovna came rushing in, her face flushed.

"Comrades, the purge is about to start! The Commission has already gathered."

Everyone began talking noisily all at once. "Who's the third member of the Commission?"

The secretary looked around at the assembled employees. "The third member will be Comrade Babloyan."

The officers all clapped and cheered. Babloyan was an easygoing sort who often helped the Foreign Department. Like all top Party officials, he held down several posts at once and organized the work of Soviet trade unions abroad, an activity that brought with it many material benefits.

"Drachenblut's a smart one!" exclaimed Valakhov with admiration. "So, that's where he's been these last few days—drinking vodka with Babloyan and luring him over to our side."

"Excellent!" Zharkov rubbed his hands together. "Babloyan hates Yagoda as much as we do. It won't be in his interests to destroy us."

Alov, it appeared, was the only one not delighted at the news. He was suddenly struck by the thought that Babloyan had deliberately put himself forward to carry out the purge to get rid of Alov and take Dunya for himself.

6

The bolt rattled shut after Galina. She took a step toward the drooping figure sitting motionless in the chair.

"We haven't finished yet!" barked the Mincing Machine as she glanced angrily toward Galina. Her red fringe bristled over her forehead like the comb of a rooster.

"I can take over for you," said Galina in a faint voice.

She went up to the table and, steeling herself, took a look at Klim. He sat with his head bowed low. His ashen face wore the stubble of several days, his hair was stuck together in clumps, and his lips chapped.

Klim stared at Galina with an anguished expression. "Hello."

Galina flinched. What was going on in here? Had they all gone mad?

The Mincing Machine pulled a pistol from her belt. Pushing Galina aside, she rushed up to Klim. "What did I hear you say? Are you looking for a girlfriend in here? Is that it?"

She put the barrel of the gun under Klim's chin and pushed upward, making him throw back his head. Galina noticed a long, thin contusion on his neck—it looked like the mark of a garrote.

The next moment, the Mincing Machine smashed Klim in the solar plexus. He gave a muffled groan and doubled up, gagging.

"Alov said you weren't to beat him!" cried Galina.

The Mincing Machine turned at the sound of Galina's voice. She put down her pistol on the desk and thrust her chest forward menacingly in Galina's direction.

"And just who do you think you are? Perhaps you'd like me to smash your face?"

The door opened, and the warden came in with a glass of tea. "Here you are. Careful. The water's boiling."

The Mincing Machine took the glass. "Merci."

As soon as the door closed behind the warden, she went up to Klim and pressed her foot down on his.

"Now, listen. This is the last time I'm going to ask this. Where is Kupina hiding?"

She undid the buttons on Klim's shirt and put her hand inside it, fumbling at his chest.

"Make your mind up while all this down here is still soft and warm. Or I'll pour boiling water on you, and there won't be an inch of skin left."

Klim flinched.

"Stop!" sobbed Galina.

"So, you won't speak?" said the Mincing Machine in a sing-song voice as she raised the glass. "This calls for operational intervention."

But before Klim's tormentor could do any more, Galina grabbed the pistol from the desk and shot her in the head.

7

As Klim was bundled back into the holding cell, a deathly hush fell, and the inmates stared at him in horror.

He staggered to the basin, but his hands were shaking so badly that he was unable to turn on the tap.

Ahmed came darting up to help him fill a mug with water. "There, there…. It'll be all right."

Klim took a deep draught of water, his teeth chattering against the rim of the mug. Half the contents of the mug spilt onto the floor.

"Hey…" called Billiard. "Why are you covered in blood?"

"Two women were killed just now," Klim replied.

"By the guards?"

Klim nodded. He sat down on the platform and tried to take off his shirt, but his fingers would not obey. Somebody helped him.

"You lie down now," Ahmed was still fussing about. "Don't worry. You'll feel better soon. We'll sit here at your feet to shield you so the warden won't see you. You know yourself it's forbidden to sleep in the daytime."

Klim lay down and covered himself with his coat, pulling it right up over his head. There was an awful throbbing and ringing in his temples, and the faces of the intelligence officers kept floating up in front of his eyes. How many of them had questioned him over the last forty-eight hours? There must have been at least ten of them.

At the moment when Galina had raised the pistol, Klim had shut his eyes. *This is it,* he had thought. A shot had rung out, and he had felt something warm spatter onto his face. The red-haired woman who had been standing over him fell to the floor, spilling the glass of boiling tea all over herself. A red hole gaped where her eye had been.

After that, everything became muddled in his memory—the smell of gunpowder, the sound of boots in the corridor, a shrill scream, the door bursting open. Then there had been a second shot, which left his ears ringing. He had seen Galina slide slowly to the floor. Behind her on the wall was a bloody smear.

If only he could erase all these memories from his mind! If only he could go to sleep, never to wake up. He hadn't the strength to endure anything more.

Now, Klim heard the sounds of voices. The priests who had been brought in to the cell were chanting something, but he could not make out the words.

Elkin was done for, and now, Galina was dead. She had wanted to save Klim, but that was as impossible as trying to dig somebody out from an avalanche with a teaspoon.

Now, the intelligence officers would clear away the dead bodies, wash the floor, and put Klim back on the "conveyer belt."

36. THE GREAT PURGE

1

The purge was to be carried out in the so-called "Red Corner," the OGPU employees' reading room. A table had been brought in for the chairman, and chairs were gathered from all over the building.

There were so many people packed into the room that the atmosphere was stifling. Alov found himself a place in the far corner just behind Diana Mikhailovna. His nerves had brought on fits of coughing again. He tried to restrain himself as long as possible, his face turning crimson, before finally giving in and hacking into his fist.

Ivanov, an elderly, disheveled man with a goatee, addressed the assembled employees. It was time, he announced, that the OGPU rid itself of ideological backsliders who were sabotaging the efforts of the government to build a new world.

Alov stared blankly ahead of him at the ornamental comb in Diana Mikhailovna's hair, dreaming about the precious tablet, now out of reach, that would have stopped his coughing.

"Now, comrades, to business," said Babloyan, consulting his list of employees. "First, we have Valakhov."

Valakhov stood up, flushed with embarrassment, and

began to give an account of his career. His greatest achievement so far had been the time he had discovered a wounded officer of the White Army hiding out in his neighbors' shed and reported it to the Reds. The filthy White had been shot, together with those who had sheltered him, and Valakhov had been recommended for the district division of the secret police. Soon, he had been transferred to Moscow and had come to Drachenblut's notice. And that was it.

"Any questions?" Babloyan asked the assembled officers. Everybody had fallen silent.

Ivanov studied Valakhov's files for some time.

"It says here that you are a member of a three-man stewardship team for the Communist University for Chinese Workers. What stewardship duties do you undertake in connection with this position?"

Valakhov looked around at his colleagues nervously. "Well, I do different things. Ideological work, that is."

There were sniggers from the audience. Valakhov had recently bragged about his visits to female students dormitory and how he had forced his way into the women's changing rooms when he was drunk.

As it turned out, Valakhov did not have the faintest idea of basic political science or political economy and was completely ignorant about international events.

"It's a disgrace!" Ivanov addressed the audience. "Just look at the level of political awareness among your fellow employees!"

Valakhov put his hand to his heart. "But I'm on duty for days on end. I don't have time to mess about with books!"

"I think Comrade Valakhov is the kind of man we need," said Babloyan in a conciliatory tone. "Not so long ago, he couldn't read or write, and now, he is being entrusted to carry out serious work. He has definitely made progress. We shall have to hope that in the future, he'll become better acquainted with the theoretical side of his work."

It was decided by two votes to one (Babloyan and Drachenblut against Ivanov) to allow Valakhov to keep his Party membership card.

There were sighs of relief all around.

However, things did not go so smoothly for everyone. One female officer, who was about to go to Paris for a clandestine mission, was expelled from the Party because her father had been a member of the clergy. Diana Mikhailovna, on the other hand, was allowed to keep her membership, even though her father had been a senior civil servant in the Tsarist administration.

At first, nobody wanted to put any questions to their colleagues; they were afraid it would put them in the firing line when it was their turn to be interrogated. But as time went on, employees who had escaped the purge began to point the finger at each other, reminding of illegally acquired trips abroad or the use of office telephones for private conversations and flirtations.

Eteri Bagratovna informed on an employee from the finance office who had posted a notice advertising foreign shoes for sale. "She's a profiteer!"

It turned out that none of the assembled employees were able to explain the difference between a Trotskyite and a loyal Party member. All these people who had been so zealously engaged in fighting counter-revolutionary activity had no idea what it actually involved.

Ivanov clutched the remnants of his gray hair. "And this is the Foreign Department, the pride of the OGPU!"

With each new case, it became clearer exactly what sort of people worked for the secret police: opportunists looking for easy money and ordinary bureaucrats—petty, ignorant, and vindictive.

They had taken up residence in the citadel of the Lubyanka like hyenas in caves. They went out to hunt because they needed to eat, and they hung on to their positions because everyone was afraid of the OGPU and because they themselves feared nothing and no one except the hyenas in the lair next door.

2

Alov had not raised his hand nor asked any questions. It was quite obvious the views of the employees had no effect on the decisions of the commission. Drachenblut and Babloyan had already decided in advance who would be "drowned" and who would be "saved" and settled all questions with a vote of two to one.

The meeting had been going on for three hours.

"Oh, why don't they hurry up!" whispered Diana Mikhailovna barely audibly. "Now all the stores are about to shut, and I've got no food in the house."

Alov tried to get away to go to the bathroom, wanting to check up on Rogov at the same time, but he was not allowed to leave.

"You should have thought about going to the bathroom earlier," muttered Ivanov.

Only Eteri Bagratovna, was allowed to leave the room once in a while to bring in a fresh carafe of water or replace a broken pencil.

Once, on her return, she walked up to the chairman's table and said something to the members of the commission. Drachenblut and Babloyan glanced at one another.

"Well, then," said Ivanov in an ominous tone, looking around at the silent officers. "Let's have a look at Alov's work record."

Babloyan picked up Alov's files and began to shower him with questions that had nothing to do with Marxism and was all about Dunya and the theater group.

Alov, stifled by his cough, was unable to defend himself.

"I fear our friend Alov has absolutely lost his consciousness of class war," pronounced Babloyan.

"Where does he get this haughty attitude toward the efforts of the proletarian youth?"

Ivanov nodded in agreement. "His actions fail absolutely to answer the demands of our ideology."

Drachenblut listened patiently as they talked gibberish about imperial chauvinism and poor moral character.

"Which of you supports the opinion that Alov has cut himself off from the masses?" Drachenblut asked.

Those officers who had not yet been questioned immediately realized that Alov was a clear candidate for dismissal. His name could take up one of the spaces on the quota for expulsion, and they all began to attack Alov.

Even Zharkov joined in. "For some time, Alov has been a man without a societal face."

Not a single specific accusation was made against Alov. Everybody merely called him names that signaled something bad. What could he say in return? "It's not true! I do have a societal face!"?

Alov stared dully at Drachenblut. *Help me!* he implored silently. But Drachenblut was looking the other way.

"Unfortunately," he said, "Alov has not been able to win foreign journalists over to our side. As a result, he has been making enemies of potential friends of the USSR. I am of the opinion that Alov does not deserve to be a member of the Communist Party. Let's put it to a vote."

The decision was passed unanimously.

The meeting was over, and the officers took chairs and went back to their offices—some content, and others in a state of near desperation.

Alov caught up with his boss as Drachenblut was leaving the room. "Babloyan attacked me because of my wife. He's a womanizer—everybody knows it. He spreads it around that he's impotent, but you've seen for himself what he does and—"

"That has nothing to do with me," Drachenblut cut him short and tried to push past.

Alov stood in his way. "Let me finish the job I have in hand! I have Rogov in a cell right now. Galina Dorina is working on him now, and by evening, we'll have a witness statement."

"Forget about your Galina," Drachenblut said. "She's been shot. It happened just now. She went berserk and killed that woman—what's she called?—the Mincing Machine."

Alov felt the room swim before his eyes. "What?"

"Go home and take care of that cough," Drachenblut told him. "And hand in your pass at reception. As from today, you're dismissed."

3

Klim was shaken awake just before dawn. "Rogov? Get your things and come out."

"Get your things" either meant a transfer to another prison or execution, but Klim felt nothing but dull apathy and emptiness. There was a heavy feeling in his heart too—was he about to have a heart attack? How absurd that would be….

The other prisoners watched in silence as Klim pulled on his dinner jacket onto his bare body.

"God rest your soul," muttered Billiard, turning over onto his other side.

"So long," mouthed Ahmed silently.

Klim went out into the corridor.

"Straight ahead. Right. Down the stairs," the guard gave out curt commands in between yawns.

Klim was led into a room on the ground floor where a duty officer sat behind a counter. The officer passed him a form certifying his release from prison. "Sign this please!"

Klim couldn't understand what was going on. Was it some sort of trick? Some plot thought up by the OGPU?

With rigid fingers, he took the pen, dipped it in the inkwell, and wrote his signature.

The duty officer piled up all the confiscated things on the counter: braces, keys, and so on.

"Our apologies," he said. "You were arrested by mistake."

Klim glanced at his wallet. Not even the money had been touched.

He was taken outside the gates and left.

While Klim had been under arrest, snow had fallen, and Moscow had been transformed. He too now bore little resemblance to the old Klim Rogov. He was still not fully aware of all the changes that had taken place in him, but there was definitely something wrong. The pain in his chest was still there, and he kept hearing a ringing in his ears like the chiming of distant bells.

Klim had always been cautious about any signs of illness, but now, he felt no anxiety neither did he have any wish to run to a doctor and find out what had happened to him. He just set off home.

On Krivokolenny Lane, Klim saw a small crowd reading a notice that had been posted on the gates. On it was a list of those who had been deprived of their electoral rights and were to be evicted immediately.

A young man in a coat too short for him was stabbing at the blacklist with his mitten, protesting indignantly that he was a useful member of society. "I'm not a lishenets! I'm studying to be a draftsman. I can show you my student card!"

The crowd said nothing. Only the steam of their breath rose up into the air above their heads.

There were other lists on other doorways. Clearly, the Kremlin had taken the decision to expel all potentially dangerous citizens from Moscow. They were carrying out a general purge of society.

Klim had to make a plan of action quickly. If the Party had already begun a wide-scale assault on counter-revolutionaries, the fact that Klim had been set free had been merely a happy accident—a bureaucratic error which had not been noticed in time.

Klim rubbed his cheeks, trying to concentrate. *They'll probably try to arrest me in another few hours,* he thought. *First, I have to find out what's happened to Kitty, and then we can work out what to do next.*

4

"Sir!" cried Afrikan when he saw Klim coming in at the gate. "You've come back!"

"Where's Kitty?" asked Klim urgently.

Afrikan looked at his feet. "Magda took her away. She sent Kapitolina back to the village immediately and gave me a ruble to drink to the October Revolution."

Klim felt his heart thaw a little at this news. What angels some women were!

"They sealed your apartment straight away," Afrikan informed Klim as he followed him up to the upper floor. "But today, some others came—in uniform—went in and stayed in there a long time. Then they cut the seal off the door as if nothing had happened."

Klim opened the door to his apartment. It was obvious a search had taken place. The skirting boards had been torn away and sections of the parquet floor wrenched up, and then everything had been fastened back any which way. The floor was covered with the prints of muddy boots, and a pall of plaster dust lay over everything.

The packed suitcases were still where they had been. On one lay a large envelope with an official seal. Klim tore it open and pulled out the letter.

You are hereby informed that Comrade Stalin will receive you at the Kremlin on 13th of November at 7 p.m.

Klim was at a loss to understand what was going on. So, the guardian angel that had released him from prison was the general secretary of the All-Union Communist Party himself. But why had he not been informed that Mr. Rogov was a spy? And that he no longer worked for United Press?

Klim turned to Afrikan. "Would you bring up some coal for the boiler, please? I need to wash and change."

When Afrikan had left, Klim picked up the telephone and called Magda.

"I'm at home," he told her.

5

Kitty flew into the room and threw her arms around Klim's neck.

"Daddy… Daddy…" she kept repeating.

Magda gazed lovingly at the two of them with tears in her eyes. "I thought I would never see you again," she sniffed, overcome by emotion. "I've brought you some food. I expect you're hungry."

There was no kitchen table—Kapitolina had taken it with her, so Magda began laying food out on a newspaper spread out on the lid of the grand piano.

"I had a telegram from Seibert," she said. "Nina arrived safely in Berlin, but Elkin never appeared with the money."

"He was caught on the border," explained Klim and gave Magda a short account of what had happened to him at the Lubyanka.

"I really don't know why Stalin decided to save me," he added.

"It wasn't Stalin; it was me—and Babloyan." Magda laughed, handing Klim a piece of bread and butter. "When I left you after the political rally, I remembered about the face cream I use for my freckles. I really need it, and Friedrich is always forgetting to bring me any. I wanted you to meet him in Berlin and remind him to get some. I ran after you and saw you being arrested."

Magda had gone to Chistye Prudy and taken Kitty away with her, and then she had set off to see Babloyan at a celebratory dinner.

"You can't imagine how happy I was to find out he spoke English!" she exclaimed, beaming. "I hinted that if he didn't get you out of prison, you would tell everyone about the bribe he had taken. So, he persuaded Stalin to give you an interview and explained to the OGPU that you were a very important person who had the confidence of the General Secretary himself. Only he asked if you could keep quiet about the arrest. The last thing he needs is a row with the OGPU."

"I don't know how to thank you—" began Klim, but Magda waved aside his gratitude.

"It was nothing. So, when are you going to do the interview?"

Klim was silent for a moment.

"I'm not going to meet Stalin."

"Why on earth not? A chance like this only comes across once in a lifetime. You can build your whole career on it. After all, Stalin has never once given an interview to a foreign correspondent."

"I just hate the whole idea of talking to the man," Klim said. "Stalin and his henchmen behave like common criminals and then act as if nothing has happened."

Klim patted the polished case of the grand piano. "It looks fine, doesn't it? Like an instrument in good working condition?"

He lifted the lid to show Magda a heap of loose hammers and a tangle of broken strings. "This is what I found after the apartment was searched. And that's just the way I feel inside."

"You're a terrible romantic," Magda sighed sympathetically. "As a journalist, you're doing something unforgivably stupid."

"But as a person, I'm averse to the idea. If I were to go to Stalin and not ask certain questions, I'd be taking part in a conspiracy of silence. And if I do ask them, I'll be arrested again immediately."

"Then you need to get out of Moscow as quick as you can," Magda said. "Friedrich is flying to Berlin today. You'll have to hope and pray he has room in his plane. Do you have a valid passport and exit visa?"

"I think so, yes."

"Then there's no time to be lost. I'll get you a taxi now."

Magda threw down a half-eaten piece of bread and ran out of the apartment.

Klim called out to Kitty. "We're going, little one."

He buttoned her coat and helped her put on her boots.

"What's that, Daddy?" asked Kitty, pointing at the red mark on Klim's neck.

He hurriedly adjusted his collar. "It's nothing. It will heal soon."

The mark from the telephone cable that the OGPU woman had used to throttle him was in the same place as Galina's scar.

"We're going to see Tata now," said Klim. "We have to talk to her."

6

"They rang yesterday from the morgue," Galina's neighbor, Natasha, told Klim. "They asked if anybody was going to pick up Comrade Dorina's body or not. But what could we do with her body? We couldn't afford to bury her, anyway. Tata and I went to say our goodbyes, and they took poor Galina off to the crematorium. It was all paid for by the state. We were told she died in the line of duty."

"Is Tata in her room? " asked Klim.

Natasha nodded. "She's locked herself in, and she isn't answering. We're fed up with pounding on the door. I told her, 'You need to go to an orphanage. Who's going to feed you?' But it's all the same to her."

Tata only opened the door when Kitty knocked and called her name. But as soon as Klim came in the room, she darted into the closet and began to whimper like a sick wolf cub.

Kitty ran to her. "Oh, please don't cry!"

"Tata, we have very little time," Klim said. "So, you need to make a decision quickly. Either you go to an orphanage, or you come abroad with Kitty and me. This minute."

"I'm not going anywhere!" yelled Tata in an angry voice.

Klim sighed. "All right then. Kitty, let's go."

Reluctantly, Kitty tore herself away from Tata. "I love you very much!" she told her friend.

Klim and Kitty left the apartment and set off down the stairs.

"Wait!" Tata's voice echoed around the stairwell. "I can't go to an orphanage! I remember what it was like in the boarding school."

"Come with us!" Kitty cried, her words echoing off the high ceiling.

Tata ran up to them, her worn slippers falling off her feet, and then stopped as if she had hit an invisible wall.

"How can you take me with you? You need documents, don't you?"

"I can write your name in my passport," said Klim. "That will be enough."

Tata gawped at him, unable to believe her ears. "What? Are you going to adopt me?"

"Your mother saved my life."

"When? How?"

"I'll tell you later. Get your things together now. The taxi's waiting."

37. THE PLOT AGAINST STALIN

1

Alov could not bring himself to tell Dunya about the results of the purge, and Valakhov was not at home; he had been sent out of town on an urgent mission.

The following day, Alov surreptitiously observed his wife, convinced that her feminine intuition would tell her something terrible had happened to him, but she showed no signs of having sensed anything. Or then again, perhaps she had known all along? Was she in cahoots with Babloyan?

Alov knew that everything was over for him. He would never find another position now. Who would associate with a pariah who had been expelled from both the Party and the OGPU? In his mind, he went through all his acquaintances, wondering if he could ask any of them for help, but he could think of no one. The only person who had always helped him and never expected anything in return was Galina.

When Dunya came back from work, the solicitous neighbors were quick to let her know that her husband had been lying about at home all day. Only then did she realize Alov had been dismissed from his post. However, to his surprise, she was not in the slightest bit dismayed at the news.

"I'm glad you're not working at the Lubyanka anymore," she said.

"Are you out of your mind?" yelled Alov. "Don't you understand? We don't have enough money to live on. We'll be evicted from this apartment, and we won't be able to rent even a corner of a room on your miserable wages."

Dunya took out a small cloth purse from her shopping bag and held it out to Alov. Inside was a brand new banknote, bearing the portrait of an elderly man with a prominent forehead.

Alov had only ever seen a hundred-dollar bill once before in his life—when he had been shown the contents of Klim Rogov's wallet.

"Did Babloyan give you this money?" he asked in a shaky voice.

"Yes," replied Dunya. "And there's no need to stare at me like that. It's payment for my performance on the anniversary of the October Revolution."

Now, Alov understood what had happened. Rogov must have used the foreign currency to bribe Babloyan, and Babloyan had handed the note on to Dunya.

2

Alov was lying in wait for Diana Mikhailovna when she came out of work.

Finally, she appeared from the gate. Alov ran up to her and grabbed her sleeve.

"Help me, for God's sake! Could you check the number of a banknote against the list given to Oscar Reich?"

Diana Mikhailovna stared fearfully at her former boss. "I don't know if I'm allowed."

"Please! I helped you when you needed work. Don't you remember?"

She agreed in the end to check the number and went back inside the building. Fifteen minutes later, she came out again.

"Yes, that's one of ours," she said.

Overcome by emotion, Alov kissed her hand. "I'll be indebted to you till the day I die. Now tell me, what's happening with Rogov?"

"They let him out today."

"What? Who let him out?"

"It was Drachenblut who signed the order. He said the charges were fabricated. Rogov was just the victim of slander by some scoundrel."

Alov clutched at his head. So, that was it! Babloyan had had Alov expelled from the Party simply to get his crony out of prison. Babloyan must have made a deal with Drachenblut, agreeing to support him during the purge and creating an alliance against Yagoda. And as Alov might have objected to their plan, they had sacrificed him like a pawn in a game.

But why had Drachenblut agreed to such a deal, Alov wondered. After all, his former boss had been adamant about locating the money stolen from Reich. And he knew that the registered banknotes had been found in Rogov's wallet.

Suddenly, Alov felt his blood run cold. *But maybe Drachenblut didn't know about the banknotes,* he thought. *Not if I didn't include it in the report!*

On that day, Alov's damned illness had made it impossible to work; he must have neglected to fill out the necessary papers and then forgotten all about it.

Alov took his leave of Diana Mikhailovna and ran back to the gate. He had to speak to Drachenblut urgently.

3

At first, Drachenblut refused point blank to speak to Alov, but then he relented.

"What is it?" he demanded gruffly when Alov came into his office.

"Why did you let Rogov go?" asked Alov, trembling all over.

"Comrade Stalin invited Rogov for an interview. That doesn't happen to just anyone."

Alov clutched at his chest. "But Rogov was planning an assassination attempt! He won over Babloyan and used him to get close to Comrade Stalin."

Then Alov told Drachenblut of the hundred-dollar bill and of the money that had been found in Rogov's wallet.

"I didn't manage to finish the report," Alov said, "because I was sick. But you saw for yourself the portrait of Comrade Stalin with a hole in his forehead. It was a prearranged signal!"

It turned out that Drachenblut had seen nothing of the sort. He had only read Elkin's testimony. The envelope containing the postcards had turned up on the following day.

"We have to save Comrade Stalin!" cried Alov. "All Rogov has to do is to smuggle in some poison powder into Stalin's office inside a button or a fountain pen and scatter it before he leaves. Surely you know that?"

Drachenblut summoned Eteri Bagratovna. "Find out the time of Rogov's interview at the Kremlin!" he ordered.

A few minutes later, the secretary reported back that the meeting with Stalin was scheduled to take place at seven o'clock. It was now already half past six.

Cars were dispatched to Chistye Prudy and to the Kremlin visitors' pass desk.

Alov sat fidgeting nervously while Drachenblut smoked one cigarette after another, every now and again picking up the phone to make a call. "Have you found him yet? No? For Chrissakes!"

At 7:30 p.m., a call came in from the Kremlin to say that Comrade Stalin had canceled the meeting with the correspondent from the United Press as he had not turned up.

"I don't understand," Alov kept saying. "Was Rogov so

delighted to be let out of jail that he went on a drinking spree? How could anyone fail to turn up to a meeting with the Comrade Stalin?"

Drachenblut ordered an investigation of Rogov's friends and acquaintances and a search of the city hospitals, stations, and local bars. Rogov was to be found, dead or alive.

At half past eight, the message came in that he had flown out of the Moscow.

"What do you mean 'flown out'?" Drachenblut roared at his secretary.

"He got on a plane," answered Eteri Bagratovna calmly. "He left for Berlin this afternoon. His documents were in order."

Alov jumped to his feet. "We need to tell Comrade Stalin everything. He needs to know that Babloyan is taking bribes—" Alov caught Drachenblut's icy stare and fell silent.

"Calm down," said Drachenblut. "We can't touch Babloyan. If we start a scandal now, Yagoda will get involved, and he'll almost certainly work out what's going on with the money from union fees paid overseas."

Alov slumped weakly back onto his chair. How could he have been such a fool? He might have guessed!

OGPU agents working abroad were paid in foreign currency, and as they used it to pay their union dues, large sums of currency were piling up in foreign bank accounts. Drachenblut and Babloyan must have agreed to appropriate the money for themselves, meanwhile transferring the payments back to the state in devalued rubles, which were worth only half the official exchange rate.

All senior Soviet officials were like servants stealing from their employer's storerooms. They would strike up deals to make it easier for them to steal and then go to the boss to report on each other in an attempt to keep their enemies from the feeding trough. This was the substance of their "struggle for a bright future."

"You know, Alov, we were maybe a bit hasty to expel you from the Party," said Drachenblut thoughtfully. "I can see you're a reliable employee and a vigilant agent. We'll send you out to Cuba to carry on the good work."

Alov understood everything. His superior was prepared to turn a blind eye to any crimes committed by Babloyan and Rogov. Meanwhile, Alov, as an unwanted witness to those crimes, was to be dispatched abroad to keep his mouth shut.

Drachenblut picked up the telephone receiver. "Put me on to the administrative department of the People's Commissariat for Foreign Affairs.

"Ah, good evening, Comrade Fyodorov. We need to send one of our men to Havana. Do we have a position as commandant? No? Well, then he can be a registrar. I'll send him to you with a note from me, and you get him settled in, all right?"

He hung up the phone and turned to Alov. "You were dreaming about having your own room, weren't you? Now you'll have one with a view of the sea and palm trees. And take that woman of yours along too so she doesn't make a nuisance of herself here."

"So, you're just going to let Rogov and Kupina go?" said Alov in a faint voice.

"Don't worry about them," said Drachenblut. "We'll find them all right."

4

Klim realized it was madness to take Tata away with him. What would Nina say when she found out he had decided to adopt another child, and the child of his former lover at that? Tata would run them all ragged with her awful character, but Klim could not bring himself to abandon her to her fate. If it had not been for Galina, the OGPU woman with the red hair would have maimed him for life.

They were in luck: there were seats left on the plane, and they passed through passport control and customs without incident.

A young airport employee led Klim and the girls out on to the airfield where a bright red blunt-nosed plane stood waiting.

"Isn't it pretty?" cried Kitty in delight. "Just like a model plane!"

It was true; the airplane looked like nothing more than a toy. It was difficult to believe that this shed with wings would actually be capable of taking off.

Klim cast an anxious glance toward Tata, but thankfully, she said nothing.

At that moment, Friedrich jumped down from the cockpit. He was wearing a leather coat and a helmet with earphones.

"Good Lord!" he said when he saw Klim. "You're still alive! And who are these young ladies?"

"These are my daughters."

Friedrich looked nonplussed. "Ah well, you can tell me everything later. Let's go into the cabin. We're leaving in fifteen minutes. First stop—Smolensk, then Kaunas, then Konigsberg. And after that, it's just a short hop to Berlin."

In the cabin were four leather armchairs with headrests. There were hooks for coats on the walls and rolled-up blinds at the rectangular windows with rounded corners. In the back end of the plane, behind a barrier, various crates and suitcases were being loaded noisily. Every time a new piece of baggage was thrown on board, the plane would shudder and rock.

"It's going to be noisy," Friedrich told Klim. "Don't forget to put in your earplugs. You'll find them in the pocket in the sides of your seat. And if you get sick, use the paper bags."

Tata and Kitty sat in an armchair together and spent a long time fiddling with the belt, trying to work out how to fasten it.

"Aren't you afraid of flying?" asked Tata.

Kitty shook her head. "No."

Lucky thing, thought Klim, sighing to himself. He was struggling to suppress a sense of dread. He had read so many reports of plane crashes in the papers!

The door flew open, and another passenger came on board.

"Oh, I see I won't be flying alone!" he exclaimed in English, catching sight of Klim.

It was Oscar Reich. He was red in the face, his coat was undone, and his hat askew.

"I'm delighted to see you," he said to Klim. "Are these your children? They'll have a rough time of it, I'm afraid. These planes bounce you about terribly. I would never get into a plane for the life of me if I didn't have urgent business to attend to."

He put his briefcase under the seat and banged on the wall that separated the cabin from the cockpit. "Hey, Friedrich! Have you had the heating fixed? I almost froze to death last time I flew with you."

A man with a shaved head appeared in the doorway.

"Yefim, come in and sit down," Oscar patted the seat next to him. "You and I are flying with these young ladies today."

Klim forced himself to shake both men by the hand. What bad luck to have to fly with Reich for company! He was glad, at least, that it would be noisy during the flight, so there would be no need for conversation.

"Ready everyone?" called Friedrich from the cockpit. "Off we go then!"

5

They reached Smolensk without mishap, not counting a sudden fit of tears from Tata, who had remembered that she had forgotten her father's ashtray at home and that she had not said goodbye to her cat, Pussinboots. It had suddenly hit her that she was leaving Moscow forever and would never be able to go back home.

When the plane took off again, it began to bounce about horribly, and Tata was immediately sick. Kitty was frightened and began to cry, and Klim, at a loss as to what to do, tried to calm first one and then the other.

Oscar and Yefim screwed up their faces and moved their legs away squeamishly from the remains of Tata's breakfast.

During refueling at Kaunas, Tata hid in the ladies' lavatory, declaring that she would not get back into the plane for anything in the world. Klim was forced to carry her out—to the horror of the polite Lithuanian ladies in the queue.

"I've been kidnapped!" Tata yelled, bucking like a crazed calf.

Klim set her down on the ground. "Tata, look at me. Please, for goodness' sake, don't make my life even more complicated! I can't leave you here. We've already crossed the border. If Kitty and I leave without you, where would you go?"

"I hate airplanes," sobbed Tata.

Klim was sorely tempted to leave her with the Lithuanians. He understood the problem: Tata had had a difficult childhood, she had lost her mother, and now, she was flying to some unknown destination with a stranger—and a stranger she didn't trust, at that.

Perhaps a Soviet orphanage would not have been such a bad option after all for Tata, he thought.

He took her hands and squeezed them tight. "I owe a huge debt to your mother. I promise I'll look after you just as I look after Kitty. Just as long as you trust me, everything will be all right."

Klim had already enough on his plate. There was a dull ache in his chest, and he was afraid it might be something serious. He was not enjoying being bounced around for hours in a small plane side by side with his worst enemy. And on top of that, only the day before, he had been held in a cell and subjected to torture. But none of this was likely to make Tata come to her senses. It was useless to expect any compassion or understanding from her.

She only calmed down eventually when Klim reminded her that it was a Young Pioneer's duty to be strong and brave at all times.

"We're going to Germany now," he said sternly. "A capitalist country. We might face all sorts of dangers and deliberate provocations. I'm entrusting Kitty to your care. Whatever happens, you must make sure you get her to safety."

Tata dried her eyes and nodded quickly. "All right. I understand."

Klim gave Tata five Deutsche marks and a piece of paper with Seibert's address written on it. "Show this to no one. This is the address of our coconspirators' apartment. You can always go to them if you need help. Are you ready for the fight?"

"Always prepared!" said Tata, giving the Pioneer salute.

It is better this way, thought Klim. If he had a heart attack, at least the girls would be able to find their way to Nina.

6

A brief item had appeared in the *Berliner Tageblatt* stating that the timber being used to build German railway sleepers was produced in Soviet labor camps. Not long after this, a cable from Seibert had arrived in Moscow: "Stop stalling on counter-propaganda. Questions being asked about the provenance of Russian timber. Unforeseen consequences likely."

Gritting his teeth, Drachenblut had allocated an additional budget of ten thousand dollars and ordered

Oscar Reich to fly out to Germany immediately.

Oscar had hoped to get to Berlin before nightfall, but on arrival in Konigsberg, Friedrich announced that his plane had developed engine noise, so they would be taken on by a German plane that was flying out the next morning.

Klim and the two girls set off for the airport hotel while Oscar and Yefim went to the Soviet Consulate.

All this time, Oscar's thoughts had been dwelling constantly on Nina. How could some commoner have managed to trick him into believing she was a baroness? He should have handed her over to the OGPU straight away instead of putting himself at risk, creating a jealous scene. If Nina had been just a little stronger, she could have smashed his skull with that starter handle.

It was clear from Elkin's testimony that Nina Kupina was in Germany. What if she decided to go to the press and tell the newspapers about the private life of the famous Mr. Reich? It was essential he found Nina and got rid of her!

But it was no easy task to locate a young lady who had arrived in Germany on a false passport. In Moscow, all you had to do was go into some establishment and show your OGPU credentials, and immediately, you would find out everything you needed to know. But in Berlin, it was difficult even getting a list of guests from a hotel. And how many such hotels were there in this city with its population of millions?

The Soviet consul, a fussy, stout man with dark eyebrows, took Oscar and Yefim into an office with pale wooden walls.

"Take a look at the message that just came in," he said.

He handed Oscar a diplomatic cable stating that on November 13, 1928, a dangerous criminal by the name of Klim Rogov—the husband and accomplice of Nina Kupina—had fled the USSR.

"But we were on the same plane with him!" cried Oscar and began to read the cable aloud: "Rogov is to be captured immediately and returned to the USSR. If it is impossible to take him alive, destroy him. His departure will demonstrate our utter defeat and constitute a serious blow to the reputation of the Soviet Union. Deploy all possible means to achieve this mission."

"Our plane has broken down—otherwise, we could have ordered Friedrich to turn back," muttered Yefim and turned to the consul. "We need to arrest Rogov immediately. How many free men do you have?"

The consul shook his head. "There's no one I can call on."

"There'll be no end of trouble with the kids," said Oscar, frowning. "Let's get to Germany and seize him there. He'll probably go straight to Kupina, so we can take the two of them together. Wire the envoy's office in Berlin and have them send their men to the airport. Then we'll take Kupina and Rogov to Hamburg and put them on a Soviet ship. They won't get away from us after that."

38. THE REICHSBANK

1

The plane circled the new airport of Tempelhof. Gazing out of the window, Klim saw a building stretching the length of the airfield and dozens of planes—some modern and some veteran fighter planes from the last war.

As it landed, the plane sped past aircraft hangars and towers with flags. When the plane's engine had stopped, two servicemen in dark blue boiler suits wheeled up a sloping gangway.

Klim jumped down to the ground and took a deep breath of the cold air. Thank heaven they had arrived!

The freight handlers began to take the baggage out of the hold and load it onto trolleys.

"Goodbye!" Oscar waved to Klim and hurried toward the large glass doors of the airport building.

Yefim set off at a run, following him.

Klim took both girls by the hand. "How are you feeling?"

The girls were exhausted from the journey, but nonetheless, curiosity got the better of them. Tata stared wide-eyed at the technicians driving about the landing strip on motorized carts.

Klim went through passport control, and a customs officer checked his baggage.

"All in order, sir. Welcome to Berlin!"

Klim found a stand with a plan of the airport and located the taxi rank on the map.

"Here are some of my fellow Russians!" the exclamation came from a tall, fair-haired young man in a thick sweater and quilted pants who was bearing down on them. "Delighted to meet you. I'm Sergei. Can I take you anywhere? I have a taxi waiting just outside." Without waiting for a reply, he grabbed Klim's suitcases. "Come on. It's just a step away. Are you from Moscow? I'm from Suzdal myself. My parents brought me to Berlin when I was just a little boy."

Chatting and laughing, Sergei led them through to an empty passage between two hangars where a small yellow van stood waiting. It was emblazoned with a picture of a pike with staring eyes and the inscription "Fresh Fish" in Russian and German. Beside it stood a burly man with gold teeth, holding a tyre lever.

Klim looked around in alarm. This van was clearly not a taxi. Where had they been taken? Who were these people? Thieves?

Sergei, quite unperturbed, was securing Klim's cases to the baggage rack.

"Take a seat, Mr. Rogov, please. Let's go!"

And how on earth did this man know his name?

Klim picked up Kitty. "Tata, we're going!"

But they had barely taken a step when Yefim came around the corner of one of the hangars, holding a revolver.

"Get into the car this minute!" he ordered quietly.

The two girls set up a terrified wail.

Sergei and Yefim sat Klim between them on the back seat. Tata was ordered to take Kitty and sit in the front next to the driver with the gold teeth.

"Where does Kupina live?" Sergei asked Klim.

Klim kept his head down and said nothing.

"Do you think we're here to play games with you?"

Sergei grabbed Klim by the shirtfront.

Klim pulled away, and a scuffle broke out. The children began to wail even louder. Then Yefim took a brass knuckleduster from his pocket and dealt Klim a blow to the back of the head, knocking him out.

2

Tata huddled in close to Kitty's shoulder, which was shaking with sobs.

Who were their abductors? Tata thought. *White Russian émigrés? Surely it had to be! Nobody else would be capable of such a vile act!*

The van kept circling the streets aimlessly while the gangsters argued about whether they should head to some "envoy's office" or drive to Hamburg.

Once, Tata plucked up the courage to look around. Uncle Klim was lying unconscious at the feet of their abductors. Good grief! Maybe he was dead already?

"How on earth will we find out Kupina's address now?" Sergei asked Yefim angrily. "Who told you to knock him on the head?"

"You started it with your questions!"

"Quiet!" snapped the driver. "Make up your minds where we're going."

The abductors were silent for a minute.

"Let's make for Hamburg," said Yefim. "We'll hand Rogov in there and work out what to do after that. In any case, we can't take these kids into the envoy's office. There'll be no end of fuss."

Trying to appear casual, Tata put out a hand to touch the lock on the door.

The car was traveling down an elegant street lined with tall buildings adorned with balconies and sculptures. All around, car horns sounded, and bicycle bells rang. Street merchants were selling newspapers, balloons and—oranges!

Suddenly, their road was blocked by a column of demonstrators. They were dressed in what looked like army uniforms: battered peaked caps and military trousers and belted tunics. The demonstrators kept clenching their fists and raising their right arms to the regular beat of a drum.

"*Rot Front!*" their cries echoed over the street.

"Oh my god! That's the Union of Red Combatants!" Tata whispered. "The military division of the German Communist Party!"

The demonstrators had come to a stop, and it was impossible for cars to pass. The driver with the gold teeth stuck his head out of the window to see how long they would have to wait.

"Damn it all!" he cursed. "It looks like we're stuck."

At that moment, Tata tugged at the chrome door handle, and she and Kitty tumbled out onto the pavement.

"Run!" shouted Tata.

"Hey, stop!" yelled the driver. "Get back here this minute!"

He set off after them at a run, but the girls had already dashed ahead through the lines of demonstrators and soon outstripped him.

"We left Daddy behind!" Kitty kept sobbing, but Tata pulled her relentlessly through the crowds.

Breathless and tear-stained, they stopped before a strange building that looked like some ancient temple.

All around, Tata saw men and women dressed up to the nines looking like profiteers. All the signs were in German, and Tata couldn't understand a word, even though she had learned German at school for several years.

Everything here was foreign and unfamiliar. A barrel organ grinder stood on the pavement, singing something in a nasal voice. Two soldiers in silly looking helmets were buying sausages from a street vendor. The only thing that reminded Tata of home was the pigeons fussing about in the gutter. But they were pecking at white bread! Who would toss away anything so delicious?

Kitty had not stopped wailing.

"Please try not to make so much noise!" Tata implored her.

She put her hand in her pocket and pulled out the note that Uncle Klim had given her. He had told her that this address was a safe place for them. But where was it? And how would they get there? They were surrounded by Germans and could not even ask anyone the way.

An old man with whiskers carrying a bucket and a roll of paper under his arm went up to one of the advertising columns and began to paste up a poster decorated with a red star and the inscription "*Kommunistische Partei Deutschlands.*" Tata knew what those words meant: "The Communist Party of Germany."

At last, there was somebody they could trust—a member of the working classes! She ran up to him.

"*Kamerade*…I…*Ich habe, haus*…Oh, I don't know how to say it in German!"

"Please, speak Russian," said the old man with a smile.

Tata was alarmed. What if the old man was a traitor, like Sergei? But he seemed to have a kind face.

"Dear Mister, are you a Communist?"

The man squinted up at the poster with the star. "Good heavens, no! But I'll put anything up if they pay me for it. I have a family to feed."

Another White Russian émigré, thought Tata desperately. *An unprincipled degenerate from a previous era.*

She dithered for a moment, unsure what to do, but then decided to show him the piece of paper with the address. "How do we get to this house?" she asked.

The old man took a pair of spectacles from his pocket, perched them on his nose, and read the address.

"You need to take the metro," he said.

"What metro? Where is it?" Tata said in alarm. "We're lost. We've only just arrived in the city, and we don't know anything."

The old man grabbed his bucket and motioned them to follow him through the doors of the temple-like building.

"Here—this is the metro," he said. "Come on. I'll show you the way."

They went inside, and Tata stopped, struck dumb by amazement. Sunlight poured through the glass roof of the metro station. The tiled walls were hung with panels bearing advertisements for cabarets and sports equipment. And there were kiosks along the walls, selling all manner of goods.

The old man helped Tata to buy a ticket and explained to her where to go and how to know when to get off.

"Thank you!" said Tata and led Kitty down the stairs.

It was hard to believe this was all really happening to her. Only yesterday, she had been sitting in a cupboard bemoaning her unhappy fate, and today, here she was with Kitty, roaming about the metro beneath the city of Berlin. And all alone without any adults!

The girls emerged onto the dimly lit platform and sat down on a bench.

The old man must have been a Communist after all, thought Tata. A White Russian sympathizer would never have helped out strangers as he had. It was just that Tata was a stranger, so he hadn't trusted her enough to tell her. After all, in Berlin, there were any number of children of aristocratic émigrés, not to mention young fascists.

A train came roaring by, and Tata and Kitty clapped their hands over their ears. A group of schoolgirls standing nearby burst out laughing and began whispering and looking in their direction.

"I want my daddy!" sobbed Kitty.

Tata squeezed her hand. "Don't be a scaredy-cat! You and I are brave Pioneers."

They got onto the train and traveled for a long time, counting off the stops as the old man had told them.

Suddenly, the train came out over the ground, and the whole car was flooded with sunlight. On they went, between unfamiliar German buildings, parks, and stores until at last, they stopped at the station at the end of the line—*Tilplatz*.

Tata and Kitty stepped out onto the open platform and looked around them.

"This way!" declared Tata, pointing to a group of apartment blocks painted in different colors. "We'll ask someone. Even if we can't understand what they say, they can point us in the right direction."

3

Seibert received two telegrams from Mr. Reich, one after the other. In one, Oscar promised Seibert that he would bring the money on Tuesday. In the other, he apologized and asked if he could postpone their meeting to the following day at five o'clock.

On Wednesday morning, Seibert sat down at his typewriter and began to write a lengthy article on labor camps in the USSR. He had decided that if he did not get the money from Oscar today, tomorrow he would send his piece to the press.

The article turned out well. Seibert wished he could show it off to Nina, but unfortunately, she could not appreciate the elegance of his German prose.

Several days earlier, she had received a telegram from Magda that had hinted at Klim's arrest. Ever since, Nina had been going out to Charlottenberg every morning. She had told Seibert she was looking for work, but he had his doubts. In his opinion, this young lady was capable of just about anything. Perhaps she was trying to find desperate White Russians to help her in some plan to cross the Soviet border and put a bomb under the Lubyanka?

It was eleven o'clock, and Seibert was feeling in need of a little sustenance. As it happened, there was an excellent restaurant just around the corner that sold fried sausage and cabbage cooked with apple.

Seibert put on his coat and hat and wound a scarf around his neck, but no sooner had he opened the door of his apartment than Nina came rushing in, accompanied by Kitty and another girl wearing a coat decorated with squirrels.

"Henrich, we're going to rescue Klim!" declared Nina, grabbing the keys to his Mercedes from the shelf.

"You leave those keys alone!" shouted Seibert, but Nina took no notice.

"Tata, you girls sit here. Henrich and I are going to find Uncle Klim. Don't open the door to anyone!"

The unknown girl nodded. Nina pushed Seibert out of the apartment.

"Klim's here in Germany!" she exclaimed breathlessly. "He's been kidnapped by a bunch of thugs, and they took him to Hamburg."

"What thugs? What are you talking about?"

Nina took Seibert by the hand and pulled him down the stairs with surprising strength.

"I met the girls at the station," she said. "They told me everything. There's huge traffic in the city because of the political demonstration, and we might be able to catch the kidnappers on their way to Hamburg. They're traveling in a van that's easy to spot: it's yellow with a picture of a pike fish on it."

"Give me back the car keys!" yelled Seibert.

Nina wheeled around and eyed him furiously. "I'm going no matter what—with you or without you. If I smash up your car, I don't care. You won't stop me!"

She ran downstairs, and Seibert ran after her, quite beside himself. This crazy woman would be the end of his glorious Mercedes!

4

The little white Mercedes sped along the highway, past trucks, cumbersome family cars, and farmers' traps.

Seibert sat at the wheel, alternately lamenting and shouting at Nina in German. She paid no attention to him but kept a sharp lookout at every car they passed.

Nina had no plan in her head and no idea how to rescue Klim. Tata had told her that they had been abducted at the airport and that a man called Yefim had hit Klim over the head and knocked him out.

The abduction must have been arranged by Oscar Reich—Nina was sure of it. He had an office and some warehouses in Hamburg, and he was probably planning to hide Klim there. How on earth could she find him? Could she appeal to the police to help? But while the officials spent their time gathering statements and writing out arrest warrants, Klim would either be killed or taken to the harbor and put on a Soviet ship—beyond the reach of any police.

"Faster! Faster!" Nina pleaded, grabbing Seibert by the elbow.

He gave her a dirty look. "What's your problem? Do you want to end up in a ditch? Like that lot?" He pointed to a yellow van which had come off the road into a field. It had a picture of a pike on the side.

"Stop!" cried Nina.

The brakes squealed, and the Mercedes came to a halt at the side of the road.

"It's them!" said Nina, trembling all over. "Please, Henrich, go up to them and ask what happened."

"Go yourself!" snapped Seibert. "I don't want to get mixed up with a bunch of gangsters."

"I can't! Yefim will recognize me. He knows me!"

"For God's sake! This is the last thing I need!" Seibert groaned, but still, he got out of the Mercedes and set off toward the yellow van.

Nina covered her face with her hands. *Please let Klim still be alive,* she prayed. *Only let him be alive!*

The next few minutes seemed to go on for hours. At last, Seibert returned.

"A fine bunch of gangsters!" he snapped. "They barely speak German, and they can't drive either."

"What about Klim?" Nina interrupted him. "Is he with them?"

"I don't know. I expect he's with them, but I didn't see what was going on in the back of the van."

Seibert put his hands on his hips and looked sternly at Nina. "These Russians are asking me to tow them to Oscar Reich's office. They don't know where it is as they've never been there before. So, I think I'll take you all to the nearest police station. After that, I want you to get out of my car, and I never want to see you again."

"But if Yefim realizes you've tricked him, he might kill Klim!"

"What do you suggest? That I start a fight with them? You should be grateful I'm helping you at all."

"Sorry, I am grateful. Thank you," said Nina in a shaky voice.

Seibert tied the two cars together with a tow rope and got in behind the wheel.

"Henrich, do you know Hamburg well?" asked Nina.

"I suppose so," muttered Seibert. "What's it to you?"

"I think it might be a better idea not to go to the police."

5

"Aha, he's waking up," Sergei nudged Klim with his boot.

Klim raised his head, which was splitting with pain. "Where are the girls?"

Sergei and Yefim glanced at one another. "They're in a safe place."

They lifted Klim back onto the seat. He felt the wound at the back of his head. His hair was matted with congealed blood, and a large lump had swelled beneath the skin.

Everything was swimming before his eyes, and his thoughts were in disarray. He did not register at first that the engine was no longer running and that they were swinging too far from side to side. Up ahead, he could see an elegant white convertible with a raised leather top. Apparently, they were being towed by this car.

Klim was entirely at sea. Where were they? Where were they going?

A dreary succession of concrete walls and industrial buildings was passing by the window.

Oh, God, he thought. Now they were going to take him to some deserted factory and torture him until he gave them Nina's address.

Presently, the industrial landscape gave way to ancient buildings with turrets, weather-vanes, and red roof tiles.

The car up ahead crossed a bridge and stopped before an elegant light gray building ornamented with bas-reliefs and sculptures.

Sergei stuck his head out of the window. "What is this? Is this Oscar's office?"

"Look up there. It's on the sign: 'Reichs,'" said the driver, pointing to the huge sign under the roof.

Yefim wrapped the hand holding the gun inside his coat and put a hat on Klim's head to conceal the wound.

"Out you get," he ordered. "Take one step to the side, and you'll get a bullet in your back. Understand?"

Klim clambered painfully out of the car and looked around him. The doors of the building were wide open, and richly dressed visitors in coats with fur collars were walking in and out. A black, red, and yellow flag fluttered against the blue sky, and beneath, in a semicircular panel, was a coat of arms with the word "Reichs" on one side and "Bank" on another.

This building has nothing to do with Oscar Reich, thought Klim. It was a branch of the state bank of Germany!

"Keep moving," said Sergei.

They walked past the white car. Inside sat a woman

with a hat pulled low over her eyes and—good god—Seibert!

"*Danke!*" said Serge and Yefim, waving to them.

In answer, Seibert gave a tortured smile.

They entered the ornate lobby, furnished with mosaic-covered columns and octagonal light-fittings with elaborately ornamented frames. Bank clerks hurried to and fro, carrying files.

"I think we've come to the wrong place," muttered Yefim, bewildered.

Just then, there was the sound of footsteps behind them. Klim looked around and saw Nina and Seibert.

"Hands up! This is a robbery!" Seibert cried in a shrill voice.

Klim shoved Yefim and dived to the floor. A shot rang out, and the next minute, sirens wailed, women screamed, and all the exits were swiftly closed off with steel shutters.

The armed robbers—five men and a woman—were apprehended by the security guards. Ten minutes later, the police arrived to take away the detainees to the cheers of onlookers.

Klim smiled over at Nina. The handcuffs looked rather incongruous on her.

"I have to thank you and Seibert for rescuing me," he said, "but now, we're all going to go to prison for ten years."

"I hope they put us in the same cell—without Seibert," said Nina, trying her utmost to put on a brave face.

39. EPILOGUE

1

Seibert did not come to meet Oscar Reich as planned. In the evening, he rang from a hotel and said he had been obliged to leave for Hamburg on business.

The next day, Oscar found out all the details from the newspapers. It turned out that Seibert had rescued two White Russians, Klim Rogov and his wife, who were being hunted down by OGPU agents with false passports and smuggled weapons.

Oscar was beside himself with fury. Seibert, without even realizing it, had put Oscar's head on the line: thanks to his tip-off, the police had arrested Yefim, and there was a good chance Yefim would tell the investigating officers exactly who had given him the order to kill Klim Rogov.

Oscar thought of a new plan. He would catch Seibert out with a bribe, and then when he had him backed up against the wall, demand that he change his statement. Seibert could present Rogov and Nina as swindlers who had slandered employees of the Soviet envoy's office and forced Seibert to do the same. White Russian émigrés had a bad reputation in Germany, and it was easy enough to pin any number of crimes on their heads.

Reich's secretary tried to reach Seibert by telephone all day. At long last, Seibert answered.

"Are you already in Berlin?" asked Oscar. "Let's settle

our business. Could you come to see me at my hotel?"

Seibert, however, announced that he did not want to carry a large sum of cash on him as he went about town and proposed that they meet at a branch of the Deutsche Bank and put the money straight into a safety deposit box.

"Very well. Come at five o'clock," grunted Oscar. "I'll book a meeting room. See you then."

He counted out the money himself and checked the numbers of the banknotes. Then he called a private detective by the name of Koch and two journalists who were in the pay of the USSR and ordered them to come with him to the Deutsche Bank.

"Make sure that there's an adjoining room next to the meeting room," Oscar told his secretary. "And leave the door ajar so you can listen to what we say."

Seibert arrived exactly on time.

"Here's the sum you asked for," Oscar told him, taking the money from his wallet.

Seibert counted the money and then went off to put it into the safety deposit box. Five minutes later, he returned.

"Thank you very much. That's everything sorted; now, we can discuss our plan of action."

The door to the adjoining room opened and out stepped Koch, the detective, a grim-faced fellow of about forty in a double-breasted suit and a Homburg hat.

"I'm a private detective," he said, "and I've been hired as a witness to an act of extortion. We have a note of the numbers of the banknotes you just received from Mr. Reich and three witnesses who can confirm it."

"Excuse me, but what exactly can these witnesses confirm?" asked Seibert with a puzzled air. "Mr. Reich has just given me money for the Association for Aid to the Volga Germans. The money will enable us to charter a ship to take them to Canada. I already paid the bill to the shipping company, you see."

Oscar jumped to his feet. "What are you talking about? What Volga Germans? What ship?"

"You said yourself that you wanted me to clean up your image in Germany," Seibert told Oscar. "That's exactly what I'm doing."

The journalists in the doorway looked at one another and took out their notebooks.

"Put those away!" snapped Oscar. Grabbing Seibert by the shoulder, he led him from the room.

"I'll see you in your grave, do you understand?" he whispered maliciously when they were alone.

Delicately, Seibert moved away from him. "It's not in your interests to see me in my grave," he said. "If I ever have a problem with my health, you'll run into some problems too, concerning the inheritance of Baron Brehmer. Nina Kupina has told me one or two details of your biography."

"Are you trying to blackmail me?"

"Why, my dear fellow? I'm only reminding you of the fact that businessmen must come to agreements with one another."

Oscar wanted desperately to say something in reply, but words failed him.

2

Seibert sat in his dining room, totting up his gains and losses.

The story of the Volga Germans had led to a sequel, and this was a source of some decent political capital—that was one nice gain.

The shipping company had paid Seibert a commission in return for chartering the ship, and that was another gain.

He had made his peace with Oscar Reich too. Reich had realized that his old friend Henrich had done the right thing by presenting him as a champion of the interests of Germans abroad. The deal on Russian timber had been signed and sealed by the authorities. And meanwhile, Seibert's in-depth article about Soviet labor camps had been locked away in a safe.

But besides these gains, there were losses, and as far as Seibert was concerned, all these losses could be laid at the door of Mr. Rogov. Klim and Nina had been arrested in Hamburg, and while the police were investigating them, Seibert was left looking after their children.

The two little girls were driving him mad. The older one kept preaching that art and icons were immoral. Meanwhile, the younger one would scribble pictures and icons straight onto the wallpaper.

Seibert had already put together a list of all his expenses: food, soap, coal, and new stockings for Tata—to replace her old ones that were torn. Altogether, it had added up to quite a sum.

There was a clatter of feet, and Tata and Kitty rushed into the dining room. "Uncle Henrich, we need an evil, greedy capitalist prince for our game!" they shouted.

Seibert tucked his list into his pocket. "Go away! I don't have any princes for you!"

The girls looked at one another. "That's just right!" said Tata. "That sounds just like a capitalist. We've found some gold on your land and—"

"What gold?" asked Seibert, alarmed.

He had remembered his collection of Imperial coins, which he had hidden away in a musical box. He started to feel slightly sick. Could the girls have discovered it?

"Gold isn't a toy!" he protested. "You leave it alone!"

"But we don't have anything else to play with!" said Kitty.

At that moment, the doorbell rang. Seibert went to open it, hoping desperately that it would be Klim and Nina.

And indeed it was. There the two of them stood, looking disheveled and anxious but apparently happy.

Kitty squealed with delight. "Mommy and Daddy are here!"

Seibert made himself scarce as they all began to kiss

one another and exchange meaningless endearments and exclamations.

He went out onto the balcony, lit up a cigarette, and then dug in his pocket and took out the list of services he had performed for Klim, wanting to check it one last time.

Down below, Frau Hauswald was sweeping the snow from the porch. When he caught sight of her, Seibert forgot everything and let go of the piece of paper. It flew out of his hands, and the wind caught it and dropped it at her feet.

"I think you've dropped something," said Frau Hauswald. "Is this your list?"

He shook his head. "No, no. It has nothing to do with me. Please just throw it away if it's no trouble."

It wouldn't do for Frau Hauswald to read what was written on the list, he thought. She might think he was a miserable skinflint.

"We've been neighbors for some time now," said Seibert. "And yet I still don't know your first name. Mine is Henrich."

"I'm Gertrude. Please to meet you."

Seibert grinned from ear to ear. In the USSR, the name Gertrude had a particular meaning—it was short for "*Geroinia Truda*" or "Heroine of Labor."

I'll wait for my uninvited guests to leave, he said to himself, *and then I'll ask her in for cocoa.*

Please support the *Russian Treasures* series with your reviews on Amazon and Goodreads.

It will help a lot—people make buying decisions on the number of reviews, making every one of them precious.

SUBSCRIBE TO A NEWSLETTER

The only way to know immediately when a new book by Elvira Baryakina comes out is to subscribe to her newsletter at www.baryakina.com/en/

Join and get *The Shaman*, a prequel to the *Russian Treasures* series, for free.

THE SHAMAN
A short story

Klim Rogov, the sole heir to the fortune of a noble family, has disappeared without a trace. Only his fifteen-year-old cousin has any idea what has happened, but she is keeping silent. There is little point trying to explain to adults the nature of the mysterious force that has commanded Klim to leave home, come what may.

If you'd like to talk about life and good books, please join Elvira Baryakina on her Facebook — http://facebook.com/elvira.baryakina

THE PRINCE OF THE SOVIETS

ELVIRA BARYAKINA

RUSSIAN TREASURES SERIES

Russian Treasures Book 1

White Ghosts Book 2

The Prince of the Soviets Book 3

Made in the USA
Middletown, DE
02 July 2019